THE
WITCH
HUNTER

MAX SEECK

WELBECK

Published in 2020 by Welbeck Fiction Limited,
part of Welbeck Publishing Group
20 Mortimer Street, London, W1T 3JW

Copyright © Max Seeck 2019
Translation copyright © Kristian London 2020
Cover design © Nathan Burton 2020

Original edition published by Tammi Publishers in 2020,
UK edition published by agreement with Max Seeck, Elina Ahlbäck at the Elina Ahlbäck Literary
Agency and Rhea Lyons at HG Literary

A CIP catalogue record for this book is available from the British Library

Paperback ISBN: 978–1–78739–479–7
E-book ISBN: 978–1–78739–502–2

Printed and bound by CPI Group (UK) Ltd., Croydon, CR0 4YY

10 9 8 7 6 5 4 3 2 1

For William.

It will take some time before I let you read this.

And once (and if) you finally do, do know that
Dad wasn't as crazy as the book may indicate.

Chapter 1

THE WIND HAS PICKED UP, AND THE CORNERS OF THE massive glass-and-skimmed-concrete house wail restlessly. The tap-tap carrying from the roof has gradually intensified; the faint pops call to mind the spitting of an open fire. The incredible speed with which the accumulation of white dunes on the patio now vanishes speaks of the gusts' force.

Maria Koponen knots her cardigan tightly around her waist and stares out the wall-to-ceiling windows into the darkness. She gazes at the frozen sea—which at this time of year is remarkably reminiscent of a vast, flat field—and then at the path plowed down to the dock, illuminated by knee-high yard lights.

Maria curls her toes into the plush carpet that reaches almost to the edges of the expansive floor. It's warm inside the house, cocoon-like. Even so, Maria feels uneasy, and even the tiniest grievances strike her as unusually annoying tonight. Like those damn expensive yard lights that still don't work the way they should.

Maria is roused from her reverie when she realizes the music has stopped. She walks past the fireplace to the enormous bookshelf, where her husband's collection of nearly four hundred records has been organized in five neat rows. Over the years, Maria has gotten used to the fact that, in this household, music is not played from a smartphone screen.

Vinyl just sounds a hell of a lot better. That's what Roger said to her years ago, when she paused in front of the collection for the first time. There were more than three hundred albums then, a hundred fewer than now. The fact that the number of records has grown slowly, comparatively speaking, during their shared existence makes Maria think about how much life Roger lived before her. Without her. Maria was with only one man before Roger: a high-school romance that had led to marrying young and ended with her meeting the famous writer. Unlike Roger, Maria has never tasted the single life. Sometimes she wishes she'd also had a chance to experience irresponsible floundering, finding herself, one-night stands. Freedom.

Maria is not the least bit bothered by the fact that Roger is sixteen years her senior. But a thought has begun to nag at her: that she might one day wake up to a sense of restlessness, the sort that will not die until you have plunged into the unknown a sufficient number of times. And Roger already had the chance to experience that in his previous life. Now, suddenly, on this stormy February night Maria spends pacing alone around their massive waterfront home, she sees this as a threat for the first time. An imbalance that could cause the ship of their

2

relationship to list dangerously, were they ever to drift into the eye of a true storm.

Maria lifts the needle of the record player, takes the vinyl disk between her fingertips and slides it carefully into its cardboard sleeve, where a young artist in a brown suede jacket and a black-and-white-checked scarf looks directly into the camera, self-assured and surly. Bob Dylan's *Blonde on Blonde*. Maria returns the record to its place and picks a new one at random from the end of the alphabetically organized collection. A moment later, after a brief crackle, Stevie Wonder's honeyed, compassionate voice reverberates from the speakers.

And then Maria sees it again. This time out of the corner of her eye. The yard light closest to the shore drifts off for a second. And comes back on.

It goes dark for only a fraction of a second, just as it did a moment before. Maria knows the lighting elements glowing inside the fixtures were replaced before Christmas. She remembers it well, because she is the one who paid the electrician's tastelessly inflated invoice. And for that reason, this trivial matter kindles an inordinate pique in her.

Maria grabs her phone and taps out a message to Roger. She isn't sure why she feels the urge to trouble her husband with such a matter, especially since she knows he is on a stage addressing his readers at this very moment. Perhaps the cause is a fleeting flurry of loneliness, mingled with a dash of uncertainty and unjustified jealousy.

Maria watches her sent message for a moment, waiting for the little arrows at the bottom edge to turn blue, but they don't; Roger is not paying attention to his phone.

At that moment, the record gets stuck: *What I'm about to. What I'm about to. What I'm . . .* Wonder's voice sounds uncertain, thanks to the bit excised from the beautiful sentiment. Some of Roger's records are in such poor condition they aren't worth keeping. *Doesn't anything in this goddamn house work?*

And then Maria feels a cold wave wash over her. Before she has time to make sense of what she has just realized, she looks out the sliding doors and sees something that doesn't belong there. For a moment the contours line up with those of her reflection. But then the figure moves, transforming into a distinct entity of its own.

Chapter 2

ROGER KOPONEN SITS HIMSELF IN THE CHAIR UPHOLSTERED in a coarse, perspiration-inducing fabric, and squints. The spots hanging from the ceiling of the conference center's main auditorium are shining right into the eyes of those onstage. For a moment all he sees is blinding light; he forgets that before him and his two author colleagues sit four hundred curious readers who have packed into this auditorium to listen to their favorite boozers' thoughts on their latest works.

Roger understands that the event is important in terms of promoting his book. He understands why he would bother to drive four hundred kilometers in heavy snow to spend the night at a serviceable dump slapped up on Savonlinna's main square, its mediocre fast-food restaurant on the ground floor dolled up with tablecloths and table service. But what Roger doesn't understand is why the good people of Savonlinna would bother to show up on a night like this. Even though his books have sold millions of copies worldwide, he is never going to be an idol besieged by shrieking fans. Few people ever reflect that musicians and authors do very similar work—same shit, different package—but only the former inspire middle-aged women to toss their panties onstage. But people still show up. The majority are seniors, tilting their heads slowly to one side and then the other. Aren't they tired of the sportscaster-style banalities and superficial analyses authors spew about their own work? Apparently not, as it appears to be a full house: not a single empty seat.

Roger's latest psychological thriller, launched the previous spring, is the third and final book in his enormously popular *Witch Hunt* trilogy. His books have always sold relatively well, but the *Witch Hunt* series blew up. No one anticipated this sort of mega-success, least of all his agent, who originally held a skeptical view of the entire project, or his former publisher, whom Roger dumped prior to the publication of the first installment due to their lack of confidence in its prospects. But in the space of a few years, translation rights to the trilogy have been sold in almost thirty countries and more deals are in the pipeline. Although he and Maria were doing fine before, now they can buy themselves whatever they want. Suddenly all possible luxuries and pleasures are within reach.

The evening goes predictably; Roger has heard the questions hundreds of times during his promotional tours and answered them in four different languages, intermittently modulating his cadence, intonation, and minor details with the exclusive aim of keeping himself awake amid the fog of bright lights and forced laughter.

"Your books are quite violent," a voice says, but Roger doesn't look up from the pitcher he's using to fill his water glass for the third or fourth time. He hears this a lot too, and there's no denying it: brutal murders, sadistic torture, sexual violence directed at women, and nightmarish dives into the depravity of sick minds are described in Roger Koponen's works in graphic detail.

"It reminds me of Bret Easton Ellis, who has said he processes his angst by writing detailed depictions of violence," the voice continues.

Now Roger shifts his gaze to the man sitting halfway back in the auditorium, microphone in his hand. Roger raises the glass to his lips and waits for the man to ask his question. Instead, there's an awkwardly long pause as the man collects his thoughts.

"Are you afraid? Is that why you write?" the man finally asks in a flat, reedy voice.

Roger puts down the glass and takes a closer look at the balding scarecrow of a man. Surprising and interesting. Almost brazen. Now, this is a question he has never heard before.

Roger leans in, bringing his mouth closer to the flexible microphone on the table. For some reason, he feels a pang of hunger at this instant. "Am I afraid?"

"Have you written your own fears into your books?" the man asks, then lowers the microphone to his lap. There's an annoying smugness to the guy. There's not a hint of the jittery respect, the certain reverence fame brings and that Roger has grown accustomed to.

"Right," Roger says, and smiles thoughtfully. For a moment he forgets the person posing the question and allows his gaze to wander across the sea of faces. "I think that something of the author always finds its way into the work. You can't help writing about what you know about or think you know about. Fears, hopes, traumas, things left undone, and then, of course, the things you did and justified to yourself too easily . . ."

"You're not answering the question." The gaunt man has raised the microphone up to his lips again.

Roger feels first surprise and then irritation cutting through him. *What is this, a fucking interrogation? I don't have to listen to this shit, regardless of the circumstances.*

"Could you please be more specific?" Pave Koskinen, the ineradicable literary critic who organized this event and is serving as moderator, has intervened. He no doubt feels that he has handled his role with panache and gusto but is now afraid that his star guest, the red-hot thriller writer who has written three international bestsellers, will take offense.

But Roger raises a pacifying hand into the air and smiles self-confidently. "I apologize. Perhaps I didn't understand the question. Do I write about what I'm most afraid of?"

"No. The other way around," the man says in an unusually cold tone. Someone in the front row coughs maddeningly.

Roger hides his confusion behind an idiotic smile. "The other way around?"

"Yes, Mr. Roger Koponen," the man continues mechanically, and the way he utters Roger's name is not only sarcastic, but vaguely chilling. "Are you afraid of what you write?"

"Why would I be afraid of my own books?"

"Because truth is stranger than fiction," the thin-faced man replies. An awkward silence falls over the room.

Ten minutes later, Roger takes a seat at a long table covered with a white tablecloth in the lobby, which is abuzz with people and chatter. The first fan in the line of those hoping for an autograph is Pave Koskinen. Who else?

"Thanks, Roger. Thanks. And sorry about that one knucklehead. You handled it beautifully. Unfortunately, not everyone is blessed with social skills . . ."

Roger smiles. "No worries, Pave. There's one in every crowd. The only thing any of us is responsible for in this world is our own behavior." He registers that Pave has lowered all three books of the trilogy to the table for signing.

As he scrawls out something ostensibly personal along with his name on the title pages, he glances up at the snaking line in front of him and silently notes that the thin-faced crackpot is nowhere in sight. Luckily. He wouldn't necessarily be able to handle a face-to-face provocation as diplomatically.

"Thank you, Roger. Thank you. We have a table reserved at the hotel restaurant at nine. They make a mean rack of lamb." Pave smiles and stands there in front of Roger, books clutched to his chest like an eager schoolgirl.

Roger nods slowly and lowers his gaze to the table, a prisoner who has just received his sentence. It shouldn't be hard for Pave to realize that Roger would rather retreat to his room. He has come to despise the banal chitchat and forced wine swilling that, as far as he can tell, has zero impact on sales of his books. He could just as easily decline the invitation and allow himself to be branded an asocial asshole.

"Sounds great," Roger says wearily, twisting his face up in an almost credible smile. Pave Koskinen nods in satisfaction, revealing teeth that are more or less white, thanks to new crowns. He seems unsure of himself.

Then he steps aside, making way for the winding centipede of book-cradling readers.

Chapter 3

SERGEANT JESSICA NIEMI TIES BACK HER SHOULDER-LENGTH black hair into a ponytail and pulls on a pair of leather gloves. A bright signal sounds as she opens the passenger door; the engine is still running.

"Thanks for the ride."

The man at the wheel yawns. "It's probably best if no one knows who dropped you off."

They look at each other for a moment as if each is expecting a kiss. But neither will make the first move.

"This was so fucking wrong."

Jessica steps out of the car and narrows her eyes; the icy wind scrapes her face. It has snowed heavily, and the plows rumbling over at the school haven't made it to the waterfront yet. Jessica shuts the car door and sees a large contemporary house looming before her: a compact front yard, an arborvitae hedge clipped at eye level, a wrought-iron gate. Two police vans are parked on the street out front, and based on the sirens howling in the distance, more are on their way.

11

"Hey there." A man decked out in heavyweight blue police coveralls steps out from behind one of the vans and walks up to Jessica. "Officer Koivuaho."

"Jessica Niemi." She shows her badge, but her colleagues in uniform have already recognized her. She has caught a few of the nicknames in passing. *Sergeant Sweetcheeks. Lara Croft. PILF.*

"What happened?" Jessica asks.

"Goddamn it . . ." Koivuaho takes off his navy blue cap and rubs his bald head.

Jessica waits patiently for the officer to pull himself together. She glances over at the house and sees that the front door is ajar.

"We picked up the call at ten fifteen. Taskinen and I were pretty close, so we were the first patrol to show up." Koivuaho gestures for Jessica to follow him through the gate. She does, acknowledging the officers waiting near the van with a nod.

"What did dispatch say?"

"We were told that there was a suicide threat at this address," Koivuaho says, as they step up onto the porch. A puddle of melted snow has formed on the flagstone floor of the entryway. The wind dies for a second, and Koivuaho continues: "The door was open, so we went in."

It is only now, under the bright porch light, that Jessica sees the depth of the fear in the husky man's eyes. She curls and uncurls her aching fingers and allows her mind

12

to form an image of the situation based on the little she was told a moment ago on the phone.

"So there's no one else in the house?" she asks, even though she knows the answer is negative.

Koivuaho solemnly shakes his head and puts his wool cap back on, pulling it down to his ears. "We checked both floors. I have to say, my heart has never pounded so hard. Plus there was that damn music coming from the speakers."

"Music?"

"It was, like, inappropriate for the situation . . . too mellow." Koivuaho hands Jessica the basic protective gear: gloves, face mask, a pair of disposable shoe covers. She bends down to slip the blue plastic booties over her black sneakers. Her holster slides a hair toward the floor.

"Where's the body?"

"We tried to leave the place uncontaminated," Koivuaho says, then coughs into his fist.

Jessica brushes a strand of damp hair from her forehead and walks toward the picture windows giving onto the sea. She passes a powder room and the kitchen and enters the living room, where the walls are all glass. The emergency lights glaring through the enormous panes make the furnishings pulse blue in time to her heartbeat. The room looks far too much like an aquarium to be comfortable, but when Jessica sees the figure sitting at the head of the table, she abruptly stops assessing the room's aesthetic dimensions.

Jessica pauses and tries to figure out why the woman sitting almost upright in her chair looks so incredibly unnatural. She takes a few steps closer, and her stomach drops.

"Have you ever seen anything so creepy?" Koivuaho asks, somewhere behind Jessica, but she doesn't hear the question.

The dead woman's face is twisted up in a hysterical grin. Even her eyes are laughing. The expression is in utter contrast to the fact that this woman lost her life just a moment ago. She's wearing a black cocktail dress, its most prominent feature a plunging neckline, and her crossed hands rest on the table. The table is otherwise bare. No phone, no weapon. Nothing.

"I felt for a pulse. I haven't touched anything else," Koivuaho says, and now Jessica turns to look at him. Then she warily steps up to the woman and leans in to examine the face distorted in an unnatural grimace.

"What the hell . . . ?" Jessica mutters in a voice so low that the only one who could hear her would be the woman, if she were still alive.

Jessica glances down and quickly observes that the bare feet have been crossed underneath the chair, and a pair of matte black Jimmy Choo spikes have been placed tidily on the floor next to the chair. Both the toenails and fingernails have been painted a glossy black.

"Koivuaho?" she finally says, returning her gaze to the forced euphoria of the woman's face.

"Yes?"

"You called this in as a homicide. Even though this doesn't seem like your typical suicide, it—"

"Shit." Koivuaho gulps, takes a few steps toward the table. A trickle of sweat runs down his knobby temple, behind his ear, and vanishes between the thick neck and the collar of his coveralls. He appears to avoid eye contact with the lifeless woman as he tentatively continues: "Didn't they tell you? The call to the emergency number—"

Jessica is getting impatient. "Yes?"

"She didn't place it." Koivuaho pauses for a few seconds to lick his parched lips.

Jessica knows what he's about to say next, but even so, hearing it makes her shudder.

"It was called in by a man."

Chapter 4

ROGER KOPONEN TOSSES BACK THE REST OF HIS CALVADOS, swishes it gingerly around his mouth, and doesn't catch the tiniest hint of apple or pear. Cheap crap. And yet the meal itself has been a positive surprise, for which thanks is not due to the organizers, but to Alisa, the thirty-something manager of a local bookstore. A hot little number who has capitalized on a beautiful face and melodious laugh by keeping her figure in mint condition. *CrossFit.* She mentioned it earlier when she was explaining how her ex-boyfriend had forgotten the keys to his third-floor apartment, and they had climbed in by piling up garden furniture and . . . blah blah blah. *Who gives a shit?* Roger watched the discreetly gloss-moistened lips form the words instead of paying attention to the details of the story. The germane point was that some months ago, the boyfriend who featured in the story had, by either his, her, or mutual decision, earned the prefix "ex."

The way Alisa has been looking at Roger is the way single women in their thirties—who are wavering between eternal youth and the burgeoning urge to reproduce—do in the best-case scenarios. Roger relishes the attention. He

16

was never a ladies' man in his youth. Just the opposite, as a matter of fact. His interaction with the opposite sex had gotten off to a miserable start during early adolescence, and it had taken nearly two decades for him to repair those original disappointments. As a young man, Roger had been too weird and different for women his age, and it was only upon reaching his forties that Roger had genuinely started to have confidence in his appearance and charm—so that nowadays he could actually accept that the woman sitting across from him was batting her eyes at him and not the Shia LaBeouf look-alike standing behind him, pouring more crapple-flavored hooch.

Age has brought Roger success, money, self-confidence, and, above all, the sort of charisma that a spray tan, shirt-stretching abs, and a thick head of hair are incapable of producing on their own. Women want him. Like many inveterate oat-sowers, he has found his segment, the type of woman he never fails to get. Maria eventually joined this happy club. And Alisa the bookstore manager is inevitably going to be included in it too.

"Am I the only one who hasn't read the *Witch Hunt* books yet?" Alisa asks with a laugh. The sycophants sitting around the table bray their ironic disapproval and join in the laughter. Alisa takes a sip of her wine and shoots Roger a playful look from behind her glass, shrugs conciliatorily as if she had just pelted him in the back of the head with a snowball. She is flirting through provocation. And Roger finds it incredibly sexy. He feels a swelling erection and considers the possibility of rising from the table and visiting the men's room. Alisa would follow him; there's no doubt about that. He could take the little bookseller for a real ride without having to look at her lying next to him in the bed of his hotel room afterward. Without having to come up with something private and profound to discuss when there was nothing left to talk about.

"You're in the minority, Alisa," Pave Koskinen says at her side, his spoon filled with melted ice cream from his dessert plate, and continues: "It feels like everyone has read them. Even people who never read detective novels."

Roger lowers his glass to the table, smiles at Pave, and is certain that his phony grin has failed to conceal his revulsion. The old fart has shed whatever remained of his dignity by refusing to drop the toadying and trying to rescue his star author from a jab that, in his deplorable lack of social insight, he does not recognize as a mating dance.

"I'm going to powder my nose." Alisa dabs at the corners of her mouth with her napkin, as if etiquette required her to do so, and stands. She's a step ahead of him.

Roger's eyes trail her as she walks around the table in her high heels and, when passing Roger, discreetly brushes against his back. An unnecessary gesture; the game is obvious. Roger takes a moment to eye the dinosaurs sitting around the table and sees that only Pave has raised his uncertain gaze to follow Alisa. *So you have a pulse too, Pave.* Roger strokes the stem of his Calvados glass and considers his next move. It's been over six months since

18

the last incident. He has since promised himself countless times that he would never fool around behind Maria's
back again—at least in situations where the risk of being
caught exceeds the temptation. This is a borderline case.
The desire blazing in the young woman's eyes makes her
particularly intriguing, and over the course of the dinner,
it has become clear that there's no point expecting a deeper
connection. Wham bam, thank you, ma'am. A couple of
minutes is all he needs.

Roger pushes back his chair, lets out an almost percepti-
bly excited sigh, and stands. He glances at the clock on his
phone and notices that he has received three calls from an
unknown number and a WhatsApp message from Maria.
Two hours ago. The yard lights still don't
work! Beneath it a crying emoji—and an orange angry face.

Roger feels a wrenching in his gut. The fact that he
suffers pangs of conscience for his behavior doesn't make
him feel like any less of an asshole. Roger suddenly understands that it was wrong for him to commit to Maria simply because he doesn't want anyone else to nose in on his
kill. He knows that any middle-aged man would give one
of his kidneys to be able to grow old next to a woman
like Maria. And despite that, he's rushing off after the girl
from the bookstore.

Don't stress. I'll handle it tomorrow.

Roger waits for a moment to see whether Maria reads
the message, but when she doesn't, he returns the phone to
his pocket.

"Please, excuse me," he says, not offering more of an alibi, and stalks off. It's only after he steps out of the private dining room that he hears the flies gradually dare to continue their buzzing. Going on about what a great evening it has been and how they're sure Roger thought the event was a success too. The restaurant is otherwise empty, and Roger crosses the deserted dining room toward the toilets. He passes the reception desk, nods at the desk agent who has just answered the phone, and spots the door to the ladies' room. It has been left slightly ajar. His heart pounds harder, and in his mind's eye, he sees how in no time flat he'll be hiking the black-and-white dress up to waist height, pulling the panties to the side, and thrusting himself into that young woman, putting a hand over her mouth to prevent her from arousing the curiosity of other guests.

But just as he's reaching for the door handle, he hears a voice behind him and freezes, like a teenager who's about to sneak out for a party and is accosted by the angry tone of his mother. But the tone of this voice isn't scolding; it's somehow apologetic. It belongs to the woman from the reception desk.

"Excuse me. You're Roger Koponen, aren't you?" she says from a safe distance.

"Yes," Roger replies, wondering whether he can still claim, with any credibility, that he misinterpreted the symbol representing a shepherdess' silhouette.

"There's a phone call for you."

Roger registers that the desk clerk seems concerned. *A phone call? Amazing fucking timing.* And before he can ask, she continues: "It's the police."

"What?" The question blurts rudely from Roger's mouth; he is simultaneously surprised and disappointed.

The sound of high heels clacking against the tile floor carries from the ladies' room.

"The police are on the phone. They said someone is on their way."

"Wh—"

"Your wife. It's about your wife."

Chapter 5

JESSICA NIEMI HAS REPLACED HER BLACK LEATHER GLOVES with a pair made of thin elastic rubber. As she smooths out the wrinkles, her superior Erne's words creep into her head: *Gloves protect the evidence from the investigator, but they also protect the investigator from the evidence.* It feels particularly apt in this instance. The cause of the woman's death is impossible to determine by visual examination of the body. No external wounds, signs of strangulation, or other clues. The table—or, more likely, the entire room—may be contaminated by some toxin invisible to the naked eye.

"Tech is here." The voice belongs to Yusuf Pepple, one of the investigative team's senior detective constables.

Jessica turns and sees Yusuf nod at the open front door. Jessica can't see the street, but she hears an engine idling and the side door of a van being pulled shut. Yusuf is a couple of years Jessica's junior, an athletic man with big eyes whose roots are evidently in Ethiopia. Not that Yusuf has ever set eyes on the country: he was born and raised in Söderkulla, an idyllic area in the Helsinki commuter town of Sipoo. He has the demeanor of a sweet country boy, almost overly so.

22

"Has the husband been contacted yet?" she asks, shutting her eyes. The wind is making the large house moan; it sounds as if it were trying to tell its own story about what happened.

"The police in Savonlinna contacted him. Someone's on the way to the hotel where he's staying as we—"

A mobile phone blares out, ringing, cutting Yusuf off. Jessica opens her eyes and scans the room.

"Where is it?" she mutters, and watches Yusuf approach a sofa set across the room.

"It's here next to the remote; it slipped between the cushions—"

"Wait!" Jessica says, unintentionally snapping at Yusuf. She strides over. The iPhone on the sofa is playing a vaguely familiar melody as a picture of a man flashes on the screen. Rouzer <3.

"Rouzer?"

"Roger. Roger Koponen," Jessica says, huddling over the phone.

"He looks really familiar . . ."

"Guess you're not much of a reader?" Jessica asks laconically as she lowers her gaze to the floor.

Yusuf studies the smiling middle-aged man on the screen for a minute before realization brightens his face.

Jessica pulls down her mask, takes off her right glove, and answers with the middle knuckle of her forefinger. Then she turns on the speaker.

"Hello?"

After a brief silence, a firm but fearful voice speaks: "Maria?"

"Roger Koponen?" Jessica asks, bringing her face closer to the screen.

"Who is this?"

"This is Sergeant Jessica Niemi with the Helsinki police." Jessica pauses for a few beats. The man at the other end of the line doesn't say anything. But Jessica could tell from the tentativeness in his voice that the bad news has already reached him. "I'm sorry."

"But . . . what happened?" Roger Koponen's voice isn't breaking, but it's searching for its intonation.

"I'm sorry. It would be best if you came home." Jessica feels her throat constrict in empathy. She hasn't had to have many of these conversations over the course of her career; responsibility for informing loved ones has fallen on her shoulders on only a few previous occasions. Not that it necessarily matters: her colleagues assure her that the task doesn't get any easier with repetition. How do you tell someone the words they dread hearing more than anything else in the world?

For a fleeting second, Jessica considers how and from whom she heard them herself the first time. Might it have been one of the ER doctors? Or her aunt Tina?

Jessica swallows to lubricate her dry throat and is on the verge of speaking again when the line goes dead; Koponen has ended the call. The wind conveniently stops wailing, and for a moment she and Yusuf can clearly hear the investigators talking outside the house.

"Did you say the husband is in Savonlinna?" Jessica asks without looking up. The screen of the phone goes black. Jessica tries to turn it back on, but her attempt is foiled by the request for a PIN code. Suddenly the device is nothing more than a useless hunk of black metal.

"That's what I was told."

"Damn it," Jessica mutters again, prompting her colleague to prick up his ears. What a case. The wife of Finland's current number-one export, the thriller writer Roger Koponen, has died in circumstances that are, at the very least, suspicious. The husband is conveniently halfway across the country, which eliminates the statistically most probable scenario. And then there, right in front of their faces, is the phone from which the man who murdered Maria Koponen had, in all likelihood, called the emergency number just a moment ago, before making his way into the frigid, blustery night. The perpetrator can't be far. But then Jessica realizes she is rushing to conclusions.

"Was the call to the emergency center placed from this number?" she asks, feeling an irresistible urge to look over the back of the couch to where Maria Koponen is laughing hysterically. Or that's what it would look like in a photograph, a burst of overacted hilarity. But it's not a photograph. Everything else in the room is living in this moment. The blue lights, the wind, Yusuf, and the leafless trees swaying outside. But Maria Koponen is stone-dead.

"I don't know," Yusuf says, unzipping his coat. Frigid, freezing air is flowing in through the open door, but the room is still hot.

"Could you please call and find out? Now."

As Jessica speaks, three figures in white coveralls waddle slowly into the living room, as if trying not to wake the princess sitting at the table from her eternal slumber. Jessica watches the forensic technicians go about their business in such a routine fashion that they might just as well be engaged in some mundane chore, like emptying the dishwasher. By any standard, these protective-suit-wrapped human burritos have seen plenty; it takes a lot to throw them off. Even so, Jessica can't help but notice how each one stops in turn to eye the corpse and the configuration of its pretty face, which is more reminiscent of Jack Nicholson's Joker than anything else.

"That's it for the first one," one of the techs mumbles from under his hood and mask. Based on the footfalls echoing from the hallway, he has just come downstairs from the second floor, and he stands there in front of Jessica, scanning the room as if he has nothing better to do. The three other techs are working at the body, deep in concentration.

Jessica looks at the tech and narrows her eyes to indicate that she doesn't grasp his meaning. She has a hundred percent confidence in these people's competence; not once

26

has she had to intervene in crime-scene practices over the course of her career.

"What?" she says, but the tech is already turning around; she sees him disappear into the hallway.

Jessica steps past the table and toward the bookshelf burdened with LPs. She walks past the long row of records, allowing her rubber-skinned fingertips to dance across the album covers' slender spines. Dozens and dozens of albums; the couple must really love music in its analog form. An author's bookshelf full of music.

Jessica stops in front of the record player and registers that it's a brand-new piece of equipment and presumably connected to the home's wireless sound system. The needle has risen from the surface of the record, and the PVC disk is resting, motionless, on its overlarge platter. It's a forty-five. A single. The cover is there on the wooden side table next to the player: a black-and-white image of John Lennon, eyes hidden behind round sunglasses, looking at the camera. *"Imagine." Released as a single for the first time in the UK.*

Jessica picks up the cover and turns it over. Two sides. Two songs; one per side. "Imagine." Jessica feels a cold wave shudder through her as she remembers what Koivuaho told her when she first showed up. *That damn music.* If the song was still playing when the patrol arrived, someone must have lowered the needle to record just before the police entered the house.

Jessica lets the cover fall to the side table and slips her hand under the bottom of her coat before she has time to register the true significance of her insight. She wraps her hand around the polymer grip of her Glock and turns to look at the white angels tending to the body. There are three of them. There have been only three this whole time, and none of them ever went upstairs.

Chapter 6

JESSICA STRIDES BRISKLY DOWN THE SHORT HALL TOWARD the front door. She unsnaps her holster and tilts the gun slightly toward her body, releasing the locking mechanism. She feels a throbbing at her temples; her rhythmic, ever-intensifying heartbeats make her feel incredibly alive, a body running on automatic functions. When she reaches the door, Jessica sees three officers in uniform, two police vans, the tech van, and the hearse, which just pulled up. The ambulance, called in pointlessly, is leaving. The flashing blues and reds of the emergency vehicles dominate the color scale of the nocturnal idyll; they draw their strokes across the neighboring lots and the buildings, where lights indicating curiosity are coming on in more and more windows.

The officers notice Jessica's alert state before she can even open her mouth.

"Is everything—"

"Where did he go?" Jessica barks.

"Who?"

"That CSI!"

"Oh, him . . ." one of the officers says, raising his thumb to indicate the street leading down the hill. "He just headed—"

"Running?"

"Walking."

"One of you come with me, now!" Jessica orders, taking a few backward steps down the road, illuminated by street-lamps swaying in the wind.

"Was he—"

"And you, call dispatch and tell them the killer fled the scene on foot just a moment ago. We need more bodies and fast!" Jessica speaks emphatically, pulling her pistol out of the holster. The dramatic gesture makes the bearded officer start, as if this was what it took to convince him Jessica is dead serious.

They drop down the snow-blanketed street, where the deep tire tracks look as if they could carry a streetcar. A densely spaced line of fresh footprints is clearly visible on the sidewalk. The man in white coveralls has indeed walked away: the tracks of a running person would be farther apart. They'll be able to catch up to him if he's not expecting them to follow him soon. Even so, confusion bores into Jessica's mind during the few seconds it takes them to hustle to the corner where the footprints lead. The murderer knows they will chase after him. It's what he clearly wanted: a moment before, he marched up to Jessica and opened his mouth, despite the fact that he could have simply strolled out of the house without anyone being the wiser. If she had only understood during the encounter that he was no CSI . . .

Jessica feels goosebumps form on her skin. She has seen the shit who murdered Maria Koponen, looked him in the eye. And now the asshole is out here somewhere, on the loose and triumphant.

"He can't have gotten far," the officer says. Despite his beefiness, he is keeping up without the slightest shortness of breath.

Jessica grips her pistol in both hands as they approach the intersection; her line of sight to the cross-street is blocked by a tall, snow-crusted spruce hedge. She slows down, shoots a glance at the officer at her side, whose movements are a mirror image of her own. Jessica peers around the hedge and sees an empty street with a pileup of cars parked on either side.

"Motherfucker," Jessica mutters, scanning around for the footprints. There's no sign of them. The road has been plowed, and by walking down the middle of it, the fugitive has been able to continue on his way without leaving any easily discernible trace.

Jessica hears the sirens of approaching patrols. The clank and growl of a snowplow carry faintly from somewhere in the distance.

"He could be hiding behind the cars. Or under," the officer whispers confidently, then calmly advances toward the closest parked vehicles.

Jessica replies at normal volume: "He'd only do that if he had to hide in a hurry."

"Doesn't he?"

Jessica doesn't answer. She softly curses the long seconds it took her to grasp that the killer had just walked out of the police-cordoned crime scene on his own two feet.

"Maybe he had a car parked here," the officer says. It's not a totally off-the-wall idea. But, at first glance, there are no parking spots melted by a car or tire tracks merging into the driving lane.

"What's your name?" Jessica asks as they advance cautiously, car by car.

"Hallvik. Lasse Hallvik."

"OK, Lasse. Check the cars. Stay on your guard. Reinforcements are on the way," Jessica says, and starts jogging down the long, brightly lit road.

"You're not going after him alone, are you?"

Jessica doesn't make any sign of responding; instead, she pulls out her phone and lifts it to her ear, pistol still in her other hand. She runs down the middle of the street, cars on either side, fully confident that Hallvik is covering her. At least for this stretch of road.

"Hello?" The alert voice that answers belongs to Erne Mikson, who just half an hour before was made investigative lead on the case.

"I'm not sure if you got the message from the switchboard, but we have to close the interchanges leading to the

Kulosaari bridges. Fast." Jessica can hear the tension in her own voice.

"What's going on there?"

"I'm trailing the killer on foot . . ."

"With who?"

"No one."

"Jessica!"

"He went this way just a minute ago . . . I have to see if . . . Shit, hold on . . ."

Jessica slips the phone into her coat pocket and holds the Glock with both hands again. For a second she's sure she's looking at a person lying on the ground. But the white coveralls shivering in the street are empty, like a Michelin Man who has been pricked with a dagger. One leg flutters in the wind, as if indicating the direction its owner has in all likelihood continued on in his journey. Jessica glances back, sees Hallvik crouching between cars a hundred meters away. She puts her fingers in her mouth and whistles to get his attention.

"Lasse! Make sure no one drives over this!"

At first Jessica isn't sure if he heard her yell since it was flying into a headwind, but he stands and hurries over. Jessica continues down the road and is considering her next move when she registers the sirens growing louder. Some ineffable instinct prompts her to stop and whispers the unfortunate truth. They're not going to catch him. Not tonight. She lets out a deep sigh and feels the sting in her lungs. Then she puts her hand back in her coat pocket.

"Erne?"

"Goddamn it, Jessica! I was already thinking—"

"Erne, I screwed up."

She hears her boss' voice, but her mind has already leapt onto a spinning merry-go-round with no room for new thoughts to jump on in the middle of the ride. The man who conjured up a smile on Maria Koponen's lifeless face might be watching them at this very moment from the depths of the darkness. There's no sign of him. And yet he's everywhere.

Chapter 7

CHIEF INSPECTOR ERNE MIKSON HAS BEEN DOWN FOR over two weeks with a nasty flu, but even so, the characteristic odor of the interior of his car—a distinctive blend of marzipan, worn leather, and burned clutch—penetrates the stuffiness in his nostrils.

Erne hears a faint beep and pulls the digital thermometer out from under his arm—*37.4. Goddamn it . . .* That's 0.3 degrees higher than it was when he climbed into the car in Pasila. Erne glances at his watch, searches his pocket for the small notebook, and jots down the reading in the next free square. The thick notebook has served him for years, and it is now on its last legs.

Erne starts when the passenger-side door of his old 3 Series opens. A thirty-three-year-old woman with black hair steps in, the angularity of her pretty face exaggerated by her stony expression and the dim lighting.

For a moment they stare straight ahead, where a dozen cars stand outside a house a hundred meters up the road. A police van closer by is parked crosswise across the street, its message underscored with the blue-and-white cordon tape of the Helsinki Police Department.

"Looks like the circus has come to Kulosaari," Erne eventually says, shoving the notebook back into his breast pocket. He pops a piece of nicotine gum out of the foil and into his mouth. The calming effect of the cigarette he smoked ten minutes earlier with the window cracked has dissipated. Besides, by now, at the latest, it's high time to cut back. Or even quit. Although it may not do any good.

"Aren't you coming inside?" Jessica says quietly, then leans her head back against the headrest.

"No. Seeing as how I don't have to." Erne's eyes appear to be yawning. He unrolls the window a little. "Male, forty, average build, relatively broad-shouldered, a hundred and eighty centimeters, and . . . lightly dressed, considering the weather?"

"I don't think a heavy coat would have fit underneath the coveralls."

"We have six guys who fit the description, but they're all wearing big coats. One from the street, three from the pub at the shopping center. And two more from the bus stop on the expressway. We set the radius for apprehending potential suspects based on how far he could have gotten at a run. Five more minutes and we would have had to push it out to the Herttoniemi waterfront too. And that means we would have run out of resources." Erne turns to Jessica and continues: "Jessica, you did everything exactly the way you were supposed to."

Her boss' words elicit a grunt from Jessica, but they offer no consolation. Erne is speaking to her like a soccer coach talking to a kid he has pulled out of the game after the first half. His compassionate tone doesn't change the fact that things on the pitch didn't go as intended.

"Tell me, Erne." Jessica gulps audibly before continuing: "How long have you been at the unit? And over that thousand years, how many times has an investigator talked with the killer at the scene of the crime and then let him go?"

"You can see it that way if you want to torture yourself."

"How the hell am I supposed to see it?"

"Well, for instance, that he could have pulled a gun and shot all of you if you'd begun to suspect something. No one would have necessarily had time to react." Erne turns down the radio. From the look on Jessica's face, he can see there's a seed of truth in his words. They thought they were safe, and he could have easily hurt anyone who was in the house. Not just Maria Koponen.

"Six suspects?" Jessica finally says, unzipping her coat.

"The fibers from the coveralls will be compared to their DNA."

"What about the mask?"

"We didn't find it. Probably in a trash can somewhere. Or with the perp."

"That makes no sense," Jessica says softly.

"Because he left the coveralls on the street?"

37

"Yes."

"Listen, Jessie," Erne croaks, cutting off pointless speculation. He focuses his gaze on the man stepping through the gate of a yard across the street, whom Yusuf is gesturing to stay away. The nosy neighbors have caught the whiff of carrion. "Do you think you'd recognize his voice?"

Outside the car, one of the investigators starts to take a statement from the neighbor, who's wearing a parka, pajama pants, and low boots.

"Sure. But I'll bet you none of them is the perp."

"A pessimist is never disappointed." Erne reaches into the back seat for his leather satchel and pulls out a tablet. A second later he hands it to Jessica. "Six videos. Same sentence six times." *That's it for the first one.*

Jessica watches the clips, listens to the voices, and looks deeply into the eyes of each suspect, wanting to believe she would recognize the culprit. The creep who, just forty-five minutes ago, was standing in front of her at Maria and Roger Koponen's record shelf.

Two of the men in the digital lineup are clearly intoxicated, which has been confirmed with breathalyzer results recorded in the comments at the bottom of the screen. One is incredibly—if not particularly suspiciously—relaxed; the other three seem annoyed. And Jessica can't blame them: who wouldn't be pissed off, having to stand in the glare of bright lights, reciting a phrase fed to them by the cops without the slightest idea what was going on. Someone has more than an idea. But just as Jessica guessed, it's none of the men from the video.

"No," she says, and hands the tablet back to Erne.

"Are you sure?" Erne says, knowing full well that the question doesn't warrant a response.

After a moment of silence, he rakes a hand through his thick gray hair and coughs to open up his voice. The wheeze carrying from deep within his throat does not disappear with the coughing, however.

"Here. Rasmus has gathered all the relevant info on Maria Koponen," Erne says, handing Jessica a printout. The dead woman's curriculum vitae, all the basics on her interrupted life.

Jessica takes hold of the sheet of paper and starts reviewing it, line by line.

"'Age: thirty-seven . . . Education: PhD in pharmacy . . . Profession: VP, product development, Neurofarm Inc . . .'"

"I don't know if you're going to get anything useful out of that."

"That remains to be seen," Jessica says, then folds the paper up and slips it in her pocket. A white hare bounds across the road. Maybe she should interrogate it too.

"I have to head over to HQ to prepare a press release," Erne continues.

"Lucky you."

"The circumstances are pretty unusual. We need to warn people."

"How? *Don't open your door for a criminal investigator?*" Jessica grumbles as she strokes her knuckles.

Erne lets out a joyless chuckle. Black humor is part of the job, and Jessica is a master at taking it to the extreme.

They sit there for a moment longer, collecting their thoughts.

"We need to expand the investigation. And then there's interrogating Roger Koponen," Erne eventually says, rolling up the window. "I'll handle all that. Your job now is to figure out what the hell happened in that house. It looks like we're already talking to the neighbors. Maybe one of them saw something."

"OK." Jessica opens the passenger door. "Try not to have a heart attack, Ser Davos."

"If anyone's going to give me one, it's you, Arya."

Chapter 8

ROGER KOPONEN SITS AT A TABLE, FINGERS WRAPPED around an empty water glass, staring at the forehead of the woman sitting across from him. The social worker who just stepped out informed him that she'll be waiting in the next room if Roger wants to discuss what happened. Chief Inspector Sanna Porkka from the Savonlinna police force reaches for the glass pitcher and pours him more water. Sanna is a forty-two-year-old single woman and lifelong resident of this eastern Finnish city whose life revolves around her police work, hunting, orienteering, and three old Finnish Hound bitches.

"I should probably start heading back to Helsinki," Roger says, his glazed eyes not budging from the spot where the ceiling hits the wall.

"I understand," Sanna says, then calmly leans back in her chair. "But first we'll need you to blow into the Dräger. I'm assuming you had some alcohol with dinner . . ."

Koponen's tone is incredulous: "Are you fucking kidding me?"

"Actually, we'd prefer you'd spend the night in Savon-linna, just as you planned."

"Why?"

"The news you just heard would be a big blow for anyone. You have a long drive in lousy weather ahead of you, and there's nothing you can do in Helsinki tonight to help."

"True. I suppose it's a little late for that." Roger's voice is barely louder than a whisper. He smiles faintly, but only with his mouth. In every other way, his expression is pained.

Sanna knows that the family members often behave in strange and erratic ways due to shock; you can rarely deduce anything useful from their reactions. But glazed, unmoving eyes, pallid skin, and accelerated breathing indicate genuine distress.

"Have they caught him?" Roger asks now with a little more determination, his trembling hands raising the glass of water to his lips.

Sanna takes a quick glance at her notes to check how much the victim's husband has been told. Apparently Roger Koponen has been informed that his wife has died at their home in the Helsinki neighborhood of Kulosaari and that the police have probable cause to suspect that it was a homicide. Then her thoughts refocus on Koponen's question.

"Excuse me, but do you have some reason to assume that the perpetrator is a man?" she asks, doing her best to avoid a cross-examiner's tone. At this point, the police have no reason to assume Roger Koponen had any part in his wife's death, but fully excluding the possibility may become notably more difficult if careless mistakes are made during questioning. The truth of the matter is, Sanna has no role in the investigation; her sole task is to keep an eye on the celebrity author who has just lost his wife. The temptation to ask him some basic questions is too over-whelming, however.

"I don't know. Isn't it pretty likely?" Koponen says slowly, lowering his glass to the table. His eyes brighten a bit, as if he were proud of his observation.

Sanna purses her lips and nods. He's right, if the matter is considered from a statistical perspective. In nine out of ten cases in Finland, the murderer is a man. The ratio is even higher if the perpetrator and the victim are strangers to each other.

"Our only aim now is to catch the perpetrator. And the police in Helsinki think the place you'd be of most use is at this computer. Here, in Savonlinna, at this station, where we'll do our best to make you comfortable. Not in your car, tired and in shock, where you'll pose a threat to yourself and possibly other travelers on the road." Sanna purses her lips again and hopes she projects enough empathy. Then she taps in the password for the laptop.

Koponen frowns. "How am I going to be of use at a computer?"

"The lead investigator in Helsinki, Chief Inspector Erne Mikson, would like to talk to you. We'll set up a video call," Sanna says calmly, folding her hands on the table.

Roger Koponen blinks a few times, as if this proposal were utterly absurd. Nevertheless, his body language does not speak of outright opposition.

"A video call?" Roger mutters, appearing to furiously ponder the idea.

"As I said, our only goal is to—"

"You said *aim*."

"Excuse me?"

"A second ago, you said your only *aim* is to catch my wife's killer. Not *goal*." Koponen scratches his eyebrows with a fingernail; a flake of dead skin floats down to the table and comes to rest next to the glass.

"Right. You're right. I did." Sanna tries to smile understandingly. She considers whether she ought to give him some time alone to compose himself. But there's no time. Just half an hour ago, she received word that the suspect is still at large. The minute hand on the square wall clock pulses a notch ahead, coming to a brief rest on top of the twelve. "Would you excuse me for a moment?" Sanna says.

After a few seconds, Koponen nods his apparent approval.

Sanna shuts the door behind her and gestures to the officer on duty to keep an eye on it. She glances at the young social worker standing near the deafening grind of the coffee machine and heads for her office.

"Is he ready?" Erne Mikson's weary voice asks over the phone. The sound of a car engine hums in the background.

"He's pretty shaken."

"We have to talk to him."

44

"I know." Sanna walks over to the window. The bare birches staring back from the darkness wave their wispy branches at the warmth inside.

"Of course we'd prefer to do it face-to-face," Erne says, and Sanna hears the rustling of foil. There's a pause as the jaws at the other end of the line concentrate on chewing gum. In the end, the hoarse voice continues: "Somehow it feels a little disrespectful to talk through a screen to a man who just lost his wife, but . . . we have to get as much information as possible immediately."

"Gotcha." Sanna's word choice makes her feel like an insecure adolescent who understands the language of adults but doesn't know how to speak it.

"Fifteen minutes and I'll be online. Take good care of him in the meantime."

"Sorry. There's one thing . . ." Sanna interjects before her colleague in Helsinki cuts off the call.

"Yes?"

"Koponen . . . he says he really wants to see his wife. Maybe even a photograph from the scene . . ."

"Of course," Erne says after a brief silence. The hum of the car engine stops and Sanna thinks she catches the sound of spitting. Then a car door slams shut, there's the click of a lighter, and a deep inhale as Erne draws the smoke into his lungs. "Of course he fucking does. But trust me when I tell you you're going to want to hold him off for a little while."

Chapter 9

JESSICA PULLS ON A FRESH SET OF SHOE PROTECTORS, WHITE coveralls, gloves, and a mask. Suddenly being in the house feels unsafe, even though after the most recent incident it has been checked thoroughly. She steps into the living room again, sees that the techs have expanded their evidence gathering and moved on from the table. Maria Koponen is still sitting staunchly in her seat, the same lunatic grin on her face. It looks as if the hostess is the only one who hasn't gotten the memo about the murder.

Normally, the body would have been zipped in a bag and removed from the scene by now, but apparently there are still too many questions in the air—the kind where finding the answers could be critically impaired by moving the woman's lifeless body.

"Do we have the slightest idea what happened here?" Jessica asks. She has waved over the tech in charge of the crime scene, this time one she knows for a fact is part of the investigative team. The murderer in disguise has put her on edge.

The tech is a good-looking guy named Harju, and he looks at Jessica reassuringly with his brown eyes. He sighs and takes off his mask. "The very slightest."

"So basically nothing?"

"The only thing we know for sure is it wasn't a break-in. The perp entered through the sliding door in the living room. Then shut it behind him. It wasn't locked. As a matter of fact, it's still unlocked."

"It wasn't locked . . ." Jessica mutters.

"Or else the victim and the perpetrator knew each other and the victim let th—"

"Somehow that's a little hard to believe. The perp had white coveralls with him and . . ." Jessica steps past Harju and continues: "Whatever he used to create this work of art here."

"Her face is rock-hard."

"What?"

"It's as if it's been artificially locked into that position. It's hard to say . . ."

"Was something injected into her face?" Jessica squints and now notices that the victim's head is slightly tilted. It must have been this whole time.

"That's my guess. But we won't know for sure until after the autopsy."

"Let me know right away if you come across anything else out of the ordinary."

"Sure thing."

"Thanks." Jessica turns back toward the hall. Down at the far end, the front door is still open, letting in a flood of lights and sounds. The house is cold as hell. Nor do the white canvases with their minimalistic brushstrokes hanging from the white walls give off any warmth, just the opposite—they emphasize the frosty ambience.

Jessica walks past the record shelf into the hall and steps into the spacious kitchen for the first time. An incredibly long countertop cut from a single slab of marble runs between the black cabinets and drawers. Jessica lowers her rubber-gloved hand to the cold stone. Everything is spotless, gleaming. Poggenpohl. The matrix of marble, expensive wood, appliances, and hardware that serves as the heart of this home has cost twice the annual salary of the average police officer. Jessica knows, because the kitchen in her apartment is almost identical. It's the apple of her eye and one of the dozens of reasons she could never invite her colleagues to her place. To the place where she really lives.

Jessica allows her gaze to slide from the west-facing windows past the fireplace toward the bookshelf, which holds a huge collection of stories and ideas bound between covers. Her first impression is that the literary offering appears astonishingly one-sided. The same name is repeated on the spine of every single volume. The books diverge from one another in terms of size and color, but every single one has been penned by the same man. Roger Koponen. Upon closer inspection, Jessica realizes that the abundance is not due to the author's prolificacy. Most of the books

48

are translations. *Witch Hunt, Häxjakt, Hexenjagd, Caccias alle streghe.* Jessica knows Koponen's thrillers have found an international readership. That is what has made all of this possible for the Koponens: the luxurious waterfront home and contemporary comforts, including a kitchen that costs as much as a good-sized German sedan. Jessica feels a sharp pain at her temple, as if reminding her that it's not her job to ponder what built the couple's life together, but what tore it apart just a moment ago.

There's a click from the fridge as the compressor automatically starts up, and a low hum fills the kitchen. Jessica picks an English-language volume resting at eye level and studies the cover. The image of a woman in black bound at the stake and the Gothic-script words arcing over it—**Witch Hunt**—look like a heavy-metal poster to her. Jessica flips the book over. *Over 2 million copies sold worldwide.* She pictures the Finnish paperback sitting on her own dresser. A friend gave it to her as a present years ago, but it has remained unread due to lack of time and inertia, as well as some sort of bias Jessica harbors against fiction, the ingrained idea that when you read, you should always be learning something new and useful, that stories welling up from someone's imagination are a waste of time in this hectic world.

Jessica's fingertips are sweating inside her rubber gloves. *A serial killer . . . going after witches.* Jessica doesn't fully understand why she has gotten stuck on the back cover and the plot summary there. A moment later, she flips the

49

book back over and stares at the picture on the front cover. The book thunks to the floor. Jessica doesn't drop it on purpose; it slips from her grip as she starts scanning the other prints of the book. Japanese, Polish, Cyrillic characters. It looks as if every publisher in every country has chosen a different cover image for their edition, but almost every single one portrays a suffering witch. The exceptions are the few featuring nearly identical wintry seascapes of the Gulf of Finland, frozen white. *Nordic noir.* But most of them are of a witch being burned at the stake. Flames. A young woman dressed in black, writhing in agony. The cover of *Hexenjagd,* the German edition, shows some sort of torture rack to which the victim is bound by the wrists and ankles. In her finery. And when Jessica now, for the first time, looks more closely at the woman on *Hexenjagd,* she notices that what she a moment earlier interpreted as agony is the most monstrous grin imaginable. There's a lunacy to the smile, a forced smugness. Jessica can feel her pulse in her ears, the rush of blood.

Erne answers his phone, and it takes Jessica a moment to realize that during those few seconds she has instinctively called her boss' number.

"Jessica? Has tech—"

Jessica can hear her shortness of breath as she interrupts: "Listen. Have you read Koponen's books?"

"Can't say that I—"

"Goddamn it, Erne. It looks like the killer has."

50

Chapter 10

ROGER KOPONEN IS STANDING AT THE WINDOW, LOOKING out into the darkness. The blinds between the panes of glass are partway shut, but Roger doesn't bother to twist them open with the long wand resting against the window frame.

"OK, it's time," Chief Inspector Sanna Porkka says probingly, pouring Roger a glass of sparkling water. The beverage is room temperature; some idiot left the crate of water bottles on the break-room floor instead of stocking them in the fridge to cool.

Roger's eyes remain glued to the window.

"Excuse me, but we have the lead investigator on the line now," she reiterates, and now Roger glances back lazily.

"Then I guess we'd better get started," he says, before returning his gaze to the snow-dusted treetops. He stands there, hands behind his back, eyes locked on the emptiness where his traumatized mind may be trying to see the meaning hiding behind the sting of agony. Roger's stance reminds Sanna of a dictator holed up in his secret bunker, pondering his next move.

A moment later he spins around and walks slowly over to the table, anguished and pensive, looking like he's just decided to pick up the red headphones and launch a nuclear weapon.

Then he speaks again: "Lead investigator?" For the first time, there's a hint of irritation in his voice. Keeping this guy here could grow more challenging by the hour.

"Yes. His name is Erne Mikson," Sanna says, and starts the video call with a few clicks of the mouse.

Apparently the name offends Roger's sensibilities, because he frowns skeptically. Roger can also hear Mikson's Estonian accent, which vaguely calls to mind cruises to Tallinn and the boats' tax-free announcements. Sanna turns the laptop toward Roger and rises from her chair to ensure that the parties on the call can see each other.

"Roger Koponen," Erne's voice says. His face appears on the screen, and it takes a moment before the grainy image comes into tolerable focus. The voice lags a few fractions of a second behind the image. "First of all, I'd like to offer my deepest condolences on your wife's passing."

Roger settles for a laconic thank you, although the term Erne has used to describe Maria's death—"passing"—must strike him as absurd.

"I'm Chief Inspector Erne Mikson, and I'm leading the investigation."

"So I've been told." Roger takes a sip of his raspberry-flavored mineral water. The temperature of the beverage seems to make no difference to Roger, prompting a sigh of relief from Sanna.

"Unfortunately, there's nothing we can do to make things any easier right now. We have to jump right in and make sure we catch the perpetrator."

"How?" Roger asks, but it sounds as if his tongue catches for a moment in his throat. Then he gulps audibly and continues: "What happened to Maria?"

"You can have a look at the patrol's report in a moment. The cause of death will be discovered during the postmortem, which will be conducted without delay."

"Goddamn it." Now Roger is speaking at a near hiss. In the space of a few seconds, he has turned from a deer caught in the headlights into a predator bearing its fangs. "You've seen Maria's body, haven't you?"

"Yes, but—"

"So then tell me what happened to her."

"We don't know yet—"

"Fuck! Tell me something! In your own words! Was she shot? Strangled? Was she . . ." Roger lowers his quavering voice, and his trembling fingers clench into fists. "Was she raped?"

"As I said, the cause of death remains unknown. No indications of sexual violence have been detected yet. But the investigator at the scene has found similarities to—"

"Similarities to what?"

"One of the books from your *Witch Hunt* series." Erne pauses, gives Roger a moment to process this information. "Or more than one. I don't know, because unfortunately—"

"What fucking similarities?" Roger barks.

Sitting across the table, Sanna has no trouble identifying with his outburst. Her colleague in Helsinki is speaking in riddles, even though Koponen deserves to hear the unvarnished truth.

"May I call you Roger? I'm going to send you a photograph now. I understand it's . . . What you will see is shocking. But we have cause to suspect that the perpetrator has been inspired . . . that he has copied his method from your book."

On the screen, Roger sees Erne lower his hands to the keyboard. He doesn't reply; he breathes heavily and waits. A moment later, a bright bing sounds. Sanna is just getting up from her chair to help Roger open the attachment, and then she sees him raise his hand to his mouth in a way that lets her know there's no need.

"What the hell?" Roger's eyes have widened into saucers. The hand wanders from the mouth, up the nose, and grips the furrowed brow. Sanna hasn't seen the picture, nor does she, despite her burning curiosity, think it would be appropriate to circle the table to satisfy it. She'll know how the woman died soon enough.

"I'm sorry to have to show this to you. But could you confirm that you described a female victim in exactly this same way in the first book of the *Witch Hunt* trilogy?"

"Does Maria . . . Is Maria wearing a black dress?" Roger asks, and in a flash he has regressed into the cautious, fearful man who just a moment ago was looking out the window into the disconsolate February darkness.

"Yes," Erne answers.

"Are her nails painted black?" Now Roger's voice sounds as if he has made a firm determination to keep himself together. But his eyes are fixed on the image of his dead wife taken at the scene of the crime.

"Yes."

"Goddamn it," Roger whispers, and grabs at his hair, lets his head tilt backward as if another hand were pulling his hair. Then he sits up straight and takes hold of the computer screen with both hands. His Adam's apple bobs briefly up to his chin. "Have you . . . have you been down to the shore?" he asks, even whiter now.

"The shore?"

"Yes. The shore! Have you been . . ."

"Our investigator found tracks, and we have reason to believe that the perpetrator entered the property from the ice . . ."

"Haven't any of you read the goddamn book?"

Seconds pass without either one of them speaking.

"What's at the shore, Roger?"

"If some goddamn lunatic wanted to reconstruct the scene exactly the way it's described in the book, then Maria isn't the only one . . ."

"What do you mean? What do you mean, she's not the only one?"

"Because there were two witches the whole time. And one of them is buried under the ice."

Chapter 11

I'M SORRY FOR YOUR LOSS. THE WORDS ECHO SO VIVIDLY in Jessica's mind, it almost feels like she said them out loud. She passes the kneeling olive-skinned figure whose grief-stricken gaze is glued to a name etched in the white stone. The man lowers his head, sobbing quietly, and rubs his tear-dampened eyes with the heel of this thumb. A tattooed neck peers out from under the black ponytail, and the loose collar of his T-shirt reveals muscular sun-bronzed shoulders. Then his gaze returns from his knees to the grave, and his fingertips touch the flower-decorated door behind which the deceased rests, now ash. Jessica noticed the man from a distance as she meandered down the paved path between the urn vaults, but only now, as she approaches him, does she see how handsome he is.

I'm sorry. The words catch in her throat again, and Jessica steps past the man without him noticing her, let alone turning to look at her. Jessica quickly glances over her shoulder and is relieved she ignored the impulse to stick her nose where it doesn't belong. It would have been inappropriate. And yet she finds herself yearning for something. The man's eyes. As refined and beautiful as the man's profile had been, she did not see his eyes. They must be brown and mournful.

The air is hot, oppressively so; Jessica can feel the electricity in it, a moist touch on her skin. The black clouds looming in the distance omen a thunderstorm. Twenty minutes earlier, Jessica had leaned against the railing of the *vaporetto*, gazed out at the inky horizon, and reflected that the rain made the city of a hundred islands even cozier.

Jessica's trip from Murano to the historical center of Venice was interrupted when the *vaporetto* stopped at San Michele. On a whim, she stepped off the boat and onto the dock of the cemetery island sheltered by a brick wall and cypresses.

Now Jessica is walking unhurriedly between the massive tombs, marveling at all she sees. At San Michele, the dead rest on top of one another in above-ground catacombs reaching up as many as nine stories, just like the residents of concrete apartment buildings. The overall effect is stunning: almost every vault is adorned by bouquets of flowers and photographs of the dead embedded in the stone. In many of the pictures, the faces are stern; the black-and-white shots in particular emanate severity, but there are plenty of smiling faces as well. Occasionally a corny, forced shot has been chosen for the grave, making for a final resting place that's vaguely embarrassing, even sad. But loved ones presumably choose a picture in memory of the deceased that shows them the way they want their kin

57

to be remembered. Maybe some people simply don't have enough photographs to choose from.

The first rumble of thunder bursts and Jessica feels a warm breeze on her face. She climbs a few stairs to a sand path running past a semicircular row of tombs and gazes at the trees rising amid it, their leaves dancing in the gusts of wind. Jessica loves cypresses and the pines and especially the palms reaching heavenward; they remind her of her father, mother, and little brother. The sand crunches under her sneakers, but when Jessica stops, perfect silence falls over the little plaza. Even the dove that was cooing a moment ago, somewhere hidden from view, has fallen silent.

Jessica remembers the signs at the cemetery entrance: *Vietato fotografare, bere e mangiare.* She glances around, but there's not a soul in sight. She would wait to eat the snacks she packed in her shoulder bag in the *vaporetto* to Venice, but she wants to record some personal memento of this one-of-a-kind island. She raises the camera hanging around her neck and snaps a few pictures of the charming clearing and the vaults surrounding it. Then she lowers the camera and lets it dangle from its strap, slowly circles the curving building, and carefully peers into the open mausoleums. Everything is tasteful and well-tended, graced with time's beautiful patina.

Jessica steps into a doorway and her gaze strikes upon a female figure, life-sized, a crown of thorns visible under the hands clasped to her breast. The figure has trained her wistful gaze down and to the side, as if pondering the answer to a difficult question; there's something compelling about the ghostly eyes. Jessica is burning with desire to step into the chamber, to touch the Virgin Mary's cheek and feel the contrast between warm thought and cold reality. She enters warily, registering that the air inside the thick stone walls is cooler than it is outside. Jessica pulls her thin jacket more tightly around her and approaches the wall of white marble where the names of the dead have been carved in gilded lettering. Some of the dates of death are recent, while for others no date has been marked. People have reserved places next to their loved ones. The thought feels simultaneously beautiful and macabre.

Jessica extends a hand and lets her fingertips lower to the knuckles of the statue, carefully, so her painted fingernails don't accidentally scrape the holy woman's paper-white skin. For a fleeting moment, she feels some sense of belonging, as if two totally different worlds and times have come together, the sort of comfort only shared sorrow can provide. Now Jessica wraps her fingers around the statue's, and the marble fingers do not feel cold; they are exactly what she has been longing for. The support they offer is frank and unadorned. The intimate moment with Mary is like a drug; it punches full force into her consciousness, its rush like the lightning of the storm rolling in the distance. No one can understand what it feels like. No one can comfort her. Everything is here and now.

Jessica lets out a deep sigh, gradually releases her grip on Mary's fingers, and runs the back of her hand across the smooth cheek. *Thank you. And forgive me for intruding.*

At that moment, Jessica hears an ominous blaring from outside. She hurries out but doesn't see anyone. Then she hears an angry, shuddering voice speaking Italian. Jessica tries to understand where it's coming from. Then she realizes: the cemetery speakers. There's something spine-chilling about the message echoing from the amplifiers; it reminds Jessica of World War II movies, soldiers marching in formation, hands raised in the Nazi salute. Jessica glances around in a panic; maybe she has broken the rules by entering the tomb. But after listening she understands that the message blasting from the speakers is a recording: the cemetery is closing. The next *vaporetto* must be the last one.

Chapter 12

JESSICA STRIDES BRISKLY THROUGH THE GATE AND TOWARD the dock. She has noticed the masses of dark clouds approaching from the south and shoves her camera in her shoulder bag as she walks. She sees the *vaporetto* splitting the waves in the distance, forming white crests off Murano, and slows her footsteps. The warm breeze sets her hair dancing in her eyes. She brushes it away and simultaneously feels her stomach drop curiously. A man is standing under the shelter at the *vaporetto* stop. Alone. The beautiful profile she had already banished from her mind is there before her once again. A titillating anticipation and excitement wash over her. She is not the type to fall for anyone easily, but there's something compelling about this man, perhaps a sensitivity born of sorrow.

The man turns and for the first time reveals the square jaw and the brown eyes, bloodshot from crying. They are precisely as sympathetic and melancholy as Jessica imagined.

"Buona sera," he says after looking at Jessica for a moment, then wipes his eyes as if to make sure he hasn't left any tears on his face. The voice is surprisingly youthful but pleasantly low.

Jessica answers his greeting with a cautious smile and steps under the shelter. The man turns back to the sea, hands on his waist. For a moment they stand there near each other without saying a word. Jessica is ashamed that she has come to the cemetery out of sheer curiosity, to find something to paste in her photo album, while this man has come to visit a person he once loved and lost. Luckily she put the camera away, she thinks, and, out of the corner of her eye, spies the ring on the man's left ring finger.

The *vaporetto* on the horizon is making its approach to San Michele. The man turns back to Jessica. *"Sta per piovere,"* he says with a slight smile. *It looks like rain.* There's an empathy in the way he looks at her, as if they were in the same boat. A moment later they will be, literally. Jessica adjusts her shoulder bag.

"Sì purtroppo," she replies, and knows her accent has given her away. Jessica's Southern European style and dark features, black hair, and bright green eyes could easily be those of a local. And while the love of the language she developed in high school has made her Italian fluent, it is by no means flawless.

The man looks momentarily taken aback before nodding, and this time the gaze does not turn back to the sea. He eyes her from head to toe as if searching for the answers to questions he hasn't asked yet. But the cautious assessment conducted by the sad eyes doesn't feel intrusive to Jessica. Instead, she feels like she has been noticed.

"This is a beautiful place," Jessica continues in Italian to break the silence.

The man nods again and rakes back his hair with both hands. Sinews and thick veins bulge against the browned backs of his hands. His biceps tense against the fabric of the white T-shirt; as the sleeves hike up, more ink etched into skin is revealed.

"It is," he answers, lowering his gaze to the tips of his shoes.

The ball is in his court; it's the only way the encounter will continue naturally. But the man doesn't say anything. His face is still marked by grief, and he appears to have to wrestle with it, over and over again.

During the silence, Jessica watches the *vaporetto* come in; its arrival is both irritating and liberating. The captain puts it into reverse to slow the vessel, and the rumble of the engine buries the next clap of thunder. The sides of the *vaporetto* bump against the pier as the vessel clumsily docks. The boat hand, a young woman in a turquoise polo shirt, lassos the rope to the piling and tugs the water-bus up to the dock. *Benvenuto.* The idling vessel's engines burble like a pot of porridge; the heavy reek of diesel fills the air.

The man's fingertips have stealthily crept up to Jessica's shoulder and now they gently nudge her onto the deck of the *vaporetto*.

"After you," he says in English. And as she steps onto the boat, Jessica feels the butterflies in her stomach again, the Virgin Mary's white knuckles on her skin, and the electrified air all around them.

63

Chapter 13

THE *VAPORETTO* IS ALMOST EMPTY, AND AS THE MAN SEATS himself, he leaves the aisle between him and Jessica. Sitting side by side would have felt awkward. "Colombano," he blurts out, then wipes a bead of sweat from his temple.

"Excuse me?"

"That is my name." He extends a hand.

Jessica glances at the cracked skin on the knuckles, the letters tattooed on them. She accepts his large hand and pronounces her name the English way, the way she learned to say it when she was little.

"*Zesika*. That is a beautiful name."

"Thank you."

"Is this your first time in Venice?"

Jessica nods and turns her gaze from the window to the sea. For some reason, Colombano's presence is making her shy. His entire demeanor is wholly unlike that of the insecure, overgrown adolescents she usually meets on summer nights on the terrace at Kaivohuone.

There they sit, two adults, still strangers, one of whom appears impossibly more mature than the other. And is.

Colombano must be over ten years older than she is, maybe more.

Colombano breaks the silence. "Are you traveling alone?"

"No," Jessica says, and the lie gives her goosebumps. "My friends are back in Murano. They were too tired . . ."

"To go to a cemetery with you? You young people sure are strange these days." Colombano flashes a dazzling smile, and Jessica instantly regrets not telling the truth. Then she sees an emptiness creep into his face, not because of Jessica's answer, surely, but because the roller coaster of his emotions has plunged him back into a dark tunnel.

Who are you mourning, Colombano? Jessica thinks as the spray from the open window splashes against her face. She unzips her shoulder bag, pulls out her pocket-sized city guide, and turns through the pages to give Colombano space to collect his thoughts.

When she stepped out of her hotel on Murano an hour earlier, she had been planning to see all the main sights: the Doge's Palace and the Basilica San Marco, as well as the Canal Grande and the Rialto Bridge crossing it. But the spontaneous visit to San Michele has thrown her plans into chaos.

Eventually Jessica can tell from the way her bench is shaking that the captain is easing off the gas. She closes her guidebook and puts it back in her bag.

"Your stop?" Colombano asks.

"Yes. I guess," Jessica says, then bites her lip.

"You guess?"

"I mean . . . I don't know the city that well . . ."

"I understand. I know it extremely well, and still I am not sure."

"About what?"

"If this is my stop." Colombano laughs and sighs deeply.

"Well," Jessica says. The soles of her feet are tingling. She slips her bag over her shoulder and stands: "Is it?"

It's hard to say what's happening. The question sounded like an attempt at flirtation, even though she didn't mean it to. Or did she? Jessica hopes that the heat suddenly spreading across her face hasn't turned her cheeks red.

"No," Colombano finally says, almost coldly. "I am going to continue."

Jessica feels her throat constrict. It feels as if someone just pulled the rug out from under her feet. She looks at Colombano, not sure how to bring the conversation to an end. The dock appears outside the windows. The engine rumbles again, and the *vaporetto* lurches as it thuds against the pier.

"*Arrivederci, allora,*" Jessica says with a smile, and turns toward the stairs leading up to the deck. What was she thinking? The man is either married or just barely widowed. What the hell is she—

"*Zesika?*"

She hears the voice behind her and stops. Colombano has followed her, and when she turns around, Jessica catches a whiff of strong aftershave.

"I don't know if maybe you and your friends like classical music." Colombano hands her a flyer. "Vivaldi's *Four Seasons*. I am performing tonight."

Jessica looks at the flyer in surprise. A picture of a string quintet. In the middle stands a handsome man, a violin resting in his powerful arms. "I . . . I'll ask my friends."

"I can arrange two free tickets. The others have to pay."

"Thank you." Jessica smiles and folds the flyer twice. Then she spins on her heels and steps ashore. The air is humid, oppressively so, and the fabric of her T-shirt is clinging to her perspiring back.

Even so, she feels lighter than she has in ages.

Chapter 14

THE BEAMS FROM THE HIGH-POWERED FLASHLIGHTS LICK the yard as the police officers holding them plunge toward the shoreline. Two helicopters hover farther out over the sea, looking for tracks on the ice.

"Form a line and watch your feet!" Jessica shouts, her gaze firmly focused up ahead. The group tramps down the left edge of the property, the same track that the investigators and the patrol have already followed to the water once. The shoe prints that have been photographed and modeled for further investigation range down the path running through the middle of the large yard.

Jessica stops the others by raising her fist into the air and slows her steps as they reach the frozen water. The shore is a confusion of snowfall-softened footprints, presumably those of the suspect. According to the CSI's report, they lead from the Koponens' waterline to a long-distance skating track plowed a hundred yards out on the ice.

"There's got to be some sort of contraption out here somewhere. Something to keep it in place," Jessica says, stopping at the edge of the ice.

Officer Lasse Hallvik stops at her side. His face is serene, as if he had received confirmation that carrying out his duties could get no stranger tonight.

"Contraption?" he asks, resting the butt of the long flashlight against his shoulder.

"That's what Koponen said. Otherwise no one would be able to find it."

"Find what?"

"The second body." Jessica draws her lungs full of the stinging icy air. Her gaze scans the shore. A wooden dock stands at the middle of it; a few meters out, two red snow-hooded buoys are locked in place by the ice. The suspect's footprints approach in a dead-straight line from the south, pass the dock, skirt it, and climb ashore. Then they zigzag back and forth in a ten-meter radius right at the waterline.

"Wait here," Jessica says as she steps onto the frozen sea. Three meters from the shore, a patch of snow cover a square meter in size has been disturbed.

"Goddamn it," Jessica whispers, warily approaching what suddenly looks like a trap. It's a hole in the ice that someone has done their best to cover up. In Koponen's book, the witch is anchored to the ice. Erne's recent words echo in her ears.

"Hallvik," Jessica calls, bending over the now-wet snow. The hole sawn into the ice is not much bigger than a beach ball in radius. Jessica hears Hallvik approach but cannot help herself: she takes action. She tries to jam her fingers between the hunk of ice covering the hole and the sea ice surrounding it, but the water has already frozen.

"Try this." Hallvik removes a multi-tool from his belt, his experienced hands quickly transforming it into a knife. He kneels down at Jessica's side, striking at the ice with sharp blows, and a moment later the frozen mass rises, like the cover of a well. "Crap," Hallvik says. A horrified disbelief has crept onto his face.

Jessica gulps and feels the shivers run down her spine. Hallvik looks at the jury-rigged mooring lodged in the hunk of ice he's holding: a piece of plastic with a thick cord tied around it. Jessica feels nauseous.

"Call the guys over," she says quietly. "We'll need help hauling it to the surface."

Hallvik folds up the multi-tool and puts it back in its case at his belt, maintaining a firm grip on the line. Then he stands and hands the rope to Jessica.

"Someone get over here and give us a hand," Jessica hears him say.

The line is wet and ice-cold. She wraps it around her gloved fist and looks at the hole in the ice: the water is black; it's darkness in liquid form. In all likelihood, a dead woman rests somewhere down there in the depths of the frigid water, and the only thing between Jessica and her is the rope. A bridge between life and death. Despite wearing a down parka, Jessica suddenly realizes she's shivering.

"Do you want to hand that over?" Hallvik says, rousing Jessica from her reverie.

She turns and passes him the end of the rope, sees the line tauten ominously. There really is a body down there. She stands and only now realizes that her knees have gone numb from the icy surface bleeding through the thin denim of her jeans.

Hallvik and another officer in uniform pull the rope up out of the water. Flashlights illuminate the operation from all sides. The procedure reminds Jessica of pulling a crab trap out of the water. The rope is long; first a meter spools onto the ice, then another. And finally a dark, algae-like clump rises to the surface.

The woman's hair is jet-black, just like Maria Koponen's.

Chapter 15

THE SHARP WIND SENDS THE DRIFTS OF POWDERY SNOW swirling across the ice as Jessica watches the body bag being transported to the ambulance on a stretcher. She shuts her weary eyes for a moment, but the image of the woman's wide brown eyes and pale skin is burned onto her retinas.

"Quite a night," Yusuf says behind her, and lights up a cigarette. Yusuf plays Division II floorball in his free time and rarely smokes, only when he's extremely stressed.

"Let me get one of those," Jessica says.

Cigarette in his mouth, Yusuf shakes his head, nods at the uniformed officers smoking at the police van. He takes a drag, then offers the cigarette to Jessica.

"Forget it." Jessica sighs and shoves her hands deeper into the pockets of her parka.

"Any word from Erne?" Yusuf asks, exhaling the smoke in short, quick puffs.

"He's talking to Koponen. They're going through all the murders described in his books. MO, place . . ."

"Shit. How many are there? Murders, I mean."

"I don't know. These two were at the beginning of the first book."

"Jesus," Yusuf says, tugging the zipper of his jacket all the way up. "What next?"

"Erne should be calling any minute now." Jessica gestures for Yusuf to step to the side, away from curious gazes.

Even though it's past midnight, the reporters crowded behind the police cordon have been joined by bystanders. Half a dozen police officers are watching the street and the property to ensure that no one trespasses into the scene. A tension fills the air. The evening's unexpected turns have put everyone present on edge.

"There's not much we can do right now," Jessica says in a low voice, coming to a stop at the Koponens' fence. "All we know is the perp approached the property from the skating track."

"So we have no way of figuring out what direction he came from."

"If it's not impossible, it's going to be really damn hard. It's been snowing all evening. Tech is checking the skating track right now."

"Did the medics say if she drowned or . . ."

"We'll know soon," Jessica says, watching the smoke escaping from Yusuf's nostrils into the biting air.

Yusuf glances discreetly at his phone. "No one has been reported missing,"

"Not yet. But the victim was carefully selected. Based on her appearance, she could have been Maria Koponen's twin sister."

Yusuf drops his cigarette butt to the ground, suddenly alert. "Does she have one?"

"What? A sister? No."

The rotor blades of a helicopter thunder closer. Jessica eyes the facade of the luxurious house and sighs. She knows what it's like to grow up in a home with so many rooms, it could be a small hotel. She suddenly remembers the leathery smell in the back seat of the black car, the tall metal fence, the fat, friendly man who dressed like a police officer even though he worked for a security company. There aren't any booms, fences, or guards like that in Finland; there's not a single gated residential development in the entire country. Anyone at all can ring anyone else's doorbell without getting into trouble. The Kulosaari waterfront is one of the most expensive neighborhoods in all of Finland, and even so, someone entered the house without anyone noticing and murdered Maria Koponen.

"Jessica?" Yusuf says, rousing her from her reverie. He nods at the police officer farther down and across the road who is waving for them to come over. He's talking to an elderly woman in a parka.

They hurry over.

"Detective Niemi," Jessica says, extending a hand toward the old woman. As they shake, Jessica feels the brittleness of the bony fingers. The woman's wrinkled face is dotted

74

with liver spots and her voice drags, but her gaze is keen. Jessica notices the little eyes shift and pin themselves on Yusuf, the suspicion flashing in them.

"I'm sorry I didn't come out earlier," the woman says in a feeble voice, and then looks at the Koponen house in concern. "But I was sleeping so soundly that—"

"No need to apologize, ma'am," Jessica says. She glances at the green metal gate and the steep driveway rising behind it and wonders how the old woman managed to toddle down to the street without slipping and falling.

Jessica gives the woman a moment to collect her thoughts. She glances at Yusuf, who looks a little disappointed. And for good reason: it is highly unlikely that an old woman who was deep in sleep a few minutes ago would have seen or heard anything relevant at the time of the murder.

"It's the oddest thing," the old woman finally says, and shrugs up her shoulders inside her coat. It makes Jessica think of a shivering turtle. The old woman's eyes are suddenly fearful.

Jessica takes a step closer. "What's that, ma'am?"

"You'll have to come with me. I can't remember . . ." The old woman gestures for them to accompany her.

Jessica and Yusuf exchange perplexed glances and then follow as the woman carefully picks her way across the yard. Yusuf gestures for the patrol officer to stay put.

"Maybe her sink is clogged or—" Yusuf whispers.

Jessica shushes him as they slowly ascend the steep driveway. At the top of the large yard stands an ornamental

75

wooden house with a light on in one of the upstairs windows. Despite the disturbing events of the evening and the deep freeze, the old woman has left her front door open.

"You're going to have to come upstairs," the woman continues as they step in. She hangs her coat on a hook and swats dismissively when Jessica and Yusuf make to take off their snowy shoes. The varnished plank floor creaks under their feet. The entryway smells of old wood and damp.

"What's upstairs?" Jessica asks a little impatiently as the old woman lowers her foot to the first tread. She quickly thinks through various alternatives but cannot come up with anything useful in terms of the investigation that would be found on the second floor of the woman's house.

"You'll have to come see for yourselves," the old woman mutters, and continues up the stairs slowly but determinedly.

Jessica shoots another glance at Yusuf, who shrugs.

At the top of the stairs, there's a hall, its walls hung with dozens of black-and-white portraits. Most are group pictures in which a youngish woman and a dozen or so children and adolescents are looking at the camera. Maybe the woman used to be a teacher.

Light is shining from the open door at the end of the hall. They make their way to it, the old woman leading the way.

"This is my bedroom. I'm sorry. I haven't had time to make the bed," she says as they step across the threshold.

76

Jessica gives her an understanding smile and eyes the room. A bed, a mirror, a writing desk, an armchair. A Persian carpet, a small chandelier. Everything in perfect order. The old woman walks over to the window and stands there, back to them. Jessica discreetly glances at her watch. Maybe Yusuf was right after all; maybe old age has muddled the woman's sense of reality.

Jessica wipes strands of snow-dampened hair from her forehead. "You wanted to show us something, ma'am."

The woman slowly turns around. Her voice is now chilling, mechanical. *"Malleus Maleficarum."*

"Excuse me?" Jessica frowns and steps farther into the room.

The woman repeats herself; the words sound like Latin. A sudden eeriness falls over the room. The words surge out of the old woman's mouth as if the lips uttering them were possessed. Her face is simultaneously confused and fearful. Jessica's fingers rise instinctively toward her holster. Her body is instantly in a state of heightened alertness.

"At my age, your memory starts to be poor," the old woman says softly. "But there's nothing wrong with my vision." She points at the window.

Jessica and Yusuf warily step up to it. They're standing on the top story of a three-story home built at the crest of a hill, and they're much higher than the homes on the water. Then Jessica realizes the woman is pointing at something they could not have seen from the street.

"What the hell . . . ?"

MALLEUS MALEFICARUM. The words are there in large letters on the Koponens' snow-covered roof. Jessica raises her phone to her ear and glances at Yusuf. There's no sign of the mockery that smoldered on her colleague's face a moment ago.

Now he looks like he's seen a ghost.

Chapter 16

CHIEF INSPECTOR ERNE MIKSON LEANS BACK IN HIS CHAIR
and rubs his wrists. His desk is covered in random printouts from the internet. Snippets of text and images he
found with a quick search. *Malleus Maleficarum.* The term
refers not only to a French black-metal group, but also to
a book about witch hunts published in the fourteen hundreds: *The Hammer of the Witches.* According to Wikipedia,
this guide of questionable repute, collated by the inquisitor
Heinrich Kramer, provides detailed instructions on how
to interrogate, torture, and punish suspected witches. A
little digging reveals that a Finnish-language translation of
the book is available, and a copy is currently being rustled
up for the unit.

A moment ago, Erne got off the phone with his boss,
who at the end of the call promised more resources for the
investigation first thing in the morning. The text that was
written on the roof has deepened the enigma surrounding
the murders, especially since there is no mention of anything like it in Roger Koponen's books. This means that
the two homicides were carried out faithfully following the

fiction imagined by Koponen, but the text drawn on the roof of the house that served as the scene of the crime feels like a joke made on a whim.

Erne pops a piece of nicotine gum out of the blister pack and into his mouth. The fruity taste fades fast, and the burning sensation spreads across the back of his throat. The wind has finally died, leaving the open-plan office unsettlingly silent.

"Jessie," Erne says, swallowing down the prickling sensation.

The voice carrying through the phone's speaker is tired but determined: "Is there anything new?"

"I'm going to talk to Koponen again here in a minute. We came to the conclusion that it would be best for him to start heading to Helsinki immediately. Someone from Savonlinna is going to drive him."

"I understand."

"We're getting reinforcements in the morning." Erne can sense his young detective's impatience. He has gone against his principles and called a subordinate even though he doesn't really have anything new to report.

"Good."

"You guys go home. I'm going to need you early tomorrow. Tonight we're going to concentrate on tracking the suspect with patrols and dogs. We're going to catch that asshole."

"You think so?"

"Of course," Erne says self-confidently, and picks up one of the drawings he has printed out. It is clearly medieval in style and depicts normal people conversing with horned beings. Devils, maybe demons. The image next to it is more realistic in technique; in it, a woman with bound ankles is being hanged from her arms, and stern-eyed men in dark garb are addressing the prisoner. It is doubtless a depiction of some sort of arbitrary trial. Or torture. In any event, the woman looks terrified.

Jessica's voice reaches him amid the diabolical scenes: "If you say so."

"What?"

"We'll go get a little sleep."

"See you in the morning," Erne says distractedly, and hears Jessica end the call. He clicks open the photographs of Maria Koponen and the woman the CSIs have given the macabre but apt nickname Ice Princess. Her pale, beautiful face is tranquil, as if she were sleeping for a hundred years and she would someday wake.

Erne picks up a few of the medieval drawings of bonfires. Of women being burned at the stake. Cheering crowds. Flames. Agony. It all looks so familiar; similar images were used on the covers of Roger Koponen's books.

All of these crimes were committed by the Inquisition, the body of the Catholic Church established to combat heresy. Erne shivers. Witches never existed, of course, but even so, all of this has actually happened. Innocent women were murdered at the Inquisition's command. And now someone has started copying those abominable crimes. Is it a sadist who has struck on a theme for his murders

81

in the medieval opus and Roger Koponen's thrillers? Or could the perpetrator be so delusional that he imagines he is doing good, ridding the world of witches?

Erne sighs deeply and shuts his eyes. The thermometer bings: 37.7. The information alone makes his temples break out in a cold sweat. He has been taking his temperature for months, more or less compulsively. At the worst, Erne was shoving the thermometer into his armpit two to four times an hour and marking over fifty readings in his notebook in a single day. In hindsight, it has all been completely pointless. Now he knows it was never any use. The doctor promised to call with the results of the biopsy tomorrow. The schedule time of the call is anytime during the workday, as if it were impossible to set a more precise appointment for a call involving such a serious matter.

Pompous fucking quacks.

Chapter 17

YUSUF PULLS OVER AT THE INTERSECTION OF TÖÖLÖNKATU and Museokatu. Lit by the city's lights and the moon, the tower of the National Museum looks surreal against the black sky, like some skyscraper out of Gotham City. The snowflakes drifting through the air are tiny, a color-blocking filter in the image.

"Remind me that someone needs to talk to Maria Koponen's coworkers and boss first thing in the morning," Jessica says.

Yusuf nods. "You want me to pick you up in the morning?" The car's AC system is blasting hot air into the interior.

"No, thanks. I'll make my own way in. Get as much sleep as you can. It's going to be a long day again." Jessica glances at the time shown on the car's central console. It's one forty-seven a.m. She opens the door, and a frigid gust blasts into the warm car.

"See you at the station."

"At eight. Thanks for the ride." Jessica yanks up her zipper and steps out. A taxi is idling at the taxi stand down the block, even though the chances of some lost soul showing up for a ride at this hour are extremely unlikely on a February Tuesday.

Jessica watches Yusuf's Volkswagen Golf turn onto Mannerheimintie and disappear from view. She pulls out her mobile phone. Would Fubu still be up? Jessica is exhausted, but she knows she won't be able to fall asleep right away. She can't get Maria Koponen and the woman anchored to the ice out of her head. Two murders executed in totally different ways. Two beautiful women with dark hair.

Jessica feels a warmth spread into her fingers. The blood is circulating through her veins; she can hear the rush in her ears. She is here, and she is alive.

"Jessie?" The sluggish male voice on the phone sounds surprised.

"Are you . . . you asleep?"

"Sleeping? Fuck that. I'm ready for you."

"I . . ." Jessica sighs and crosses the crosswalk, phone to her ear. The wind tosses the streetlamps on their wires.

"Is everything OK?" Fubu asks, now more seriously. He has clearly heard from Jessica's voice that this is no ordinary call.

"It's been a crazy night."

"You want to talk about it?"

"I can't even if I wanted to." Jessica pulls her house keys out of her pocket. She hears a toilet seat thunk at the other end of the line. She can picture Fubu's filthy bachelor pad, smell the stale sheets that reek of sex and perfume—and not hers alone, someone else's too. Jessica wants to feel a man's body against hers. A man inside her. So hard and so long, she can't take it anymore, until she's so tired that sleep arrives uninvited. She wants to wake up in the morning and leave knowing she wouldn't ever necessarily be returning.

"You want to come over?" Fubu asks after a brief silence.

"Maybe. But I have to get up in five hours."

"We don't have to sleep." Jessica hears Fubu flush the toilet. She pictures him plopping down on his bed in his loose boxers. It's a warm image, safe in the way she needs right now. But then her thoughts wander back to Maria Koponen's petrified face, the perfect makeup, the cocktail dress, the painted nails. A coldness washes over her body.

"Maybe tomorrow. Thanks for picking up," Jessica says, and opens the door to her building.

"Anytime, Detective."

Chapter 18

JESSICA STEPS OUT ON THE FIFTH FLOOR AND SHUTS THE old-fashioned elevator gate. She fits her key into the lock of the door marked with a brass nameplate that reads NIEMI.

She steps in and turns on the lights in her studio apartment, where the windows give onto the inner courtyard. She takes off her shoes, hangs up her coat, and picks up the junk mail the postal carrier has slipped through the mail slot. She stands in the middle of the room, looking around, the sheaf of papers in her hand.

On some nights, especially when she's really tired, Jessica stays here in the studio to sleep. It's a kind of role play for her, like a tent in the backyard where you can leave comforts behind without being in any real danger.

But it has been a couple of weeks since Jessica last spent the night here. It was the night Fubu hit her up at last call, drunk off his ass but as charming as ever, and wanted to offer her, in his words, *the best loving of your life*. Despite the big talk, his performance had ended up being an all-time low, and in the end Jessica had settled for throwing a blanket over her passed-out guest and cleaning up the mess from a wineglass that slipped from his limp grip.

Jessica lowers the mail to the table and picks through her key ring for a second key. On the right-hand wall as you enter, next to the alcove, there's another front door. Two entrances in such a small apartment has always aroused hilarity in her rare visitors.

Jessica opens this door and steps into a second stairwell in her stocking feet. There's no elevator here, only stairs leading down to the lower floors and the airing balcony and up to the attic. There's one other door on the landing, and it's unmarked. Jessica doesn't need to turn on the stairwell lights; she hears the door to her studio close behind her.

The key marked with the green rubber ring sinks into the lock. Once again, light floods into the dark stairwell. But this time Jessica enters the code for a security system before walking down a long hallway. She enters a large room where the bay windows give onto a panoramic view: across the park to the bay and south toward the parliament building and brightly lit Mannerheimintie beyond. The decor is a mix of the latest trends and old furniture, as well as conservative and modern art. Half a dozen paintings in ornamental frames hang on the long wall behind two divans. Despite their divergent styles, the works by Munsterhjelm, Schjerfbeck, and Edelfelt are in complete harmony with one another.

Jessica walks through the living room, passes the spiral staircase leading to the second floor, and enters the spacious kitchen. She clicks on the electric kettle, takes a white mug from the cupboard, and places it on the table, then leans against the counter. Poggenpohl. Aside from the finish on the cabinetry, the kitchen is exactly the same as the one at the Koponens' house. Three years ago, it cost sixty-three thousand euros, including appliances and installation.

The water inside the chrome kettle gradually starts to simmer. Jessica opens the laptop that's on the counter, taps in the password, brings up a search engine and enters malleus maleficarum. An hour ago, *The Hammer of the Witches* meant nothing to her. But now that she has seen the text on the roof of the Koponen residence, she can't resist googling it. Responsibility for investigating the book and its history does not lie on Jessica's shoulders; Erne immediately assigned the research to the unit's nut-crackers, Nina and Mikael, who at this very moment are furiously reading through not only all of Roger Koponen's works but also everything about *The Hammer of the Witches* they can get their hands on in the middle of the night. Nina and Mikael are the homicide unit's power pair, who have an unfailing eye for detail critical to investigations. Jessica also happens to know that they see each other outside of the office, although they don't admit this to anyone. Jessica feels a pang in her heart. Nina deserves a better man—and a better friend.

Jessica clicks open the English-language Wikipedia article. It's more comprehensive than the Finnish one and features medieval drawings detailing various methods of killing. She reviews the text thoroughly; some sentences make her heart skip a beat. *It was permissible to torture a suspected witch until she confessed to being one.* Jessica knows that employing psychological or physical violence to elicit a confession is not an unusual phenomenon—it happens in plenty of authoritarian states to this day—but the idea of witchcraft as a criminal offense is absurd. How many innocent people had to suffer in such horrific ways simply because they were heretics in the eyes of the Catholic Church? How was it possible that one wrong utterance, nasty rumor, or accurate weather prediction could get anyone at all cast into the flames as a bloodthirsty crowd cheered?

Jessica unfolds the printout Erne gave her. She taps the name of Maria Koponen's employer into the search engine and browses through the clinically sleek website of the company called Neurofarm. *Contract manufacturer of neuroleptic drugs*—whatever that means. She could assign further research to the unit's propeller head, Rasmus.

The water in the kettle starts to boil. Jessica raises her glazed eyes from the screen, drops a tea bag into the mug, and drowns it in the hot water. The mug feels hot and numbs her fingertips. It has been ages since Jessica has wanted to numb not only her fingers but every single cell in her body.

Jessica shuts her laptop and rubs her eyes. She's burning with a desire to dive into the case, but her brain needs a minute. Hot tea in hand, she goes into the living room. It's like a museum she has gradually updated every year. The ancient grand piano got the boot, as did the coffee table set that had been in the family for a century. The lily wallpaper made way for pale gray paint. Still, the apartment has a split personality, as if the person living there can't decide if she's thirty or eighty. For some reason, this has been bothering Jessica lately.

A coldness fills her, as if the wind outside took up residence inside her. She finds herself regretting not going over to Fubu's. The home where Jessica was born so long ago has always felt safe, never too big, bare, or lonely.

But tonight Jessica is sure she's not going to be able to sleep.

Chapter 19

A WHISPER. IT'S NOT COMING FROM ANYWHERE NEARBY, but from somewhere too far to be real. And that's exactly why it is so unusual. Jessica opens her eyes. The living room is dark. The time on the cable box reads three thirty a.m. The wind is howling outside, setting the windows creaking. Even so, it's stiflingly hot inside.

A whisper. Jessica sits up. *Who's there?* Jessica thinks, even though she knows the voice belongs to her mother; it was once the most beautiful voice in the world. She remembers sensing it as the sun's rays penetrated her closed eyelids. She remembers the delicate hands that picked her up and held her. Their noses touching in an Eskimo kiss.

A whisper. Mom must know that Jessica is awake. So why is she still whispering? *What is it, Mom?* But her mother doesn't answer; she just sits there at the long dining table with her back to Jessica. *Am I late for breakfast? Are you mad, Mommy? Don't be mad, Mommy.*

A whisper. Jessica slowly stands. Her feet feel feather-light. Her knees are sturdier than they normally are in the morning. Nothing aches. She glides effortlessly toward the kitchen table.

"Mom?" Jessica says, and now she realizes that she doesn't recognize her own voice. It's not the voice of a child; it's an adult's voice. But her mother doesn't turn around. The black hair unwinds on bare shoulders. Her mother looks as if she were on her way to a party. A pair of gorgeous spike heels has been set out under the chair, next to her bare feet. She is wearing her black evening gown, the one she wore to her first major award gala.

A whisper. Jessica smiles when she understands that Mom is speaking a foreign language. Jessica speaks English with her friends at school, Swedish at home with her mother, and Finnish with her father. But the language her mother is whispering this morning is unfamiliar to Jessica. She doesn't understand what the words mean, and there's something ominously mechanical about the way Mom is speaking. It sounds as if she were reading something from a piece of paper, something she doesn't understand herself. Suddenly a frightening thought creeps into Jessica's mind: what if the figure sitting there with her back to her isn't Mom after all, even though she sounds like her? Jessica still can't see her face. The shoulders are alabaster. The moonlight shining through the window forms a bridge to the chair where her mother is sitting.

"Mom?" Jessica says softly as she walks toward the dining table. She wants Mom to turn around and show Jessica her beautiful smile. Take her into her arms. She wants to feel like a child. She wants the world to once more look the way it did through the eyes of a six-year-old.

John Lennon's "Imagine" carries from the speakers. The room smells sour, a bit like the stuff Dad pours into the sink sometimes. But there's no sign of Dad this morning.

A whisper. The words hiss, as if they were slithering out between teeth; they contain a measure of stifled aggression. Jessica is behind Mom now; she touches her bare shoulder. And then Mom slowly turns around. It really is Mom. But the smile is not at all the one Jessica was hoping for; it is not the smile Mom had on her lips on those many occasions she woke her daughter. It is everything but a happy smile.

Jessica feels horror wash over her body; she can't move. She tries to cry out, but all she can produce is a gasp. Mom languidly rises from her chair; her movements are stiff and unnatural, as if someone crushed every single bone in her body and randomly glued them back together. Jessica tries to take a step backward, but the soles of her feet remain firmly on the floor. She has been fixed in place.

"Look in the mirror," Mom whispers, and takes a step toward her, hands extended, fingers hooked like a vulture's claws, ready to sink into her hair.

And then Jessica feels like she's falling. Her fingers are gripping the blanket, and the sofa's upholstery is wet with sweat.

The living room is dark; the timer turned off the television. The time on the cable box reads three thirty a.m. The wind is howling outside, setting the windows creaking.

Chapter 20

ACROSS THE TABLE, THE MIDDLE-AGED WOMAN WITH sharp cheekbones gives Jessica the once-over. A moment earlier, Jessica informed her that she was attending as Colombano's guest.

"There are two tickets reserved for you," the woman says in Italian.

"I . . . I'm alone."

"Of course you are," the woman says, forcing a smile. "Welcome."

Jessica slips the ticket and the program into her purse, steps past the ticket seller, and feels the woman's critical gaze on the back of her neck.

It's pleasantly cool inside. The space is ornamental and churchlike, but wholly void of religious objects and artwork. People gradually flow into the little concert hall, some in polo shirts and shorts, others as if they were planning on attending an opera gala. A symphony of languages echoes in the high room; the majority of concertgoers are clearly tourists. According to the sign out on the street, tickets cost no more than a few dozen euros, so it's unlikely Jessica is in for a world-class spectacle.

Jessica is wearing a navy blue dress and spike heels. She knows she looks beautiful, but isn't sure if she dressed up for the event or exclusively for Colombano. As she was applying her makeup in the hotel room, she was overcome by a sudden uncertainty. The image of the weeping Colombano and the metal band on his left ring finger came back to her. The fact that he had arranged two tickets for Jessica presumably means he isn't looking for company. Would coming alone be strange and, above all, would it reveal that she had lied about her friends? Would Colombano recognize her in the crowd? Would he say hello? Would they have an opportunity to exchange a few words after the concert?

Jessica pulls out the ticket again and glances at it. The seats are not numbered. The first few rows are already full. The majority of audience members appear to be elderly, but the faces of a few young couples appear among the crowd as well. Jessica takes an edge seat midway back and lowers her purse to her lap. Four string instruments are on the stage: the bass and cello lean in their stands; the two violins rest on chairs.

Jessica tastes a sourness in her mouth. Before coming, she ordered a bottle of Prosecco at a café, sipped two glasses, and then abandoned the nearly full bottle in the falling Venetian dusk. The alcohol feels warm in her belly and calms her, like the hand of a trusted friend on her shoulder.

Fifteen more minutes pass before the last guests find their seats. The concert is clearly not sold out; empty chairs dot the room. Finally a chime echoes from the speakers. The lighting dims slightly, and the chatter dies, as if someone turned off a switch. Then footfalls carry from the rear of the hall, and the audience begins to clap. The musicians, men and women of various ages in formal wear, walk past her and to the stage, where each strides directly to a seat and takes up a reddish wooden instrument.

The sounds of tuning reverberate in the silent hall. Colombano is not on the stage. Jessica glances at the doors at the rear of the auditorium, but they're shut. What's going on? She has to be at the right place; her name was on the list. And Colombano said he was going to be performing himself.

Jessica pulls the program out of her purse. The concert hall in the photograph is the same. At least some of the members of the orchestra seem to be the same as the musicians in the photo. Why isn't Colombano here? Did something happen to him?

Now the instruments settle into the firm grip of the musicians' hands. Bows rise into the air. The musicians nod at one another. And then horsehair starts to stroke tautened strings; the bows move back and forth in a controlled fashion, creating such a bright tone that it gives Jessica goosebumps. She looks down at the program: "J. S. Bach—'Air on the G String.'" The melody is so beautiful that it takes her breath away.

Jessica closes her eyes and sees the mound with the flowers on it, herself standing at the edge of the grave, senses the people standing around her and Aunt Tina's hand on her shoulder. Tears are running down her cheeks. The floral sprays are white; that was Mom's favorite color.

The piece lasts no more than a few minutes, but for Jessica it is a heart-stopping trip into the past, an eternity that races by too quickly.

And then it's over. The audience claps again, and it takes a moment before Jessica is able to gather her thoughts and join in the applause. The sound fades for a moment, but then it starts up again. And then a smiling man walks past her toward the stage, a violin in his hand. Colombano. He is the soloist. He is the star of the show.

Jessica crosses one leg over the other and tugs down the hem of her skirt. Her soul feels light. She lowers her hands to her lap and watches the handsome man rise to the stage, place the violin under his chin, and smile at the audience.

But, above all, Colombano smiles at her.

Chapter 21

CHIEF INSPECTOR SANNA PORKKA GRIPS THE STEERING wheel and stares out at the hypnotic sight before her. The powder swirling on the surface of the highway dances in the glow of her high beams. The wedge of light illuminates not only the plowed snow at the sides of the road but the bare tree trunks that hide endless darkness behind them. They have been driving through heavy snow for an hour already, but they still have more than three hours to go before they reach Helsinki, and that's without any stops. On the phone, her colleague Chief Inspector Mikson stressed that there was no particular hurry. The important thing was to get Koponen to Helsinki safely so they can go through things in the morning thoroughly.

Sanna glances down at the navigator on the dash. Once they pass Juva, she is supposed to turn onto Highway 5 toward Mikkeli, from where their trip will continue via Lahti and on to Helsinki. The road will not turn into an expressway until they reach Heinola. Even though there is no traffic to speak of, driving down the narrow highway when she's tired is stressful. All they have come across is the occasional lorry headed in the other direction; Sanna hasn't had to pass a single vehicle.

"Tell me if you need to stop," Sanna says, looking in the rearview mirror. Neither she nor Koponen has said a word the entire drive. The author has been sitting so quietly in the back seat of his Audi that a couple of times Sanna has thought he's fallen asleep. But Koponen hasn't so much as shut his eyes; this whole time, his blank gaze has been directed at the forest flickering past like a monotonous filmstrip. A few thumb-sized bottles of liquor from the hotel's minibar have joined him for the ride.

"Stop?" Koponen says, and now turns his eyes to the front seat. Sanna can smell the whisky on his breath.

"Yes. If—"

"It's one thirty in the morning. Why the fuck would we stop?" Koponen's voice is low; he rubs the wrinkles in his forehead.

For a moment, Sanna considers answering but decides not to. She has tried to be friendly, and that's enough. It's not natural to expect completely normal behavior from anyone in this sort of situation. The guy must be in some sort of shock; he probably just wants to get home, sit next to his wife on the couch, and tell her how crazy everyone else is. But Maria Koponen is dead. And now Sanna knows what Koponen and her colleagues were talking about; she glanced at the image Chief Mikson sent. The frozen euphoria on the woman's face has been etched onto

Sanna's retinas. She can picture it amid the snowflakes scintillating in the car's headlights.

"I'm sorry," Koponen says with a sigh.

A twist cork cracks open in his hands, and Sanna emerges from her imaginings. The speedometer shows a hair past a hundred; it's over the speed limit and otherwise too fast, considering the weather conditions, despite the all-weather tires.

"I don't mean to be rude," he continues in a weary voice, then raises the bottle to his lips.

Sanna isn't sure drinking is what's best for Koponen at the moment. On the other hand, it could calm him, maybe even help him fall asleep. Mikson's instructions didn't include any specific requests: just pack Koponen into his car and drive him to Helsinki.

"No worries," Sanna says with a quick glance over her shoulder. It's too fleeting to catch Koponen's face in the darkness, but she assumes his expression is conciliatory.

Sanna takes her foot off the gas. The V-6 purring under the hood of the Audi drops its revs. Her fingers stroke the tooled leather on the steering wheel. A magnificent machine. Maybe someday she'll be able to get herself a car she wants, not just one she needs.

"We'll be in Helsinki at four thirty at the earliest," Sanna says, jamming a pillow of snuff into her upper lip with the tip of her tongue. Her passenger doesn't respond, but Sanna sees him lean his head back against the headrest.

Sanna hasn't been to Helsinki in ages, and she doesn't have any intention of staying there any longer than absolutely necessary this time either. But she's scheduled for duty today anyway, and it's all the same to her where she spends her workday: at the station in Savonlinna or on the road, chauffeuring a just-widowed bestselling author. Besides, it's not often that she gets a chance to sit behind the wheel of a brand-new luxury car.

"Have you read my books?"

"No," Sanna answers quickly. Further explanation would feel strange.

Koponen lets out a deep sigh. "There are totally crazy things in them . . . If everything that . . . I can't even imagine."

"You'll have a chance to talk about all that once we get to Helsinki," Sanna says calmly.

A few moments pass in silence. Then she starts to hear sobbing from the back seat. Sanna isn't sure if her passenger's sudden outburst is due to the fact that the thought of his wife's death has finally sunk in, or if he is silently reviewing the horrors his imagination has produced between the covers. Grisly fantasies that have inspired some sick individual to kill his wife. Sanna has the urge to say something comforting, but nothing feels right. It has all been said already. The distance to the back seat feels farther than a light year.

A lorry blows past, and the current of air from the massive vehicle rocks the Audi. Snow tumbles across the asphalt, whips into frenzied swirls. And then Sanna sees a bright light creep into the rearview mirror.

Chapter 22

THE WHISKY BURNS HIS THROAT, BUT IT ISN'T NUMBING him. Not enough. The police chief at the wheel of his car has her eyes on the road. Roger feels the blood course through his veins boiling hot, and then it abruptly recedes somewhere, leaving his fingertips ice-cold. The monotonous wooded landscape racing past outside the window, the absolute ennui of snowy conifers is making him nauseous. He is burning with the impulse to take his driver up on her offer and ask her to pull over. He wants to sprint into the forest, to plunge between the trees like a waterbird diving into a weed-choked pond. He wants to disappear in that nondescript mire, to press himself to the earth, to bury himself in the snow. He wants to drift off into hibernation like a bear, giving no thought to the upcoming spring.

It's his fault. He has murdered Maria. The thought releases something inside him. He feels the tears stream down his cheeks and his mouth twist up in inconsolable weeping. He has achieved everything he ever wanted: literary success and a beautiful wife waiting for him in a big house on the water. But now it all feels final, as if he was living and writing for Maria alone, living through her reactions, seeing himself from her perspective. Admiring himself from wherever Maria was standing at any given moment. And now Maria is gone. For good.

Did he love her? Maybe. At least in his own way. He was prepared to make sure she lacked for nothing. Was that love, or had Roger just been keeping his aquarium clean and his fish fed? He doesn't know the answer, and that makes him feel a strangling guilt. And now it's too late to find out; lost happiness will gild those memories forever.

A big truck drives past them. The car rocks; the automatic windshield wipers wave for a second like hands at a rock concert. The car is only six weeks old. Or new. Every single detail, down to the accessories and the leather upholstery, was carefully selected last year. But it doesn't smell like a new beginning anymore. It smells like death. It's like a casket being drawn by 340 horses.

"Turn them off, goddamn it."

"What?" Roger asks with a sniffle, and raises the bottle to his lips.

The police chief glances in the rearview mirror. A bright light is blazing through the car's rear window. "That car behind us has its high beams on," she says, then flips her rearview mirror down.

Roger wipes the corner of his eye on his sleeve, glances over his shoulder, and is instantly blinded.

"Goddamn . . ." Roger mutters, and quickly turns back around. He saw enough to know the car is only a few dozen meters away.

A moment later, the car's lights dim.

"And now they're going to pass us," the police chief says to herself, both hands clenching the steering wheel.

Roger looks over as the car pulls up alongside them. The police chief has decelerated; they're not even going eighty now, but the car doesn't pass. Roger sees the hood of an SUV gliding along steadily, keeping pace with the rear window of the Audi.

"What the hell is he doing?" The police chief at the wheel turns to shoot a flinty look out her window. There's a portable blue light in the passenger seat. It's hooked up and ready to use; the police chief brought it along just in case. The bullshit in the car driving next to them would come to a quick stop if she turned it on.

Roger glances at the console; their speed has dropped to seventy. The SUV is a shadow; it clings to them like a sidecar. The long stretch of road opening up before them is deserted.

The detective's fingers grope for the portable police light. She lifts it up to the dash and turns it on. A band of blue light licks the windows of the vehicle dogging them from the side. And then the rear window of the SUV rolls down. The mini bottle of cognac slips from Roger's fingers. He recognizes the thin face staring out of the open window, the question formed by the black maw gaping at its center.

Are you afraid of what you write?

Chapter 23

THE RINGING MINGLES WITH HIS DREAM. IT TAKES A minute for Erne to wake up and haul himself up to sitting on the well-worn leather sofa. The air conditioning is blowing cold air on his face, and his neck aches. His fever has probably gotten worse. The number flashing on the screen belongs to Sanna Porkka, the police chief who they agreed would drive Koponen down from Savonlinna. It's three fifteen a.m., and the open-plan office is deserted.

"Hello?" Erne has a hard time finding his voice and can't help coughing.

"Respice in speculo resplendent," a female voice says. It sounds like the chief inspector, but the voice is sluggish, shaking.

"What?"

Then silence. There's a rustling in the background. A woman sobbing. Erne tries to process what he's hearing; his thoughts are still confused from sleep.

"Porkka?"

"Respice in speculo resplendent."

"I don't understand," Erne mumbles, and sits up. He is too out of it to make any sense of what's going on. "What's wrong?" His grip on the phone tightens. "Where's Koponen?"

Then there's shouting, and the call cuts off. Erne looks at the screen of his phone for a moment, then goes into his recent calls and brings up Sanna Porkka's number.

The number you are trying to reach is not available.

Fuck. Erne also saved Roger Koponen's number a couple of hours ago but can't get through to it either. Something is seriously awry. Erne rubs his face hard and stalks into his office. He selects the next number from the phone's menu and presses the call icon.

"Savonlinna police . . ." answers a male voice, alert, considering the time of day.

"Mikson, Helsinki homicide. What time did Porkka and Koponen leave Savonlinna?"

"Just a second . . ."

"What time did they start driving toward Helsinki?" Erne snaps, and now he hears fingers leap into action on the keyboard.

An agonizing ten seconds pass.

"According to the log, they left the station at one-oh-three a.m. But weren't they supposed to take his car?"

"Yes. Why?"

"My understanding was they had to pick it up from the parking garage at the hotel, so it would have taken a while before they actually got on the road." The on-duty officer falls silent.

Erne sits down at his computer and feels the pulse at his throat.

"Isn't Porkka answering her phone?" the on-duty officer asks.

"No."

"But . . . if anything happened on the road, we would have been informed . . ."

"If it were an accident."

"What else . . . ?"

"Call me right away if you hear anything," Erne says, and hangs up. He can hear the blood rushing in his ears. The bare branches of the birch scratch against the window.

Erne brings up a map on his computer screen. Did Porkka and Koponen ever leave Savonlinna? *One-oh-three a.m. . . . plus twenty minutes . . . They've been driving for two hours max . . .* Erne drags his cursor along the route from the Sokos Hotel in Savonlinna and stops it between Mikkeli and Heinola.

"Fuck. Fuck. Fuck," Erne whispers to himself, and looks up the teleoperators' dedicated number for the authorities. He lifts the phone to his ear again, at the same time trying to remember what Porkka said just a second ago on the phone. *Respis . . . Damn it.* The words didn't mean anything to him in the first place.

The night-shift worker at the emergency line answers the phone, but Erne stammers, has a hard time explaining what he needs. A cold wave washes over him.

Porkka was speaking Latin.

Chapter 24

JESSICA IS SITTING ON THE EDGE OF THE COUCH, STARING at the dining table. She has turned on the floor lamp next to the sofa, as right now darkness is a racetrack that sends her imagination galloping.

Jessica doesn't remember ever having experienced anything similar. Her dreams have never felt this real.

There's something unusual about this case she's working on. Maybe it's the murderer's twisted MO. Maybe Jessica was more traumatized than she realized by coming face-to-face with him at the scene of the crime a few hours earlier. Maybe both.

Jessica straightens her knees and stands. Her joints ache; she feels a sharp stabbing at her hip. Sometimes she wonders if there's anything else she could do about the pain, but the intensity is rarely bad enough for her to mention at the doctor's office. Pain has followed Jessica for so long that it has become part of her. Her head dealt long ago with what happened, but she intends on giving her body as much time as it needs. She owes it that much.

Jessica passes the chair where her mother was sitting in the dream. She glances at it out of the corner of her eye and returns to the troubling nightmare for a moment, the woman at its heart who was reminiscent of her mother but wasn't her. *Look in the mirror.*

The parquet creaks beneath her feet. Jessica pauses at the kitchen door and feels her stomach drop. *What the . . . ?*

Adrenaline surges through her body. Her black bathrobe is hanging from the backrest of a barstool, right where Jessica left it after her shower. There's no one in the kitchen. Just the bathrobe, which, all things considered, formed a surprisingly effective optical illusion in the darkness. Jessica bunches it up and drops it to the counter. She can hear herself breathing heavily.

The electric kettle clicks on. The clock radio flashes the time. Three forty-six a.m. She needs to get a little more sleep; otherwise the upcoming day will be far too long.

Jessica shifts her gaze to the window and sees the reflection of the kitchen bathed in light, with herself in the middle of it, in sweats and a T-shirt. Her black hair has been tied back into a ponytail. It's hard to make out her facial features.

Look in the mirror.

Maria Koponen has manifested to Jessica in her dreams, in exactly the same position and same clothes Jessica saw her in at the scene of the crime. But the face was her mother's. Jessica has never bothered to interpret her dreams, despite being forced to occasionally discuss them in therapy. Still, she can't help thinking that the words her mother uttered in the dream meant something.

Her stomach growls. She hasn't eaten anything since a late lunch the day before. She grabs the bread from the breadbasket, drops two slices into the toaster, and turns it on high because she doesn't want to wait a second longer than necessary. The water is burbling in the kettle. The laptop is still on the counter. Jessica takes a fresh white mug from the cupboard. As she's pouring water for her tea, she feels her phone vibrate in the pocket of her sweats, and her pulse spikes. Erne wouldn't be calling her in the middle of the night unless it was deadly serious.

"Erne?"

"You're awake."

"I am."

"Sorry. I meant what I said earlier. That you guys should get some rest . . ."

"What's going on?"

"We have two more bodies."

"OK." Jessica realizes that Erne's news, as horrible as it is, doesn't surprise her. Something else was to be expected. Jessica forces herself to wait and let Erne choose his words. All she hears for a long time is heavy breathing.

Eventually Erne speaks: "Call Yusuf and have him pick you up."

Jessica walks over to the kitchen window. Step by step, her reflection grows more distinct, more familiar. Jessica feels a curious relief, as if she has been afraid that window would reveal something she doesn't want to see.

"Erne?" she finally says. "What happened?"

"Two bodies were found in the woods in Juva, near Salajärvi Lake. Sixty kilometers west of Savonlinna . . ."

"Savonlinna . . ." Jessica says softly. She places her fingers against the window. The glass feels cold, as if the icy wind were traveling through it and into her body.

She listens silently to Erne's words, even though she already knows what he's going to say. Koponen's abandoned Audi. Chief Inspector Porkka's mobile phone, a strange call. Then Erne sighs dramatically: "We have every reason to assume that the bodies belong to—"

"What do you mean, assume? Haven't—"

"Jessica. The bodies aren't easy to identify. They've been burned."

"Holy sh—"

At that moment, a sharp pop explodes in the kitchen, and Jessica's heart skips a beat. The phone drops to the tile floor.

A burned smell fills the kitchen. Jessica stares at the toaster, which just disgorged two hunks of blackened bread.

Chapter 25

THE CONFERENCE ROOM SMELLS OF CIGARETTE BUTTS, despite the fact the last time smoking was allowed there was somewhere around the beginning of the millennium. It's early morning, the wind has settled down, but it's still dark out. The window gives onto a view of the gargantuan construction site enveloping the Pasila rail yard, deserted despite the glare of bright lights. Towering cranes rise skyward, like dinosaurs sleeping on their feet.

Jessica intertwines her fingers around her mug and raises it to her lips. With the exception of Erne, the whole team is present: Yusuf, Nina, Mikael, and Rasmus, who, as usual, reeks of sweat. According to the joke going around the station, Rasmus' deodorant is the worst friend in the history of the world, because it betrays him every day. It's pretty amazing that the gibe hasn't reached his ears yet, because if it had, he might have done something about it. Rasmus Susikoski, the same age as Jessica almost to the day, is an attorney by training and hasn't spent a single day in the field. In spite of this—and thanks to his keen observations and

113

encyclopedic general knowledge—he has proven worth his weight in gold during many investigations.

Nina Ruska is tapping blithely at her phone, as if she will return to the spartan conference room at police HQ and a reality more gruesome than a fairy tale only after she has pressed Send. Nina is fortyish, with strong features and a generous sprinkling of freckles; despite her daily uniform of jeans and a hoodie, she always looks beautiful.

Mikael Kaariniemi, sitting at her side, chomps on his gum furiously. Micke is the same age as Nina and has recently given up the battle against hair loss; his dress shirts are always surprisingly well pressed. He raises an eyebrow at Jessica, and she quickly turns away.

"Good morning," Erne says, shutting the door behind him. The other five attendees mumble responses. "The press briefing starts at eight. By then, we have to sketch out at least a preliminary line of investigation."

Erne uses the remote to turn on the video projector. The room fills with the subdued hum of the device hanging from the ceiling.

"You first, Rasse," Erne says, and leans against the table.

The foul-smelling man clears his throat and prods his glasses more firmly onto his nose with his forefinger. He glances quickly at the others and begins haltingly: "We've read through Koponen's trilogy and started a second round, to see if we might catch any details we missed the first time. We found a total of eight homicides, seven of which can be considered ritual murders. For each of the homicides under investigation, a corresponding crime is described in Koponen's story."

Rasmus' words break the tension that permeated the room. They confirm what everyone already knew, deep down.

"Do the crimes in the book take place in this same order?" Erne asks, surprisingly calmly, as he folds his arms across his chest.

Jessica glances at her superior and then turns back to Rasmus, who is sitting at her side.

"No." Rasmus nervously fiddles with the temples of his eyeglasses. "The murders have not been carried out in the same order as in the book. Or, I mean, the first two were, but if we want to view the two middle-of-the night killings as burnings at the stake . . . I have copies here for everyone . . ."

Rasmus pushes a slim stack of papers out into the middle of the table, and everyone grabs their own. Jessica looks at the list and frowns.

Murders committed in Roger Koponen's **Witch Hunt** *series:*
  Book I
Woman, drowned (under the ice)
Woman, poisoned (body positioned in a manner identical to Maria Koponen's body)
Man, stoned to death
  Book II
Man, stabbed with a dagger

Man, burned at the stake
  Book III
Woman, crushed to death (gradually, by heavy stones)
Woman, burned at the stake

"Just a second," Erne says, looking up from the sheet of paper. "Has poison been confirmed as the cause of Maria Koponen's death?"

"Not that I know of," Rasmus replies unhesitatingly; his tone is uncertain. "But with the others, the crime matches the depiction in the book. And the victims match the books' descriptions to a T: dark hair, beautiful."

"Fine," Erne says, picking up his printout from the table and raising it closer to his eyes.

"And these two *burned at the stake*—" Yusuf begins, and Erne replies with a pregnant nod.

A moment of absolute silence falls over the room; everyone appears to be reading the printouts over and over. Jessica sips her rose hip tea; it tastes like iron.

"If we assume that the perpetrator or perpetrators intend on going through the entire list, we can expect three more murders."

"Perpetrators?" Nina asks, jotting something down at the upper edge of her printout.

Mikael glances at her and then at the text she has scrawled there. Jessica looks at the couple and momentarily wonders if Nina wrote herself a note or if she was scribbling a message to Mikael. But their faces are serious.

116

"It's likely that the killer in Juva is different than the one who fled from the Koponen residence," Erne says, ducking the blue rectangle created by the video projector. "But it's by no means certain. The Kulosaari perp slipped away at eleven-oh-four p.m. I received Sanna Porkka's call from Juva at three fifteen a.m. If the perp immediately jumped in a car at Kulosaari and headed for Savonlinna, he could have made it to the vicinity of Juva to ambush Koponen's car, despite the challenging weather conditions."

"Maybe skipping town would be a smart choice anyways," Yusuf says, voice slightly hoarse.

"I still don't think it's the same guy."

"Why not?"

"There's one fundamental flaw with that theory: how would the killer have known Koponen is going to be driven to Helsinki? And at what time?" Erne says, eyeing Yusuf, who shakes his head thoughtfully. "It's hard to believe the guy would have just jumped in his car and driven off without a careful plan, spotted the oncoming Audi at Juva, and then turned around to follow it. Besides, snow was falling heavily last night. Visibility would have been shit."

Erne sits.

"And still, whoever it was got a bonfire to light in the forest," Jessica says softly, eyes glued to her piece of paper.

No one laughs. Not that that was the intent.

A siren bursts out howling on the street. Jessica's thoughts turn to Fubu, who gets skittish every time he hears the sound of an emergency vehicle. *You can take the man out of eastern Helsinki, but you can't take the eastern Helsinki out of the man.*

"The more likely scenario is that someone followed them from Savonlinna. Someone had to be aware of every move they made. The decision to start driving Koponen toward Helsinki wasn't made until around midnight." Erne's Adam's apple trembles the way Jessica knows so well; that decision was made by Erne. In hindsight, it's easy to say it's obvious Koponen needed proper protection during the return drive. Erne is presumably blaming himself for what happened, at least subconsciously.

"A few things to note here," Erne says gravely. "In the first place, Sanna Porkka had her gun with her. Even so, she wasn't able to defend herself against the assailants. Why not? Were the assailants also armed? With more firepower maybe?"

Except for the hum of the video projector, the room is utterly silent. Even Mikael's jaws have momentarily stopped moving.

"In the second place," Erne continues, frowning as if forming the words hurts, "Koponen's Audi was found undamaged at the scene of the crime. So there was no collision, and it wasn't forced off the road. Either Porkka turned onto the dirt road herself, or by that point the car was driven by someone else. Who? Last of all, only one type of footprint was found at the scene. In other words, if there were multiple perpetrators, they were all wearing the same size forty-five combat boots fresh out of the box. The

118

number of footprints at the scene indicates the potential for lots of traffic."

"But the footprints at Kulosaari are—"

"Exactly the same. But, like I said, I believe the perp there is someone else."

"Wait a second," Mikael interjects, rubbing the bald crown of his head. "Multiple perps at Juva. Plus the guy at Kulosaari. Are we assuming now that—"

"Yes," Erne says, and inhales deeply. "Everything points to there being three perps. Or more."

Jessica shifts her gaze from the printout to her warm mug. The tea bag has dyed the water red. She tastes the iron on her tongue, and for some reason, her brain raises the specter that she has prepared herself a cup of blood. For an instant, everything is red: the walls, the screen at the front of the room, the table, the faces of the people sitting around it.

She feels like she's going to retch.

Chapter 26

FINGERS GRIP THE EDGE OF THE SINK. JESSICA TAKES DEEP breaths. She knows the nausea is the result of exhaustion and stress and vomiting won't make her feel any better. She sips water from the tap and raises her head. Her eyes look tired, and despite the minute she took to apply her makeup, her face is etched with worry. She ponders her reflection, which has felt somehow alien since the day before, not at all like her own. Jessica leans closer to the mirror, her features grow sharper, her pupils expand, and staring out at her from the mirror is her mother, her mouth twisted up in a vicious smile.

"Jessie?" Erne's concerned voice carries through the door, followed by an eruption of the dry, deep smoker's cough that has grown chronic over the past few months.

"I'm fine," Jessica says, yanking a sizable length from the roll of paper towels and wiping her eyes. One final glance in the mirror. The sick grin instantly vanishes, but it forces Jessica to close her eyes. It is etched onto her retinas. A few deep breaths. Then she opens the door.

"Are you?" Erne is leaning against the wall. When Jessica doesn't stop, he follows her down the corridor, coughing into his fist. "You're not—"

"I'm not what?" Jessica stops and whirls around so fast that Erne nearly slams into her.

"I'm just not used to seeing you—" Erne stammers.

"See me what? Weak?"

"Not weak, just—"

"What? Is it against departmental policy now to be sick in the morning?" Jessica snaps, hands on her hips. She sees something in Erne's eyes shift as she utters the words. "Fuck. And no, I'm not pregnant." She stalks off toward the conference room.

"Jessica!" Erne growls. His tone has instantaneously turned to one of annoyance. Jessica stops. Erne walks up and takes her by the arm. "For all I care, you can be as nauseous as you want and expecting triplets. But I want you to have your head on straight. Is it?"

"Yes."

"Say it."

"My head is on straight."

"Say it again."

"What is this, some fucking rock concert? Do you want me to shout it so everyone around here thinks I'm crazy?"

"OK." Erne steps aside as the usual anxious smile reappears on his face.

The second she sees it, Jessica regrets her outburst. For some reason or other, Erne has been losing his temper just about every day lately, but she can never be angry with him for more than a minute. Erne's big heart compensates for his deranged need to coddle his subordinates. To coddle Jessica, who she figures is the daughter Erne always wished he'd had.

"The case on our desks right now is the most unusual one any of us has ever dealt with. You understand I'm under incredibly intense pressure to solve this case," Erne says.

"Of course."

"I need results fast. So I need to take everything into consideration—including my team's physical and mental well-being."

"I understand."

"There hasn't been much time to digest the scale of this case. Last night when we talked in the car, there was one body."

"Now there are four."

"And if the signs are accurate, there will be three more before long—"

Erne's sentence cuts off when a door at the end of the corridor opens and clipped footfalls fill the quiet space. They see a woman in a skirt suit enter the conference room, along with a tall man wearing the uniform reserved for the brass.

"Lönnqvist from the National Police Board. A total prick," Erne says in a low voice. "He's coming to the briefing for the press. Along with someone from the ministry—"

"What if there *already are* seven of them?" Jessica says quietly. Her eyes fix on the unbuttoned button on Erne's dress shirt.

"What do you mean?"

"What if the murders did take place in order after all, and we just haven't found the other bodies yet?" Jessica can tell from the look in her boss' eyes that the notion is painfully fresh—and not at all out of the question.

"Either way, I'm sure we'll be finding out soon," Erne says.

"I was thinking of taking Yusuf and going out to the drug-manufacturing facility where Maria Koponen worked."

"The medical examiner should be here in a minute. Wait until after."

"Who was on duty last night?"

"Who do you think?"

Chapter 27

YUSUF LEANS BACK IN HIS CHAIR AND WATCHES AS JESSICA and Erne re-enter the room and take their seats. Photographs of the body fished out of the water are being projected on the screen. The devastating darkness that formed the backdrops of the previous photographs has been replaced by a clinically cold aluminum table and white sheets. The woman's face is pale, serene.

Yusuf unzips his cardigan. The air in the room has grown stuffy. More people have gathered there: two technical investigators, a guy from the National Police Board, as well as the medical examiner conducting the autopsy, Sissi Sarvilinna.

"Our preliminary findings confirm drowning as the cause of death . . ." Sarvilinna says, and moves on to the next slide with the click of a remote. The laser pointer bounces restlessly around the screen.

Yusuf has never met Sarvilinna before, but he has heard she is aloof, stupefyingly direct, and not the least bit fun, despite an idiosyncratic form of black humor. In her religious-conservative attire, she is the stereotype of a no-nonsense medical examiner.

Yusuf squints and wonders how a dead person can look so peaceful. You'd think suffocating would have left traces of fear and panic on her face.

". . . but diatom analysis indicates she was drowned elsewhere." Sarvilinna scans the dumbfounded faces in the room, as if taking the mystery to the next level gave her pleasure. Mikael and Nina are the only two who don't seem caught off guard by the information.

"And then *buried under the ice*," Erne whispers. "I knew the way Koponen expressed it during the video call sounded somehow strange."

"The lungs are full of fresh water," Sarvilinna continues as if Erne didn't interrupt her. "Tap water, to be exact."

"When did she die?"

"Between six and nine p.m., by rough estimate. Furthermore, I can say with relative certainty that she was in the freezing water for a couple of hours, maximum."

"So she was drowned somewhere yesterday evening and then brought almost immediately to the Koponens' shore," Jessica says, jotting down her observations.

"And after the perp drilled through the ice, dropped the body into the water, and covered the hole in the ice with snow, he walked across the yard and into the house, then murdered Maria Koponen," Yusuf says, glancing uncertainly at the medical examiner like a schoolboy who's unsure of his answer.

Sarvilinna doesn't make the slightest indication of responding; instead, she glances at her watch in apparent boredom. It's not her job to confirm the detectives' guesses. She came here to present the facts. The. Cold. Hard. Facts.

"How did it happen in the book?" Jessica asks, and inquisitive faces turn toward Mikael.

He rustles a little blue plastic bag and pops a piece of gum into his mouth. Then he shoots a look at Nina and begins: "In the book, the suspected witch is bound at the wrists and ankles. Then she's thrown into a pool. It's a medieval method of testing whether someone is a witch—either that or a barbaric trial. Take your pick. If the suspect floats even after she's tied up, it's definite proof she's a witch, and she's immediately sentenced to death."

Jessica shakes her head incredulously. "On what goddamn basis?"

"There are two answers to that question. Many believed that, because witches rejected their baptism when they joined the devil's legions, water would repel them. Another belief was that water repels the witch because it symbolizes purity. The craziest thing is if the victim sank to the bottom and drowned—which logic would argue would have been a pretty common result—she was freed from suspicion. But the test had to be performed to acquire the necessary proof. Shitty deal, but hey, at least they did it."

Yusuf dries his sweaty palms on his jeans. "Jesus Christ. That makes no sense."

"So our victim died as a result of one of these tests?" Erne asks.

126

"It's possible. If the murderers copied Koponen's novel. That's how the crime takes place in the book."

"Marks on the body support this theory. There are signs of binding at the victim's wrists and ankles," Sarvilinna says, and clicks onward, bringing up a close-up of the deceased's face.

"Where did this trial take place? In the book, I mean?" Jessica asks.

"At the home of the chief inquisitor," Nina says. She and Mikael exchange glances and sigh more or less simultaneously; they're about to be bombarded with more questions. "Everyone involved in the investigation should read the books. There are some similarities, but . . ." Nina shuts her eyes.

Mikael picks up where Nina left off. "That's just it. There are similarities, but only up to a point."

"Look . . . at this juncture, it's critical we make one thing clear for everyone." Nina sits up straighter. "Koponen's books are part fantasy: supernatural things happen in them. There are women suspected of being witches, and then there are *real* witches too. For instance, in Koponen's version, the woman sitting at the table has already been killed, but then she appears at the head of the table, all dressed up, with the blood-chilling smirk on her face."

"So the killers didn't copy the book's murders exactly? They took inspiration from the events in general?" Erne asks.

The man from the Police Board, leaning against the rear wall of the room, massages his eyebrows.

Nina undoes her blond hair just to tie it up again. "That's how it looks."

Erne makes a note in his little pad. "What about the immolations at Juva?"

"In the series, they're two totally different events. The sole similarities to last night's murders, aside from MO, are that that the victims are a man and a woman," Mikael says, twirling his gum on his tongue.

"Do we know for a fact that the Juva victims are Porkka and Koponen?" Nina asks.

Jessica raises her hand. "I can take this one. The male victim's teeth were removed, apparently to hinder identification, for some reason or other. But DNA tests have already confirmed the victims' identities. DNA lifted from hygiene products at the Koponen residence matches DNA samples taken from the male body."

A few seconds pass before anyone says anything. It's official: Roger Koponen is dead.

"To go back to the Ice Princess," Jessica says, and immediately regrets using the macabre shorthand in the full conference room. "Is it true we still have no idea as to the victim's identity?"

"No. No one matching the description has been reported missing."

"What about a non-match?"

"The murderers could have made up and dressed the victim however they wanted, but I'm sure we're not going to find some ninety-one-year-old Alzheimer's patient underneath, if that's what you're getting at."

"Fine. What about Maria Koponen? How was she killed?"

"There are no external wounds," Sarvilinna says, crossing her arms. "In all likelihood she was poisoned. But it will be some time before we know for sure."

"But what about that smile?" Erne asks.

Sarvilinna brings up a slide of Maria Koponen. Then a second and a third. She advances through the images until a photo of some sort of contraption made up of tiny parts appears before them.

"Those are plugs we found in the cheeks. They were joined by a fine line of wire tied around her head. The line was hard to see, because heavy makeup was applied over it, as well as a sealant to produce the rigid effect on the face," Sarvilinna explains with a scratch of her earlobe.

"Insane," Erne says.

The next ten seconds pass in collective head-shaking.

Eventually Jessica sees the tall man decked out in the uniform of a high-ranking officer glance at his watch and gesture Erne over. Erne rises slowly from his chair, and the two of them step out into the corridor.

Jessica can sense her superior's distress. Erne's role as director of investigations is anything but easy. Four bodies within the course of a few hours is rare by any measure. *Serial killer.* Everyone who has investigated serious crimes knows such cases are extremely rare in Finland.

The country's criminal history knows only a handful of instances that, loosely interpreted, meet the criteria: two or more homicides carried out as distinct actions. Even in this instance, the use of the term is, at the very least, questionable; the facts seem to indicate that, despite certain similarities, the murders in Kulosaari and Juva were committed by different individuals.

"We'll be receiving the preliminary laboratory results within the next few hours." Sarvilinna pulls a thick folder from her leather satchel. "Everything we already know is in here. You know where you can find me."

Tentative murmurs fill the room as Erne steps back in. His boss' tongue-lashing has been brief but intense. The stress shines from Erne's face. No one says anything.

Yusuf opens a tabloid app on his phone, even though he knows it will simply compound the agony. The headlines are confused; the reporters don't know where to begin. *Police. Bestselling Author. Wife.*

A moment later, the fluorescent tubes in the ceiling flicker as Sarvilinna shuts the door behind her.

Chapter 28

THIS MORNING, THE AUDITORIUM AT POLICE HQ IS LIKE another dimension: a lively, brightly lit cell in the otherwise drab body of a government building. Erne seats himself on the outermost chair at the long table, the only one still free. Sporting his blue uniform, Jukka Ruuskanen stares straight ahead without making the slightest sign of greeting Erne as he takes his seat. It's a stressful situation for everyone, but Ruuskanen has been standoffish and full of himself for years. It seems like an eternity has passed since the camaraderie and drunken escapades of the two men's academy days.

Microphones and recorders of all sizes and colors are strewn across the table. Beyond them open up rows of seats, which have been filled by a groggy but attentive audience. Flashes go off; the largest cameras are transmitting the footage live to websites and television. Erne can't remember a time the auditorium has ever been this full; the case has an extraordinary number of compelling elements.

Erne coughs. His mouth feels dry, and no water has been set out on the table. He swipes his nose and catches

131

on his fingers a whiff of the cigarette he smoked five minutes ago.

"All right, folks, it's eight o'clock. Let's get started," Ruuskanen eventually says, and the murmur dies. Meanwhile, the glare of the camera flashes intensifies, as if starting the event has in some way made the police officers sitting there more photogenic.

"I'm Jukka Ruuskanen, chief of the Helsinki Police Department. To my left are Deputy Chief Jens Oranen and Joonas Lönnqvist from National Police Board headquarters." He pauses to look out at the cameras snapping in front of him. For a moment, Erne is sure Ruuskanen has forgotten his existence. But then he finally shifts his gaze to Erne: "And to my right is Detective Superintendent Erne Mikson from the Helsinki Criminal Investigations unit and investigative lead on the case."

Erne feels the cameras turn toward him and accelerate their tireless documentation. Now it's official; once again, he has given a face to the investigation, to the mistakes that will be made and the potential lack of results. The flashes reveal the furrows in his face and emphasize the years that have accumulated in them. Erne knows he looks frail. Time has done its job, but acknowledgment is also due to Rumba, the paper-rolled Estonian poison he's been inhaling into his lungs over the years, perhaps in greater amounts than pure oxygen.

Ruuskanen begins his summary of the events of the previous night. The sweat is running down Erne's back, and his armpits are drenched. He turns toward Ruuskanen, only to avoid looking out at the lenses that are ogling him like big black eyes.

Roger Koponen . . . wife . . . police . . . Ruuskanen speaks laconically.

Erne isn't listening; he could catalog these same details by rote. Instead, he studies the men sitting on Ruuskanen's other side, who have donned the dark blue uniforms of commanding officers, which would look perfectly appropriate at a formal ball. Erne is the only one onstage who has felt free to toss on black jeans, a dress shirt, and a tweed blazer that has seen better days. They are his uniform; the workwear of the Estonian errand boy. Erne is also the only member of the group who will have to take the reporters' calls once the press conference ends; the other three will return to their politicking and activities that have nothing to do with actual police work.

Jens Oranen is clearly younger, but the other two commanding officers are Erne's age. One might make the assumption that Erne slipped off the track at some point, got stuck in place. But Erne has always felt that he advanced precisely the way he wanted. At the age of fifty, he is exactly where he wants to be, doing the work he dreamed of as a little boy. Even so, during moments like this, a certain career anomaly and aberration are plain.

". . . and questions regarding the investigation itself will be taken by the investigative lead," Ruuskanen concludes.

Several hands shoot up in the air before he has even reached the end of the sentence.

"Do the police have any suspects at this time?" asks a woman sitting in the front row. Erne knows she works for public broadcasting. As usual, the questions begin from the most obvious, but Erne knows from experience that they will grow trickier as the briefing progresses.

"We have a description of a suspect in the Kulosaari homicide. At this point, I can say that the suspect is a white male and a native Finn," Erne says, lowering his gaze to the microphone. He has been ordered to release this morsel of information; the Minister of the Interior made it clear he wanted to nip any speculation regarding foreign terrorists in the bud.

"So there are no suspects?"

"As I said, we have a description. No one has been arrested in connection with the case, and we will continue searching for this individual based on information we acquire during the investigation." Erne clenches his fingers into a fist. The halogen lights on the ceiling feel like they're growing brighter.

"What about the killing of the police officer in Juva? Are you certain the perpetrator is a different individual?"

"Considering the distance, it's extremely likely."

"Could it be more than one perpetrator working together?"

"At this point, that is not out of the question."

134

"Had Roger Koponen or his wife received threats in the past?"

"We are not aware of any such threats."

"How were the victims in Kulosaari killed?"

Erne blinks a few times. This is when he needs to call on that infamous poker face. "Due to investigative reasons, we cannot—"

"Is the MO similar to the killings in the woods outside Juva?"

"As I indicated, I cannot—"

"Do you suspect the method of killing is based on Roger Koponen's works?"

There it is. The inevitable has happened, despite the efforts expended to keep details of the crime tightly under wraps.

"At this point, I cannot, nor do I want to, take a stance on the methods used in these homicides."

Erne knows he didn't answer the question. The audience, which consists of professionals who throw curveballs for a living, isn't satisfied.

"Were the bodies burned in the woods?"

His hands are sweating. The word is out.

Ruuskanen presses his knuckles into Erne's ribs, leans toward Oranen, mutters something in his hear, and then nods at Erne.

"Yes. The victims' bodies were found burned," Erne says. He reaches for his water glass, only to realize none was ever brought out. Every word makes his voice box

135

hurt. Over the next few seconds, the orchestra of cameras, laptop keyboards, and whispers swells to a roar.

"People are burned in Koponen's book. Isn't this a clear parallel?"

"Our investigators are currently reviewing Roger Koponen's literary works. If there is a connection between the homicides and the contents of those books, we will strive to find it and make use of it during our investigation."

"Is there a literary template for the Kulosaari murders?"

"Answering that question would contradict what I just said."

"Are we talking about a serial killer here?"

"At this point, those criteria have not been met."

"Do the police have any reason to believe this man will strike again?"

"No."

Ruuskanen and Oranen exchange whispers again. More hands rise, even though no one is calling on audience members to ask any more questions. No immediate reprieve is in store for Erne.

"Why are the police—"

The question ends when the lips of the scraggly-bearded man posing it stop prematurely. For the first time during the press conference, the room is still. The reporter's gaze is glued to his laptop screen, as are those of everyone else. Then a disbelieving murmur starts to spread and rises to wholly new levels. The journalists grab their phones and start tapping at the screens. Those still in the dark peer over seat backs to spy on the screens of those nearby. The faces in the audience are shocked, disbelieving. Excited even. The initial drowsiness has lifted.

Ruuskanen bites his bottom lip and glances around, as if demanding an explanation for the sudden change in mood. Erne pulls out his phone; he hasn't received any new messages from his team.

"What's going on out there?" Ruuskanen growls. It's apparent from his voice that he's supremely irritated at being the only one out of the loop.

"A video was just uploaded to Roger Koponen's YouTube account," the public radio journalist says in a loud voice. "A video of his wife."

Erne wraps his fingers around the fat microphone. He shuts his eyes and sees a face distorted in an unnatural smile drawn onto his retinas.

Chapter 29

MALLEUS MALEFICARUM. MALLEUS MALEFICARUM. MALLEUS MALEFICARUM.

Jessica is sitting at her desk. Yusuf is next to her, leaning in to see. The computer screen is open to Roger Koponen's YouTube channel, on which a dramatic video was uploaded just a moment before. The vertical, slightly unsteady footage has clearly been shot with a phone. It shows Maria Koponen at her familiar place at the head of the long table, lunatic grin on her face. "Imagine" is playing in the background, in addition to which it's possible to make out a didactic, flat male voice mingling monotonously with the rush of white noise. *Malleus Maleficarum.* The voice repeats the words over and over in an unvarying tone. The video is sixty seconds long; all you can see is the face of the dead woman. It was presumably shot only minutes before the perpetrator called the police. Either that or the call had already been made when the footage was shot.

"Fuck. What a creepy voice. Is it a recording?" Yusuf asks.

"That's what it sounds like."

"How long will it take for YouTube to take down the video?"

"It doesn't matter. The video has already been seen, downloaded, and disseminated." Lips pulled tight, Jessica scrolls down. Despite his global success, Koponen's channel only has several thousand followers, but the video has spread like wildfire. There are hundreds of comments.

A sound approximating a whistle emerges from Yusuf's mouth. "Goddamn. Erne warned us we were heading into a shitstorm, but he didn't see this coming."

"How could he?"

Jessica gulps; the sight is chilling. Most of the commenters view the whole thing as a joke, some sort of belated Halloween prank or a marketing stunt for the writer. But the minute-long recording is long enough for viewers to tell that something is very wrong. Maria Koponen isn't breathing. In addition, she exudes an ineffable finality, something almost impossible to fake. Despite this, the comments are anything but empathetic. People can be so cruel. And stupid. Winston Churchill is said to have once remarked that the strongest argument against democracy is a brief conversation with the average voter. These days, you could replace the second half of the quip with *a glance at the comments field in social media.*

"What do you want to do?" Yusuf asks.

"Call IT. We have to find out the IP address the murderer used to log in to Koponen's YouTube account."

"OK." Yusuf exhales and is about to make a discreet exit when Jessica drags her face away from the screen.

"Yusuf . . . somehow I'm getting the sense that heading out to Neurofarm is a waste of time. Will you ask Erne to send one of the guys from the NBI instead, since they offered their assistance?"

Yusuf nods and continues on his way.

Jessica scrolls back up to the top of the screen and clicks the replay button. She has already watched it three times, and it's unlikely the rerun will reveal anything new. The footage is relatively steady, but the slight shakiness reveals that the camera was not supported against the table; who-ever was doing the shooting held it in his hand. *Malleus Maleficarum. Malleus Maleficarum.* The repetitive voice is chilling, but Jessica doesn't mute the sound. She has to hear it over and over; she has to try to understand what the man who entered the house has been trying to com-municate through his actions and the video. Jessica looks at the woman's face, frozen in its wide smile, and the eyes seem to be simultaneously crying for help and jeering at her malevolently.

Chapter 30

THE AUDIENCE HAS EXITED THE AUDITORIUM, BUT JESSICA is still sitting in her seat. The timeless strains of Vivaldi are echoing in her ears. She's not a big fan of classical music, but today the Venetian composer's concerto series, irrefutably his best-known work, has made an indelible impression on her. Of course, another reason for the experience being unforgettable was the soloist: Colombano is not only ravishingly mysterious and handsome, but a true virtuoso with the violin.

Colombano didn't ask Jessica to wait. He just shot her a quick glance as he stepped off the stage and made for the doors at the rear of the room. Nevertheless, something inside Jessica has persuaded her to remain seated. Would Colombano really have invited her to the concert if he didn't have the slightest intention of saying hello to her afterward? But as the banks of lights in the hall go off one by one, it's starting to seem as if Colombano wasn't interested in a date. Maybe he just wanted a bigger audience for his concert.

"We're closing," a woman's voice says in Italian.

Jessica starts and feels the blush spread across her cheeks. "I understand." She wraps her restless fingers around the leather straps of her purse. She turns and sees the woman with the sharp cheekbones, whose face reminds her of a bird of prey. But the coolness that marked the other woman's face before the concert has vanished; it has been replaced by empathy. Perhaps even pity. The expression seems to be saying: *Don't take it personally. You're not the first. And you're not the only one.*

"You should go now," the woman says with a shrug.

Jessica feels her stomach lurch in disappointment. She stands and discreetly nods a goodbye to the woman, who is walking between the rows of chairs, gathering up the programs that were left behind. Jessica's footfalls echo in the large space; her legs feel heavy. The sedative effects of the sparkling wine evaporated during the concert, leaving a hollow sensation in their wake. Jessica isn't sure if it's because of hunger, the letdown, or a combination of both.

Jessica pushes the heavy door open and realizes it has started to rain again. The little drops are light and warm. The humid breeze smells of the sea and vaguely of metal and urine. The voice of a tenor singing a familiar melody carries from somewhere in the direction of Piazza San Marco.

Jessica steps onto the wet cobblestones and nearly loses her balance. Her ankles feel weak, and the pain that preys upon her nerve endings has reappeared out of nowhere. It starts above her ankle, then travels up her leg toward the knee, all the while boring deeper into her leg, like a slender nail being tapped through the bone with sharp hammer raps.

Jessica knows she ought to turn around and take hold of the heavy door handle, lean against it, sit down next to it to wait for the episode to pass. But pride prevents her from doing so. She wants to shake off that ornate concert hall, which, this evening, has served as a stage for humiliation and disappointment.

The pain intensifies with every step. Jessica sees a fountain across the street and starts wobbling toward it like a long-legged doe on slick ice. More nails appear, one in the calf, another in the thigh. In the end, the pain is unbearable. Jessica knows her legs will not carry her all the way to the carved-stone fountain. She crouches down on her burning legs and places a hand on the wet surface of the street.

And then someone takes hold of her. Powerful fingers press into her ribs, wrap her arms so she can feel their rock-hard rifts against her skin. The embrace is not gentle; it is resolute and unhesitating. She is in the grip of a force that makes no apologies.

"Zesika," the voice says softly, supporting her the last few meters to the fountain.

Colombano lowers her to sit at the fountain's edge. Jessica reaches down to slip off her shoes and then dips her naked feet into a puddle that has formed in a hollow in the street. Only then does she raise her eyes to her savior. There he is. For her and her alone.

A tear rolls down her cheek. It is a sign of pain and relief. Of joy and shame.

"What's wrong?" Colombano asks, glancing discreetly somewhere behind Jessica. Her embarrassing reeling has to have aroused the concern and scrutiny of other passersby too. Even so, no one else rushed to her aid. Only Colombano.

"Where did you leave your violin?" Jessica finally asks. She didn't mean it as a joke, but it sounds like one.

Colombano smiles in relief. Then he grows solemn, licks his lips, and raises his eyes to the sky, as if to better feel the rain drizzling from its heights. Jessica closes her eyes, and when she opens them, Colombano's gaze has returned. He has edged a bit closer.

"Why did you leave?"

For a moment they just look at each other.

"Did you like it? The concert?"

"Why did you invite me?" Jessica registers that the pain in her legs has disappeared almost as quickly as it appeared. All that remains is a titillating tension. And a dash of embarrassment.

Colombano bursts into warm laughter. As he laughs, his cheeks pinch his eyes into delicate arcs, and the broad mouth reveals a row of white teeth reaching all the way to the back.

"Tante domande, Jessica, ma nessuna risposta."

Chapter 31

YUSUF IS ROUSED BY JESSICA'S MUTTERING AND SHIFTS his attention from his sweet roll to her. "What did you say?"

Jessica raises her eyes from her phone and shoots Yusuf an inquisitive glance. The ballpoint pen in her hand clacks against the tabletop, the way it does whenever she's lost in thought.

"Are you speaking in Latin now too? *Domande . . . Risposta . . .*"

"No . . ." Jessica whispers. She clears her throat. Did she really say the words out loud? "It wasn't Latin; it was Italian. It means: *So many questions, but not a single answer.*"

"Nicely put. A great aphorism," Yusuf says with a nod. Then he turns back to the treat waiting in front of him.

Despite the morning's chaos, Nina has managed to pick up some sweet rolls from the local grocery store. Coffee break has turned into a regular ritual at the homicide unit, ever since they realized it serves as fertile ground for conversation. Considering the nature of the crimes the unit investigates, outside eyes might see the tradition as gratuitously casual and unhurried. But that's the whole point.

Jessica rubs the sugar from her palms and collects it carefully on a paper plate. The detectives sitting around the table are munching on their sweet rolls; no one is talking. Mikael has pasted four photographs to the board, one of each of the people found dead the previous night: Roger and Maria Koponen, Chief Inspector Sanna Porkka, and the beautiful brunette fished from the ice, whose identity remains a mystery.

The door opens, and Erne walks in with a tablet under his arm. The room was just aired out, and now a pungent tobacco reek wafts in again. Rasmus quickly pops the rest of his sweet roll in his mouth, as if he were afraid of being punished if he was caught eating it.

"Sit down," Erne says, walking around to the head of the table. He leans his palms against it, drums its wooden surface with his splitting fingernails.

Jessica looks at him. The two of them have known each other for a long time, been in plenty of tight spots together, but she doesn't remember ever having seen Erne this stressed before. Could the publicity the case has garnered and the pressure from the brass actually be eating at him this badly, or is he suffering from an extraordinarily aggressive man flu?

"Jessica is going to take the lead on this," Erne says. Everyone nods. As the detective on duty, Jessica was the first to be called in to the scene, so there hasn't been any ambiguity about this. Any other decision would have been a clear statement of no confidence in Jessica.

Erne's phone vibrates in his jeans pocket, but he pays it no mind.

"The tabloids have already published the first clickbait. They have christened the crimes ritual murders, and, my guess is, speculation about potential new victims is underway." Erne puts his hands in his pockets and walks over to the middle of the table, where he reaches over to retrieve the last sweet roll. "I want you all to forget about the media. I'll handle that. We have every chance of making a rapid breakthrough. We have Eastern Finland PD helping out, and because one of the victims is a police officer, the National Bureau of Investigation is also involved."

"But we're in charge, right?"

"Yup. The crimes are presumed to be related. The NBI and Eastern Finland are on the Juva case, but they answer to us and will keep us informed about the progress of their investigation."

"OK," Jessica says. She feels her fingers start to tingle. It's a huge case, and as principal investigator, she's responsible for solving it.

"Do we have anything new, Jessie?" Erne munches on his roll and wipes the sugar from the corner of his mouth as he speaks.

Jessica sits up straighter and tries to project as much decisiveness as possible. "We have to find out what device was used to log in to Roger Koponen's YouTube account this morning. Because no mobile phone was found in the vicinity of the burned male body, it's possible, maybe even probable, that the video was uploaded from Koponen's own phone."

"Call data?"

"The phone was last traced to a base station located near the site of the murder. Within the next thirty minutes, we'll find out if the phone was powered on again this morning."

"If it turns out the video was uploaded from Koponen's phone, we have even more reason to suspect that the murderers from Kulosaari and Juva are working together," Erne says.

Everyone nods.

Erne reaches for his wool blazer, which is hanging from the back of his chair. His movements are somehow stiff and slow, and have been for quite some time.

"The good news is, we don't have to come up with a communications strategy. The perpetrators have handled it for us," Erne says as he steps toward the door. "The media and the public will draw their own conclusions about the case. We ought to prepare ourselves for some measure of panic."

Jessica stands too. "We need suspects. And fast."

"Start with the publisher," Erne says.

"Why?"

For the first time in ages, a cautious smile creeps onto Erne's face. "As far as I'm aware, they're the only party benefiting from this mess. I overheard at the press briefing that Koponen's *Witch Hunt* books sold out online in all Nordic countries in a couple of hours."

148

Chapter 32

JESSICA ENDS THE CALL AND PRESSES HER PHONE TO HER chest. The NBI agents who went to Neurofarm talked to Maria Koponen's boss and a few colleagues but didn't come up with anything out of the ordinary.

Jessica sits back down at her computer and looks at the dark screen. She is on the verge of rattling her mouse to rouse it, but her arm stops mid-movement. She stares at her blurry reflection. It reproduces the contours of her head, but leaves the features in the center indistinct. The experience is like a repeat of the night before, when Jessica gazed at her reflection in the window. It's as if someone were looking back at her from the other side of the glass. Some stranger from a cold, dark universe reminding her she has yet to find her place in the world. She will never be normal, even if she has a government job and pretends to live on the salary the police department deposits in her bank account every month. *Fake. Liar. Hypocrite. Fraud von Hellens.*

"Jessica!" Yusuf barks as if he were calling a dog. But the face that appears over the room divider is sympathetic. He continues more softly, but still clearly pumped up: "Call data."

Jessica taps her computer screen to life, then walks around to Yusuf's workstation. It's as messy as ever. At least six or seven dirty mugs, rims ringed with coffee stains. No wonder she can never find clean dishes in the kitchen. Behind the stacks of papers stand two trophies: Yusuf took them home for winning the department's go-kart championship and is more than happy to show them to anyone and everyone who wanders past his desk.

"Roger Koponen's phone was on between eight-oh-two and eight-oh-nine this morning," Yusuf says, arms folded across his chest.

"Where?"

"Helsinki Central Railway Station. Maybe underground, at the metro station."

Jessica's fingernails sink into the upholstery of Yusuf's chair. "Great. There are tons of people there—"

"We'll go through the tapes," Yusuf says, tapping a number into his phone.

Jessica stands up straight and fills her lungs with the stale air the station's tirelessly exhaling AC system has perfumed with its signature scent: a blend of vacuum cleaner bag and metal. Jessica rubs her wrists and finds her pulse, which seems to have remained elevated since the events of the previous evening. She hasn't been able to get her encounter with the murderer out of her mind. The coverall-hooded face; the eyes whose color she can't remember. The words she still doesn't understand. *That's it for the first one.* She can't help but think *the first one* refers to something they haven't even thought of yet, something the perpetrator wants them to know. Or, to be more accurate, guess.

"Jessie?" A remote connection to the CCTV cameras at the railway station has appeared on the computer screen. "It might take a minute," Yusuf says. "Going through the tapes, I mean."

"Leave it to—"

"The lovebirds?" When he sees the surprise on Jessica's face, Yusuf smiles. Then he shakes his head. "What? You think I didn't know Nina and Micke are screwing? You think Erne doesn't know?"

"I couldn't care less. Go tell them." Jessica grabs the parka lying on Yusuf's desk and tosses it in his lap. "Then you and I are heading out."

"Where?"

"Kulosaari. I want to see that place in daylight."

Chapter 33

THE CRYSTALLINE FREEZE HAS MELTED TO GRAY SLUSH, as if in empathy for the horrific events of the previous night.

Yusuf drives up the ramp onto the Eastern Expressway. Jessica gazes out at the construction site and the high-rise sprouting at its center, which upon completion is supposed to be the tallest residential building in Finland. Jessica remembers having seen summery illustrations of this so-called skyscraper, of a luminous white spire piercing the skies. In reality, the structure is a glum gray. Maybe it's because of the weather; maybe the material simply looked better on the architects' computer screens.

"Is everything OK with Erne?" Yusuf asks, turning the radio down.

"How so?"

"He just seems somehow—"

"Stressed out?"

"Not just that. It seems like he isn't doing too well."

"Physically?"

"Yes," Yusuf answers quickly.

Jessica watches him drive for a moment and then turns her gaze toward the road. Of course she knows what Yusuf is talking about. She knows Erne better than anyone else in the unit. She noticed a clear change in his demeanor a long time ago; he sounds and looks sick. But asking Erne about his health would be an even more pointless exercise than speculating about it. Even if he were on his last legs, her bullheaded Estonian boss would say he was in the prime of his life and accuse others of unnecessary fussing.

"If anything was wrong with Erne, we'd learn about it in the obituary," Jessica eventually says, wondering why she feels like she has to hide the fact that she's also worried about him.

"I admire his attitude. Never complaining about anything. Even if—"

"Maybe Erne doesn't have any cause for complaint. You don't know for sure." Jessica turns the radio up a notch and looks out the window. Warming temperatures have melted green patches in the white blanket covering Mustikkamaa Island. Jessica frowns. "Yusuf?"

"Yes?"

"What would the murderer have done if the sea hadn't frozen over yet?"

"Waited for a proper freeze."

"But what if they wanted to time the crime to when Roger Koponen was on the other side of Finland and Maria was at home alone? According to Koponen, this was the only night he was gone in all of January and February."

"I guess it's pretty likely the sea would be frozen in mid-February," Yusuf says, pulling off at the Kulosaari exit. "Besides, Roger Koponen was murdered too. If he had been at home, he probably would have been killed there instead. With his wife. Now he just happened to be off promoting his book, right?"

"*Happened* to be promoting his book? *His* book?" Jessica bites her lower lip. Koponen's book is the key to everything. Nothing related to it is coincidence.

It can't be.

Chapter 34

NINA RUSKA CRUMPLES UP THE EMPTY BOX OF PASTILLES in her fist and drops the wadded paperboard in the trash. A moment earlier, she sat down at the laptop and two stand-alone monitors on her desk. The middle screen displays a list of video files. There is a total of forty-five of them: one for each CCTV camera. The task might have felt impossible, especially since no one knows who they're supposed to be looking for. But the seven-minute time frame Jessica gave her is going to make things a lot easier. In addition, the location information provided by the phone's Bluetooth-transmitted beacon signal and MAC offers precise coordinates of the device's movements.

"Seven minutes," Mikael says, pulling up a chair.

"Within that time frame, he received the video and uploaded it to YouTube."

"How many cameras do we have left?"

"After narrowing it down, nine. What a pain in the ass. I have a strong suspicion the guy was standing on the metro platform. That's why this feels so damn hopeless."

155

"What do you mean?" Mikael asks, swirling a spoon around in his mug.

"The guy knows we're using the CCTV cameras to look for someone holding a phone. So he goes somewhere there are shit tons of people standing around—"

"And just about everyone is glued to their phone."

"Not *just about*. Every single one." Nina opens one of the files with a click of her mouse. "Look. It's depressing in so many ways. Even the people walking onto the platform with someone else are staring down at their hands."

"Pretty dystopian sight, I admit."

"So I'm sure the guy we're looking for is visible in this footage. We just don't know which one of them it is. There are at least a hundred people on that platform."

"When did you get so pessimistic?" Mikael says, snatching the mouse out of Nina's hand. "Besides, that doesn't make any sense."

"What doesn't make any sense?"

"You said the guy knows the phone's movements can be traced. Even so, he turned it on in a place that has one of the highest concentrations of CCTV and security cameras in the country. What do you think that means?"

"That . . ." Nina sighs deeply and smiles. "That he wants to be seen."

"Seen but not necessarily recognized," Mikael adds with a wink.

Nina leans back in her chair and looks at Mikael. Years ago she fell for the unshakable self-confidence he exudes, even when it's not justified. Maybe that's why she didn't dare approach him at first. She thought his nonchalance and coolness were a sign that he was satisfied being single, that he didn't want anyone at his side—and even if he did, there was no way it would be a close colleague who sweats her ass off in judo five times a week. Then, five months ago, Mikael finally made a move on her at the end of an exceptionally intense stint at work. They sat drinking at a bar until last call, discussing all sorts of things they had never exchanged a word about at work. And they came to the realization that there was chemistry. That there had been for a long time.

"So it's some sort of sick game?" Nina says.

"Of course. It has been this whole time. The perp is taunting us. Arranges the bodies in a way that forces the entire unit to read mediocre fiction with a magnifying glass. Writes a message on the roof of a house. Talks to the principal investigator face-to-face at the scene of the crime. Uses the victim's phone to upload a video to the net, even though he knows we'll trace it." Mikael raises his mug to his lips.

Nina clicks open the next file. "That's a disturbing thought."

"What?"

"That we're following the tracks the perp specifically wanted to leave for us. It's like sticking your head into a mousetrap. Or your dick into a tank full of piranhas . . ."

"But right now it's all we have. Besides, no matter how well-drawn a treasure map is, the drawer may have made

157

mistakes. No one's perfect. And the perp doesn't necessarily have a clue what the police are capable of these days."

Nina smiles. "Are you sure about that?"

"No," Mikael says after a long pause. "Maybe he's on the National Police Board."

"Lönnqvist? An evil white wizard?"

"The entire board?"

"Bingo!"

"There's a real bunch of witches right there," Mikael says, tentatively lowering his fingers to Nina's thigh.

Nina discreetly swats at them. "You just focus on that video now."

Chapter 35

JESSICA AND YUSUF CLIMB OUT OF THE CAR IN FRONT of the Koponens' house. The cordon has contracted, and there's only one patrol directing residents entering or leaving the area. The apocalyptic chaos of the previous night is nothing but a faded memory.

Jessica inhales the cool air and microscopic water droplets permeating it and looks around: slushy tire tracks running along an unplowed street, tall pines bravely bearing the growing burden of wet snow. She raises her gaze toward the wooden house on the hill, the upper-story window from where they looked down at the words stamped onto the roof: **Malleus Maleficarum**.

They slip on shoe protectors, even though the house has been inspected from floor to ceiling during the night. As they step into the house, Jessica suddenly remembers the music that was playing when the patrol showed up: John Lennon's "Imagine." The song has found its way into her dreams. Jessica sees the large mirror in the entryway and has a compulsive urge to pass it without looking at it. As if doing so would reveal something not hoped for. Even so, she registers her reflection out of the corner of her eye. The figure looks like her, but everything is backward: emotions, motives, intentions. What flashes past in the mirror is a shell, an expertly fashioned wax doll. *It's you.*

Jessica feels a stabbing pain in her neck. She presses her fingertips into it and forces herself to concentrate.

It's cold inside the house. And it's no wonder: the front door was open all night and into the wee hours of the morning. But somehow the raw air suits the ambience; the impression the house gives of being a huge icebox is reinforced by its color scale and cold decor.

Hands in her pockets, Jessica steps across the hallway into the living room and looks at the now-unoccupied dining table. But the sight of the glamorously dressed, eerily smiling woman has been so deeply ingrained into her consciousness that the body could just as easily still be there.

"Did you hear me?" Yusuf says. Jessica closes her mouth and gulps. Her eyes froze for just a little too long, just long enough that Yusuf felt the need to wake her up. "How did he access the roof?"

"Maintenance ladder. Side of the house," Jessica says. She then turns toward her younger colleague.

Yusuf has pulled a stack of photographs out of his coat pocket, one of which was taken from the old woman's window. Spotlights and streetlamps illuminate the words written on the roof. "Not a single superfluous shoe-print. The words were formed by stomping into the snow. By placing one foot in front of the other," Yusuf says. "The text is evenly spaced across the full width of the roof. All the letters are the same height."

"Neatly done, I have to admit. Did you have a point in there somewhere?"

"If I got drunk and decided to write '*shit*' or '*dick*' in a field or the roof of my sauna," Yusuf begins, looking satisfied that he has elicited a little smile from Jessica, "then I'd be happy if it were even semi-legible to some hang glider."

"What are you getting at? That the perp wasn't drunk off his ass? Or that as an artist you don't have much to say?"

"No. Either that a hell of a lot of time went into creating this work of art, which isn't really possible, considering the chain of events. Or someone practiced it beforehand. And that someone knew the exact width and length of the Koponens' roof," Yusuf says, handing the photograph to Jessica.

"I never thought it was improvised. I'm sure everything was planned in advance."

"What if the words were stamped into the snow earlier? When there were no time constraints—"

"No. It was done last night. Tech looked into the precipitation levels and snow strata for the past few days." Jessica steps toward the dining table, which for some reason or other looks longer now that no one is sitting at it.

"Fine. But it doesn't matter. Because if someone practiced making them, we'll find the same text somewhere else."

Jessica raises her chin and crosses her arms.

"In exactly the same size," Yusuf continues, looking a touch relieved.

Jessica frowns and eyes Yusuf. Maybe it's worth looking into. Not that it makes a lick of sense. But neither does anything else right now. And if they want to solve this insane crime spree, they might have to rely on more creative and crazier ideas.

"What do you suggest?" Jessica asks, and sees her colleague's beautiful eyes burn with enthusiasm. Yusuf has always been cute, but she has strictly relegated him to the friend-slash-little-brother zone. Maybe because Yusuf was already dating his fiancée, Anna, when Jessica met him. The two of them have always seemed so innocently in love that knocking on the window of their idyll would be a true mortal sin. As long as Anna and Yusuf are together, there's hope for all of them.

Yusuf gathers his thoughts, hands on his hips. "I think Erne should have a copter comb the area. Or maybe send up some drones. Worst case, the chopper wastes a few hours flying over fields for no reason. But the weather forecasts are predicting more snow for tomorrow. So if we want to do some looking before dark, we'd better hustle."

Yusuf shrugs; Jessica sighs deeply. At the same time, her phone rings.

"Hi, Micke."

"Are you ready to shit your pants?"

"Nice opening. I'm surprised you got fired from your telemarketing job."

"Because there's something really fucking weird going on. Nina and I reviewed the files from the CCTV cameras. And I think we found the guy we're looking for."

"Is it possible to identify him from the footage?"

"It sure is. And that's what so damn creepy," Mikael says, then coughs.

"Well?" Jessica says as Yusuf takes a step closer, an inquisitive look on his face.

"The guy is . . . He's like a carbon copy of Roger Koponen."

"What?"

"And if the DNA testing hadn't proved he burned to a crisp in the woods outside Juva last night, we'd even swear it's him."

Chapter 36

ERNE MIKSON BLOWS ON HIS COFFEE BUT DOESN'T EVEN try it. He takes a few drags from his cigarette, and it shrinks by about a third. Despite the warmer temperatures, it's damn cold, and the sharp breeze makes the wet chill unbearable. Oddly enough, it reminds Erne of the fortress of Carcassonne in southern France, of the December day years ago when he stood on its walls, underdressed, his then-wife at his side. The icy rain lashing his face, the masses of snow plopping down from the tree branches and the roof gutters. His wet shoes, his sore throat. At the time, he could blame a passing flu; this time there's more to the symptoms. This damn cough.

As he takes his final drag, his lungs start to burn; they've had enough. He's been testing his body's tolerance for too long: when he was young, out of a belief in his immortality, and later out of sheer habit. Alcohol has taken its toll but also given a lot to this shy man. Erne has never enjoyed spending time alone with his own thoughts, let alone in the company of others; a drink has always been welcome in both instances. It's ironic that the liquid nerve toxin that is now killing him has perhaps made it possible for him to live such a long, rich life. A good life, considering how it began. Two sons who have grown into smart adult men, a respectable job with the police force, and a number of tolerable colleagues, Jessica the closest and dearest of them.

The cigarette falls to the bottom of the ashtray bolted next to the door. The fact that the ashtray is empty makes Erne feel guilty. Maybe it was just emptied. Or maybe he's the only smoker in all of Pasila. He hopes it's the former.

For a moment, Erne is filled with yearning and a longing for the good old days. Maybe this wave of nostalgia was set in motion by the stubbed-out cigarette and today's almost smoke-free police HQ; maybe by the fact that he has, over the past months, gotten more used to the idea of his own mortality. Nascent old age and the attendant physical frailty are remote bogeymen until they come knocking at your door. Erne is fifty, and his father never lived to be this old. Ever since the big birthday he celebrated in November, Erne has been overtaken by the thought that something changes fundamentally in a man when he lives longer than his father. Erne spent more time on this planet than his old man did, which means he must be more mature, wiser. It's as if he had made the transition from journeyman to a master. Now his dad would be the one seeking advice and life wisdom, if he still existed in some form. And if he did, all this would negate itself.

The thermometer beeps again. *37.3. Not a catastrophe. But alarmingly high.*

Erne slips the thermometer into his pocket and grabs the door, which is vigorously pushed open at the same time. It's Mikael, standing there in the doorway like a bouncer.

"Erne? Why aren't you answering your phone?"

"What do you mean?" Erne says, then remembers he left his phone on his desk. He wanted just ten minutes completely to himself. "What's going on?"

Chapter 37

ERNE IS STANDING NEXT TO THE TABLE IN THE CONFERENCE room, arms folded across his chest. He's watching the large television screen, on which Mikael just started playing the CCTV footage. Nina is sitting at the table, swigging juice. She has taken off her hoodie, revealing the athletic arms under her T-shirt.

"Something here doesn't add up," Erne says, glancing at each of his subordinates in turn.

Mikael zooms in again on the man standing right at the edge of the metro platform, smartphone in his hand. The figure, who bears an astonishing resemblance to Roger Koponen, turns his head and looks more or less directly at the camera. The image is crisp and leaves no room for conjecture. The expression on his face is guarded but calm.

"Fucking fucking fuck," Erne says, rubbing his forehead. A moment later, he looks up, and his shoulders start to jiggle, at first almost imperceptibly, then harder. A burst of laughter erupts from his mouth.

Mikael and Nina exchange glances.

"Well, I'll be . . ." Erne says, wiping the tears from the corners of his eyes. Then, in a surprisingly swift transformation, he's serious. "I'll be damned. This is something else."

"Another passenger must have noticed Koponen in a fully packed metro," Mikael says tentatively, casting a discreet glance at Erne. "After all, the guy is a celebrity. And even if the news of his death didn't make it into the free rush-hour papers, it was already online by then."

"Picture yourself reading about some famous person's death on your phone and you look up and there he is, sitting across from you in the subway, live and in the flesh," Nina says, lowering her empty mug to the table. "I'd probably pull the emergency brake."

"The first thing I'd think is, man, that looks a lot like him. And that's what's going on here too. It has to be," Erne says.

"Because the DNA from the burned body was compared to DNA found on Roger Koponen's belongings?" Mikael asks laconically.

"Yes."

"Can we be sure the guy from Kulosaari didn't seed the house with those things after he murdered Maria Koponen? Razor blade, toothbrush, deodorant . . ." Mikael strokes his knuckles. "For some reason he wanted us to believe one of the bodies from Juva was Roger Koponen's. Maybe that's exactly what the guy dressed as a CSI was doing upstairs."

Erne's eyes are nailed to the ghost on the screen. "Where does he get off the metro?"

"Rasse is looking into that right now."

"Good," Erne says, then leans over the table so his dirt-brown tie slips out from under his blazer.

Nina sees Mikael stop his gum under his tongue. She hears Erne's raspy breathing in the otherwise quiet room. He strokes his gray beard thoughtfully.

"What if Roger Koponen didn't die last night, but arrived in Helsinki in perfect health, uploaded that sickening clip of his dead wife to YouTube while waiting for the metro . . . ? It would mean Koponen is the devil himself."

"There's one thing I don't get." Nina knots her hair up in a ponytail, only to let it fall free again. "Why would anyone go through so much trouble to stage Roger Koponen's death if they knew he was going to show up, with his phone, at a metro station during rush hour, just a few hours later?"

"Koponen might be in on the plot—"

"The question still stands," Nina says.

Silence falls over the room.

"Does Jessica know about this?" Erne eventually asks.

"Yup. She went to Kulosaari with Yusuf. She called in techs to lift more DNA samples. Ones that really are Koponen's."

Chapter 38

JESSICA STOPS OUTSIDE THE SLEET-SPLATTERED GLASS doors and scans the yard opening up before her. In the darkness of night, a body was submerged down at the water, after which someone crossed the yard and entered the house. And then left through the front door. Eventually the yard was filled with bright lights, police investigators, and dogs. Jessica feels shivers run up her back.

"Tech's here." Yusuf steps in, followed by a whiff of freshly smoked cigarette. Everyone deals with stress in different ways. And right now stress is the one thing they all have in common.

Jessica stretches her neck. "Let them know what we just talked about."

"What are you going to do?"

"Go down into the yard."

Jessica inhales the biting sea wind through her nostrils. She pulls the sliding-glass door shut behind her, glances at the handle and lock. *There was no break-in. But the killer walked in through these doors.* Maria Koponen presumably knew the perpetrator; maybe it was someone who had dined at the Koponens' table, watched television on their couch, slept in their guest room. Maybe climbed the maintenance ladder to the roof at some point. Someone who had a reason to be on their deck on a winter's night. Someone Maria was expecting.

In the light of day, the yard looks larger than it did last night. Jessica eyes the hedge bounding the yard, the stunted stumps, the two tall pines that were spared when the other trees were felled to offer an unhindered sea view. The path leading from the shore to the terrace has been cordoned off with blue-and-white tape.

Jessica takes hold of the black iron railing and cautiously descends the few stairs. Wet snow sloshes underfoot. Her tennis shoes were perfect in the previous night's below-zero temperatures, but when the weather gets slushy, they absorb water, and her feet freeze.

Jessica glances back up at the house and sees Yusuf talking with the CSIs. The knowledge that Roger Koponen may be alive has rattled Jessica. Suddenly the man assumed to be one of the victims is one of the suspects. Could Koponen himself have cold-bloodedly uploaded the video of his dead wife to YouTube, then hopped on a metro? And now no one knows where he is. Maybe he's on his way home.

The wind eases its hold on the pines' boughs. Jessica's cell phone bursts out ringing; she doesn't recognize the number.

"Jessica Niemi."

"Hi, this Pave Koskinen calling from Savonlinna. Or actually I'm already on my way back to Turku and—"

"What does this concern?" Jessica says coolly, and watches two crows dive from the crown of one pine to the other. She thinks she can make out the scratching sound as the birds' claws seize the branches. Their furious breathing, the sequence of light slaps as they shake the water drops from their feathers. They look back at her.

"I got your number from the investigative chief. Mikkelsson—" the voice says after a moment's hesitation.

"Mikson."

"Of course. Exactly. We're in utter shock over this. Roger Koponen was a superb writer and . . . it feels insane that just last night he and I were sitting down to a nice meal at the end of a pleasant evening. After his engagement at Savonlinna Hall—"

"What can I do for you?" Jessica is trying not to sound rude, even though it's the second time she has interrupted the caller. She closes her eyes. She feels tightly wound; all her senses have sharpened. She looks up at the crows but isn't able to make them out among the dense branches. Maybe she was hearing things the whole time.

"The thing is . . . something occurred to me that might be related to the murder of Roger Koponen and his wife, but I don't know if it's of any use—"

"Anything could be of use."

172

"I probably wouldn't have remembered otherwise, but now—"

"What?" Jessica can no longer conceal her impatience. Now she spies the crows. They have settled side by side on the pine's lowest bough. Their heads bob back and forth nervously.

"At last night's event, where Roger was speaking, a rather unusual question was asked by an audience member. The man who asked it was very self-assured, even a little aggressive. And in hindsight, also somehow threatening. He asked . . ."

The caller pauses to consider his words, and Jessica decides to give him time to collect his thoughts. In this instance, rushing him would just cause problems.

"Argh, I had it formulated a moment ago, but—"

"Take your time. It's important that you try to remember everything as accurately as possible."

"Well, in the first place, the person asking the question was a man. Middle-aged, bald, thin . . . a somehow antisocial and scary-looking guy." Koskinen prattles away as Jessica presses the phone to her ear with her shoulder and pulls her pen and notebook from her pocket. The caller has captured her undivided attention.

"What did he ask?" Jessica says, clicking out the tip of her ballpoint pen.

"He asked . . . if Roger is afraid of his own books."

"If he's afraid of them?"

"Yes. It was a very strange question, and I don't think Roger completely understood it either. Maybe that's why he didn't quite know how to answer. At least at first."

"What else did this man ask?"

"He asked the same question a few times. Repeated it in slightly different words."

"In your view, did the man mean Koponen ought to be afraid of his fiction coming true?" Jessica immediately regrets having asked the question. It was too leading. She turns to look at the house. From the yard, it looks even bigger than it does from the street. That was hard to discern in the darkness last night.

"Well, that's just it . . . That's exactly what it sounded like, even though it was only these ghastly events that made me think that . . . that, after the fact, the question sounded almost like a threat." Pave Koskinen's voice is trembling.

"Is there a video or audio recording of the event? Were there any journalists present?"

"I don't think so. I don't know about journalists. Maybe one or two. I was just the moderator."

"Great. What do you think . . . It's Pave, isn't it?"

"Yes, Pave Koskin—"

"Would you be able to identify the man from a photograph?"

"I don't know. Maybe. Yes, I believe so. He was sort of an unusual-looking fellow."

"Good. Do me a favor, Pave. Keep your phone on all day. I'll give you a ring back."

Jessica ends the call and brings up the caller's number. She jots it and Koskinen's name down in her little notebook and then shoves her writing supplies in her coat pocket. If there are cameras at Savonlinna Hall or its immediate vicinity, they have a chance of finding the guy. In and of itself, the question doesn't prove anyone's guilt. Even so, the tip feels like it has potential.

Jessica pulls her beanie down over her ears. She can't help but feel like a chump. Everything they know about the case has been offered to them on a silver platter. But experience has taught her that the crumbs suspects toss the police are usually inedible; there's always something poisonous about them. Otherwise they wouldn't have been offered to the police in the first place.

Unfortunately, they have few clues to go on otherwise: a skinny man in the audience and Yusuf's gauzy theory that they might find the words *"Malleus Maleficarum"* somewhere else, perhaps written in the snow. She has the urge to phone Erne but decides to wait to talk to him until she gets to the station. Even though he's the sweetest guy in the world, by some trick, he inevitably manages to sound like an asshole on the phone. More than one conversation has gone off the rails simply because the warmth Erne exudes in person doesn't come through on the phone. To like Erne, you have to meet him in person.

Jessica slogs the remaining few dozen meters of wet snow to the shore and pauses on the dock. The crows scream behind her. The two snow-frosted buoys jut up on either side of the dock, frozen in the ice. To the left of the dock, she can see the hole from which the Ice Princess was fished out last night. The hole is still unfrozen; its frigid heart is as black as oil.

Jessica looks at the long-distance skating track running down the middle of the strait. The tracks indicated that was where the suspect made his approach the night before. The unbuilt rocky cliffs of Kruunuvuori and Kaitalahti loom beyond it. Like other teenagers, Jessica spent drunken evenings there long ago.

Jessica turns her gaze to the right. A few hundred meters away, a figure is standing on the ice between the skating track and Laajasalo. There's no sign of a dog or ice-fishing gear. Perhaps it's an eager journalist with a camera and a .5-meter lens.

Jessica feels a curious shudder in her gut. Suddenly she regrets having come down to the shore alone.

Jessica squints. Something starts pushing up from the figure's shoulders. For a moment, Jessica thinks he's slowly raising his hands, but then she realizes it's a pair of horns, and that they've been there this whole time. The figure has raised its head. Now it's looking at the end of the dock, where Jessica is standing.

She smells the fetid stench of Venice's canals, a mix of silt and salt.

Jessica's fingers wrap around her pistol grip; she is otherwise paralyzed, staring at the strange creature. She feels like shouting, like ordering the creature not to move, then chasing it down. She is burning with a desire to call Yusuf, the uniformed officers out on the street, but her lips won't part.

The figure raises its right hand in the air, as if it were about to wave. But the hand doesn't move. And just as Jessica releases the gun from its holster and starts off across the ice, she hears something.

The sound grows louder. Behind her. Air bubbles are burbling in the ice hole, as if the water has started to boil.

"What the hell—"

She freezes as the words escape her mouth. And then, as if she was only watching the eerie preview to a nightmare, Jessica hears an animal scream, sees a head rising out of the hole in the ice, plastered with glossy hair, followed by bluish fingers, their nails scrabbling at the slushy snow.

Chapter 39

COLOMBANO THRUSTS OPEN THE DOORS TO THE FRENCH balcony; light floods the apartment. The outboard-motor sputter of the boat slipping through the narrow canal mingles with the blows of a rug beater. A salty tang wafts in, and Jessica can distinguish the odor of canal mud exposed during low tide.

"You know what, Zesika?" Colombano says, stepping over to the balcony doors. "If we were Vivaldi's *Le quattro stagioni*, this morning, this very moment, would be '*La primavera.*' Spring."

Jessica smiles. "Is that a good thing?"

"Of course it's a good thing, silly. That means that we're at the beginning of something new, but better things await. We still have summer to look forward to."

"But autumn will come someday. And winter."

"'*L'inverno.*' It's inevitable. But in the right company, winter can be gorgeous," Colombano says, gazing out the French doors. "You know what I would like to do today?" Colombano glances over his shoulder. He has lifted his powerful hands to the doorframe and now he thrusts out his chest, stretching his upper back. The flood of light clearly reveals the distinction in his shoulder muscles, as if Jessica were looking at da Vinci's sketch *L'uomo vitruviano,* the skillfully executed shadowing of details.

Jessica tugs the sheet higher and sweeps the hair out of her eyes.

"I'd like to go out on the water." Colombano turns around. His naked skin is covered by a dozen prominent tattoos. But they don't make him frightening. On the contrary. Colombano's body is like an illustrated collection of bedtime stories with warmhearted morals. Jessica has studied them, traced their dark green contours with her fingertips. Asked and heard dozens of stories.

"Out on the water?" Jessica asks, intrigued. In Venice, water is so omnipresent that referring to it specifically strikes her as peculiar. Boats are transportation mode and tool here. They're in a space station, and Colombano wants to take her for a rocket ride.

"Why not?" Colombano shoots Jessica a look that she has come to know over the past few days. The crooked smile is not purely tender; it is maybe the tiniest bit malicious. "Hasn't little Zesika had her fill of playing indoors yet?" Colombano takes two long strides, dives into the bed, and wraps Jessica in his arms. "Is my Arctic princess insatiable?"

"No, let's go out on the water." Jessica smiles, shuts her eyes, and accepts a long kiss from Colombano. Their lips, tongues, and teeth touch. The kiss must be their millionth, but it still feels like the first one.

"Good. I have the feeling that we must go out on the water. Right this instant." Colombano pushes himself up from the bed so quickly that for a second Jessica is lying there alone, thinking they're still kissing. "I have a boat," he calls from the bathroom a moment later. He twists on the shower taps. "Twenty horsepower. Ferrari of the seas."

Jessica stretches her hands and tosses off the thin sheet. She has spent two days in this apartment, or three nights, to be exact. During the day, they have toured the city by foot or gondola, gliding down Venice's hundreds of canals; they have cuddled as the gondoliers steered their vessels with long oars; they have leaned against each other and sat in silence. Jessica's life has turned into the world's biggest cliché: she's living an unexpected love story set in the cradle of romance, taken on the role of protagonist in the middle of her lonely journey.

There's a momentary break in the ecstasy of infatuation that casts all rational thoughts aside, and Jessica remembers the ring that adorned Colombano's left ring finger while they waited for the *vaporetto* at San Michele. The ring is no longer there. All that remains is the strip of pale skin it left behind, and that only if you know exactly what you're looking for and where to find it.

A surge of guilt washes over Jessica: she knows she's standing on someone else's toes. Whoever she is, she isn't here. Perhaps she's dead; perhaps Colombano was shedding tears for her at the cemetery. The thought makes Jessica feel like a vulture. She knows she is no thief; if anyone asked her to return Colombano, she would do so instantly and be on her way. But she hopes with all her heart it won't happen. She is young, free, and her entire body is vibrating from the force of falling in love.

"I'm supposed to check out of the hotel today," Jessica calls out, but Colombano can't hear her through the shower's blast. A fresh soapy scent wafts through the bedroom.

Since the night of the concert, Jessica has gone back to her hotel in Murano only once, to pick up clothes. Even then, Colombano didn't ask what Jessica's friends thought about her disappearing trick. Maybe he knows there are no friends. Ultimately, it makes no difference.

Time has flown by. Talking, eating, drinking, exploring the city, making love. It wasn't until last night that Jessica, after waking up in the dark and hearing Colombano's snoring, stopped to think that she knows almost nothing about him. Asking significant questions is a true art: at the onset of a romance, prying can feel intrusive and premature, and after a few days of ecstasy the stakes are so high that one inevitably chooses one's words carefully.

Jessica sits up and looks around the sun-drenched room. It's not very large; as a matter of fact, the entire flat is very compact, in the old Central European style. The furniture is cheek to jowl; there's stuff crammed everywhere. Not a square meter to spare.

Still nude, Jessica rises from the bed, feels the worn wooden planks beneath her heels, and walks over to the antique bureau. Colombano is singing something that sounds like an Italian *schlager* in the shower. Jessica strokes the ornamental frames there; a skim of dust clings to her fingers. There are over a dozen pictures. A few faded black-and-white photographs of people she assumes are Colombano's grandparents. The other photographs are more mundane; they have clearly been taken spontaneously without much preparation. Colombano and a string orchestra, Colombano and his violin, Colombano with a group of guys, Colombano and a woman cheek to cheek.

Jessica reaches for the rearmost photograph and cautiously picks it up. A glistening blue sea and a blazing sun in the background. Two beautiful people posing for the camera. The man appears no younger than the one Jessica has gotten to know over the past few days and who looks at Jessica in a way that lets her know there is no one else. That there never has been.

Once again Jessica remembers Colombano crying at the cemetery of San Michele and reflects that, actually, she's not supposed to know everything. They've just met, they barely know each other, and maybe that's the way it's supposed to be. Maybe everything will end just as quickly as it began. Maybe Jessica will board the train to Milan today, as she originally planned.

The rush of the shower dies. The singing continues. Jessica puts the picture back down, but it topples on the cramped bureau, setting off a domino effect that knocks over the entire arrangement of photos. Jessica can feel her cheeks color with embarrassment; she barely stops the photograph at the front from crashing to the floor.

She hears Colombano's footsteps, draws her lips up into a smile, and prepares to say something apologetic, but he is already grabbing her shoulder, jerking her backward. The movement is unexpected and rough. His fingers press painfully into her shoulder skin.

Her voice trembles from being startled: "I'm sorry . . ."

Colombano is at the bureau, towel in his hand, righting the framed photographs one at a time. He doesn't say anything, doesn't so much as glance at Jessica. Water drips to his feet from his wet body. His movements are clipped with anger. Then he unclenches his fist, lets the towel drop to the floor, and turns toward Jessica, who has retreated to the bed and wrapped the sheet loosely around herself.

"What am I going to do with you?"

"What?" Jessica stammers, and for a moment she feels like she ought to be somewhere else, in some other place, maybe on a train to her next destination.

But Colombano doesn't look angry anymore. Jessica eyes him warily. There's an unsettling passion in his gaze. It's hard to say what he's feeling. Maybe it's love.

"What am I going to do with you?" Colombano repeats calmly, then steps slowly up to Jessica and wraps his rough fingers behind her neck, sinks them into her hair.

"What do you mean?" Jessica asks. The strong scent of shower soap assaults her nostrils. The dark green doves entwined on the muscular chest draw close to her face.

183

Colombano presses his lips to Jessica's forehead. She senses his damp breath in her ear. And then the hand grips her neck harder, the sheet drops, and Colombano's fingers push into her crotch. Jessica cries out, the touch feels good even though it lacks any of the tenderness Colombano has shown toward her thus far. And when he presses her back down on the bed face-first, Jessica sees herself in the mirror hung next to the bathroom door. Her dark hair has tumbled over her face; her dark nails are clenching the sheet; her lips are parted in a moan. Colombano's muscled stomach moves rhythmically above her buttocks. She doesn't recognize herself in the reflection; she looks at it as if she were a complete stranger she is meeting for the first time. And a moment later, when she's on the verge of orgasm, she thinks how razor fine the line is between pleasure and pain.

The bottomless uncertainty, fear, and loneliness don't come until after.

Chapter 40

JESSICA STANDS STILL FOR A MOMENT AND TRIES TO MAKE sense of what she's seeing. There's a person in the water. A woman. Jessica breaks out into a run; she bounds across the dock and jumps to the ice.

"Yusuf!" she roars at the top of her lungs, then drops to her knees next to the floundering woman. It takes Jessica a few seconds to run through her options in this incomprehensible situation and pull herself together. She sees black hair plastered to a bluish face distorted in horror. The woman alternates between coughing up icy water that has made its way into her lungs and screaming as loudly as she can.

The sound of running footsteps carries from the shore. Jessica grabs the woman's arm and exerts every ounce of her strength in an attempt to pull her out of the water. The woman's struggling makes it a challenge. The water is ice-cold; Jessica's grip slips.

And just when the task starts to seem overpowering, the woman thrusts out of the water as if on her own, and starts twitching on the ice like a landed fish.

"What the fuck!" Yusuf shouts, running up.

Jessica takes off her parka and wraps it around the shivering woman. "Something pushed her out! I felt it . . . There was someone under the ice!" She grabs her gun and rises to her feet.

Yusuf lifts the shrieking, dripping creature into his arms. "We have to get her warm!"

Jessica's frantic gaze moves between the hole in the ice and the woman's face, the black curls and the terrified eyes peering out behind them. "A diver . . . There's someone under the ice, goddamn it!" she shouts, pointing at the open water.

Yusuf pauses and stares at Jessica in alarm, then starts jogging toward the shore, the woman in his arms.

"A diver brought her here—"

"Come away from there," Yusuf says, at first calmly, but then he raises his voice when the woman starts screaming again. "Get the fuck away from there, Jessica! We'll take a look in a second. We have to get her inside." He turns toward the Koponens' house.

Jessica circles the hole and aims her gun at the water, traces the imagined route under the ice with the barrel, and then raises it toward the place where just a moment earlier she saw the horned figure.

It has vanished.

Chapter 41

ERNE CAREFULLY WIPES HIS FEET ON THE DOORMAT. The action immediately feels pointless and absurd.

"Where's Jessica?"

"In the living room," Yusuf replies, and steps around his boss in the entryway.

Erne strides across the hallway into the living room, where there are now almost as many people as the night before. Jessica is sitting at the long table, in the chair last occupied by Maria Koponen. Her clenched fists rest on the table in front of her; her face is grave.

Erne walks up to her. "Are you all right?"

"Who, me?" Jessica's eyes are boring into the table.

Erne looks out to where a half-dozen SWAT team members are guarding the shore with their submachine guns. Another half-dozen armed figures are combing the ice farther out.

"This is no normal murder investigation, Erne," Jessica says, slowly unclenching her fists.

"That's been clear since last night." Erne lowers his fingers to Jessica's knuckles. Her eyes follow the gesture, but the expression on her face remains impassive.

"They're toying with us . . . with me . . . It can't be a coincidence that I was at the shore just then—"

"This isn't personal. It could have been any of us down at the shore. Yusuf, me . . . one of the patrolmen . . ."

"I wouldn't be so sure, Erne. There's something really weird going on . . . I can't stop thinking about it."

"But now you have to. Otherwise the investigation will suffer."

"I suppose," Jessica says, slowly extracting her hand from Erne's grip.

Erne stands and walks over to the sliding doors. "The woman—"

"Is she—"

"She's in good shape, considering. Suffering from hypothermia, in shock. But the doctor said she'll survive."

"When can we talk to her?"

"Soon, I think. She was just booked into Töölö Hospital."

"What about security—"

"Handled. No one is going to be able to get to her," Erne says, and lets his gaze slide across the living room. He hears Jessica curse softly and shake her head.

"What the fuck was that creep with horns—"

Erne sighs: "Jessica—"

That's all he has to say.

188

"You don't believe me?"

Erne doesn't answer. There's no point debating the point. He has seen Jessica in this state only once before, almost fifteen years ago, and neither of them has been the same since.

"Well?" Jessica asks insistently.

"The area is being combed. As of yet, we haven't found anyone in the vicinity who matches the description."

"Great, so no one has seen a guy with horns wandering around . . ."

Jessica sighs, eliciting a grunt from Erne.

"Nor was there another hole found in the ice where a diver could have entered the water with the victim. The coast guard has taken over that aspect of the search."

Jessica rubs her forehead. Yusuf steps into the room, pulling on his coat. Erne gestures for him to sit next to Jessica, and Yusuf does as ordered.

"Listen up, you two. Even though the case is unusual, we can't get discouraged and just lie down and give up. We have five victims now, the last of which survived—"

"Because, for whatever reason, they didn't want to kill her," Jessica says, tracing a figure eight on the tabletop with her finger.

"I just talked to command over the phone. They've given us more manpower. Yusuf, you're going to be the point man with the folks from NBI."

"Got it," Yusuf says, arms crossed.

"What about the man we saw on the security-cam tapes?" Jessica says. "Now it looks like it really is Roger Koponen, as incredible as that seems."

"What's our strategy for dealing with the media?" Yusuf queries.

"It's being resolved as we speak."

"Is Koponen our prime suspect now?"

"That's a call we have to make ASAP."

Chapter 42

JESSICA PULLS THE DOOR SHUT BEHIND HER AND HEARS Yusuf's car cough to life at the side of the road. Once again, the Koponens' front yard looks like the set of a Hollywood movie; hordes of people and equipment have been brought in with large vehicles. The circus came, packed up, and then returned to Kulosaari. *Encore.*

Jessica zips up the coat she's wearing; it's not hers. Her parka is racing to the hospital in the ambulance, wrapped around the woman who rose out of the water. That means Jessica's wallet, phone, and the notebook where she wrote down the name of the man who called from Savonlinna are headed toward the hospital too.

Jessica's fingers feel stiff, and her joints are prickling. Her hands were only submerged for a moment, but it feels like the blood still isn't circulating properly through them.

Yusuf pulls up at the Koponens' gate, and Jessica trudges over and opens the passenger door. She climbs in, casts one last glance over the house, and pulls the door shut.

"Töölö Hospital?"

191

"Yup," Jessica says, letting her head fall back against the neck rest. Despite the gauze of clouds veiling the sun, it's brighter out than it was earlier.

"I've never seen anything like that before," Yusuf says, closing the center console. Jessica catches a glimpse of a red cigarette carton. "Those aren't mine."

"I'm not your big sister, you know."

"That's pretty obvious from the difference in our tans."

Yusuf smiles and waves at the patrol officer who's making sure outsiders don't cross the perimeter.

"Smoke all you want. As long as you can still run from one end of the floorball court to the other," Jessica says. She looks out the passenger window at the man with the thin face and the police-issue beanie pulled down over his bald head.

The car drifts down the route the murderer masked as a CSI fled on foot the night before. Jessica vividly remembers her furiously pounding pulse and the bite of frozen air in her lungs. The coveralls fluttering in the middle of the street. Her fear and disappointment. The anger that washed over her once the fear eased. The man was clearly playing some sort of game with her. She is certain it's the same man. It's no coincidence that Jessica was the one who encountered him inside the house last night and on the ice today. He wanted to be seen; good for him. Next time, she's going to shoot him.

"Stop the car," Jessica says as Yusuf turns at the intersection. She has thought back to the phone call she received right before her encounter with the horned figure on the ice. *Middle-aged. Bald. Thin.*

Jessica opens her door.

"What is it now?" Yusuf asks. But Jessica is already gone.

As she hustles back to the house, Jessica makes sure her pistol is at the ready. She hears a car door slam shut behind her, followed a second later by Yusuf's footfalls running after her.

"Hey!" Jessica calls out, and whistles at the police officers controlling access in front of the house. There's no sign of their skinny, bald colleague. Jessica feels her senses sharpen. *Where did he go?*

"Forget something?" one of the officers asks. There's a hint of sarcastic insubordination in his voice.

Jessica looks him in the eye, then turns to his partner. Yusuf runs up, a little out of breath, and looks at her, perplexed.

"Where's that other guy?" Jessica asks. Suspense is gnawing at her guts. "Where's the tall, thin guy?"

"Huh?"

"The one who was standing next to the cordon a second ago!" Jessica snaps, prompting the patrol officers to exchange amused glances. "Where is he?" Jessica insists.

Yusuf takes a step closer and is opening his mouth to say something, but then quickly shuts it again. Jessica hears a cough behind her.

"Looking for me, Detective?"

Jessica whirls around. In the doorway to the Koponens' house stands the police officer who a moment earlier allowed Yusuf's car to exit the cordon.

"Sergeant, ma'am . . ." he says, raising his hands in a pacifying gesture, "am I in some sort of trouble?"

One of the patrol officers laughs.

Jessica looks down and realizes she's holding her pistol in her right hand. She shoves the gun into her belt. "Can I see your badge?"

"Sure," he says, opening his breast pocket at a leisurely pace.

"What the fuck are you rolling your eyes at me for?"

"Sorry, but I don't understand—"

Jessica takes the badge. Her eyes flit between the name, the photo, and the face in front of her.

"I just went for a piss and all of a sudden—"

Jessica hands the badge back. "Come on, Yusuf."

Jessica starts walking back to the car. Behind her, she hears soft laughter leaping from man to man like wildfire. *Fucking schizo.*

"Care to tell me what that was all about?" Yusuf says, shifting into higher gear, once again hopelessly late. The way he punishes his poor engine annoys Jessica to no end.

"I got a phone call when I was out in the backyard. Just before . . . what happened happened."

"Who was it?"

194

"Some guy from Savonlinna. Interviewed Roger Koponen last night or something. He said someone in the audience asked Koponen *if he was afraid of the things he wrote.*"

"Pretty incriminating, when you consider everything that has happened."

"Bald, thin, weird-looking . . . middle-aged," Jessica says, shooting Yusuf a pregnant look.

He sighs. "I get that this is really hard on you. It's hard on all of us, but—"

"But what? Are you doubting me too?"

"Too?"

"There was a guy with horns out there on the ice, and he was there because of me."

"OK. But I didn't see him."

For a second, they sit in silence.

"No, you didn't. And you don't see the whole point either."

"Which is?"

"If we hadn't gone to the Koponens' house, that woman wouldn't have been in the sea to begin with."

Chapter 43

NINA RUSKA'S EYES TRAIL THE MAN DECKED OUT IN HIS commander's uniform as he stalks sourly past the unit's workstations; he doesn't expend the slightest effort to greet the police officers toiling at their desks. It's almost one p.m., and Erne has been preparing a new press briefing for the brass.

Nina drums her fingers against her desk. She watches as Mikael pours himself a cup of hot water in the kitchenette, shovels two big spoonfuls of instant coffee, then drops them on the surface of the water.

"It's better if you put the coffee in first," she says.

"Bullshit. If you put the coffee in at the end, it has time to air before it gets wet and mixes with the water. The result: a delicious cup of instant coffee."

"You don't believe that yourself."

"What I don't believe is that you really care which order I put the coffee and water into my cup."

"Apparently some people aren't capable of following even the simplest recipes," Nina says as Mikael sits down next to her.

"I've been thinking," Mikael says, stirring his coffee.

"Apparently about something other than making coffee?"

Mikael glances around surreptitiously and lowers his voice: "I've been thinking it would be fun to actually be together."

"Really?"

"So we wouldn't have to sneak around anymore. I mean, damn it, we can't even go to a movie together."

Nina lowers a hand to Mikael's thigh. "I thought sneaking around was the fun part?"

"It was. For a hot minute. Everything gets old after a while."

"Even me?" Nina pulls her hand back and shoots Mikael a look of exaggerated outrage.

"Even you. Yes, if I have to spend one more Christmas party watching Ahonen try to hit on you. I'm not man enough to watch that from the sidelines. I want to own you. I want to say you belong to me and kick Ahonen's butt if he tries something anyway." Mikael whispers these last words in Nina's ear.

"Own me? What sort of goddamn caveman are you?" Nina says, pulling back from Mikael. His warm breath on her ear has sent the blood surging through her veins and set her heart pounding.

Mikael takes her hand and places it back on his thigh. "I want you."

"And I don't want to lose my job."

"I could give a rat's ass. I can become a motorcycle cop. You can keep this job."

"Why are you bringing this up now, Micke?" Nina lets her hand slide down his thigh to the knee. Squeezes it the way she knows he likes.

"I don't know. Maybe this witch case has put me on my guard. The world is such a sick fucking place. I want you close to me. I want to take better care of you."

"I don't need anyone to take care of me. I have a black belt in judo."

"That's just it. I want to be the only one you put in a lock."

"I'm going to pin your butt to the mat if you don't watch yourself." Nina can't help it; a smile spreads across her face. "We can talk about it later."

"When?"

"After this case is solved."

"OK. That was a promise," Mikael says, and pulls back from Nina when her phone beeps.

"Showtime. We get to watch a video."

"Of what?"

"The parking lot at Savonlinna Hall."

Chapter 44

JESSICA BREATHES THROUGH HER MOUTH, TRYING NOT TO smell the odor of dried bandage and disinfectant. It makes her think of death and the long, lonely weeks at the hospital decades ago. The elevator is packed with people, some of whom are dressed in hospital gowns. Closest to the door sits a middle-aged woman with an oxygen tank strapped to her wheelchair. Jessica saw her out in front of the hospital a second ago, smoking.

Jessica and Yusuf exit the elevator on the sixth floor and follow the red line taped to the floor. At the end of the corridor, they see a muscle-bound man in a dark blue tracksuit with an earbud in one ear. Jessica recognizes him; they were on a bodyguard gig together a few years ago—and continued getting to know each other off the clock. At Jessica's studio.

"Hey, Teo." Jessica extends a hand.

"Detectives," Teo says in a raspy voice, and shakes both of their hands. Jessica knows the raspiness is the result of a laryngeal injury Teo suffered during his bouncer days, when a dissatisfied customer whacked him in the neck with a wine bottle.

"This is Yusuf Pepple. Maybe you guys have met."

"Maybe," Yusuf says, giving the other man a flinty look.

Teo is the prototypical intimidating security guard; even the smile that flashes across his face isn't sincere but picked up during some class. "I doubt it. How's it hanging, Jessica?"

"As low as the bass in that earbud. Nineties rap?"

"You know it."

Both grin wearily. Yusuf glances at them in surprise. The nostalgic moment born of the inside joke passes quickly, however, and their faces grow serious.

"Where's the attending physician?" Jessica asks before Teo can nod in the direction of the footfalls echoing down the corridor. A tall, bearded man is approaching, tablet under his arm. Turquoise scrubs flash beneath his white lab coat.

"Dr. Alex Kuznetsov," he says. Jessica looks at him, thrown; she knows she has seen him before somewhere.

"Detective Sergeant Jessica Niemi."

"Yusuf Pepple."

"Before we enter the room, I'd like to discuss a few things regarding the patient's condition."

"Of course," Jessica says. Teo considerately steps to the side.

"The patient told us her name is Laura Helminen; it matches the social security number she gave us."

"Have you reached the family yet?"

"Not yet."

"How is she doing?"

"Well, all things considered. Her body temperature didn't have time to drop fatally . . ." Dr. Kuznetsov says, scratching the side of his nose. "Do you know how long she was in the water?"

"No. I was hoping you might be able to give us an estimate." Jessica glances at her watch. Time seems to be sprinting by surprisingly fast; it's nearly evening again.

"The rate at which the body cools is affected by the temperature of the water, as well as the patient's physical condition, age, body type, and potential earlier exposure to cold water—if they have built up a certain tolerance through, for instance, ice swimming. Because the water was close to freezing and the patient is twenty-five and appears to be in good health, I'd say under fifteen minutes, no question. Any longer and she would have presumably lost consciousness. The fact that she was shouting and splashing when she rose to the surface could indicate an even briefer period."

"What about the lungs? Was there water in them?"

"Not much. According to her, she had a snorkel." Dr. Kuznetsov shoots Jessica an inquisitive look. "I'd love to know exactly what happened to her."

"It sounds as if some sort of diving equipment was used, a mouthpiece and an oxygen tank," Yusuf says.

Dr. Kuznetsov casts him a lingering evaluative glance. "I see."

"What else did she tell you? For instance, did she mention how she ended up in the water?"

Dr. Kuznetsov shakes his hand and folds his arms across his chest. "She wasn't able to say. But I believe it will be easier to talk with her now than it was a moment ago. Shock can affect the memory. I'm sure events are starting to click into place for her."

"So she's ready for us?"

"As I said, she's suffered a shock but is recovering from the physical strain, which is why I'd recommend our hospital psychologist participate in any questioning—"

"We know how to be tactful," Jessica says.

"I'm not saying you don't."

"Where's the psychologist?"

"She'll be here within half an hour."

"Unfortunately, we don't have time to wait that long. We have cause to believe this incident is part of a series of ongoing crimes. This woman may have seen the perpetrator."

"Do you mean—"

"We have to talk to her right away if we want to prevent further crimes from happening."

"Fine," Dr. Kuznetsov says, taking a step toward Jessica. "But I'm going to start the conversation by ensuring the patient is up to it."

Jessica's mouth draws into a taut line. She glances at the tips of her shoes and nods. Then she spins around and follows the doctor toward the door Teo has already opened.

Chapter 45

JESSICA HEARS THE DOOR BEHIND HER CLOSE. SHE DOES A quick scan of the room but doesn't see the coat she wrapped around the shivering woman an hour earlier. The coat rack next to the sink is empty. The coat must be at the nurses' station, unless the medics left it in the ambulance.

Yusuf pauses next to Jessica in the doorway, hands on his hips; Dr. Kuznetsov calmly walks over to the patient. Laura Helminen is resting in her bed, which is surrounded by machines measuring her vital signs and IV bags hanging from stands. Her eyes are shut, and her mouth is open, as if she fell asleep on the couch watching TV. Dr. Kuznetsov coughs tentatively into his fist, and Laura opens her eyes.

"How are we doing here?" Kuznetsov asks in a mild voice, stroking his beard.

The patient smacks her mouth, while the doctor shoots a glance over at the detectives, then turns back to check the drips and the monitor.

Jessica looks at the woman lying in the bed and then at Dr. Kuznetsov. Now she remembers why he looks so familiar; the similarity is downright remarkable.

Père Tanguy, Vincent van Gogh. The painting hanging at the Musée Rodin.

"Are you feeling any better?"

"Umm . . . I feel kind of weird . . . like my muscles have grown; they feel really hard—"

"That's a completely normal sensation for someone in your situation. Your muscles had time to freeze. You might feel some pain and tightness for a few days," says the doppelgänger for the late-nineteenth-century Parisian shopkeeper. Dr. Kuznetsov then slips his tablet into the pocket of his lab coat. "There are two individuals from the police here. They would like to ask you a few questions if you have the strength."

Laura gives the doctor a look of exhaustion.

"It won't take long," Dr. Kuznetsov says, patting her shoulder lightly.

"I've started remembering . . ." she says. Her lower lip starts to quiver, and her eyes pinch shut.

Dr. Kuznetsov shakes his head and looks reproachfully at Jessica, as if it were her fault Laura is laid up in the hospital. And then the terrible thought crosses her mind again: could it be true? Is all this happening because of her?

"That's a good sign. It's good things are coming back to you," Dr. Kuznetsov says, then turns towards the door. He stops in front of the detectives; Jessica has to raise her chin to look him in the eye. "Five minutes. The patient needs her rest."

It's not a suggestion; it's an order from the attending physician, and ignoring it means major problems for the police. Jessica slowly lowers her gaze from the doctor's eyes to his beard, from his shirt collar to his white lab coat and name tag. It strikes her as strange that he felt the need to underscore his authority by standing so close.

"We're sorry we have to bother you," Jessica begins as she steps past Dr. Kuznetsov and toward the bed. "But it's critical we hear what has happened to you."

Laura sobs softly, then wipes her tears on the back of her palm and looks up at Jessica. She seems to focus her eyes for a moment, like a camera lens seeking the appropriate distance from the subject of a photograph. Then the sadness and shock give way, and her face twists up in a mask of horror. Before Jessica can react, an ear-splitting cry has filled the tiny room.

"What—" Jessica exclaims before Dr. Kuznetsov lunges past her.

Laura's screams grow louder and louder, and she falls out of the bed, taking an IV stand with her. After scrambling to the corner of the room, she raises her hands to shield her face.

"It was her!" she shrieks.

Jessica glances at Yusuf, who looks as dumbfounded as she is. Behind them, Teo opens the door.

Dr. Kuznetsov crouches down next to the woman huddled on the floor, making reassuring sounds.

"It was her! She's the devil!" The woman is now screeching at the top of her lungs and pointing at Jessica. "I remember her face!"

Jessica senses it again, the taste of iron on her tongue. And then the entire room feels like it's starting to spin.

Chapter 46

ERNE MIKSON GLANCES AT HIMSELF IN THE MEN'S-ROOM mirror and straightens his tie. The collar of his dress shirt is pressing against his tender lymph nodes, but he's just going to have to deal with the discomfort. The pale blue dress shirt used to fit better; it's one of three shirts Erne ordered from a tailor. And, aside from a few pairs of trousers, they're the only articles of clothing he regularly takes to the cleaners. Beautiful, expensive shirts that should have stood up better to the ravages of time. He intentionally leaves the frayed cuffs, which once bore an *E. M.* embroidered in dark blue thread, hidden under the sleeves of his brown blazer.

Erne thrusts the door open and nearly collides into Mikael. "Micke?"

"Great. I found you."

"I didn't know I was lost."

"Yusuf called a little while ago and said that a tall, thin man had been asking Koponen strange questions last night at Savonlinna Hall."

"Where did this information come from?"

"A guy named Pave Koskinen. He was the event's moderator. The Eastern Finnish PD started looking for this mystery man, but no one recognized him," Mikael concludes with an enigmatic smile.

"But?"

"There's a security camera with recording capabilities outside the building."

"And does this man appear in the footage?" Erne swallows, but the lump in his throat doesn't disappear.

Mikael nods. "We can even see the car he gets into. And the license plate."

"Holy hell."

"Of course, it's a little early to celebrate. As far as we know, all the guy did was ask a few tough questions and—"

"Shut up, Micke. Who is the car registered to?"

"Torsten Karlstedt, lives in Espoo." Mikael clicks his tongue against his palate and hands Erne a still-warm printout. It's s photocopy of Karlstedt's passport. But the man in photograph isn't thin, bald, or in any way odd-looking.

"It's not the right guy."

"No. But maybe Karlstedt was driving. Because the camera recording shows the bald guy climbing into the back seat of Karlstedt's car."

"So the car was waiting for him?"

"For twelve minutes."

"Goddamn it. This could be a breakthrough. Did you call Jessica?"

"I tried. She's on her way to the hospital with Yusuf."

"OK. Tell Rasse to find out everything he can on Torsten Karlstedt. Make sure he has all the help he needs."

"Should we bring him in for questioning?"

"Not yet. Let's do a little digging first. We don't have anything that actually ties him to the crimes. Just the opposite. When it comes to Maria Koponen's murder, he has the best alibi one could hope for. But have someone find out where he is. Under no circumstances can we let him escape."

Chapter 47

A TALL NURSE IS PUSHING AN OLD PATIENT ALMOST entirely swathed in bandages down the corridor. The metal sides of the hospital bed shudder as the wheels hit the seams in the floor.

Jessica is pacing the corridor. Yusuf has returned to Helminen's room to sort things out with Dr. Kuznetsov and the nurse who rushed in.

"Everything all right, Jessica?" Teo asks, arms crossed over his chest.

"I don't know." Jessica presses her back against the wall. She's going to have to try to calm down, despite the dozens of questions ricocheting through her head.

"That woman has clearly been through a lot. Whatever happened in there—"

"Stop. Please just stop." Jessica raises a hand in a gesture of rejection. "I don't need to be fucking consoled all the time."

"OK," Teo says in a subdued voice, adjusting his earbud. Maybe because the fit is off, but more likely because the abrupt end to the conversation made him fidgety.

For a little while, the corridor is completely silent. Then Jessica shakes her head and looks up from the floor. "Sorry, Teo. Everyone's nerves are pretty shot."

"I understand. Compared to your job, this guard-dog gig is pretty low-stress."

"You know that's not true. I know it too."

Teo grunts. "It depends on the case, I guess. They're all different."

The elevator doors open, and suddenly Teo is on the alert. The nurse pushes the bed into the elevator.

"It's been a while, Jessie."

Jessica avoids eye contact. "It has. How have you been?"

Teo turns his head from side to side, as if making sure no one will have time to run from the elevators to the door of Helminen's room, at least during the sentence that's to follow. "Fine, fine," he says blandly, raising his banded ring finger. "Wife and twin daughters, five months old."

Jessica takes a deep breath. "That's . . . that's great."

Teo sighs and shakes his head almost imperceptibly. "It's pretty exhausting, to be honest. And I'm not just talking about the babies. Not that they don't know how to . . . But this job. It's not enough. I have to take the occasional bouncing gig. Last week, I was shoveling snow from roofs in Eira. You probably know what I'm talking about?"

Jessica starts making a sympathetic comment when she's overcome by a strange sensation: it's as if Teo knows something. Who knows? Maybe there's a strange but persistent rumor going around the ministry about a millionaire police officer who does everything she can to keep her wealth a secret, to hide the fact that she could pay not only her own but the entire department's wages for the next fifty years. All it would take to start a rumor like that would be one loose-lipped tax officer, asset manager, attorney, or shrink. "The more mouths there are to feed, the—"

"Looks like I'm going to have to start playing the lottery again." Teo smiles bitterly.

Jessica frowns. Deep down, she knows her intuition is right. "Tell me about it."

"Do you have any?"

"Kids?" Jessica's laugh even catches herself off guard. Now, that's a question she hasn't heard in a while. "No, no, I don't."

Teo nods and rolls his shoulders back, pulling himself up straighter, a habit Jessica was once fond of.

Jessica glances at her watch again, then waves and heads toward the elevators. "Listen, tell my colleague I'm waiting for him downstairs in the cafeteria."

"Take care of yourself, Jessie."

"You too."

And while you're at it, take care of your family, and leave me the hell alone.

212

Chapter 48

EVERY LAST TABLE IN THE CAFETERIA IS FILLED WITH patients and their visitors. Jessica has managed to down the contents of her mug by the time a harried Yusuf takes a seat across from her.

"Am I a suspect now too?" Jessica wraps her fingers around the mug. Even though it's empty, it's still warm.

"Laura Helminen was abducted from her house in Laajasalo last night, only a few hours prior to Maria Koponen's murder. She remembers watching TV on her couch when the doorbell rang. What happened next is a little less clear. She said she came to in some dark, musty place where there was another woman."

"The other woman being the Ice Princess?"

"You got it. Helminen ID'd her from a photograph. But she didn't know her from before."

"What else?"

"His Bearded Holiness said we could continue questioning her in a minute. That because Helminen couldn't describe the perpetrators—"

"Nothing?"

"All she could say was there was more than one abductor. Men, based on their voices."

"So why was she afraid of me, then?"

Yusuf falls silent and starts stroking the disposable tablecloth. "There was a painting hanging on the wall of the room where she woke up."

"What painting?"

"Helminen said it was a painting of a woman with dark hair—"

"And this painting . . . was of me?"

Yusuf chuckles. "Jessica, hey, she's confused. She's still in shock. Come on, think about it."

"Goddamn it, Yusuf. What if it really was me? What if the victims were shown a picture of me? Maybe this whole show was put on just for me; maybe someone wants to get back at me."

"I don't buy that for a second." Yusuf reaches across the table and lowers his fingers lightly to Jessica's knuckles. "We're going to solve this case. Soon. We'll catch those lunatics, and you'll see none of this has anything to do with you."

"Maybe I should ask Erne to take me off it."

"What do you mean?"

"For the first time in a long time, I'm starting to feel like I can't keep it together." Jessica looks up at the fluorescent tubes on the ceiling. Her ears can almost pick up the sound of mercury vaporizing. Her cheeks are burning; she can't stop blinking.

"You have to pull yourself together, Jessie. We need you." Yusuf takes a pack of cigarettes from his pocket and stands. "I'm going to have a smoke. And then I'll wrap things up with Laura Helminen."

"OK. Maybe it's better if you handle it alone."

"In the meantime, look for your phone. Everyone keeps calling me because they can't get hold of you."

"Is there something new?"

"The lovebirds found a lead from the surveillance camera at Savonlinna Hall. It has to do with the creepy bald guy."

"OK. Don't leave without me."

"I won't."

"And, hey, my wallet's in my coat too. They said I could pay when my friend got here."

Yusuf grunts, pulls out his wallet, and lays his debit card on the table. "You know the PIN. Don't empty the display case," he says, then beats a quick retreat toward the elevators.

Chapter 49

"KNOCK, KNOCK."

Erne looks up and sees Rasmus Susikoski in the doorway. He's wearing a gray turtleneck and is carrying a laptop and a sheaf of printouts.

"Come in, Rasse."

"Funny, it feels colder in the office today than yesterday, even though it's warmer outside." Rasmus sits down, an awkward grin on his face. Erne can see Rasmus' mouth moving, but his brain refuses to register the vacuous small talk emerging from it.

"How can I help you, Rasse?"

"Where's Jessica? I tried to call her a couple of times—"

"Her phone is on the lam. You can get in touch with her by calling Yusuf."

"OK." Rasmus nods and starts unpacking his gifts on Erne's desk. Erne crinkles his nose, despite the fact that Rasmus' heavy sweater is surprisingly effective at checking the sweat swell. Erne can't help it: every time he sees Rasmus, his nostrils pick up a fetid odor, even if the guy just stepped out of the shower.

"In the first place, I have to say things are progressing pretty smoothly. We finally have enough people. If only we always had this many helping hands—"

"And in the second place?" Erne growls.

"Right, so I'm working on two tasks . . . In the first place—"

"First place already went."

"The presumed Roger Koponen boarded the metro to Mellunmäki at the Central Railway Station at eight-oh-eight a.m. The phone powered off a few minutes later. Here's CCTV footage from the metro car." Rasmus turns the laptop so Erne can see the screen. "The first door at the bottom," he continues, pointing at the opening sliding doors.

Erne slips the reading glasses hanging around his neck onto his nose and leans in to study the clip. A moment later, Roger Koponen steps into the car. The image is crisp and the camera so close that there's no doubt as to the man's identity. Unless he's Koponen's identical twin, who, as far as they know, doesn't exist.

"Well, I'll be damned . . . And no one recognizes him."

"The funny thing about writers is that if their face isn't on TV all the time, on *Have I Got News for You* or whatever, no one recognizes them. Not even if they've sold tens of millions of books. Would you recognize J. K. Rowling if you saw her in the tube without makeup—"

"Who?"

"Never mind. Wait," Rasmus says, and clicks the screen; the image speeds up.

For the next few seconds, the doors open and close a few times; people scurry in and out like worker ants. But Roger Koponen just stands there.

"At eight sixteen, Koponen steps out of the metro."

"Which stop?"

"Kulosaari."

"Goddamn it. Was he seriously going home?"

"Somewhere in the vicinity, at least. Unfortunately, he moves out of range of the CCTV cameras the moment he steps off the metro platform."

"Car parked in the lot there?"

"No. That we would have noticed."

"Shit."

"But there's been a minimum of one patrol outside the Koponen residence since last night, and they would have reacted if Roger Koponen had shown up there. Besides, why would he have done that . . . revealed that he was alive?"

"Maybe . . ." Erne says, then buries his face in his hands. "Maybe he doesn't even know he's dead yet."

"What?"

"Maybe he doesn't read the news. Hell, I don't know. We need to think about this carefully. Thanks, Rasse. I have to make a couple of calls." Erne pushes his office chair away from his desk and directs his gaze out the window; an airplane is flying across the sky.

"There was still that second matter . . . regarding Torsten Karlstedt." Rasmus shuts his laptop, and Erne turns back, intrigued.

Rasmus moistens his fingertip on his tongue and slides it between the sheets in his stack of papers. "A truly interesting case. Finnish, fifty years old. No criminal record. Lives in Westend, three young children. CEO, chairman of the board, and sole shareowner of an IT company named Tors10 Inc. Turnover a nice two-point-four million euros, nearly half of that profit."

"And the car seen in Savonlinna belongs to him?"

"Porsche Cayenne, twenty-eighteen model. The newest of the new."

"You said just a second ago that he's an interesting case. So far he strikes me as your average rich jerkoff . . ."

"He's anything but. He appears to be some expert on the occult. He has published two works on the subject. The books cover, among other things, secret societies, esotericism, magic, and even witchcraft. Their Finnish publisher is the same company that published Roger Koponen's trilogy."

"Slow down," Erne says. "Is occult the same as supernatural?"

"To simplify, yes. The term comes from the Latin word *'occultus,'* which means 'hidden.' The occultism explores a world that exists outside of everyday reality. The purpose of occultism is to build a bridge between realities, between our mundane world and the world of secrets. In order to achieve this aim, practitioners of the occult employ various rituals and objects, such as amulets, rabbit feet, you name it. Or even spells and magic."

"What's the point of all this mumbo jumbo?"

"Secret knowledge only accessible to a few has all sorts of amazing potential. It helps practitioners understand the meaning of life. Impact its course. Perhaps conquer death."

"So the aims of occultism are positive?"

"There are all sorts of magic. And while the aims of white magic are good, the aims of black magic—"

"Are bad. I get it. So what we're talking about here is some sort of religion?"

"There are similarities. But there's one fundamental difference between magic and any major mainstream religion. And that's where the fascination with the occult lies."

"Which is?"

"Anyone can believe in God if they want to. Religions compete for members; they push their beliefs on people in the form of missionary work and other dogmatism. But secret knowledge is, as the name indicates, exclusive—in other words, information intended solely for a select few."

Erne draws his mouth into a taut line and looks at Rasmus. "And as an expert in the occult, Torsten Karlstedt made a special trip to Savonlinna to hear Roger Koponen talk about his novels, which deal with the same topics?"

"I doubt it. Roger Koponen spoke three times in Helsinki last week. At the Casino, Pörssitalo, and Paasitorni. Why drive four hours to Savonlinna just to hear the same twaddle?" Rasmus murmurs.

"Maybe Karlstedt wasn't able to make it to the Helsinki events. Or maybe he's a serious fan."

"Koponen was supposed to speak at a few bookstores in the Helsinki area next week too."

"If Karlstedt knew Koponen was going to die, he knew he would be seeing his last appearance."

"Or else he knew that Koponen wasn't really going to die."

"Fuck, what a mess. What if he didn't just drive there and back after all? Maybe Karlstedt is still in Savonlinna."

"His car is parked outside his house in Westend."

"That means he might be mixed up with the burnings outside Juva. It's possible, at least from a logistical perspective."

"That's true." Rasmus takes a few deep breaths. His demeanor is more relaxed than earlier; it feels like the progress in the case has gotten him to loosen up. "As I mentioned, Karlstedt wrote two books." He sets two printouts on the desk, each with an image of the cover of a book.

Introduction to the Occult, Torsten Karlstedt (2002)
The Hermetic and Esoteric Sciences, Torsten Karlstedt, Kai Lehtinen (2007)

"Who's Kai Lehtinen?"

"I couldn't find much on him right off the bat. As far as I could tell, this is the only project he was involved in, and he hasn't published anything else. I called the publisher and asked for information on him. They didn't tell me anything worth mentioning. But I did get his social security number from them." Rasmus slides out the bottom-most sheet of paper from the stack. The photograph is of a bald man with a vaguely threatening appearance. The glaring eyes seem to be concealing something unpredictable and uncontrollable within them.

"Kai 'Kaitsu' Lehtinen, forty-eight years old. General contractor, lives in Vantaa. No family."

"So this is the guy who asked the weird question, then climbed into Karlstedt's car?"

"I sent the photo to Pave Koskinen and he said he's ninety percent sure."

"Good work, Rasse. Give me ten minutes to chew on this," Erne says, reaching for his mobile phone.

Chapter 50

THE ELEVATOR DOORS OPEN ONTO THE SIXTH-FLOOR corridor. Jessica can sense someone's gaze on her temples: Teo must still be standing outside Laura Helminen's room. She walks over to the nurses' station, where the glass hatch slides back before she can knock on it.

"Yes?"

"Jessica Niemi, Helsinki police."

A broad-faced woman looks at her suspiciously from behind a pair of thick glasses.

Jessica reaches under her sweater and pulls out the badge hanging around her neck She slips it through the hatch, and the nurse studies it carefully. Which she should, of course.

"Laura Helminen, room fourteen. She was brought here by ambulance a couple of hours ago," Jessica says, looping the lanyard around her neck again.

"Yes . . . she came to us directly from the ER."

"I'd like to know where her belongings are. Her clothes and so on . . ."

"Her clothes?"

"I lent her my coat to keep her warm . . ."

"Just a moment." The woman draws the hatch shut, as if she doesn't trust Jessica not to steal her stapler and markers. Then she rises slowly from her chair and ambles lazily into the back room.

Jessica looks around, on a whim pumps a few squirts of hand sanitizer into her palms and furiously rubs them together. She doesn't really have a phobia when it comes to germs; after all, she has spent plenty of time in hospitals and morgues due to the nature of her work. But right now she has a dread of inaction, of standing around twiddling her thumbs. Since yesterday, she has felt naked and vulnerable, a target: that's why she doesn't want to stop, wants to keep moving. A moving target is harder to hit. All the victims have resembled her in a number of ways: the women have been relatively young, dark-haired, slim. Furthermore, she knows she has enemies.

Last October, she received some measure of publicity after having been the principal investigator in a case in which two members of a motorcycle gang were arrested on suspicion of murder. But the more Jessica thinks about it, the surer she is that whoever is behind these witch hunts, it's not gang members with a grudge or anyone else Jessica might have ticked off by sending them to prison. Seeing the horned figure on the ice has revived an incident she has been trying to forget for nearly fifteen years.

"My colleague says the coat was already picked up."

The words sink gradually into Jessica's consciousness, and it takes a few seconds before she can formulate her thoughts into words.

"What? Who?"

"A man—"

"Why the hell would you give it to someone else?" Jessica feels herself losing her voice.

"Wait a second. I'll ask—"

"Tell your colleague to come out here. This instant!" Jessica snaps, leaning against the counter. "And leave that hatch open!"

Alarmed, the nurse rises from her chair more speedily this time and disappears into the back room again.

Jessica's nose picks up the industrial odor of the anti-bacterial gel; it reminds her of regular visits to the doctor, X-rays, MRIs, cortisone shots, screws, braces, neurological tests, osteopathy, acupuncture.

"Where the hell is my coat?" Jessica demands, now almost at a shout, and bangs her fist down on the counter.

"Here, Jessie! I . . . picked it up for you."

Jessica turns and sees Yusuf, stares at his fearful face for a moment. She sees the coat under his arm, the phone in his hand. Down at the end of the corridor, Teo has turned around to look at them.

Chapter 51

THE DROPLETS ON THE CAR'S WINDOWS MEAN WARMING temperatures. Jessica pulls the door shut, and Yusuf starts up the engine. They've walked to the parking lot in utter silence. Jessica is scrolling through the unanswered calls on her phone.

"I just wanted to help," Yusuf says.

"I know. I get it. I didn't mean to . . ."

The windshield wipers whisk rhythmically across the windshield but leave some drops undisturbed. Apparently the blade on the right-hand wiper has seen better days.

"What did Helminen say?" Jessica finally asks, sweeping a strand of hair back from her forehead.

"Let's listen to it," Yusuf says. He pulls a recorder out of his pocket.

Yusuf Pepple: . . . first of all, I can assure you that Detective Niemi is in no way involved in the crime.

Laura Helminen: It was that woman . . . They said she's the one who's behind everything. (crying)

226

YP: (long pause) We'll come back to that soon. I want you to understand that you're completely safe now. There's a really strong, sharp guy standing guard outside that door. No one is going to do anything bad to you. Do you understand?

LH: (sobbing)

YP: Can you tell me what happened? Why don't you start from the very beginning?

LH: I don't remember . . .

YP: What's the last thing you remember?

LH: I was at home . . . The doorbell rang . . .

YP: You were alone?

LH: I live alone.

YP: Who was at the door?

LH: I don't remember . . . That's all I remember. And then I was in this gloomy place. It was sort of like a basement or—

YP: So there weren't any windows?

LH: It was dark in there. And there was this musty, moldy smell.

YP: Good. You're doing really well. What else did you see there?

LH: My clothes, they weren't mine.

YP: A black evening gown?

LH: I don't own . . . It wasn't mine.

YP: (pause) What else do you remember?

LH: Down in the basement, there was (sobbing) another woman. I didn't know her, but she was also wearing a black evening dress and expensive shoes.

YP: So you two had been dressed the same way.

LH: And then that man came in. (bursts into tears)

YP: Can you describe him?

LH: Horns . . . He was like an animal or something. A goat or a sheep . . .

Jessica looks at Yusuf. The sounds of crying and consoling come from the recording. Then footsteps. Dr. Kuznetsov says something.

YP: What happened next?

LH: He was speaking Latin . . . I know it was Latin because I took a semester once.

YP: Did you understand what he was saying?

LH: No . . . I was so fucking scared. But then . . . a moment later, he started dancing . . . and waving this wand or something around. It was like some crazy, sick ritual. Both of us were scared out of our wits. And then another man came in. He was wearing a mask with horns too. (pauses)

YP: Please go on.

LH: They took down this cloth that was hanging on the wall. And I saw the painting. It was of a witch. The witch that was here in this room a little while ago. (crying)

YP: (long pause) What did they say?

LH: (crying)

YP: Laura, you have to focus now. We need to get as much information as possible so we can catch them.

LH: They dragged us into the next room. There was this big wooden tub in there, like one of those wooden hot tubs but huge. I heard one of them splash the water with his hand. They said it was time to perform a test and that if we didn't have anything to hide, we had nothing to be afraid of. And then . . . (long pause) That's all I remember.

YP: Do you remember where they took you under the ice? This is important, Laura.

LH: Maybe I woke up underwater . . . It's almost as if someone was swimming with me through ice-cold water. (sobbing) But maybe I'm just imagining things. (soft crying)

Alex Kuznetsov: All right. This is a good place to take a break. It sounds like all the essential questions have been asked now.

YP: OK. Thank you, Laura. And if you think of anything else, anything at all, tell the doctor. He'll call us . . . (pause) call *me* back in. Do we have a deal? Good.

Yusuf stops the recording. The wipers rub against the windshield. Heavy snow falls from the hospital roof; the thud when it hits the ground carries into the car.

"You did a good job, Yusuf. There's nothing else you could have gotten out of her."

"This job bites, Jessie." Yusuf's eyes are glazed over. "When I was in there, I was just concentrating on getting all the essential information. It's only now that I'm listening to the recording that I get how terrified she really was." Yusuf closes his eyes.

Jessica glances over. Yusuf is sitting at her side, pinching his nose between his fingers. Sometimes she forgets how sensitive he is. Bodies, blood, and guts don't get to him. But human tragedies, the agony of loved ones, the trauma of those who survive brutal attacks—they often shut him down. The year before, he took a few weeks of sick leave after having worked on the murder of an eight-year-old girl. She had been killed by her father. Yusuf had a hard time accepting it; he hasn't liked talking about it to this day. And why should he?

"So Laura Helminen passed the test," Jessica says a moment later.

"But that doesn't make any sense . . . Isn't the whole point of the test that witches float and innocent people sink?"

"Yeah, I think that's what Micke said."

"I doubt either of those poor women actually floated."

"Not likely."

"So Helminen was spared for some other reason?"

"The Ice Princess wasn't as lucky," Jessica says as Yusuf pulls out into traffic.

Chapter 52

37.5. DAILY AVERAGE: 37.4.

Erne Mikson is sitting at the long table, sipping the weak coffee Rasmus brewed. He's studying photographs and his cracked knuckles, which have been whittled sharp and angular by the years.

"Jessica and Yusuf are on their way," Mikael says, sitting down. Also present are Nina and Rasmus, who has gotten a jolt of fresh energy from his discoveries. He looks more enthusiastic and animated than he has in ages.

"What's wrong?" Erne says without lifting his eyes from his hands. Over the years, he has become a master at sensing changes in mood. Minor things, gestures, words. Just now, his team is radiating negative energy. "Well? Spit it out, Micke."

"I think we should bring in those two guys for questioning right away." Mikael pops his gum between his teeth, arms folded across his chest.

"I see," Erne says, not the least bit surprised.

"They clearly followed Roger Koponen and Sanna Porkka from Savonlinna and sent two people up in flames. We could bring them in on probable cause—"

"Roger Koponen is alive."

"So?"

"If Karlstedt and Lehtinen really followed the car Porkka was driving from Savonlinna and stopped it in Juva and killed two people, one of whom we haven't been able to ID yet in light of new information we've discovered, we can assume Roger Koponen continued his journey to Helsinki with the two of them afterward."

"Of course."

"That makes Koponen a suspect. And if we want to find Koponen, we ought to keep eyes on Karlstedt and Koskinen for a while."

"And ears," Rasmus says, raising a tentative finger into the air.

"It's been handled. I just got a warrant from the courts. Rasse, you take the baton on that. I want you to listen to every single phone call and report anything even remotely related to the case or that otherwise strikes you as off.

And, of course, it's vital you use base-station data to figure out if the men's mobile phones traveled from Savonlinna to Helsinki, and if they stopped for a while in the vicinity of the killings."

"Got it," Rasmus says, smiling in satisfaction. Erne knows from experience that Rasmus loves a challenge. His head has really been in the game today.

"And meanwhile, Micke, it's critical that neither man disappears from our field of vision. There can be no gaps in the monitoring. No stupid mistakes," Erne says.

Nina has raised her hand, and now Erne nods, giving her the floor. "I don't disagree with you, Erne. I think it's a smart approach . . ." she begins, drawing an invisible square on the tabletop.

"But?"

"But I think what Jessica has called to our attention several times today needs to be taken into consideration. I'm talking about the fact that we're hopelessly a step behind these people. And that we have been from the beginning."

"Continue," Erne says, looking darky at Nina.

"It feels like everything we've found out . . . is things they've wanted us to find out."

"I see your perspective. But, on the other hand, my dear colleagues," Erne says, now in a sharper tone, "there's the danger here that we are overestimating the intelligence of this cabal and their ability to mislead us. Let's take a step backward: why does it feel like we've been given crumbs of information?"

"Because the '*mistakes*'"—and as she says the word, Nina holds a brief pause and draws air quotes around it, a habit that has always irritated Erne immensely—"these suspects made are so fucking stupid. Why make it seem like Roger Koponen is dead, if the next morning he's uploading a video of his murdered wife in a location where there are a hundred and twenty security cameras? You don't have to

233

be the best-informed layperson to know phones and other smart devices can be easily tracked. These jerkoffs wanted us to see them."

"Which is why we need to bring them in right away," Mikael interjects emphatically.

"I'm positive they also knew about the camera at Savonlinna Hall. Even so, Lehtinen asked a question from the audience. A question that didn't go unnoticed by anyone present. And then stepped out in front of the camera and into a brand-new Porsche whose license plate they didn't make the slightest effort to cover. Totally fucking stupid mistakes. Without that provocative question, we wouldn't even have the names of these occultists."

"Fine," Erne says, and stands. "You guys feel like we're dumbasses and they're leading us along by a leash wrapped around our necks."

"Our balls," Mikael says.

The others nod.

"It's all a fucking show. This is exactly what we're trying to say, Erne. We need to stop dancing to the tune of these sadistic murderers and make our own move." Mikael spits his gum out into a wad of paper toweling.

Erne surveys the investigators sitting round the table. He has no problem with dissenting opinions; he has always encouraged his team to think critically. It might be the very reason the unit's success rate has always been higher than average. He buttons the top button of his sport coat and pulls the sleeves over his frayed shirt cuffs. "Thank you for your thoughts. I still want to hear Jessica's views on the matter. Until then, your job is to make sure we don't miss the tiniest move or phone call those two make."

Then Erne stalks out of the conference room.

Chapter 53

DUSK HAS FALLEN OVER HELSINKI AGAIN. THE SUN SPENDS so few hours glowing through the veil of gray clouds this time of the year that it feels as if someone were turning the dimmer first clockwise and then counterclockwise.

Jessica and Yusuf are just climbing out of the car in the garage at police HQ in Pasila when Jessica's phone rings.

"Sergeant Niemi. I am. Yes. Good. Could you send me the report . . . ? Great. Thank you."

Yusuf watches his colleague's terse exchange with interest.

Then Jessica lowers the receiver from her ear. "That was Sarvilinna. We have an ID for the Ice Princess."

Yusuf leans his elbows on the car's roof. "OK."

"Her name is Lea Blomqvist. Twenty-nine years old."

"Who ID'd the body?"

"Apparently her brother, who reported her missing this morning."

"Is the brother still at the morgue?"

"Yes. We need to talk to him right away."

"Erne wants us to meet with him first," Yusuf says, slamming the car door.

"I guess we'd better do that, then."

The door is open, and Jessica and Yusuf walk into Erne's cramped office without knocking.

"You two have had a busy day," Erne says, gaze glued to his computer screen. His forefinger is tapping at the mouse.

"You can say that again," Jessica says quietly. She unzips her coat. "Did Sarvilinna call you too?"

"She did. She had tried to get ahold of you earlier, but you didn't answer."

"My phone was misplaced for a sec."

"So I understood."

"So you heard the Ice Princess has been identified."

Erne frowns. "Huh? I don't care for that nickname."

"We don't either. And now we don't have to use it anymore," Jessica says as Yusuf takes a seat in the corner.

"So now we know the identities of all victims, aside from the man in Juva," Erne says, releasing the mouse.

"Yup." Jessica lightly massages her kneecaps. They are tingling ominously. It has been months since her episode, but she still remembers the paralyzing pain that put her out of commission for multiple days.

"What's your plan?" Erne asks.

"To talk to Helminen's and Blomqvist's family members. Maybe Maria Koponen's closest friends too."

"Why?"

"I'm positive there's a connection between the three of them. Something aside from the fact that some sick fuck thought they were witches."

Erne smiles. Jessica knows all three of Erne's smiles; the one she just saw indicates satisfaction.

"Excellent," he says, then starts coughing uncontrollably. Jessica looks at him in concern. When did Erne get so old and decrepit?

Jessica waits for his coughing fit to subside before she continues. "Both Helminen and Blomqvist were drugged and taken to a basement, where they were dressed in identical clothes. Then, evidently, the witch test was performed on both of them, the one Micke told us about. The women were submerged in a large wooden tub or tank."

"And all this is based on what Helminen told you?"

"Yes. She also claimed the abductors were wearing some sort of animal masks, just like that creep I saw today on the ice." After saying this, Jessica casts a long glance at Erne and studies his reaction. If he didn't before, now he has to believe the horned man on the ice wasn't a figment of Jessica's imagination.

"So you believe Helminen is credible?"

Jessica shivers. She was wrong. Erne doesn't trust either report. "What do you mean? I don't understand why she wouldn't be."

"After a shock like that, the imagination can make up all sorts of things."

Jessica's fingers clench into fists of vexation in the back pockets of her jeans, and she is emphatic: "Like I just said, her account fits perfectly into the overall picture." She looks at Yusuf, who takes a moment to realize he's part of the conversation.

"Damn right, Erne," he says, despite the uncertainty in his voice. Yusuf has been in the unit for only a couple of years and is still afraid of saying something that might antagonize his boss.

But now Erne chuckles good-naturedly. "Damn right," he repeats softly, and then turns his attention to his papers. Jessica sees a thick stack of printouts on the corner of the desk: Koponen's books and Karlstedt's work *Introduction to the Occult*, which Erne has managed to get his hands on from somewhere. Eventually he speaks again: "I agree there has to be some connection between the women other than a trim figure and dark hair. I think it's a good angle of attack."

"I haven't had time to talk to Micke about what happened on the ice today . . ." Jessica begins, and feels hunger searing her stomach. She hasn't had a chance to eat.

"You want to know what it has to do with Koponen's book?"

"Of course."

"There's a pretty exact parallel. In the book, one of the women suspected of being a witch passes the test. In other words, she sinks instead of floating. The inquisitors pull her out of the water and set her free. It's likely that

239

Laura Helminen is playing that poor woman in this grisly drama."

"Don't you find it odd that some of the crimes that take place in the books have been copied to a T, but in others the connection to the text is pretty superficial, like in the case of Laura Helminen?"

"You're right. But you have to remember, we're the ones who made the assumption that this group is copying the events from Koponen's book. Even if it were true, the criminals don't necessarily have any rule about following the plot word for word."

"I see," Jessica says, then pulls her notebook from her coat pocket and jots down something. For a moment they sit there in silence. The only sound in the room is that of Erne's heavy breathing.

"Then there's one thing I'd like you to take a stance on as principal investigator, Jessie," Erne says. He rises lazily from his chair. "Karlstedt and Lehtinen. We don't have any information on the car's movements last night. In theory, it's possible the two of them are in some way involved in the burning deaths in Juva. And if they are, we can't shut out the possibility that the two of them are working in concert with Roger Koponen."

"But there's nothing concrete? Other than the question Lehtinen asked?" Jessica says, clicking the end of her ballpoint pen.

"Exactly. Both of them are under constant surveillance. We have eyes on the cars in Westend and Vantaa. We've received warrants to monitor their telephones, and the lines are singing. But even so, Nina and Micke think we should bring them in immediately for questioning."

"You want to know what I think?"

"Desperately."

"Isn't our main goal to find Roger Koponen? In which case we ought to hold off and wait for one of those two guys to contact him—or vice versa."

"I agree," Erne says, looking a little relieved.

"But we can't focus solely on Koponen. He was demonstrably in Savonlinna at the time when Maria Koponen and the Ice Princess . . ."

"She has a name now, Jessica." Erne steps behind his desk and looks out the window.

". . . Lea Blomqvist were killed in Kulosaari."

Erne presses his fingertips against the windowpane. "So even if we find Koponen, the murderer would still be on the loose."

"Exactly." Jessica takes a deep breath. "So it would be downright dumb to bring Karlstedt and Lehtinen in now."

"Jessica saw a guy with horns out on the ice," Yusuf begins, deep in thought. "At the same time, someone was under the ice with Laura Helminen, bringing her to the hole."

"And?"

"Were Karlstedt and Lehtinen under surveillance by that point?"

"No. But very soon thereafter, we placed Karlstedt at his house in Westend and Lehtinen at his workplace in

241

Kivistö. I suppose it's theoretically possible, but really damn unlikely, that they would have been at Kulosaari at that time. Roger Koponen, on the other hand, got off the metro in Kulosaari at eight sixteen a.m."

Jessica lowers her head and feels a tremendous shudder convulse through her body.

Chapter 54

JESSICA IS LEANING AGAINST THE BACK OF ERNE'S OFFICE. Mikael, Nina, and Rasmus have packed into the small room too. For some reason, Jessica doesn't feel the need to stop breathing, even though Rasmus is standing right in front of her. Evidently, someone has finally delivered him an anonymous message encouraging him to invest in his personal hygiene.

"That's settled, then," Mikael says, clapping his hands together. A moment earlier, Erne bulldozed his opinion that Karlstedt and Lehtinen should be brought in immediately, but Mikael doesn't seem the least bit bitter. That's what he's like: Mikael has an opinion on just about everything, but no trouble at all respecting his superior's decisions. He is well aware that the one who makes the decisions also carries the responsibility for their consequences.

"Then there are some other things," Erne continues. He's the only one in the room who's sitting. "First of all, Yusuf and Jessica just suggested we search for other instances of the words 'Malleus Maleficarum' by helicopter."

"Actually it was Yusuf's idea," Jessica says, unsure whether she made the clarification out of politeness or to save her own skin in case it's a crap idea.

"What does that mean?" Nina asks, kneading her trained shoulders with her fingertips.

"The text stamped onto the Koponens' roof might have been practiced somewhere—as Yusuf suggested—or there might be more of them. Left as clues for us," Erne explains.

Mikael shakes his head. "Left as clues for us. So we're going to keep playing these assholes' game."

"These assholes might have, for instance, marked the location of a new victim this way. In which case it's in our interests to find it," Erne says crisply, and now they catch a flash of the old Erne: the man whose firm, decisive delivery leaves no place for ifs, ands, or buts.

Erne interlaces his fingers on the desk. "Secondly, for the time being, we will not be informing the media that Roger Koponen is alive. There's a razor-thin chance the witch hunters don't know what we know. Let's go with that, at least until tonight. Thirdly: talking to the victims' family members and friends begins immediately. Jessica and Yusuf will handle that; if necessary, you two call on folks from the NBI for help. And don't be shy to ask if you need more hands or a fresh pair of eyes." Erne waves a finger in the direction where he presumes the folks from the NBI are sitting.

"Fourthly: Rasmus, I want a report of everything we can assume will happen if these witch hunters have decided to carry out every crime in the Koponen books. Not just of murders, of which, to my understanding, there are still three to come . . ."

Rasmus nods and counts on his fingers as he speaks: "A woman is crushed under rocks, a man is stoned to death, and another is killed with a dagger."

". . . but also all of the other events that meet the criterion of a crime. Abductions, assaults, rapes. Stepping in dog shit. Everything. Everything that's in the book could happen one way or another."

A momentary silence falls over the room.

"Nina and Mikael. Try to find all the buildings in Laajasalo and the nearby vicinity that have basements. Based on what Laura Helminen told us, we're not talking about some bike storage in an apartment building. It has to be a space no one could stumble on by accident. A place where you could make as much commotion as you wanted without having to worry about the neighbors calling the police. A bomb shelter, a private storage space, the basement of a house. While you're at it, check with tub import companies to find out who they've sold or delivered wooden tubs to. Check gag shops for those masks. Even the tiniest leads are valuable now. And, as with Jessica, use the guys from the NBI as a resource. They're waiting for your instructions."

Everyone in the room nods. The division of labor is efficient and clear. Erne growls out his orders once a day, then usually sets his team loose to do their thing without interference.

Mikael raises a finger, as if asking for the last word, and Erne nods. "Laura Helminen said the tub was really big. What do you think that means, more or less?"

"Are you asking how big a really big wooden tub is?" Jessica says, raising her eyes to the ceiling.

"Yes."

"If a person has to be able to float in it without their limbs touching the bottom . . . in other words, if it's possible to drown in it . . . I'd say—"

"Maybe two thousand to three thousand liters?" Rasmus interjects. "My mom has a fifteen-hundred-liter hot tub on her deck in Hanko, and it would be almost impossible to drown in it."

"Really? Did you try without your floaties when your mommy wasn't watching?"

Mikael's jab manages to visibly disconcert Rasmus, who furiously rubs the temples of his eyeglasses.

Erne shoots Mikael a warning glance: *Knock it off.*

"What are you getting at, Micke?"

"If we assume the crime spree didn't start until yesterday, isn't it likely the tank was just filled recently? The coroner's report says the water was tap water."

A smile spreads across Nina's face. "I like the way you're thinking. How much water does the average Finn use?"

"About a hundred and fifty liters a day."

"So, in a two-person household, filling a tub like that would mean a thousand percent spike in water consumption."

"Can we find it?"

"I'll call the water department."

"Have them start by focusing on Kulosaari and Laajasalo and, if necessary, expand outward into the rest of metropolitan Helsinki." Mikael claps his hands together in satisfaction.

"Good! I want you to report back to Jessica on all fronts," Erne says. He gropes at the breast pocket of his sport coat; the look on his face says his cigarettes are still there. "And, oh yeah," he says, and the high pitch of his voice clearly catches him off guard too, "Sissi Sarvilinna's report on both Maria Koponen and the Ice Princess—"

"She has a name," Jessica says coolly with a wink at Erne.

"—Lea Blomqvist, God rest her soul," Erne continues, shooting Jessica a supposedly murderous glance. He puts on his glasses and grabs a piece of paper resting on the table. "In any case, certain substances have been identified in both victims' blood that, if misused or consumed in large amounts, are lethal. Thiopental, pancuronium bromide, and potassium chloride. In addition, it looks like chloroform was used to render them unconscious."

A low murmur spreads through the room.

"The death-row cocktail. I just read a book called *Hammurabi's Angels,* where the killer supposedly used the same combo," Mikael says, intrigued. "Roger Koponen isn't the only author the killers have been reading."

Nina frowns. "So the MO can be considered to be somehow . . . humane?"

"Maybe not humane. But painless," Jessica says, pulling out her notepad again.

"Laura Helminen was also drugged with chloroform. Apparently the women were thrown into the tub when they were unconscious, which means the drowning was painless too," Erne says.

Suddenly the room is still enough to hear a pin drop.

"It's a comforting thought," Rasmus says, shoving his hands into his pockets.

"A slender silver lining on this humongous shit cloud. Nina and Mikael, find out all the places in Helsinki where it's possible to get your hands on those toxins."

"Done."

"That's it. Thank you," Erne says, and a low murmur fills the room again.

Jessica opens her notebook, looks at the name and number she jotted down on the last page: *Pave Koskinen*. She made notes on the earlier meeting with Erne below. When she turns the page to write down the toxins Erne mentioned, the pen slips and falls to the floor. A cold wave surges through her lower limbs. Suddenly everything is murky. She can hear her own heavy breathing; the others' voices echo distantly in the background.

This isn't possible.

"What's wrong, Jessie?" Erne has appeared at her side; Jessica feels his hand on her shoulder.

"This isn't . . ." Jessica whispers, clutching the notebook to her chest.

Yusuf takes hold of the notebook. "Show me."

Jessica lets go of the notebook and clasps her hands behind her neck. "I didn't write that—"

The look on Yusuf's face says it all. *Malleus Maleficarum.*

Chapter 55

OH, THAT BREEZE IS NICE.

The breeze is warm and humid. The boat rocks in the light swells off of the lido sandbar east of the city, and a two-kilometer-long beach spreads out across from them. Jessica thinks about her mother's words; it was one of those rare remarks she remembers coming from her mother's lips more than once. At their pool in Bel Air, the only time the breeze felt cool was on her wet skin, in that moment before Dad would wrap her in a big towel. Usually the breeze was warm, almost as warm as the heavy, still air, and yet it was still refreshing, especially on the oppressively hot summer days. Jessica remembers how the wind would toss the fronds of the tall palms, how their trunks would bend thrillingly but never snap, even though she watched them, hands over her ears, waiting for the crack.

"What are you thinking about?" She feels Colombano's voice at the base of her ear. His fingertips wander through her hair, rough and strong, stroke the scalp in a way she can feel in the pit of her stomach.

"Nothing." Jessica turns her head so she can see herself in the lenses of Colombano's aviators. She looks beautiful, even though the salt water has washed away her makeup and pasted her hair to her skin.

It has been eight days since Jessica was supposed to board the train for Milan. She has left behind her old life and leapt into an alternate reality, one that has no place for Torino, for skiing in the Alps, the train to Grenoble, the beach vacation in Marseille. Summer is at its most beautiful in Central Europe, and she's in no hurry to get home. Besides, does she even have one? Has she ever had a place where she feels safe and loved? *Home is where the heart is.* Her home is with Colombano now.

Sometimes Jessica feels like she has spent much longer at Colombano's side. During those moments when she settles into a plush chair in the concert hall to listen to *The Four Seasons,* during those moments when they fix breakfast or amble around the city, during those moments when she sits alone in Colombano's apartment, waiting for him to come home. During those moments when they kiss, make love, stroke each other's skin, or feed the pigeons at Piazza San Marco. During those moments, her ever-present detachment finally evaporates, and she is enveloped in a sense of calm.

"You want to go swimming?" Colombano says, stroking Jessica's cheek with his fingers.

"Sure." Jessica smiles and sits up, takes off her sunglasses and squints. The sun is blazing in the expanse of sky. She grabs hold of the hand bailer that had been pressing into her lower back while she was relaxing there and flings it into the bow of the boat. The boat is nothing special; there's not a hint of luxury about it. Not a hint of the St. Tropez glamor Jessica had a chance to sample the summer before when she spent a few weeks on the French Riviera. Which is exactly why it's perfect.

Jessica watches Colombano slip out of his white T-shirt and dive into the water as effortlessly as a dolphin, leaving the little boat swinging from side to side like a rocking chair. His athletic body glides through the crystalline water, and then his head and shoulders surface a few meters away.

"Come in, princess," he calls out, brushing the wet hair out of his eyes.

"I'm coming." Jessica stands. Colombano floats in a manner remotely akin to synchronized swimming, then disappears under the surface again.

Jessica is just placing her toes on the edge of the boat to push off into the water when she feels a sharp pain in her heel and drops down to sitting. She checks the sole of her foot and sees a metal ring digging into her heel; it has broken the skin. She takes hold of the band and cautiously pries it out. It's a ring. A decorative gold ring, the empty crown of which has presumably once held a diamond. Now the edges of the crown are like the tiny sharp teeth of a pike.

Jessica sits back down on the bottom of the boat, fingering the broken ring and massaging the cut in her heel at the same time. Blood is trickling out, mingling with the water, sweat, and sunscreen glistening on her skin. She hears Colombano splashing boisterously.

"Get in!"

Jessica turns the ring over. There's an engraving on the inside.

"Jessica?"

Per il mio amore, Chiara.
"I'm coming, Bano."
20.2.2003.—xx.xx.2103

Jessica looks at the cursive script. *For my love, Chiara.* Only a year and a few months have passed since the date engraved there, apparently a wedding day.

Suddenly Jessica feels the boat tilt, sees strong fingers hook over the edge, and the ring slips from her fingers into the dirty water pooled at the boat's bottom. Colombano pushes himself up onto his elbows on the side of the boat.

"What's wrong?" he asks, stretching out his neck to see the foot Jessica is now holding with both hands.

"I hit my toe on something," Jessica blurts.

"Is it bleeding?" Colombano frowns and points at Jessica's fingers. They're red.

"I guess." Jessica cautiously rises to her feet.

"Do you want to go home?" Colombano drops back into the water. Now he is floating on his back right next to the boat, looking at her.

Jessica feels the sun burning her shoulders, which just a moment ago were draped in a sheer linen scarf. The water around the boat sparkles invitingly. She can feel it wrapping her body in its cooling embrace. She loves the smell of the salt water, its taste on her tongue. But something gives her pause.

It's the way Colombano is looking at her.

"Not yet," she says. "I don't feel like swimming yet."

"Why not?" All playfulness has disappeared from his voice.

"I just don't feel like it."

"Jump in."

"I—"

"Jump in, Jessica." Colombano takes hold of the side of the boat again. Jessica feels ice-cold fingers wrap around her ankle. Colombano's face has grown suspicious.

"I don't want to." Jessica registers a quaver in her voice. The grip on her ankle tightens; the boat begins to rock. First slowly, then faster and faster. Water sloshes over the edge; droplets form on Jessica's skin. She lets out a jittery gasp.

Then Colombano's expression changes again, and the empathy creeping across his face is like a lifesaver tossed into freezing water. "OK. I was just teasing."

He lets go of Jessica's ankle and takes a few strokes towards the stern, where there's a swim ladder.

Jessica looks at the dark gray puddle. She hopes it will hide the ring forever.

Chapter 56

"WHAT DO YOU THINK HAPPENED?" ERNE SAYS. HE SHUTS the door. He and Jessica are alone in the room together; everyone else has headed off to get to work.

"My notebook was in my coat pocket this whole time," Jessica says, her eyes nailed to the blue-and-white pennant standing on Erne's desk, which shivers almost imperceptibly. "Someone must have found it either in the ambulance or at the hospital."

Erne leans against the door, hands on his hips, looking like he doesn't know what to do.

"Yusuf picked up the coat from the nurses' station . . . My understanding was the ambulance drivers had dropped it off."

"Your phone was in your coat pocket too. If someone got ahold of the notebook, they've also had access to it."

"It's protected with a code."

"Still, I want you to talk to Micke. I'm such a klutz when it comes to these things, I don't know how to determine if there are any risks involved in using the phone, or if you should switch it out and get a new one."

"I don't understand how the hell—"

"If someone got into your belongings, we'll be able to see it on the hospital's cameras. Rasse will look into it."

"What do you mean *if*? You see this, don't you, goddamn it?" Jessica opens her notebook to the page emblazoned with the Latin words. She flips back and forth for the umpteenth time to make sure there isn't any more writing. But the rest of the pages are pristine.

"All I'm saying is . . ." Erne says, rubbing his nose, ". . . it's always possible someone got hold of it earlier. And that a couple of empty pages were left in between on purpose so you wouldn't find the text until later."

"I don't know, Erne. I really don't know. But right now I feel like I'm a pawn in a sick fucking game. Think about it: I've seen the murderer twice. Yesterday at the Koponens' house, today on the ice. And now he left a message in my notebook."

"That still doesn't make this personal. You're the principal investigator on the case. The messages are presumably meant for whichever detective happens to be in charge, not a woman named Jessica Niemi." Erne slowly circles around the desk and takes a seat.

Jessica surreptitiously eyes his deteriorating mien. Erne is sick, and Jessica knows it, despite his refusal to talk about it. Even with her.

"There's more, Erne. We didn't have time to tell you everything about the hospital visit yet. Laura Helminen

256

had a shit fit when she saw me." Jessica raises her gaze to Erne, who suddenly looks more alert.

"What do you mean?"

"The painting she saw in the basement—"

"What about it?"

"Helminen said it was a painting of me."

Erne is about to say something, but frowns instead.

"She said she's absolutely positive."

"Laura Helminen was in a state of shock, for understandable reasons—"

"But if you take into consideration everything else that has happened, it doesn't seem that far-fetched anymore. I'm the target."

"I see. So you're a criminal mastermind who gets others to commit evil deeds?"

"Why else have those assholes hung a framed picture of me in the basement?"

Erne sighs; Jessica knows that nagging isn't fair right now. The situation is equally confusing for all of them.

"They know, Erne. They know what I did."

"What are you talking about?" Erne asks, brow furrowed, but then he understands. "No, Jessica. Now you're being paranoid. We never have to think about that again. Or talk about it."

"But—"

"A beautiful, black-haired woman. That's how Yusuf said Helminen described the woman in the painting.

Yes, the description applies to you. But it also applies to Maria Koponen, Lea Blomqvist, and Laura Helminen herself. And perhaps to thousands of other women in this city." Erne manages to sound convincing. It's what he does. Jessica discovered this years ago.

"Fine." Jessica sighs and turns to leave.

"But even so," Erne says as Jessica's fingers grab hold of the door handle, "I want to try something."

"What?" Jessica watches Erne rise from his chair and approach her slowly, hands behind his back. Now his face is grave.

"I want to test your theory."

"How?"

"I want you to stay out of the field for a bit. At least until tomorrow."

Jessica stares at the pennant on Erne's desk. Now it's fluttering visibly: evidently the air conditioning has come on. Erne's suggestion is both a relief and enraging. He's clearly afraid for her, which means she's not the only one thinking the way she is. And that isn't necessarily a good thing.

"Until tomorrow? So what am I supposed to? Go rock climbing?"

"Stay inside four walls. Keep your head cool. And the reins in your hands. You still have your phone and laptop."

"So you want me to go home?"

"Yes."

"Erne? Are you taking me off the case?"

258

"Of course not!" Erne snorts in amusement, then rolls his eyes the way bad liars do when they're full of shit. But Erne is neither a bad liar nor a shit talker. "I'm not taking you off the case. Just the opposite. I'm giving your theory a chance."

"You want to see if the perps follow my movements?"

"You're curious too."

"And what if I'm right?"

"If you're right and the witch hunters want to catch your attention specifically, they'll either stop murdering people or approach you, one way or another."

"So now I'm bait?"

"If you want to see it that way. Besides, it's better to be bait than a target. You're safe at home. I'll have the Security Police bring in a surveillance van to Töölönkatu."

Jessica eyes her superior probingly, as if simply by staring at him she'll convince him to change his mind.

"I don't know. This really sucks, Erne."

"Keep working from home. We have so much man-power now that Yusuf will have no trouble handling the questioning without you. We'll re-evaluate things first thing in the morning," Erne says. He looks as if he's about to lower a hand to Jessica's shoulder, but he knows her well enough to refrain. He rubs his knuckles instead. "You know this is the right call, Jessica."

Jessica shakes her head, pushes the door open, and steps into the hallway.

Chapter 57

JESSICA IS SITTING ON A STURDY OFFICE CHAIR, ARMS folded across her chest. The space known as "the quiet room" has no windows, only steel shelves covering almost every square inch of wall space, plus a table and chairs.

"This bad boy is fine," Mikael says, lowering Jessica's pistol to the table.

Jessica shoves the gun into her belt holster. "Great. So no one unloaded it while I was fishing that girl out of the ice—"

"Erne doesn't want to take any risks. Why should he?" Mikael pops his gum with his tongue. "In any case, it's been checked now."

"Yippee."

"And your phone. Does it have a strong unlock code?"

"Yeah, I think so."

"Does anyone else know it?"

"Can I answer in the affirmative without eating my words regarding its strength?"

"So no?"

"Of course not."

"OK. Could you still unlock it for me?" Mikael rubs his fingers clean of undetectable dust.

Jessica does as asked and hands the phone to Mikael. She watches him tap at the phone in concentration for a minute.

"The last time the phone's security has been bypassed is damn tricky to figure out, but we can do a different kind of check . . . *Settings* . . . *General* . . ." Mikael says, pressing the screen of Jessica's phone. "*Storage* . . . OK. Here we can see what apps you've used recently. You mind if I look, or—"

"Knock yourself out. I'm guessing Tinder isn't going to scare you."

"Aha, so you're on it too . . . Is—"

"Micke, just check to see if anyone used my phone."

"Not that we need Tinder." Mikael smiles as he taps at the phone screen.

Jessica glances at her watch. The last thing she feels like doing right now is sit in a tiny room alone with Mikael a single second longer than necessary. The hookup was a bad idea from the jump. Now, a day later, it feels like the biggest mistake in the world. A momentary lapse that left Jessica with a horrific moral hangover. The way Nina looks at Mikael, she seems so happy.

Mikael hands the phone to Jessica. "Look familiar?"

Jessica stares at the icons and dates on the screen.

Everything looks the way it ought to. In reality, the last time she used Tinder was around Christmas. That's how Fubu came into the picture.

"Looks normal."

"Good. But check through the sent messages and outgoing calls before you use it." Mikael pushes the phone across the table to Jessica. "I don't want you finding another *malleus maleficarum* when you're home alone."

"Great. Thanks, Micke," Jessica stands. "And hey—"

"Forget about it. Let's move on, Jessie."

Chapter 58

YUSUF PULLS OVER AT THE SAME EXACT SPOT IN FRONT of the crosswalk where he has countless times in the past.

"You see that van?" he says, pointing at an old dark gray Toyota HiAce with a moving-company logo taped to its side.

"Subtle. I'm surprised they didn't choose an extermination company."

"There are two guys and a camera. Plus patrols are only a couple of minutes away if necessary."

"I think I can manage."

"It's just a precaution. We're going to catch them," Yusuf says, opening his door.

"Where are you—"

"I promised Erne I'd see you to your front door."

"Are you going to come in and make sure there aren't any monsters hiding under the bed too?"

"Whatever it takes." Yusuf grunts and places a cigarette in the corner of his mouth, lights it, and takes a long drag. "You want a smoke?"

Jessica shakes her head "Not a good look for you, floor-ball champ."

"Name one person it is a good look for."

The woman who lives on the third floor steps out of the elevator, her brown dog in her arms. Edelweiss is a ten-year-old silky terrier whose high-pitched yaps reverberate through the stairwell every morning when the reluctant pooch's owner drags her out for a walk. The woman gives Jessica a friendly enough hello and glares suspiciously at Yusuf, who flashes a polite smile without the slightest reciprocation.

"Does she know you're a cop?" Yusuf asks as the woman disappears through the downstairs door into the dark blue afternoon dusk.

"Sure. The neighbors stop me in the stairwell whenever they see something they think is sketchy. Like when someone starts getting too rowdy at the taxi stand. Why?"

"She gave me a look that said that if she didn't know you were from the police, she would have called them."

Both of them smile.

Jessica pulls the elevator gate shut and presses the uppermost button. The old elevator rises slowly, wheezing and then clunking ominously as it passes the landings.

"When was the last time I was at your place?"

"May Day?"

"Oh, yeah, when we came to pick up that champagne . . ."

"Yup." Jessica glances at herself in the mirror. She looks more tired than she did that morning. The unusual day has taken its toll.

There's a whoosh when the elevator stops at the top floor. Jessica is momentarily creeped out; shouldn't have said anything about monsters under the bed.

She holds the gate for Yusuf and opens the door to her studio. There's no mail on the floor. Yusuf glances around the stairwell first, then warily steps in as if he is convinced some unpleasant surprise is waiting for them.

"Do you have an alarm?" he asks as Jessica turns on the lights.

"No," Jessica answers. *I mean, I do, but not here.*

"OK." Yusuf points at his shoes, a questioning look on his face.

"You can leave them on." Jessica walks into the room with her coat on and collapses on the sofa, as if that's what she does every time she comes home. In reality, she hasn't sat on it in such a long time that its softness comes as a surprise to her derriere.

Yusuf does a quick tour of the studio, peers into the bathroom and out the windows giving onto the courtyard. Then he stands there, arms folded across his chest, in the middle of the room.

"You want something to drink?" Jessica asks. She always keeps the fridge stocked like a hotel minibar, with a few sodas and beers.

"No, thanks. I'll head out."

"All right," Jessica says, kicking the shoes from her feet. It's pure theater; she's pointlessly trying to stress what is patently obvious: she's at home.

"Has that door always been there?" Yusuf asks.

Jessica can feel herself blush. But she laughs, brow furrowed. "No, it appeared there yesterday."

Yusuf stops in front of the white door, lowers his hand to the knob. "Where does it lead?"

"The other stairwell."

"Huh. This has to be the only studio in Helsinki with two entrances."

"Could well be." Jessica tries to seem unbothered. This is all she needs. Soon, a vanful of tech investigators and someone from her own unit will start looking into the ownership of the apartments in the building. The thought of them discovering the truth sets Jessica's pulse racing. She has carefully constructed herself a normal, unremarkable life: a government-employee salary appears in her account every month; she vacations once a year in Spain; she commiserates with her coworkers' hopes and concerns about the sustainability of the Finnish welfare state. If word of her three-hundred-square-meter apartment were to spread, the facade she has erected so meticulously would collapse, and she would be utterly alone again. Not because people would shun her wealth, but because she lied to them, to those who are not only her colleagues but her close friends.

"Is there courtyard access to this other stairwell?" Yusuf suddenly asks. His attention to detail is driving Jessica crazy. She's much more aware of it now than she usually is, when the two of them are seeing things from the same vantage point as they carry out their shared duties.

"Yup. And the only way to get into the courtyard is through the portico, which is locked and visible from the van," Jessica says, standing up. "I'm safe here. Believe me already."

"You mind if I take a look?" Yusuf asks, and opens the door before Jessica has time to respond. He shoves his head out into the dark stairwell.

"Listen, Ghostbuster, I appreciate you looking out for me, but I want you to get the hell out of here and get back to the investigation."

"Sure." Yusuf shuts the door and grunts. "Erne . . . and I, we're all a little worried about this case. About you," he continues, slowly walking over to Jessica.

Jessica bites her lip and turns away. She's used to managing on her own, and now all these uninvited visitors are barging into her life. Suddenly her world is so patriarchal. Strangers, strange men, frighten her. Men she knows open doors for her, look after her, care about her, watch over her. Just now, it's hard to separate the two. Everything feels so damn oppressive, as if her actions were being controlled by everyone but her. But Yusuf isn't the enemy, and neither is Erne. Jessica shakes her head lightly to clear her thoughts.

"Thanks, Yusuf. Let's catch those guys so none of us has to be worried. About anyone. At least me."

Yusuf's cell phone rings. He glances at the screen and mutes the ringtone.

"Please stay home now. Just for today, Jessie. I'm going to see Lea Blomqvist's brother in a minute. I'll be sure to report back if I learn anything." Yusuf punches Jessica softly in the shoulder. Then he answers his phone, disappears into the stairwell, and pulls the door shut behind him. "*Hey, honey.*"

Relief washes over Jessica. The danger has passed. Or is it just the opposite? Is it just beginning?

Jessica shuts the inner door and listens to the footsteps echoing from the stairwell. Yusuf has chosen the stairs instead of the elevator; the guy doesn't leave anything to chance. Then the stairwell fills with shrill yaps, and Jessica smiles as she pictures the woman from downstairs clutching her dog tightly as she comes across a black man in the dark stairwell, this time just the two of them.

Jessica hangs up her coat and pulls her phone out of the pocket. There's a message from Fubu.

```
How do, Sheriff? You busy rassling
up badmen? Or you got time for me
today?
```

Jessica looks at the message. Three questions Fubu has written her plenty of times before. Replying has typically led to a quick rendezvous and sex. Their sessions have helped her take a step back from tough cases, momentarily forget her hectic life and the atrocities she comes across at work. The fact that she hasn't developed romantic feelings for the guy, despite the regular hookups and palpable physical attraction, is an out-and-out miracle. On the other hand, there's a reason for it. The two of them are incredibly different. Fubu is a few years younger than her, and his no-stress attitude and chill vibe are traits a homicide investigator can't afford. Fubu is like a virginal buzz, fun a couple of times a month. A good servant but a bad master. That's why they could never be together.

```
Working. You can come by tonight if
you want.
```

Jessica sends the text and eyes the colored speech bubbles on the screen for a second, then turns off her phone. She's going to brew herself some strong tea and sketch out every bit of information they know about these witch hunters. Then she'll wait for news from the field. Good and bad.

She snatches her keys from her coat pocket and walks to her back door in her stocking feet.

Chapter 59

THE KEYPAD BEEPS AS JESSICA TURNS OFF THE ALARM. She shuts the door and sets the system to *Home*, turning off the motion sensors inside the flat but leaving on the magnetic readers at the doors. Now Jessica can sleep in peace, knowing no one can break into the apartment without setting off the alarm.

Jessica steps across the room, casts a rapid glance at the long table, and goes into the kitchen. She turns on the electric kettle and reaches into the cupboard for a mug. The chrome sink is full of identical white mugs, their insides stained a pale pink by rose hip tea. Jessica looks at the mugs, the sink, and the counter surrounding it. Suddenly the fact that her kitchen is almost identical to the Koponens' doesn't seem like an uncanny coincidence. On the other hand, she can't figure out why anyone would have gone through so much trouble just to get her attention. She opens the dishwasher, smells the funk of standing water and ingrained grease, and loads the dirty mugs onto the upper rack. They clink as she packs them in so they'll all fit. The electric kettle starts to hum.

* * *

Jessica is sitting at her kitchen table, looking at her computer screen. Her fingers are resting on the keyboard, but her police-issue gun lies within arm's reach. It's dark again. She brings up a photograph of a board crowded with notes and pictures of people and places somehow related to the case. Jessica tears a sheet out of her sketchbook and starts to trace out the mind map the unit devised as a team.

Jessica thinks about the conversation she and Erne had that morning. Are there really more murders to be expected? Or haven't they just found all the bodies yet?

Jessica zooms in on the photographs. The hysterically laughing Maria Koponen, the utterly serene Lea Blomqvist. Laura Helminen's image has clearly been culled from social media: she's posing in a yellow top that shows off her cleavage, a glass of sparkling wine in her hand. She's alive; she can still do what she's doing in the photograph. Koponen and Blomqvist cannot.

The more she studies the faces of the beautiful raven-haired women, the more plainly Jessica grasps that she herself is one of them. They could all be sisters. The thought is simultaneously reassuring and rattling. Reassuring because Helminen, after being kidnapped and languishing in a cellar, could have easily mistaken the woman in the painting; there's no way she can be sure it was a portrait of Jessica specifically. Even so, the thought makes Jessica nauseous. She feels like she's involved in something she doesn't want to be in, as if her identity and body were thrust into some risk group forming on the fly.

Jessica's thoughts wander to past centuries, to the arbitrarily defined reference groups from recent history persecuted in the name of truths that prove untrue. Heretics, infidels, subhumans, witches, warlocks. The nations and populations made targets through propaganda, whose origins, appearance, religion, or ideology have predestined them to suffer a ghastly and utterly unjust fate. Of course, genocide is a crime on an entirely different scale from individual instances of violence, but the psychological and societal effects of a rampaging serial killer can correspond to widespread persecution. Being hunted sparks uncertainty and fear, forces people to hide their identities. It makes people flee, seek safety, hope that things will one day return to normal.

Jessica glances at the large clock on her kitchen wall. Two long hands equipped with quartz mechanisms sunburst out from the center of a ring of dots glued to the wall. They show a time of five thirty.

The phone on the table starts to vibrate.

"I'm alive, Erne," Jessica says into the phone, jumping in alarm when she hears faint pops in the depths of her walls. The structures of her old building are alive too.

"I'm sure you are," Erne says. His voice has grown even raspier. "A couple of things . . ."

Erne clears his throat, and Jessica holds the phone away from her ear. His cough sounds like an ax striking frozen rock.

"Rasse is checking the hospital cameras. The medic handed your coat straight over at the nurses' station where

272

Yusuf picked it up. There are obviously blind spots the cameras don't cover, but Yusuf spoke with the nurse, and she said she didn't leave her station at any point."

"And no one had access to it at the nurses' station?"

"Highly unlikely."

"But that text was written at some point. Because I still didn't do it."

"We started from the assumption that you'd remember if you'd written it yourself," Erne says. Jessica isn't able to discern the tiniest hint of irony in his words. Erne utters them as if that alternative was considered seriously and rejected as improbable, but by no means impossible. Jessica hears Erne shut the door to his office and collapse in his chair, forcing the air out of his constricted bronchial tubes. "Is it possible someone got into your apartment?"

Jessica feels a tingling in her calves. Even though Erne knows—he's the only one who does—that she doesn't live in a tiny studio, Jessica still finds discussing the matter with him awkward.

"You know my alarm system is always on. Night and day. Besides, I never leave my notebook at home. It's either at the station or with me in the field," Jessica says, fully aware it's not necessarily the truth.

"Fine. Let's not draw any hasty conclusions."

Jessica hears her superior's words, but his question remains smoldering in her head. The possibility has already occurred to her, despite knowing no one could have gotten into the flat without tripping the alarm—except, that is, the woman who has cleaned the place once a week for several years. But almost a week has passed since the cleaner's last visit, and all her visits are recorded in the security system's log.

"But what?" Jessica says to shake off the disturbing thought.

"Kai Lehtinen's and Torsten Karlstedt's cell phones didn't budge from their homes in Vantaa and Espoo yesterday."

"But we know for certain that at least Lehtinen was in Savonlinna."

"In a car owned by Torsten Karlstedt, who potentially acted as the driver."

"The assholes left their phones at home."

"They know what they're doing. Either that or they're doing a masterful job avoiding beginners' mistakes."

"For the meantime, then, there is nothing to indicate Torsten Karlstedt was in Savonlinna yesterday?"

"No. Theoretically, he could say he loaned the car to Lehtinen. And if Lehtinen confirms it, we don't have anything on him."

"Maybe it's the truth."

"What is?"

"Maybe Karlstedt let Lehtinen borrow his car. Maybe he wasn't in Savonlinna."

"Someone was driving."

"More than one driver's license has been issued in Finland the last time I checked."

"Good point, Saga Norén."

"Isn't there anything else?" Jessica asks as she zooms in on Maria Koponen's laughing face. For some reason, she can't get enough of it; she stares at it as if she were trying to solve an optical illusion. What the hell is so goddamn funny?

"Torsten Karlstedt talks on the phone a lot. Nothing incriminating has come up during the phone calls yet though," Erne says, and coughs again.

"Fuckety fuck."

"But Micke raised an interesting point. Karlstedt hasn't mentioned a single word about the incidents, which have been all over the news today. To anyone. Which is pretty remarkable when you take into consideration that in all likelihood he himself—or at least his car with Kai Lehtinen in it—was in Savonlinna yesterday listening to Roger Koponen speak."

"That just proves he's mixed up in this."

"Karlstedt also made a call to Kai Lehtinen. Twenty minutes ago," Erne says, and Jessica can hear him flip through the stack of papers on his desk. "Karlstedt asked Lehtinen if he left his cap in the car."

Jessica sighs and rubs her forehead. "Well, did he?"

"Apparently he did. The whole conversation was brief and extremely casual. Damn it, if we could just get something concrete to grab hold of."

"Let's see how things play out." Jessica notices a second incoming call and glances at the screen. An unrecognized

275

number. "Hold on, Erne. Someone's calling. I'll call you back in a second," she says, and hangs up.

She stares at the unfamiliar number flashing on her screen. Are things playing out now? When she picks up, will she hear the voice she heard at the Koponens' house the night before? She feels prickling in the pit of her stomach.

"Niemi," Jessica answers, then holds her breath. The window frames rattle in the wind.

"A man just stepped into the stairwell."

"Excuse me? Who is this?" Jessica snaps, rising to her feet. Her fingers wrap firmly around the gun that was resting on the table.

"Uolevi, Security Police. We're posted in a vehicle outside your building."

"Right." Jessica walks into the living room, gun in her hand.

"A man, about thirty, in a heavy coat . . . stood outside the door for a second and then slipped in when an older gentleman exited. Looked like he didn't have a key to the downstairs door."

"How do you know he's coming to my—"

"We don't. He rang the buzzer multiple times. Did it ring in your apartment?"

Jessica holds her breath. *Fuck.* She has no idea if the buzzer rang in her studio, and she hasn't prepared a lie for this contingency.

"I'm not sure. I was in the shower."

"You mind if we stay on the line just in case the situation requires us to intervene?" Uolevi says mechanically.

Jessica stands in the middle of her living room, considering her next move. She's safe here, but if the guys from SUPO follow the potential intruder to her studio, it won't take long before they realize she isn't there. And then everything will come out.

"Sure," Jessica says, trying to sound self-assured. She presses the phone to her chest and thinks. She's trained and armed. All she has to do is go back to her studio and look out the peephole if and when the guy who slipped in downstairs knocks on her door. That's all. She knows how to defend herself if circumstances demand.

Jessica hurries into the hall, opens the door, shuts it behind her. She stands in the dark stairwell for a second. Her keys clink loudly in the echoing space. And then the entire bunch slips from her hand and drops to the floor at her feet. Jessica crouches down to pick it up, glancing both up and down the stairs. Anything could be hiding in the darkness. Anyone. The light switch is just out of arm's reach. Damn it. She should have stayed in her alarm-sealed palace. Maybe the whole thing is a trap. Maybe the guy calling isn't really from SUPO. Maybe—

"Hello?"

Jessica starts when she hears the voice on the phone. She finds the right key and feels shivers crawling up her spine.

"Hello? Niemi, are you there?"

Jessica holds her breath and fits the key into the lock. The door opens, and Jessica lunges into her studio.

At that instant, there's a knock at the door.

"I'm here," Jessica says softly into the phone as she takes aim at the door.

"Everything OK?" Uolevi asks. "If necessary we'll be there in a minute. But we don't want to blow the stakeout if it's a false alarm."

"There's someone at the door," Jessica whispers.

"Are you armed?"

"Yes."

"Is he trying to get in?"

"He's knocking—"

"OK. We're coming up."

Jessica hears the side door of a van slide back.

"No! Wait," she says, stepping slowly over to the door. More knocking rings out, rhythmic but not insistent. "I have a peephole," she whispers.

"Listen to me, Niemi. I want to hear the words *A friend stopped by* within the next thirty seconds. Otherwise we're coming up."

"Roger," Jessica whispers, lowering the phone to the armrest of the sofa.

She tiptoes over to the door in her stocking feet, holds her breath, and leans in to look through the peephole. And then she hears it: the familiar tipsy voice calling her name.

Fubu.

Chapter 60

YUSUF FOLDS HIS HANDS ON THE TABLE AND WAITS patiently for the young man across it to collect his thoughts. Now Timo Blomqvist rakes back his thick blond hair.

"I don't understand. Who could do something . . . ? Lea was the sweetest person in the world . . ."

"I'm truly sorry," Yusuf says, eyes lowered to the gaudy rug. He feels like he's drowning in the incredibly soft blue velvet armchair. The studio in the former working-class neighborhood of Kallio is tidy but tastelessly decorated. The dark green walls clashing with dark red wall hangings and incredibly ugly rugs are a time trip to another decade. To some lost past, although Yusuf isn't sure about that either. "You understand that it's important we don't delay this conversation." Yusuf sets the tape recorder down on the table.

"Coffee. You want some?" Blomqvist asks absentmind-edly, and stands.

"No, thanks." Yusuf glances at the figure shambling over to the kitchenette. "Do you have any idea who could have done this to your sister?"

"No. Like I said, Lea was a nice person. Bubbly and friendly . . . down-to-earth. I can't understand why anyone . . ." Blomqvist turns on the tap and fills the stovetop espresso pot.

"Have there been any new relationships in Lea's life recently? Friends? A partner?"

"Lea is . . ." Blomqvist looks at Yusuf with glazed eyes, then wipes his nose and turns back to the espresso pot. He spoons ground coffee into the filter. The hand holding the spoon is trembling. "Lea had been single for a few years. I don't think she'd found anyone. If she did, she didn't tell me about it."

"Were the two of you close?"

"Our folks live in Spain . . ."

"Meaning?"

"Yeah, we talked pretty often. I guess not so much lately. We were supposed to see each other this morning at her place in Laajasalo. I rang the doorbell for a long time . . ."

"Was there a specific reason for the meeting?"

Blomqvist looks surprised. "What?"

"Which one of you suggested the meeting? You or Lea?"

"I don't remember. It's not like there was some specific agenda. We would just visit each other a couple of times a month for coffee or—"

"Fine. Does anything out of the ordinary come to mind? Did Lea say she was doing anything special, meeting anybody?"

"We hadn't talked for a couple of weeks. We set up last night on WhatsApp."

The shocked young man slowly makes his way back to the coffee table and the two armchairs at it. Hot coffee splashes on his fingers, but he doesn't seem to notice.

"Lea was a researcher by profession," Yusuf says.

"Yes. She worked at the university."

"Got her doctorate a couple of years ago from the department of psychology?"

"She was focused on a pretty specific topic. We barely talked about work, because neither one of us understood what the other one did." Blomqvist lets out a mournful chuckle. "But . . . I have a copy here . . ." he says, quickly lowering his coffee to the table. Then he steps over to the wood-tone bookcase and pulls out a slim volume.

"What's that?"

"Lea's dissertation."

Blomqvist hands the bound manuscript to Yusuf.

Lea Blomqvist, Toxoplasmosis and Aggression. 2017

Yusuf flips through the paperbound book. "What's it about?"

"Beats me." Blomqvist bites his lip; tears are plainly not far off. "I work at an advertising agency."

"Can I borrow this?"

Yusuf rises from the armchair; Blomqvist nods and buries his face in his palms. Yusuf approaches the other man, considers lowering his hand to his shoulder. But for some reason, the gesture feels wrong.

"I'm sorry," he eventually says, and walks to the door.

Chapter 61

JESSICA OPENS THE DOOR. BEHIND IT STANDS AN INEBRIATED young man, his mouth curved up in a flirtatious smile.

"What the hell are you doing here?" Jessica says, glancing at the gun she hastily shoved onto the coat rack a second ago.

"Sorry, Detective. We were drinking in the neighborhood and—"

"I said you could maybe come over tonight—" Jessica suddenly remembers the call is still active. She peers into the empty stairwell, lets Fubu in, and grabs her phone.

"A friend stopped by," she says as she watches Fubu take off his wet coat and hang it up on the coat rack.

Roger.

"I appreciate it," Jessica says before she hangs up.

"Work?" Fubu takes off his shoes, wanders into the living room as if he owns the place, and collapses on the sofa.

"I told you I was working." Jessica grabs a glass from the cupboard and fills it from the tap.

"I lost my phone," Fubu says with an incredulous laugh.

"You just sent me a message a couple of hours ago."

"I know. And then it walked off . . . Maybe someone stole it. I don't know."

"Where did this happen?" Jessica says, draining the water from her glass.

"This bar in Kamppi. There were all kinds of sketchy people there though. Fucking hell—"

"And so you decided to come here. You know you can't file your report with me, right?"

Fubu chuckles. "I was thinking maybe we could push our date up a little."

"At least you're in better shape than last time." Jessica sits down at her little dining table.

"My bad. I was pretty lit."

"You can say that again."

"So what's good?"

"What?"

"Can I stay?"

"I have work to do."

"And you can do it. I can watch TV or something. First Netflix, then chill." Fubu smiles broadly, the red-and-blue Montreal Canadiens beanie with the big pom-pom still on his head. The rolled-up hoodie sleeves reveal thin but sinewy arms scrawled with a few intentionally tasteless tattoos.

Jessica lowers her glass to the table and massages her forehead. The last twenty-four hours have been exhausting. And every single cell in her body knows more is coming. That the attempts to frighten her aren't over. Her body and mind are screaming for a break, a tiny escape from reality. That's why Fubu is here. Her escape is there for the taking. Fifteen minutes. Hit it and quit it. But something about it feels wrong. She has seen so much death over the past twenty-four hours that giving into pleasure right now can't be right.

"Sorry." Jessica stands, hands on her hips. "You have to go. I have way too much work."

The corners of Fubu's mouth turn downward in an exaggerated show of sadness, like those of a tragic clown. Then he claps his hands together and bounces up from the couch, surprisingly spry. "Oh, well, what the fuck? I'll guess I'll take my bone and go find someone else to play with." He tramps over to the entryway. This is exactly what is so appealing about Fubu. He's self-confident, pushy to the point of brazenness, but he never whines and understands *no* the first time. He's used to getting rejected—and, as a result, to getting other things too. "I don't get it though," Fubu suddenly says as he pulls on his shoes.

"You don't get what?"

"Why you are resisting? What if I just stayed?"

Jessica feels her patience being tried. Fubu is a whiner after all.

"Go."

"What are you afraid of?"

"Now! Fuck!"

Fubu smiles and nods. "OK. But remember, Detective, that when I get to Storyville and pour a couple of pints into this sex machine, it's going to be full steam ahead . . . Some woman who's almost at your level is gonna go home with me. And then you'll be sorry. You'll be diddling yourself alone here while you're watching some German detective show—"

Jessica smiles back. "I'll take my chances."

"Call me if you change your mind," Fubu says, finally serious, then slaps himself in the forehead after he opens the door. "Except you can't call me because I don't have my phone."

Jessica takes a pen from the table, rips a strip off an old newspaper, and writes her number down on it. Then she walks to the door, pinches Fubu's nose, and shoves the slip of paper in his collar. "Never give up."

Fubu disappears into the stairwell. Jessica leans against the closed door and discovers that her heart is pounding. Hard. She takes a deep breath. She has to collect her thoughts; she has work to do.

But just now, for the first time in years, going back to the apartment off the neighboring stairwell strikes her as wrong. The luxurious home feels somehow foreign, too big for her to control. She's going to get her computer and spend the night in her studio, in the place everyone thinks she is.

Chapter 62

COLOMBANO HANDS THE MENU TO THE WAITER AND TURNS to stare at his wristwatch. Jessica waits patiently for his eyes to rise from the table and focus on her. That's all she wants. Words, beautiful or otherwise, aren't always necessary. Jessica has been alone for years and learned long ago that the less you expect from people, the easier life is. Colombano's eyes rise from his watch and circle across to the couple sitting at the neighboring table. Some tiny sign, some signal of warmth, isn't too much to ask on a beautiful day like today, is it? Jessica feels a lump in her chest.

For a few nights in a row now, Jessica has been getting the strong sense that Colombano wants to be alone, that he needs room to breathe, to do things without her. The recent weeks have been incredibly intense, and that's the way Jessica wants their shared life to continue, despite the inevitable but gradual fade of the infatuation and the first flush, the blindness to the other's flaws.

Little things that just days ago elicited a grunt of amusement from Colombano—Jessica's clumsy Italian grammar, her continuous snapping of photographs, her

287

habit of staring at her food while she eats it—are now the targets of barbs cloaked as humor. Jessica feels that, over no more than a couple of days, she has been transferred from one category to another, from adult back to child. Initially she felt mature for her age in Colombano's company, imagined he saw not only her beauty, but an interesting and intellectually challenging co-conversationalist. Now, however, he glares at her as if they were being forced to spend time staring at each other in a vacuum with no other stimuli.

But Jessica also knows erratic behavior doesn't mean Colombano doesn't love her. Mom was the same way, and she loved Jessica with all her heart.

"Is everything OK?" Jessica finally asks, and glances down at the décolletage of her dark red dress. Luckily, the cigar ash that fell on it from an old man walking past came off without a trace.

Colombano still doesn't look at her. "Why do you ask?"

"I don't know." Jessica gives him an uncertain smile, but it isn't immortalized on either of their retinas. Uncertainty is poison for a relationship; Jessica knows this from experience: the more the boys sniveled after her in high school, the less interested she was. She bites her lip and lets her fingers wander over to Colombano's hard knuckles.

"Listen, Jessica, my love," he says, and his pupils slowly turn toward her. "As you know, on Tuesday we'll start working on a totally new repertoire . . . There's a violin duet I need to spend a lot of time practicing."

"Of course," Jessica says as the waiter lowers two glasses of wine to the table, uncorks the bottle, and pours Colombano a taste. Colombano studies the color of the wine, sticks his formidable nose deep into the tall-rimmed glass, swirls the contents to release the last of the aromas, carefully regards the legs the wine leaves on the sides of the glass, and then drains it. The wine clearly doesn't make much of an impression: Colombano swallows and lets it be understood that it is swill barely worth pouring.

"You have no idea how badly I want to spend time with my princess, but I have to master the pieces perfectly," he continues after a moment, and raises his glass, which the waiter has now filled. The way he pronounces the word "*princess*" is anything but flattering.

"I'm sure it will go well," Jessica says. Their glasses clink. The wine tastes perfectly acceptable. A big German shepherd trots past the restaurant with no owner in sight.

"Is there anything you want to ask me?"

Colombano's question is like a bolt out of the blue. His eyes are now nailed to Jessica's.

"What?"

"I know you want to ask me something." There's a slight maliciousness to Colombano's smile, perhaps a dash of schadenfreude.

"I don't have anything—"

"Let's put an end to this playacting. Be honest, would you? I've seen you sneaking around the apartment, scouring frantically for crumbs of information. About who

289

I am. And what this—this here, us—could be. What it could become." Colombano presses his finger to the center of the tabletop. Despite their frankness, the words are not aggressive. They lack the necessary insolence. This makes Colombano sound indifferent. And that's even worse.

"Sneaking?"

"Yes. You sneak. And that's fine. It's fine to be curious. This is important to you. Because here you still are, even though you had planned on leaving weeks ago."

"I'm serious. I—"

But now Colombano slams his palm to the table so hard, it sets the wine dancing in its glasses. "*I'm serious. I'm serious.* Stop being so damn agreeable, would you?"

Jessica feels herself freeze; she doesn't know how to react. She looks at Colombano, whose face is determined, grim, and yet serene. "The world is a bad place," he continues. "The world is cold. You have to have the courage to get to the bottom of things you want to get to the bottom of. You can't go squeaking around like a little mouse."

Jessica fingers the stem of the wineglass. The gaze she craved so badly a moment ago has turned condescending and oppressive. For the first time, their age difference seems to be turning against her, creating a setup in which only one of them has anything to learn from the other. Jessica feels stupid, and not simply because she knows Colombano is at least partially right. But also because she harbored such high expectations for the evening. She bought herself a new dress from Marina Rinaldi, did her hair in a way she

290

thought Colombano would like, and misted her throat with new perfume.

"How do you like the wine?" Colombano asks, and the head-spinning change of topic makes Jessica feel both relieved and disappointed.

"It's good."

Colombano laughs. "Of course."

Jessica feels a pang in her gut. Colombano has turned his gaze elsewhere again, to the diners sitting on the terrace.

"We're practicing at my place tomorrow," he finally says, lowering his empty glass to the table. "So if you want to rent a car and explore the mainland . . . tomorrow would be a good day."

Chapter 63

"TOXOPLASMOSIS?" JESSICA SAYS, PHONE PROPPED BETWEEN her ear and shoulder as she tears a piece of toilet paper from the roll. The others on the conference call are Yusuf, Rasmus, and the medical examiner Sissi Sarvilinna. Jessica can hear the hum of Yusuf's car and Rasmus' eager typing in the background; Sarvilinna she imagines standing impassively with a hands-free loop in her ear, surrounded by chrome body boxes.

"Do you believe the perpetrator's motive is somehow related to the topic of the victim's dissertation?" Sarvilinna asks mechanically, reinforcing the image in Jessica's head.

"To be honest, we have no idea. But if Lea Blomqvist spent years studying the subject, we don't want to shut out the possibility." Jessica rises from the toilet seat, lowers the lid, and decides to wait before she flushes so the others don't hear.

A deep sigh serves as an accent to the hum and the typing. "Lea Blomqvist wasn't a doctor, so I don't really understand why she chose the topic of—"

"Please, Sissi. Let's save everyone's time." Jessica immediately regrets her words. So many seconds pass that Jessica is forced to check to see if the medical examiner is still on the line. "Hello. Are you—"

"Toxoplasmosis is a parasitic infection," Sarvilinna spits as if she had just been waiting to interrupt Jessica. "As a matter of fact, the most common one. It can be contracted from, for instance, uncooked meat or cat feces."

Yusuf sounds cantankerous: "Goddamn it. Doesn't sound like we're going to get anything out of this."

Jessica stands in front of the mirror, phone to her ear. Through the reflection, she looks at the bathtub and the black shower curtain hanging there. She can picture the patter of the shower, herself sitting at the bottom of the tub, her wet hair plastered to her face. She quickly gasps for air. "What does it have to do with aggression?"

"I'm not sure, to be honest. I should probably take a look at the dissertation," Sarvilinna says, and everyone on the call knows she's not kidding.

"Could it cause aggression?"

"To my understanding, the infection basically only poses a risk to fetuses and people whose immune systems are compromised. AIDS patients, for instance. I remember reading somewhere that if contracted during childhood, it can lead to abnormal brain activity. But so can many other illnesses."

Jessica takes a few steps toward the bathtub, wraps her fingers around the plastic curtain, and slides it aside.

"OK, thank you, Sissi," she says.

A moment later, Jessica sees the other woman's name disappear from her phone screen.

"It's not sounding very relevant." This is the first thing Rasmus has said during the brief call.

Jessica sighs. "We don't know what's relevant yet. Where are you, Yusuf?"

"En route to Kulosaari. There's a handwritten report of what the neighbors had to say."

Chapter 64

NINA RUSKA REACHES A HAND OVER HER HEAD TOWARD her shoulder blades and presses her elbow with her other hand. Her triceps stretch satisfyingly. Both her arms and her neck are still stiff from her match the day before yesterday. It has been over a year since her cheek was last pressed against the tatami mat and her opponent's wrist was on her neck. In addition to the muscle aches and stiffness, Nina is frustrated by the bitter fact that she lost the match to a constable ten years her junior from the Eastern Finland PD. And it wasn't even close.

"The substance we're looking for isn't thiopental," Mikael says, spinning his chair around. He has the receiver of one of the last landlines on the floor held against his chest, and now he lowers it to the table.

"What do you mean?"

"I talked to the lab. What we're looking for is thiopental sodium. It turns into thiopental in the body."

"What else did they say?" Nina asks, gradually dropping her hand.

"I wrote it all down. Wait." Mikael picks up his notepad from the desk. "Three substances . . . first, thiopental sodium renders the victim unconscious. That happens in less than a minute—"

"Hasn't the chloroform already done that? Rendered them unconscious?"

"Yes. The reason for using both substances on the victims isn't a hundred percent clear, but the lab had a pretty good theory."

"Which is?"

"The chloroform entered the victims' bodies through the respiratory passages, but the other substances were delivered directly into the bloodstream. They figured at the lab that the chloroform was used so the victims would be easier to manhandle. The cannula used to administer the other substances is damn hard to insert if the *patient* resists."

"Makes sense," Nina says as Mikael pulls a pack of gum out of his desk drawer.

"They were subsequently injected with thiopental sodium, which has ensured they remained unconscious. Then the pancur"—Mikael pops a quick series of gum bubbles with his tongue and then leans over to take a closer look at his notes—"pancuronium bromide. It's a muscle relaxant that paralyzes the respiratory organs. And last of all they were given potassium chloride, which stops the heart."

"And these last three substances were injected into the bloodstream using a cannula?"

"Yes, as indicated by the bruising on the backs of the hands."

"That demands some skill. And perhaps some sort of equipment—a regulator and stuff like that. An IV drip and a stand?"

"Exactly. The substances weren't injected indiscriminately; the dosages were precisely measured. The concentrations found in the blood of Maria Koponen and of Lea Blomqvist are almost identical. That, in turn, means the drugs were dosed according to the victims' weight. In all likelihood, the women were weighed so they could be administered the precise dose that proved effective. The poisoner knew not only how to insert the cannulas, but also how to calculate the precise dose that would prove fatal."

"Are you going to say it, or should I?"

"The perp is a doctor?"

"Or a nurse?"

"Or a vet."

For a moment, Nina and Mikael stare at each other the way they sometimes stare at each other after they've made love, lost in thought, without saying a word. But now both of them are thinking only and exclusively about the case they're investigating.

"Or not," Nina eventually says, crossing her arms over her chest. "The procedure doesn't exactly require years of specialization. You can probably find instructions in no time by searching the magical internet."

"But a healthcare professional would have a much easier time getting their hands on the substances."

"Why would hospitals stock lethal poisons?"

"None of the substances is a toxin in and of itself. Thiopental is used as an anesthetic and so is pancuronium bromide, which is used in pretty simple procedures requiring anesthesia. They're found in every hospital."

"What about potassium chloride?"

"E508."

"What?"

"It's an additive. You'll find it in the frozen pizza down at your local grocery store. The lethality is due to the large dose. In small doses, it can even be beneficial to your health."

"No shit. Maybe tracing them won't be so easy after all."

"Maybe not. But now we know the perpetrators didn't necessarily have to turn to the black market. In the case of the first two chemicals, hospitals keep detailed records of them and any related medications."

"What about Maria Koponen's workplace? Neurofarm? They manufacture drugs—"

"We can exclude that alternative." Mikael hands Nina a printout that was lying on the table. "The company manufactures neurolepts, in other words antipsychotics, which it then sells onward to the companies that manufacture the pills. Here's a list."

Nina studies it for a moment, then sighs in disappointment.

"What about Torsten Karlstedt and Kai Lehtinen?" Nina stands and walks over to the wall covered in a controlled chaos of photographs, Post-it notes, and sheets of paper. She presses the tape holding the men's photographs in place more firmly against the board. "An IT entrepreneur and a construction contractor. Does either one have any connections to hospitals or drug stocks?"

"We'll have to look into that right away," Mikael says, once more raising the receiver of the landline to his ear. But before he brings up the number, he stops to look at Nina. It's evident from her face that she isn't thinking about the case at that particular instant. Nina loves her work. When engrossed in a case, she often has the same look on her face as a high-school student aiming for top scores on her college entrance exams: thoughtful and determined. But now her face is a mask of concern. "Are you thinking about Jessica?" Mikael says, lowering the receiver back to its cradle.

Nina nods and stops in front of the mind map, hands on her hips.

"Jessica can look after herself," Mikael continues.

"I have no doubt about that, but . . . someone's too close. It feels horrible."

"We're going to solve this case."

"Have you ever considered that the chance to investigate murders from a bird's-eye view is a luxury of sorts? That it's a privilege to solve problems that aren't . . .

reactive. Dynamic. Problems that don't change as we follow the clues."

"No, but I get your point. Unfortunately, this isn't that sort of case."

"No, it's not. This is anything but. This is like some fucking super bacteria that keeps living and mutating no matter what the antibiotics do."

"Are we antibiotics?"

"Wow, you got the metaphor."

"You get this metaphor?" Mikael's voice is thick and smarmy as he curves his fingers into a suggestive gesture.

"You're such a clown, Micke. Make that fucking call," Nina says, then disappears into the corridor.

Chapter 65

THE OFFICER IN UNIFORM RAISES HIS HAND TO SHIELD his eyes against the car's headlights. Yusuf reaches for the pack of cigarettes lying on the center console, but then thinks about Erne, the raspy wheeze that sounds like a plastic pipe being cleaned with a metal brush. Maybe he's smoked enough for one day.

Yusuf doesn't kill the engine. He lets his gaze sail across the Koponens' house, its front yard. The neighboring lots and the lots opposite. Some of the houses are old, but most are new construction, built on property that has been subdivided, the majority luxurious works of skimmed concrete and glass. Not one of the residences on this street exchanges owners for under a million euros, and the Koponens' waterfront house has certainly cost several.

Yusuf looks up the slope of the tall hill. At the crest stands the old woman's wooden villa, which reminds Yusuf of the Moominhouse: not the familiar blue tower from the Japanese cartoon, but the more villa-like version that Tove Jansson built a scale model of herself. Yusuf saw it at the Tampere Art Museum while he was at the police academy; he had spent a sunny Saturday at the museum with his nine-year-old sister. Now Nezha is sixteen and isn't interested in Moomintrolls anymore, or much of anything for that matter. To be honest, Yusuf has no idea what Nezha likes and what she expects from life. It's been a while since he had a proper conversation with his sister. Yusuf doesn't know Nezha anymore, not the way he used to. He doesn't remember the last time he got a real answer when he asked her how she was doing, the kind that reveals something about the person answering.

Hey. Yusuf comes out of his reverie. A police officer in blue coveralls has sidled up to the car door without Yusuf noticing. Yusuf doesn't know him. The officer knocks on the window; Yusuf opens the door.

"Yes?"

"Umm . . . you're with homicide, right?"

"Yes." Yusuf flashes his badge just in case.

"Fine. I just came over to make sure—"

"That some random black dude didn't drive up to the crime scene," Yusuf says, and turns off the engine.

The constable gulps. "No, I—" he protests but falls silent when he sees Yusuf smile.

"I'm just giving you a hard time. I get it. There have been all sorts of weird people creeping around this crime scene." Yusuf decides to bring his cigarettes along after all and climbs out of the car. The strong wind makes the air, which has dropped below zero again, bone-chillingly cold.

"Koivuaho," the officer says, extending a hand.

"Pepple." Yusuf lights a cigarette, then lifts the hand holding the cigarette and points at the man questioningly. "Koivuaho? Weren't you the first patrol on the scene yesterday?"

"Yes." Koivuaho pulls on his gloves more snugly. "I showed Sergeant Niemi around. Is she coming by?"

"Apparently you have a report of the neighbors' responses to questioning?"

"Yup. But it hasn't been typed up yet." Koivuaho reaches into the breast pocket of his coveralls and pulls out a folded piece of paper. "We went around to all the houses a few hundred meters in every direction. Only one hasn't answered all day. We collected some of the statements last night. Like Mrs. Adlerkreutz's," he continues, looking cold, then wipes his nose and points at the wooden villa across the street. The Moominhouse, where Yusuf and Jessica looked out the upstairs window less than twenty-four hours ago.

Yusuf smiles involuntarily. "Did you say Adlerkreutz?"

Koivuaho nods and takes the cigarette Yusuf offers him. A moment later, a short stick of rolled paper glows in the fingers of each man.

"Any highlights?" Yusuf asks, exhaling in brief puffs. The freezing air condenses the smoke.

"No one noticed anything out of the ordinary. Or anyone suspicious. No one remembers having seen Maria Koponen all day, or even Roger Koponen pulling out of the drive in his car yesterday morning. The whole street has been sound asleep."

303

"You can't blame them for that." Yusuf takes the sheaf of paper Koivuaho hands him.

The patrol officer is shorter than Yusuf but twice as burly. His stubble looks so coarse that you could stick cotton pads to it. Koivuaho must be about ten years older than Yusuf, and, as a police officer, much more experienced. Even so, he's still working patrol. Yusuf knows not everyone is interested in rising to chief, or even investigator, but it never ceases to amaze him that so many of his fellow officers don't mind driving around in a van, handing out fines and chauffeuring drunks around. There isn't the slightest trace of bitterness or envy in Koivuaho's eyes. Nor does Yusuf discern any of the racism masked as locker-room talk that he's been forced to tolerate in various forms over the course of his career and life.

"Thanks. I'll have a look at these." Yusuf flicks the butt in a handsome arc to the base of Mrs. Adlerkreutz's hedge. "And hey, which house is the one where there wasn't anyone home?"

"It's marked down there. Number twelve," Koivuaho mumbles, cigarette dangling from the corner of his mouth, and points farther away, outside the bounds of the cordon. "Big old brick house. The gate says Von Bunsdorf."

Chapter 66

IT'S A FEW HUNDRED METERS TO NUMBER 12, AND YUSUF decides to make the journey on foot. When sitting in the warm car, a beanie and gloves seemed unnecessary, but after he's been at the mercy of the frigid wind for five minutes, he starts missing them badly. It was a mistake leaving them lying between the dash and the windshield.

A fat man in a red-and-black lumberjack coat approaches from the opposite direction; he wraps the leash restraining a small dog around his wrist. To the right of the road, there's a large lot with a brick house toward the rear. Yusuf stops and raises his hand as the man walks past with his mutt.

"Excuse me." Yusuf takes out his badge again. "Police."

The man pulls the dog toward him, frowns, and seizes the badge Yusuf is holding out. Looks at it long and hard. *No, asshole. It's not a forgery.*

"Under normal circumstances I wouldn't have stopped to chat, but I'll make an exception," the man says, and Yusuf doesn't understand what exception he's referring to: the fact that Yusuf is a police officer or that two homicides just happened on the street. "It's just terrible. Do you have any leads?"

Yusuf shoves his badge in his pocket. "Do you live around here?"

"Pretty close," the man says, tossing his head in the direction he came from.

"You follow the news?"

"Kulosaari's a small place. Not that there's the same sense of community there used to be. You're lucky to get a hello out of your neighbor these days. But everyone knew the Koponens. The house was empty until they bought it. When was that? Two years ago? Three?"

"How long was it empty?"

"Since it was built. A local architect designed it but got divorced right after it was finished. He put the house up for sale. Big waterfront lot in a location like that, big house . . . As I recall, the original asking price was appallingly high. Maybe four."

"Million?"

"No, thousand." The man chuckles and yanks the dog closer again. "Of course million. Then they came down by half a million. And came down more later. I don't think the Koponens even paid three for it. Then again, how would I know—"

"I see." Yusuf considers whether to make a note of this detail. The man in the plaid coat strikes him as an awful person. The kind of guy who thinks he knows things, but really—and this time to Yusuf's chagrin—doesn't appear to know anything interesting. "Here's the number for the tip line. Call it if you remember anything. Anything at all." Yusuf hands the man a card. It's the second-to-last one in his stack.

The man looks at the card and laughs out loud. Yusuf can only guess as to the reason. Then the man grows serious, pulls a poop bag from his pocket, and wishes Yusuf a good evening surprisingly politely.

Goddamn, these people are crazy. They should fence off the whole island.

Chapter 67

Yusuf presses the buzzer a few times without getting any response. He then reaches for the ornamental handle, only to notice that the metal gate, with its chipped dark green paint, isn't locked. An automatic driveway gate stands next to it, along with an old-fashioned security camera.

The front yard is surprisingly large, and a densely spaced row of arborvitae has been planted along the fence. As Yusuf walks up the paved drive, he studies the brick house rising before him, which has white window frames, a steeply pitched roof shingled in black shakes, and a tall chimney. A low flight of flagstone stairs leads to the front door. The house looks nothing like your average Helsinki residence; it's more like an upper-class manor from somewhere in the English countryside. The drive is lined with heavily pruned apple trees; behind them looms a garage big enough for at least two cars. There are no tire tracks, but the thin dusting of snow under Yusuf's feet tells him that the drive has been plowed since the storm the day before yesterday. Someone must have been home recently.

Maybe someone is at home at this very moment; at least the bright light blazing upstairs would seem to indicate so.

Yusuf climbs the few stairs and stops at the door. The upper half is rounded, and the whole frame is edged in ornamental white brick. An iron lion head the size of a fist glares out of the middle of the door, a knocker in its mouth. There is no doorbell, which is logical, since the visitors have already rung the gate buzzer. Yusuf takes hold of the knocker clenched in the lion's teeth and raps it three times. He waits. There's no answer.

Meanwhile, he feels a vibration in his pocket. It's a text message from Jessica. `Call when you can.` Yusuf locks the phone and holds it against his chin. The von Bunsdorfs—plural or singular—are not at home. He can come back tomorrow or send someone else. Or find the phone number and talk to the homeowner via telephone. It's not likely they saw anything anyway. It's a bit of a way to the Koponen house, and the army of arborvitae blocks the view, even to the street.

Yusuf shoves his hands in his pockets and walks down the stairs. He's about to bring up Jessica's number, but then his gaze lingers on something he didn't notice before. He shoves the phone back in his pocket and uncramps his fingers. *What the fuck?* Out in the yard, there's a knee-high cluster of stones, like a miniature Stonehenge. A short horned figure stands in its center. Yusuf steps from the plowed driveway into the yard, which is covered by a crust of snow a few dozen centimeters thick. Its surface has melted and refrozen; the crunch underfoot makes Yusuf feel like he's sinking into an enormous crème brûlée with every footfall.

After a minute of trudging through the snow, Yusuf squats down in front of the stones, looks at the meter-high statue, and now sees that it is a fountain. Its curved horns are attached to a goat's head; the half-naked body beneath is human. The creature's right hand is raised so the arm forms a right angle, with the fore- and middle fingers pointing upward. A pentagram hangs from the neck. Hooves take the place of feet.

Yusuf grabs the statue by the horns, shakes it, and decides it's firmly in place. He looks at the goat's grim eyes, the symbol hanging at its neck, and feels a cold wave surge through his body. He glances around. The monument has been erected in the precise center of the yard.

Yusuf's thoughts turn to Jessica, to everything she has stumbled upon during the brief course of the investigation. To how she would be the one here now if Erne hadn't ordered her to stay at home. He gulps, agonizingly aware that there's no such thing as coincidence. Not in any murder investigation, and not especially in this hellish puzzle.

The yard where Yusuf is squatting is illuminated solely by the white blanket of snow and the glow of the street-lamps peering over the hedge. He feels incredibly exposed. He looks up at the window, sees the light burning inside. Then he turns back to the half-human, half-goat, to the demon carved from stone whose dead eyes stare directly at the house.

310

Chapter 68

SOME MINUTES THAT FEEL LIKE AN ETERNITY LATER, YUSUF hears the thunk of the latch from the metal gate and sees two uniformed officers step onto the property, looking vigilant. He recognizes the one in front as Koivuaho. Koivuaho advances at a slight forward lean, like an offensive lineman waiting for the play to begin.

"What's the situation?" Koivuaho asks when he reaches Yusuf. The second officer has stayed back on the drive and is now warily approaching the garage.

"I'm not sure. But I have a bad feeling about this." Yusuf rises to his feet. His calves ache from squatting so long on his toes, and the frigid wind has made his ears numb.

Koivuaho looks at the stone statue. "I can see why."

"You only rang the buzzer at the gate earlier? You didn't enter the property?" Yusuf says, and when Koivuaho nods, he continues: "Did you notice if the light was on upstairs?"

"No. You can't even see the house from the street. Besides, it was still light out then—"

"OK." Yusuf wipes his nose on the back of his hand and tells Koivuaho to follow him. The two of them

311

trudge across the snow to the plowed area fronting the house.

"Someone shoveled the snow recently," Koivuaho whispers.

"That's what I was thinking."

Yusuf looks around and now spies another security camera over the door, similar to the one he noticed at the gate. If there's anyone home, they have some reason for not letting the police in. The junior officer is still at the garage, looking around.

"What should we do?" Koivuaho asks.

"I don't know. A statue of Satan doesn't give us cause to kick down the door."

"No, it doesn't."

"Tell your buddy to wait out front here. Let's go around the back."

Yusuf cringes at the loud crunch the coarse snow makes after each step he takes. The facade of the house is pierced by numerous windows, but they're dark and the curtains have been drawn across them. Finally, they round the corner and enter the backyard. It's much more modest than the apple orchard out front.

"Look," Koivuaho whispers. "Holy hell."

Another horned figure stands in the middle of the yard.

Yusuf takes a moment to consider the alternatives. They've trespassed on private property without cause to suspect a crime. On the other hand, the horned figures are a clear indication that the residents are involved in the case, in one way or another. Considering everything that has happened, there's zero doubt.

Yusuf turns toward the house and the large glass doors giving onto the back patio. He takes hold of his pistol and cautiously makes his way over. The blinds are open, but he has a hard time seeing inside. The sizable room is pitch-black. But there's something odd about the glass doors; there's a spiderweb-like pattern on the inside. It's as if someone tried to smash the glass. Yusuf presses his face to the glass, raises his hands to his temples. The white marble floor is dotted with black splotches that, upon closer inspection, are not flat, but craggy three-dimensional objects. Of different shapes and sizes.

Rocks.

"Koivuaho!" Yusuf barks, and he hears the other man's combat boots churning the snow as he hustles up. Yusuf remembers the list Rasmus drafted of the murders in Roger Koponen's series of books. He would remember it in his sleep.

Book I
Woman, drowned
Woman, poisoned
Man, stoned to death

"Flashlight," Yusuf says, hand held out like a dentist addressing his assistant.

Koivuaho pulls a black flashlight from his gear belt.

313

The powerful beam licks the dark room, the floor strewn with rocks. The sofa set in front of the fireplace. And the green armchair where most of the rocks seem to be concentrated. And now Yusuf catches a flash of something in the beam of light that, based on a hirsute glisten, could be the crown of someone's head. It's doming on the other side of the chair's backrest.

"Bring in another patrol. And tools to get inside the house," Yusuf whispers, lowering his hand to the door's metal handle. It's locked, and the panes are burglarproof bulletproof glass. Yusuf comes to this conclusion based on the pattern the rock blows have left on the window's interior.

Koivuaho grabs his radio.

Chapter 69

ERNE MIKSON CLENCHES HIS ARM HARDER AGAINST HIS RIBS, but the unstapled stack of papers is already sliding toward the floor. They cascade uncontrollably and skate across the laminate floor into even greater disarray.

"*Kurat!* Fuck!" Erne curses loudly, and if the situation weren't so chaotic, he would probably smile at his bilingual outburst. He lowers himself to his knees and sweeps up the papers. His lungs feel like they're collapsing every time he leans forward; the blood rushes to his head faster than it used to. All sensation disappears from his fingertips.

"Wait. Let me give you a hand," Mikael says, taking a few brisk steps down the corridor. He has just stepped out of the men's room.

"No!" Erne says, thrusting Mikael aside. "Stop, Micke."

"OK, OK." Mikael steps back, hands on his hips.

Erne gathers up his papers, taps them into a disordered, unruly sheaf, and jams it under his arm.

"Is something wrong?" Mikael asks after giving Erne a moment to catch his breath.

"Yes. Have Nina and Rasse come to the conference room. Now."

"Do you have a fever?"

Mikael points at the thermometer lying on the floor where Erne was crouching a moment ago.

Erne feels a cold wave wash through him. "No, goddamn it, I don't. I just forgot it in my pocket . . ."

"OK," Mikael says, and walks off.

"Yusuf called a minute ago," Erne says as Rasmus pulls the door shut. "We have the fifth body. An old man in Kulosaari, tied to an armchair and stoned to death. Only a few hundred meters from the Koponens' house."

Mikael's brow furrows in sympathy. "Who is he?"

"Albert von Bunsdorf."

"Doesn't tell us anything. Sounds like an aristocrat or something."

"Exactly," Erne sighs, then concentrates on corralling his renegade papers into a stack on the table. Mikael, Nina, and Rasmus are standing next to him, too agitated to sit down.

"What else do we know about the victim?" Nina asks.

"Seventy-year-old widower. Respected physician. Retired, specialized in psychiatry. A link to the case not only through the MO but also through devil statues in the yard."

"Let me see," Mikael says as Erne flips through his papers.

Erne finds a printout of a few shots of the stone statue snapped with a flash. He hands the printout to the trio to peruse.

"Baphomet," Rasmus says softly.

"What?"

"Just as I suspected. Jessica said the figure she saw on the ice raised a hand into the air. But it wasn't clenched in a fist; it was positioned like the hand in this statue. Jessica couldn't see it, because the figure was so far away—"

"Wait, wait, wait . . . Slow down a little, Rasse. Sebamed?" Mikael says brusquely.

"Baphomet. An ancient divine being of sorts. Contrary to popular belief, it doesn't really have anything to do with Satan worship. With heresy, absolutely, so one could assume von Bunsdorf was punished for worshipping it."

A deep silence falls over the room.

"There were two statues. One in the front yard and one in the backyard. Situated so they were facing the house," Erne says.

A restless murmur wells up at the corner of the table.

"The murderers brought them—" Nina begins.

"Yusuf thinks that, based on the tracks, the statues must have been there for at least a few days. Maybe they were erected before the snowstorm two days ago."

"How long has he been dead?"

"We'll know the exact time of death soon. But the body's state of absolute rigor mortis would indicate the victim was killed between nine and twenty-four hours ago."

"So the statues could have easily been brought—"

A guttural squawk emerges from Rasmus' throat, silencing Mikael. Everyone turns to look. The shoulders of Rasmus' black sweater are covered in dandruff.

"Darn it, didn't any of you hear me?" he says, rubbing his temples.

Erne glances at Nina, who smiles involuntarily. For the first time in his career as investigator, this placid man is demonstrating signs of having a will of his own. An actual pulse.

"Please go ahead, Rasse," Erne says conciliatorily, and all eyes turn back to Rasmus. "Be so kind as to enlighten us."

"You're entertaining a dangerous flaw in your thinking. Don't you understand? The murderers didn't bring those Baphomet statues to von Bunsdorf's yard. Just the opposite. In all likelihood, those statues are the reason he died."

"Sit down, all of you." Erne nods at Rasmus. "Go on."

"A goat's head has traditionally symbolized fertility. New life. Baphomet, with his human body and goat head, is a fertility god of sorts. Do you get what I'm driving at?"

"You're saying von Bunsdorf died because he worshipped a pagan god?"

"That would explain an inquisition's anger. For instance, in fourteenth-century France, Templars were imprisoned because the king at the time believed they were worshippers of Baphomet. They were tortured, and many confessed under duress."

"So the Templars worshipped Satan?"

"No. Like I said, Baphomet didn't originally have anything to do with Satan worship. But the pentagram associated with Baphomet was extracted from that context in the nineteen sixties, and a goat's head was drawn inside. This is how the Satanist symbol came about. And note, Satanism is a different thing than Satan worship."

Mikael chuckles. "How, supposedly?" It doesn't take him long to notice that he's the only one laughing.

"As its name indicates, Satan worship entails a belief in an evil force, Satan. In Satanism, on the other hand, Satan symbolizes the animal side of humanity, the natural desire for sex and other hedonistic pleasures the Church has tried to root out for centuries. It's more like Satanists are giving the finger to the Christian concept of morality instead of actually believing in the existence of Satan."

A burst of laughter incongruent with the moment echoes from the corridor as a group of police officers walks past. Once the noise dies down, Mikael asks: "OK. So you mean a Sweden-Finn psychiatrist was a dyed-in-the-wool Satanist and died for it?"

Rasmus buries his face in his hands and sighs as if to indicate that the level of the questions has dropped to a new low. "Not a Satanist but an adherent of Baphomet. For some reason or other, the perpetrators considered both Maria Koponen and Lea Blomqvist witches. They've raised themselves to the status of some sort of inquisitors who have the authority to punish heretics. That's why von Bunsdorf suffered the same fate."

"There's something illogical about that though," Nina says, studying her neatly filed fingernails. "We've been assuming the murderers believe in the occult. Now Rasse is talking about them as if they were the Inquisition, which, at least in the Middle Ages, wanted to kill those accused of occult activities. So which is it?"

"Good point, Nina," Erne says, stifling a yawn in his fist.

"How does von Bunsdorf's murder take place in the book?" Mikael asks when no one seems to have an answer to Nina's question.

"The victim is stoned to death, like von Bunsdorf. In other ways, the scenario is totally different," Rasmus says.

"If, in the perpetrators' view, von Bunsdorf deserved to die due to his presumed Satanism, where does that leave Maria Koponen and Lea Blomqvist? Were they Satanists too? Or were the women labeled as witches simply on the basis of their looks?" Nina asks.

Rasmus looks frustrated; it seems as if his explanations have fallen on deaf ears. "Interesting question. That's the assumption we've been working off of so far. That the only thing the women have in common is their appearance."

"And shitty luck," Mikael adds.

"But what if there's some worldview or philosophy underpinning all this? Something Maria and Lea had in common when they were alive . . . that could help us move forward?" Nina says.

"We've spoken with the Koponens' closest friends, and nothing of the sort came up."

Nina cracks her knuckles. "Maybe they weren't asked the right questions."

"Maybe not." Erne sighs so deeply that his lungs empty to the last gasp. "Do any of you see it?"

"What do you mean?"

Erne looks straight ahead impassively. "Lea Blomqvist was a neuropsychologist studying aggression. Albert von Bunsdorf was a retired psychiatrist. And Maria Koponen worked as a product development manager at a drug manufacturer manufacturing antipsychotics."

Mikael scratches his neck. "Now that you put it that way—"

"The connection is clear but not very specific. In this instance, at most, we can talk about a pattern in which the victims are linked by work with the human psyche."

"Exactly. Tantalizing but still pretty broad. In reality, their jobs were totally different. The victims' workplaces didn't have anything to do with each other. University of Helsinki. Neurofarm Inc., and von Bunsdorf's one-man practice, which he ran from nineteen sixty-eight to two thousand and nine."

"So not the same clients, enemies . . . anything."

"Neurofarm's clients were large drug companies. Whereas—"

"Goddamn it," Erne snaps, a stressed-out squeak escaping his lips. He shoots a sharp glance at Nina. "In the case of von Bunsdorf, let's approach it as if it were a one-off murder. What is your first thought, Nina?"

"The perpetrator is a former patient."

"Exactly. Get us a list of all of his patients. And come up with some ideas about what the link between these people could be. Did Albert von Bunsdorf specialize in some certain psychiatric problem, for instance?"

"Will do."

"And last of all: now that we've talked to everyone who lives on the Koponens' street, I want a summary of the output. A list of residents and any potential links to the Koponens."

"I can do that," Mikael says.

"I admire your initiative. Now I need to talk to Jessica. And then fart up a press release on this latest murder." Erne pulls out a pack of cigarettes. "So you get back to work, you bunch of charlatans."

Chapter 70

JESSICA WAKES UP TO NOISE OUTSIDE. THE CURTAINS DRAWN across the French balcony blow lazily. The first night of August is excruciatingly hot.

The racket carrying from the street turns out to be drunk British tourists singing out of tune. It echoes for a moment, then fades around the corner.

Jessica rises to sitting and realizes the other side of the bed is empty. Colombano told her not to wait up for him, that the last concert of the summer season always ends with the musicians dining together on one of the northern islands of the old town.

Three-and-a-half weeks have passed since Jessica met Colombano at the cemetery at San Michele. According to her original plan, she should have returned to Helsinki yesterday. And yet she is still in Venice, where her trip began, without seeing those numerous cities and beaches she had planned on visiting. But she has gotten something else in their place. She has gotten to know a man, a real man in the true meaning of the word. A man whose incredible talent and self-confidence are like something from a different world. Jessica has fallen in love with Colombano's direct way of approaching her. Touching. Kissing. There's no tentative probing to his movements, no touches unsure if they have permission, no sweaty adolescent fingertips fumbling for the right to take hold of her arm. With Colombano, Jessica feels desirable and safe.

However, in some moments, Colombano is overcome by an inexplicable darkness, like a thundercloud suddenly blowing into a sunny sky. At such times, his behavior becomes unpredictable and impulsive. Light touches become a sudden gripping at the nape, nails dig into her downy neck hairs, fingers wrap around her chin so hard that Jessica is afraid her jaw will pop out of joint. Colombano is handsome, muscular; he could have anyone. But he wants Jessica. That's why, when this happens, they do whatever Colombano wants. It's the least Jessica can do: accept his primitive, unshackled desire as is, as evolution meant it to be. Jessica has learned to read Colombano from nothing more than the look in his brown eyes. They reveal what is coming, but only an instant before the tranquility bursts into a full-scale tempest.

What in Jessica's mind was stimulating and exciting twenty-four days ago has now transformed into something else. It has transformed into love and affection. What initially aroused her desires now appeals to completely different instincts. She wants to please Colombano, give him the opportunity to express the frustration and stress inevitable to the life of an artist. She knows that those who expect perfection unavoidably end up alone, because they are hoping for the moon from the sky. Jessica wants to see Colombano through his fits of rage; she wants to tame his unpredictable nature.

And, above all, she wants to understand him.

Jessica holds her back as she gets up. The only thing she misses from her home in Töölö is the wide bed with the thick spring mattress that doesn't smell of dried sweat and oily hair. The narrow, creaking iron frame and lumpy mattress in Colombano's apartment aren't doing her damaged spine any favors.

She walks over to the balcony doors, cracks the curtain just enough to see the narrow canal and the windows of the pink building opposite, which are so close that one could easily fly a paper airplane from one window to another. She wraps her fingers around the iron railing, feels the sloughing paint prickle underneath. Then she makes her way to the bureau, the photographs that tell the story of Colombano's life. One of the pictures disappeared weeks ago: the one where two smiling faces, a man's and a woman's, are looking into the camera. Colombano and that beautiful brunette whose features Jessica can no longer recall. She looked at it closely only once, and that same night it disappeared. When she noticed, Jessica's thought was it had been done out of consideration for her feelings, that Colombano didn't want to broadcast his past in front of his new lover. And that when their relationship deepened, he would tell her about that woman, about who she had been, about how she had died.

From time to time, Jessica feels a bottomless longing for home that is, in the end, more of an itch for nostalgia, one that doesn't culminate in any certain place or time. After her adoptive parents died, there was no one left in Helsinki to rely on. Just the forced smiles of lawyers, bankers, and former guardians, and the securities accounts at a private bank that hold so much inherited wealth she could buy Colombano's entire building and the surrounding historical structures.

And Tina, of course. Mom's sister, who, after all of these years, is trying to slither back into Jessica's life. Jessica doesn't want to see Tina, who had a habit of putting Mom down. Maybe it was sibling rivalry; maybe Tina is simply so petty that she didn't want to believe in her sister's abilities, her shot at launching a spectacular Hollywood career.

Jessica thinks about Los Angeles. Her memories of the city are strongly colored by what she has seen in the movies and on television; after all, when the accident happened, she was only six years old. Even so, she remembers the palms reaching for the heavens, the warm desert wind, the mild winters smelling of suntan lotion. She thinks of the gradually falling dusk in West Hollywood, the red sun dropping over the Pacific Ocean off Santa Monica. She remembers Mom and Dad fighting, the vein at Dad's temple squirming like a fat worm, Mom's white knuckles gripping the leather steering wheel. How everything feels like it's over, even before the accident. Her squeezing her brother's hand; they're tired of the shouting and the arguing. Looking at her brother, who is two years younger and, at that moment, scared to death. As if, deep down inside, he had an intuition that the car would drive into the oncoming lane at any instant.

A tear rolls down her cheek. Loneliness and rootlessness have spurred Jessica to tour Europe on her own. Without anyone knowing where she is. At the age of nineteen, Jessica is no longer answerable to anyone. She is no one's property, not even Colombano's, even though, based on his behavior over the past few days, one might think so.

The door opens. Jessica jumps and moves away from the bureau, the only place in the flat Colombano does not want to see her.

"Zesika," Colombano says, then starts speaking Italian. He is clearly drunk. And he isn't alone.

"I'm sleeping," Jessica says in a hoarse voice, then jumps into bed and quickly burrows between the sheets.

"Not anymore," Colombano says, and from the door, Jessica can hear liquid tilting in a bottle. "Have you met Matteo?"

Colombano is now standing at the bedroom door, his tuxedo shirt on, his undone tie dangling at his neck, and an unlabeled bottle of red wine in his hand.

"What?" Jessica stammers, and Colombano erupts into a soft laugh. A bald man with a mustache, shorter but stouter than Colombano, walks up behind him.

"Ciao," the stranger says, taking the bottle Colombano offers him expressionlessly.

Then Colombano undoes his cufflinks and sits on the edge of the bed. "Princess, I'm good to you, aren't I?"

Jessica feels a lump in her chest. "I want to sleep, Colo."

"Matteo here . . . he's my brother. Not in the traditional sense of the word; we don't have the same mother, but . . . you know. Like the friend I love most in this world."

The bald man nods proudly, taps a cigarette out of the pack, and places it between his lips.

"I want you to do me a favor."

"No," Jessica says, and pulls her hand away before Colombano can grab it.

"Princess. You don't even know what I'm going to ask you to do."

"I want to sleep. Let's talk tomorrow."

"Matteo wants to watch us make love." Colombano rolls his sleeves up to his elbows.

Jessica turns her gaze to the window. She hears the man introduced to her as Matteo, Colombano's brother and best friend, pull the chair out from under the bureau. Its legs scrape against the uneven plank floor.

Jessica wants to shout, scream. Pound on the wall. But she doesn't so much as bat an eye. She is perfectly numb.

"No," Jessica says hollowly. She feels dead inside. She knows the darkness gaping within Colombano, that burned part of his soul she thought she could heal. But she also knows no words or actions will do any good now that he's stone drunk.

Colombano lies down next to her. "Matteo won't touch you, I promise. As long as you do what I say."

"Colombano. No," Jessica whispers, but she already feels the coarse fingers behind her neck. She smells his breath: red wine and cigarettes. She hears Matteo's lighter click open. Then shut. The smell of cigarette smoke wafts through the room. Colombano's tongue on her throat, teeth at her earlobe. Just like an eternity ago. How the same thing can be so different under different circumstances, like night and day. Heaven and hell. Colombano's fingers between her legs. Jessica's eyes are nailed to the ceiling, the peeling paint there.

She will leave tomorrow, at dawn.

Chapter 71

JESSICA IS BASICALLY A PRISONER. SHE IS NOT FREE. BUT first thing tomorrow morning, she will leave her home and continue living her life as if nothing had happened. Return to work, to her workstation at police HQ, go wherever she wants, and give zero fucks about all the horned creeps out there who are trying to frighten her.

Jessica looks at her studio's white ceiling, where nascent cracks are forming, despite Fubu's having painted it in January. The ski bum who boasts a cabinetmaker's training spent an entire two days on the job. Although he'd demanded to do the work for *payment in pizza and pussy*, Jessica forced him to accept a hundred-euro Stockmann gift card she claimed to have won at a workplace raffle when he finished. Ultimately, Fubu's exertions might have caused more harm than good, as the smattering of white paint sprinkles on her wood floor reminds her.

The phone rings; Erne has finally decided to call back.

"What the hell, Erne? I've called you at least four times—"

Erne's voice is tired, almost flat. "I had to give a little press briefing on the von Bunsdorf development. Have you talked to Yusuf?"

"Yes. He'll be here soon."

"Did you have something new?"

"I've had some time to think, Erne," Jessica says, rising from the sofa. "If the victim's rigor mortis was at its peak at the moment he was found, that means he'd been dead for—"

"Nine to twenty-four hours. What about it?"

"Roger Koponen. Yusuf found the victim at six thirty. Koponen left the Kulosaari metro station at eight sixteen a.m."

"Are you saying Koponen rang the doorbell and casually stoned von Bunsdorf to death?"

"Who knows? Maybe the conversation turned to politics."

"That's always risky."

"Koponen is alive, goddamn it, and is up to his ears in this case. Who says it wasn't Koponen himself who was playing Halloween out on the ice or terrorizing Laura Helminen down in that basement?"

"You're right. Besides, Koponen might well have known von Bunsdorf. They've lived a few hundred meters from each other for a couple of years."

"Maybe that's why von Bunsdorf let him in."

"Even though he and his wife were reported dead on the morning news?"

331

"According to our latest theory, our worthy psychiatrist believed in the goat god of fertility. I don't know why he wouldn't believe in ghosts or angels. Or the Dead Writers Society."

"It's Poets, but you have a point." Even though Jessica can't see Erne's face, she knows he's rubbing his forehead pensively. "How about you? Everything OK there?"

Jessica sighs and walks over to the window. She hears Erne step outside, the rush of wind in the phone's microphone.

"There haven't been any goat-man sightings on Töölönkatu, if that's what you're asking."

"That's exactly what I'm asking."

"I could get back out in the field right now."

"But you won't," Erne says. The sound of a cigarette lighting. The lighter's lid clicks shut.

Jessica closes her eyes. "You don't sound good, Erne."

"I don't sound good? Am I on the fucking *Voice of Finland* or something? Isn't Jessica Niemi's chair going to turn around?"

"I'm just saying. I'll talk to you soon." Jessica hangs up.

She turns on her laptop and opens two news sites from the bookmarks. The clickbait is firing on all cylinders, competing for catchiness and cleverness.

```
Witch Will Be Next . . . Serial Killer
Strikes Again . . . Exclusive! Coven
in Kulosaari?
```

The amount of social pornography that has been mined from the cases is downright unbelievable. On the other hand, if you think about the crimes that have taken place over the last twenty-four hours, you could say there's a lot that's still hidden from the general public.

Jessica tears a page out of her notepad and sharpens her pencil. Even though iPads and other electronic note-taking devices have made massive inroads in investigative use, Jessica still trusts in the traditional tools of the trade. She has just printed out the dissertation Yusuf emailed her; she sets it down on the table and flips to the back to see the number of pages.

Two hundred and thirty. Goddamn it.

The buzzer brays, a dead ringer for the caw of a crow. Jessica wonders whether the men from the Security Police will recognize Yusuf, or if her phone is going to ring again in a second. Or is he already in handcuffs, cheek pressed to the icy asphalt?

Jessica walks across the room and over to the buzzer. "Hello?"

"*Malleus Maleficarum*, motherfucker."

The whispering voice bursts out laughing before Jessica can even register what she heard.

"Loser," Jessica says, and presses the button to open the door.

Yusuf sits down, lowers a green plastic folder to the table, and looks at his palms. He seems tired and distracted.

"Everything OK?" Jessica asks, carrying two cups over to the table: coffee for Yusuf, rose hip tea for herself.

"No. Have a look at these," Yusuf says, opening the folder.

Jessica reaches for the photographs and spreads them across the table. They show an armchair and a figure in it, covered in blood from head to toe. The face has been battered beyond recognition.

"Oh, my God," Jessica whispers, because that's what you're supposed to say when you're presented with something so horrific. The truth of the matter is, the pictures of the man who was stoned to death don't stir up emotional turmoil in her. At most, the ugly images are part of a natural continuum that includes not only the crime spree that began the day before, but all the homicides Jessica has investigated over the years.

The man with the crushed, shapeless face is dressed in a dark blue bathrobe. A few rocks are caught between the shoulder and the backrest; the kinetic energy of the recoil from von Bunsdorf's skull wasn't powerful enough to propel them to the floor.

"Where are the rocks from? The yard?"

"Hard to say, with the snow covering the ground. But I know a place where you could collect rocks like that by the bucketful."

"The Koponens' shore. If it weren't covered in ice."

"Exactly," Yusuf says, leaning back in his chair.

"What's your hunch? Did Roger Koponen stone this guy to death himself?"

"That was my immediate reaction. Koponen was seen in Kulosaari that morning, which makes him a potential suspect."

"The thing I still don't get is why." Jessica takes a long, deep sip of her tea. "What's Roger Koponen's ultimate goal here? He knows he'll be caught at some point. He can't just stage his death, play hide-and-seek with us, then go underground. He's a public figure who's going to be recognized. Even abroad."

"Maybe he doesn't have a choice. Maybe the witch hunters are blackmailing him with something."

"With what? They started by killing his wife. I'd say that's a pretty shit strategy if you're planning on blackmailing someone. Eliminate your best leverage at the get-go."

"What about money? Koponen is a multimillionaire."

"Like how? 'If you don't stone the old guy down the street, you'll have to pay us a million euros'?"

"I don't know."

"You'd think that even a prick like Koponen places a higher premium on his wife's life than a million euros," Jessica says, then pauses to reflect on what she just said. She just talked about money as if having it made one less human. She does this a lot. It's integral to her disguise but inevitably makes her feel like a hypocrite.

"I think we still have two alternatives here. Either Koponen is one of the witch hunters, or someone else is calling the shots—"

"In other words, he's involved. Voluntarily or not."

"Otherwise he would have contacted the police."

"No doubt." Jessica sinks into her thoughts. "Unless he was avenging his wife's death?"

"So von Bunsdorf killed Maria Koponen?"

"Yes. And Roger knew somehow. And he marched into the guy's house and . . ." Jessica shuts her eyes, and Yusuf seems to do the same.

The minutes pass as they sit in silence, collecting their thoughts and sipping their drinks. Jessica writes down the names of the victims, the locations of the crimes, and other random details that occur to her. Her hands sketch out a map of remarkably straight lines, symmetrical circles and rectangles.

Eventually Yusuf speaks. "I'm starting to lean toward Micke's argument."

Jessica lowers her pencil to the table. "What do you mean?"

"Maybe we should bring in Karlstedt and Lehtinen."

"There's no point in us worrying about that. That's Erne's decision to make."

"Or, in this case, not make."

"Erne isn't incapable of making decisions, Yusuf. Just the opposite. He made the decision that we're going to wait. Maybe we'll find out something from the phone monitoring."

Yusuf shakes his head almost imperceptibly; he plainly disagrees.

Another period of silence follows as they browse through the photographs and drum their fingers against the varnished wood tabletop. Yusuf pulls a sheaf of documents from the bottom of the folder: the reports and transcriptions of the questionings of the victims' loved ones.

"You get anything from that?" Yusuf asks, nodding toward Blomqvist's dissertation.

"Oddly enough, yes . . . I think so." Jessica turns back one of the pages she has marked. "Everything in this dissertation culminates in cats."

Yusuf chuckles. "Cats? Why didn't I think of that?"

"According to this study, there's a remarkable correlation between families who have children diagnosed with serious mental health issues and having a cat as a pet."

"I mean, I'm more of a dog person myself, but cats don't drive people crazy, do they?"

"It's a simple equation. The toxoplasma parasite spreads from cat feces to humans, and those infected are twice as likely to suffer from, for instance, schizophrenia."

"Schizophrenia?"

"Which is an illness treated with antipsychotics manufactured by none other than Neurofarm."

"The link grows stronger. But it's still shaky. Did Albert von Bunsdorf treat schizophrenia patients?"

"We don't know yet. But we're going to have to look into it."

"I was thinking, based on what Rasse told us, that this Albert von Bunsdorf is a pretty clear case, with his goat statues . . . that the motive would have been heresy. But Maria Koponen and Lea Blomqvist don't seem to have any unusual interests or beliefs. Not to mention our police chief from Savonlinna, Sanna Porkka, who just seems to have been at the wrong place at the wrong time. Based on appearance alone, Porkka doesn't fit in with the other victims." Yusuf digs into the pocket of the folder and pulls out more photographs, this time of a charred figure tied to a tree. "What about him?"

"Mr. X."

"According to Sarvilinna's report, male, about forty."

"Who no one has missed yet."

"A day isn't very much time. Especially if the person in question lives alone."

"I doubt Mr. X was in the wrong place at the wrong time. The location of the murders is so remote that in order to end up there at the exact clock strike you'd have to be the unluckiest berry picker in the world."

"And dumbest. Wild strawberries are few and far between this time of year."

"Exactly."

"He must have been in Karlstedt's Cayenne the whole time," Yusuf says.

"Or in Roger Koponen's trunk," Jessica shoots back, and the thought seems to disturb Yusuf. "Mr. X's probable cause of death," Jessica continues, scanning Sarvilinna's report, "is cardiac arrest, in these cases often caused by a pain-induced surge of adrenaline. In addition, there's burning in the lungs. So he was still alive when he arrived at the scene and was burned alive. Apparently the teeth were removed after he was burned."

"Maybe the whole thing came to him as a surprise. Maybe he'd been sitting in the Cayenne with Karlstedt and Lehtinen the whole time and thought they were going to eliminate Koponen together. But then the conductor decided to have the musicians switch seats. Who knows? Maybe it came as a surprise to Koponen as well."

Jessica stretches her neck. "That's not such a far-fetched idea. Maybe Koponen was forced to watch while Porkka and Mr. X were tied to the trees and burned. Maybe he was convinced to join in the game by being assured that the same fate awaited him if he didn't play along."

"They turned Koponen into a marionette who does what he's told. That would explain why he didn't know to avoid the CCTV cameras at the metro station. Maybe he's terrified, and the notion that the police could track his phone's location simply doesn't occur to him."

"That makes sense otherwise, but Koponen looks calm on the camera. Hands steady, a face like the *Mona Lisa*." Jessica opens the video clip from the metro tunnel with a few clicks.

"You're right, Jessie. The asshole is as cool as a cucumber even though his wife just died. And even though he presumably witnessed the double murder at Juva at close proximity."

"On the other hand, that's exactly how someone in a state of shock might act," Jessica grumbles in frustration.

She leans back and stretches her arms straight up over her head.

"Are you heading back to Pasila?" she asks a moment later.

Yusuf yawns. "I don't know. Am I?"

"Yes. Talk to Rasse; he's the one listening to those calls. I want to get a clearer picture of both Torsten Karlstedt and Kai Lehtinen." Jessica shoves her chair away from the table.

Yusuf slowly drags himself to his feet. He looks at the belongings strewn on the couch. "Hey. My card."

Jessica gulps. "What?" She knows what Yusuf's talking about, but her wallet, which is where the card is, isn't in her studio. It's on the kitchen counter of her apartment next door. *Goddamn it.*

"I forgot to ask for it back."

"Argh . . . Sorry, Yusuf . . ." Jessica says, sensing the lie she came up with on the fly is already sounding lame.

Yusuf chuckles. "You have it, don't you?"

"I left it at the station. Sorry. It's probably on your desk."

"Shit. I need to get gas and . . . I was thinking I'd grab something to eat."

Jessica draws her mouth into a taut line. If she could get Yusuf to step out for a second, she could pop over and get the card, then call him and claim that she found it in her coat pocket.

"If you're not going anywhere, you could let me borrow yours—"

A cold wave washes through Jessica again. "No."

"What?"

"This sounds crazy, but . . . my card doesn't work. I don't know what's wrong with it."

"It doesn't work?"

"No. I ordered a new one."

"You have any cash?"

"No, I'm sorry."

Yusuf frowns, then shrugs and grabs his coat from the back of his chair. Jessica isn't sure her fib sounds believable, but she can't come up with any reason why Yusuf might think she's lying either. No one would ever guess in a million years that there's another apartment on the other side of the wall. Yusuf walks slowly to the door and pulls on his shoes.

"Was there something in it that didn't belong there?" he finally asks.

"In what?"

"Your wallet," Yusuf says. The question is logical, reasonable, and could mean trouble.

She takes a deep breath and stands. "I would have said something if there had been anything in it that didn't belong there, goddamn it."

"Did you take a good look? Because if someone was able to write in your notepad—"

"Yes," Jessica snaps, and her tone of voice accomplishes what it hasn't had to in a long time, especially with Yusuf: remind him of the chain of command.

"All right. Talk soon." Yusuf opens the door and disappears into the stairwell.

341

Chapter 72

YUSUF PULLS THE CAR DOOR SHUT AND LOOKS OVER AT the dark gray Toyota van across the street: stakeout central for the guys from SUPO. The van has been equipped with recording devices and eight super-sharp cameras that offer a three-hundred-sixty-degree view of the world outside via a small screen. There are two men sitting in the car. During twenty-four-hour surveillance, one watches the screen while the other one rests his eyes. The stakeout van is supplied with substantial stores of water and canned food, a portable toilet, and a reserve power source, to make days of unbroken surveillance possible. It's not a great gig: Yusuf knows the initial burst of romanticized suspense inspired by movies like *Chinatown* quickly turns into shit-stench claustrophobia.

Yusuf starts up his car. Poor Jessica. This case is making her lose her grip. She's usually so careful and conscientious, and now she's started losing things: a phone here, a debit card there. Yusuf can forget his heartwarming dreams of a to-go pizza from Manala.

He reverses a meter or two, then turns the car around and drives down Töölönkatu toward Hesperianpuisto

Park. Snow is drifting down from the sky again, and the people walking down the sidewalks have pulled up the hoods of their heavy coats to protect their heads.

His phone, which is connected to the car's Bluetooth, starts to ring. Mikael's number appears on the screen, and Yusuf sighs. He doesn't like Mikael. Not because the guy has ever done anything to him, but because they're so different. Besides, Mikael is a skirt-chaser and a cocky bastard, and Nina is going to pay the price for that if their relationship lasts. Which she does not deserve, under any circumstances.

"What's up, Micke?"

"You were right, damn it." Mikael holds a brief artistic pause.

"About what?"

"*Malleus Maleficarum.* The words were spotted from the air. This time in flaming letters."

Yusuf feels a burn in his diaphragm. "What? Where?"

"A field in Haltiala."

"You're shitting me," Yusuf says. He takes his foot off the gas, and for a second, the car slides down toward the intersection. "So a chopper spotted it—"

"The copter Erne sent up was hovering over eastern Helsinki. But Haltiala is so close to the airport that there were several sightings. The reports were passed on to the fire department as a terrain fire. There are a few fire trucks on the scene by now, but some aerial photographs were taken of the text. There's no mistaking what it said."

343

Yusuf glances at his watch. "I'm heading out there."

"Good. Tech is already on its way."

"Why?"

"A dead woman was found there, Yusuf."

The car stops at the crosswalk. Yusuf shuts his eyes; his voice has dropped to a rasp. "Out of Koponen's book? Crushed—"

"Something like that. You really need to get out there."

"Send me the address," Yusuf says.

He hangs up and tries to swallow down the lump in his throat. For some reason, the crimes over the past twenty-four hours have put him in mind of Nezha. How if some nutjob decides to target his hatred at her someday, he wouldn't be able to protect his sister.

Yusuf steps on the gas, drives across the crosswalk, and pulls over between the park's two allées. His fingers are clenched around the steering wheel; his nails are digging into the flesh of his palms. It's only when he releases his grip that he realizes his hands are shaking. Yusuf shifts into neutral, yanks up the handbrake, and turns on his yellow emergency blinkers. Then he rises out of the still-running vehicle and lights a cigarette.

The car behind passes him, horn pressed to the bottom.

Chapter 73

DARKNESS HAS RETURNED TO PASILA, AND THE YELLOW lights of the construction site once again dominate the view from the window. Nina and Mikael walk up on either side of Rasmus as he wraps up a phone call.

"What is it now?" he asks, lowering his phone to his desk.

"Karlstedt and Lehtinen. Do they have an alibi for Haltiala?"

"Do we have a more accurate time of death?"

"No, but the text was ignited just a little while ago. There were several sightings between seven fifteen and seven thirty p.m."

"Both of them were at home." Rasmus clicks his mouse. Nina can't make heads or tails of the view that opens; as best as she can make out, it's some sort of software that makes it possible to monitor, listen in on, and archive the calls of phones under surveillance. Rasmus continues: "But they just had an interesting conversation."

"Play it." Mikael pulls a free chair over and sits. Nina looks around but is forced to settle for standing.

Rasmus selects a call from the list. "This is it."

Outgoing number +3584002512585
Time of call 19:15:23
(dialing)
Torsten Karlstedt (TK): Hey.
Kai Lehtinen (KL): Hi.
(several seconds of silence)
TK: Hello?
KL: Hello?
(another lengthy pause)
TK: Is there anyone there?
(silence)
KL: Doesn't seem like it.
(soft chuckling)
TK: There's someone there. That's for sure.
KL: Let's talk soon. Everything's fine. And beautiful.
(call ends)

"What the hell was that? Couldn't they hear each other?" Nina says.

"They weren't talking to each other, Nina," Rasmus says.

Once she grasps his meaning, Nina feels like an idiot. "They . . . they were talking to us," she whispers.

"Exactly."

"This is a bunch of fucking shit," Mikael barks, then spits his gum into his fist. "We need to bring in those assholes right away."

"I'm starting to agree, but . . ." Rasmus says, but Mikael has already sprung out of his chair and is marching toward Erne's office, Nina on his heels.

"Wait, Micke. Don't get so worked up—"

"Erne," Mikael says as he pushes open his superior's door. Erne is on the other side, pulling on his coat, and the door nearly clocks him in the forehead. Nina remains in the corridor, outside the open doorway.

Erne zips up his coat. "It's polite to knock first, Micke."

"Karlstedt and Lehtinen. They know we're listening. They were fucking with us on the phone."

Erne looks at Mikael. "Was there a confession to be read between the lines of this fucking with us? Or anything else that would connect them to the murders?"

"Come on, you don't expect those assholes to confess—"

Erne slams his heavy fist into the door so hard that both Mikael and Nina jump. "What the hell is wrong with you, Micke? I'm in charge of this investigation. Do I have to send you all home to brush up on the concept of chain of command?"

Mikael's voice is quieter but still defiant: "Is that why Jessica is at home? Doing homework?"

"If you have a problem with how things are run here, you can fuck off from this unit. There are plenty of people waiting to take your place." Now Erne steps closer to Mikael.

As Nina lowers her gaze to the floor, she catches a glimpse of Erne's flashing eyes: there's not a hint of weakness on the sick man's face. Not at this instant.

"On what grounds? Because I think with my own brain?" Mikael says.

Erne stares at him for a long time, then shifts his gaze to Nina and eventually produces a weary, joyless smile. "Do you little lovebirds think I'm an idiot? The only reason you two haven't been separated from each other is that I happen to be an eternal romantic with an antipathy for bureaucrats. But, so help me God, don't test your luck."

Erne steps past them into the corridor. Nina feels her cheeks blaze bright red. She looks at Mikael, who grunts in exhaustion.

Chapter 74

JESSICA GLANCES AT THE CLOCK. IT'S ALMOST NINE. SHE'S sitting alone at the table in her studio, staring at the poster in front of her: it's formed of four sheets of typing paper held together with Scotch tape. On it, she has collated all the information about the crimes that have taken place over the past twenty-four hours.

A moment earlier, Yusuf sent her a bunch of pictures of the Haltiala victim. It's a thirty-year-old woman. Black hair, beautiful. Dressed in a black evening gown. Just like the other three victims, of whom Laura Helminen is the sole survivor.

In the photograph, the as-yet-unidentified woman is lying between two sheets of heavy-duty plywood. Large stones have been piled on the upper sheet; their weight has gradually killed the defenseless victim. Jessica compares the photographs from the scene to a historical drawing she found online, as well as to the killing in the final installment of Roger Koponen's trilogy.

Both the Haltiala murder and the scene from Koponen's book faithfully reproduce the image from the Wikipedia article "Crushing (execution)": a drawing of the death by crushing of a farmer named Giles Corey during the Salem witch trials of the sixteen nineties.

Jessica studies the close-up the CSI took of the woman's face. It doesn't appear to be in pain, more like tranquil. She must have been anesthetized when the stones were heaped on her. The thought is simultaneously horrific and comforting. Anything is better than a slow, agonizing death—and the unfathomable fear that would precede it.

Jessica looks up at the ceiling and feels the stiff muscles in her sides stretch. She has exercised less over the last six months than she has in ages. The spinal damage she suffered in the car crash when she was six no longer torments her as frequently as it once did, but it's clear that if she keeps neglecting the rehabilitation exercises tailored for her, the problems will return. Sometimes when she gets up from the couch or the bed, Jessica can't feel the first step she takes; she can't sense the contact her heel makes with the floor or the weight of her body on her calves. She doesn't necessarily feel anything when she takes an elbow to her funny bone during the unit's basketball games; the pain doesn't come until later, when she's particularly stressed. Jessica's body won't ever function normally; however, thanks to persistent training, she has achieved a level of physical conditioning that made the admissions test to the police academy child's play.

But Jessica's health records include no mention of spinal damage. There was no accident. Jessica has never been a von Hellens. She never had parents, a childhood in Bel Air, a little brother whose beautiful eyes are begging for help.

Jessica feels her brother's fingers wrap around her own. *It's OK, Toffe. Everything's going to be OK.*

Chapter 75

THE BLARE OF THE BUSKER'S TROMBONE INFILTRATES Jessica's dreams, the reel of jumbled images welling up from her subconscious. Jessica opens her eyes and grasps that she is in Colombano's arms. She has lain there all night; his powerful embrace has imprisoned her. Unable to sleep, Jessica swallowed salty tears, hoping the man's drumbeat heart would stop, that the boozy, foul carcass that trapped her would turn from warm to cold, that Colombano would die and she could finally make her escape. At some point during the night, the pain exploded in her knees, legs, and toes, and she lay there, paralyzed and sobbing in place as he pulled her closer and ran his fingers through her sweaty hair.

In the end, Jessica surrendered, because her entire body gave up. She slipped into some sort of intermediate state between sleeping and waking, a surreal torpor. She watched herself from the French balcony, peering through the curtains like an angel admiring the beauty of the romantic scene in the room but confused about her inconsolably sad face.

"Zesika."

It's the ugliest voice in the world. Jessica starts. She feels her heart skip a beat; the revulsion swells inside her. She can still hear the men's laughter, feel the blows on her bare buttocks. Colombano in her, more unrelenting and rougher than ever before.

"Zesika."

"What, honey?" Jessica whispers. The words escape her mouth of their own volition, mementoes of a time that now feels light years away. A tear rolls down her cheek. She senses the stickiness of the semen on her thigh.

"You're not angry, are you?" The grip tightens, giving Jessica a clue as to how she'd better answer.

"Is . . . is that man still here?"

"Matteo?" Colombano chuckles, gives Jessica a peck on the cheek, and rolls out of bed. Now Jessica is free, but she still can't move. "I told you he wouldn't touch you."

Jessica whimpers.

"Well, did he?"

Jessica hears Colombano traipse into the bathroom. A vile tinkling fills the apartment and Colombano groans as his bladder voids into the toilet. Jessica shuts her eyes; she doesn't know what to say. She can't remember. Maybe he didn't touch her. Maybe he just watched. Ultimately, it makes no difference.

"No," Jessica says softly, her eyes on the wall.

"Would you have wanted him to?" Colombano flushes the toilet. "Would you?" he asks again, as he returns to the bedroom. The water stops running; the plumbing squeals shrilly.

"I—"

"That's not my thing; I don't like sharing. I don't mind if someone wants to watch, but sharing is another matter altogether." Jessica feels the mattress on the iron bed sink under Colombano's weight. "But I can make an exception if you want."

Suddenly it's hard to breathe. "No."

"*No.* That's what you said yesterday, princess. And even so, we made love more passionately than ever. Sometimes it's nice being wrong, isn't it?" *Laughter.*

Jessica feels a pain in her abdomen.

"I can call Matteo right now."

"No."

"But I want to be honest with you. I would never share anything I truly loved with Matteo. You're a fun girl, Zesika. But I've come to see there's no future for us. You're immature. Just a child."

Jessica sobs; Colombano lowers a hand to her shoulder. "Honesty can be brutal, my child. But one day you'll thank me for being that. Brutally honest."

"You're . . ." Jessica says, but the tears constrict her throat and turn the words into a wet wheeze.

Now Colombano bends over her and brings his lips to the base of her ear. "As a matter of fact," he says at almost a whisper, "I suggest we make love one last time, for old times' sake. Then I'll go to rehearsals. And by the time I get back, you'll have packed up your things and gone on your way. Off on that amazing adventure you're supposed to be on right now."

"I'll go." Jessica pushes herself up to sitting. She can hear the blood rushing in her ears.

"I know you will. But before that, a proper goodbye."

Jessica feels coarse fingers on her arms and writhes free. "Don't touch me!" she shrieks, voice trembling, and pops up out of bed.

Colombano stares at her in amusement. Jessica can't look him in the eye; she focuses on the enormous tattoos that adorn his brawny torso.

"Come on. I'll be late for rehearsal," Colombano says, wiping the smile from his face.

Jessica registers that her breathing has grown shallow. The murmur of voices carries in from outside, mingling with the rataplan of the outboard motors of boats bobbing in the canal. Jessica turns, yanks open the curtains, and is on the verge of screaming for help when Colombano grabs her hair, jerks her back into the apartment so hard, her scalp feels like it's being ripped off. Then the back of her head thunks against the wooden floor and fingers wrap around her throat. Colombano's long, greasy hair licks her face, and Jessica's nostrils fill with the stench of sweat mingled with alcohol and aftershave.

"*L'inverno,*" Colombano says, spittle spraying from between the white teeth.

Winter.

Chapter 76

JESSICA GLANCES AT HER PHONE. IT'S TWENTY-TWO twenty-two, time to make a wish. In terms of probability, the rate at which people check the time during this minute is curiously frequent. Of course, it's merely an illusion, a fallacy based on the fact that we remember twenty-two twenty-two more easily than, say, twenty-one nineteen. Still, it feels especially ominous on this dark evening, when the icy wind is whistling in the chimneys and making the frames of the old windows pop.

Water is simmering in the pot. Jessica doesn't have an electric kettle in her studio. Maybe because she has never really lived there, maybe because not having one reinforces her cover story: she lives in a bare-bones bachelorette pad where the furnishings are somewhat haphazard. Besides, water tastes the same whether it is heated in a stainless-steel pan or a cream-colored KitchenAid kettle.

Jessica sips from the mug she forgot on the table; the tea is cold. Seventeen sheets of typing paper lie next to it, some torn into smaller pieces, others glued into larger wholes. Beneath the photographs of the crimes and their victims, she has copied a few phrases from Roger Koponen's books, snippets of text that have presumably served as inspirations for the killings. But have they missed something in focusing so much on scouring Koponen's books for clues? Jessica remembers what Mikael said: *We know as much as they want us to know. Only that and nothing more.* Mikael's cynicism is often irritating, but he's also often right.

Jessica drains her mug, and the last drop of tea goes down her windpipe. She coughs into her fist, and for a fleeting moment, she thinks she knows what drowning feels like: not being able to cough up liquid that has entered the trachea, and it fills the lungs, preventing the flow of oxygen.

Jessica steps over to the sink, blows her nose, and fills the mug with boiling water. She opens the IKEA cupboard and fumbles for the glass jar where she keeps her tea bags. It's almost empty, and the two bags that are left are some goddamn vanilla tea.

At that instant, her phone rings. She doesn't recognize the number; it's not the same one the SUPO guy on stakeout called her from earlier. It might be Fubu bombing her with a phone he borrowed from a friend. She's got to hand it to the guy: he's persistent.

"Niemi."

"Hello?" The woman's voice is tentative, fearful.

"Is this regarding a police matter?"

"Yes," the woman now blurts out. There's a tinkling in the background that reminds Jessica of a cowbell. Then she hears mumbling; the woman on the line has covered the receiver with her hand and is conversing with someone at the other end.

After a few seconds, there's a cough.

"I'm sorry. I . . . Yes, this is about a police matter. That's why I called."

"Fine. How can I help you?" Jessica says, sitting back down at the table. She hears the sound of a door opening in the stairwell a story or two below.

"Umm . . . my name is Irma Helle. I own a women's clothing store here on Korkeavuorenkatu . . ."

Jessica's eyes focus on the piece of paper. "What sort of clothing store?" she asks in concentration.

"A dressmaking shop. Evening gowns . . ."

The yapping of a small dog carries in from the stairwell. "And?"

"Wait just a moment, please," the woman says, and turns to talk to someone else again.

Jessica thinks back to the tinkling she just heard. It must have come from one of those bells attached to a door that announce customers entering the store.

"Is your shop open this late?"

"Of course not . . . It's already . . . But I have a dress to finish and—"

"Are you alone, ma'am?" Jessica asks, herself unsure of the question's purpose.

"I just forgot to lock the door and . . . Well, now I'm alone."

"Good," Jessica says, brushing a strand of hair out of her eyes. "What can I do for you?"

"I called the tip line about the Koponen murder and—"

"Right. Some of the calls are forwarded directly to me. I'm the principal investigator, Detective Sergeant Jessica Niemi of the Helsinki police force," Jessica rattles off, feeling the pinch of anxiety in her fingertips. She has a hunch why the woman has called; she knows it has something to do with the evening wear the victims were dressed in.

"I knew Maria Koponen." Irma Helle holds a long pause. "She was a customer. Ordered things on a couple of occasions."

Jessica sits up straighter and grabs a pen. She's bursting with curiosity, but she is determined to keep her mouth shut and listen intently instead.

"I was so shocked when I heard that she had been . . . that she had been killed . . ."

"Of course."

"But then my daughter called. She helps me out from time to time . . . She's very knowledgeable about women's clothing and fashion. She's getting a degree in textile and fashion design—"

"What did your daughter say?"

"She'd seen a YouTube video that had been spreading among the students this morning."

Jessica suppresses an itch by scratching her neck. Irma Helle's daughter saw the video of the dead Maria

Koponen. The video that YouTube had almost immediately removed from its servers, but that had nevertheless begun to live a life of its own. Jessica can practically hear the voice, its hypnotic repetition: *Malleus Maleficarum. Malleus Maleficarum.*

"My daughter thought it all seemed like some sort of sick joke. She doesn't know Maria Koponen, but she recognized the dress she was wearing."

"Did your shop make the dress?"

"Yes. I'm sure of it," Irma Helle says, suddenly sounding profoundly shocked. "Dear God. My daughter sent me a picture, but she had cropped out the face. And then I realized the picture was taken after she died, and my daughter didn't want me to see her face."

"I see," Jessica says, trying to stay as calm as possible. She takes a deep breath and presses her trembling fingers against the tabletop. This call might be a breakthrough. All female victims, excluding Sanna Porkka, were wearing identical evening gowns. Identical shoes. Even their nail polish was the same shade. She sets the phone down on the table and turns on the speakerphone. "Please, go on."

"It might just be a coincidence that Maria was wearing a dress I designed, but . . ." Jessica thinks she catches sniffling. "But when Maria Koponen came in to order it about a month ago . . . we took her measurements and picked the fabric . . ."

"Yes?"

360

"She didn't just order one. She ordered five, if you can believe it."

Jessica feels a cold wave wash over her. "Five evening gowns?"

"Five identical gowns."

Jessica knows the other four aren't hanging in the walk-in closet at Kulosaari.

"All with different measurements," Helle continues.

What the fuck? This can't be real.

Jessica drums her fingers against the tabletop. "Do you still have the measurements somewhere?"

"Yes, in my order book. All the information is there. Maria gave me five different measurements to use when sewing the dresses. She didn't tell me why, but I assumed they were for a wedding party or something. Or some other party where the women were supposed to be dressed alike—"

"So Maria Koponen ordered these dresses? And paid for them?"

"Yes."

"How late will you be at the shop tonight?" Jessica glances at her watch; it's almost ten thirty. Someone has to get over there immediately. If no one else is free, she'll go herself, no matter what Erne says.

"I'm sure I'll be here until midnight . . ." Now Jessica hears an indeterminate noise at the other end of the line, and Helle says: "What on earth does that woman want?"

Jessica is on the alert. "What is it?"

361

"That woman is at the door again."

"What woman?"

"The one who just barged in . . . Oh, my goodness, she could be Maria Koponen's twin sister . . . Wait just a moment, please."

Jessica hears the phone being laid down on the counter. "Hey! Wait!" she cries, jumping up. "Hello? Irma?"

But Irma Helle has already lowered the phone from her ear. Jessica hears footsteps, knocking, and, a moment later, the jingle of a bell.

"Don't open the door," Jessica whispers, and walks over to the window, hand on her forehead.

Next, she hears faint speech on the line: *I'm sorry, but we're closed. We'll open at nine tomorrow. Excuse me. Did you hear me? We're closed. I'm going to have to ask you to leave—*

The call cuts off, and three short tones blast in Jessica's ear.

Chapter 77

THE STAIRWELL IS UTTERLY SILENT. JESSICA OPENS THE door with the phone to her ear and pauses at the alarm-system keypad, only to realize she never turned it on in her hurry to get back to her studio earlier that evening.

"What is it?"

Jessica notes the early-morning flexibility in Yusuf's voice; her colleague has no doubt detected the hurry and tension in hers.

"I just got a call from a woman named Irma Helle. I believe she's in immediate danger. I called in a patrol; they should be there any second now."

"Who is she?"

"Owns a dressmaking shop. She's the one who sewed the victims' evening gowns. Every single one."

"What makes you think she's in danger?"

"Someone who looks like Maria Koponen just tried to enter the shop," Jessica says, striding briskly across the living room to the kitchen. Her wallet is exactly where she left it. But why wouldn't it be? Everything feels hazy and unreal. Once again, a human life is in danger.

"Looks like Maria Koponen . . ." Yusuf says skeptically after a moment's silence. "A woman?"

"Right. A woman. Maria Koponen ordered the dresses herself. What do you think that means?"

"I have to say, it sounds really strange."

"Maria Koponen gave Helle the women's dress sizes; she must have been personally acquainted with each of the victims. Or at least knew their exact measurements."

"But . . . we've been looking for a connection between the women. And so far we haven't found anything. No hobbies in common, no calls made to each other . . . They weren't even each other's Facebook friends. And Laura Helminen told us she'd never heard of the other victims, let alone known them."

"Even so, Maria Koponen knew their dress sizes."

"That doesn't mean she knew them. Someone could have given her a list."

"Who though? Were Maria and Roger Koponen in this together? Is that what's going on here? Have Maria and Roger been helping some sick prick carry out this charade?"

"Maria Koponen is still dead, Jessica. I don't think she would have intentionally aided her own murder."

"It must have been Roger who passed the dresses on."

For a moment neither of them speaks. Then Jessica asks: "Where are you?"

"I just turned the car around. I'm headed toward Ullanlinna."

"Pick me up."

"What?"

"Come pick me up. I'm coming with."

"No, you're not."

"Yes, I am."

"What about Erne?"

"Erne can kiss my butt."

"Argh, I don't know. What if you're the real target? Wouldn't it be smarter to stay out of the field for a while?"

"I'm getting the feeling that I'm more of a target here at home."

"Take a cab. Otherwise Erne is going to have my ass on a platter—"

"Goddamn it, Yusuf. If you don't drive that piece of shit up to my door—"

"You really are a witch, Jessica."

"What's your ETA?"

"Ten minutes."

"I'll come down."

"Wait," Yusuf says, and Jessica hears him turn up his police radio.

She can just about make out every word of the clearly articulated communication: . . . *the display window of the shop on Korkeavuorenkatu. We see a woman lying on the floor. She is not moving. She is not reacting to our knocks. We're going to use force to enter. An ambulance has already been called.*

Chapter 78

I GAVE YOU A CLEAR ORDER, JESSICA. DO YOU THINK I'M GOING TO turn *a blind eye to this sort of insubordination?*

Erne clicks the lighter lid shut, stretches out the first drag as long as possible, then exhales the smoke that briefly circulated through his airways in quick puffs from his big, hairy nostrils.

Erne eyes the wall of the smoking area at HQ. It's darkened by grime and exhaust, and even the snow trapped in the seams of the concrete elements isn't able to soften the ugliness. The building is so damn hideous that it makes a superb clubhouse for the unimaginative civil servants working inside, one in which they can reinforce one another's prejudices and paranoia. There's something East German about the ghastly structure; it calls to mind the Stasi or some other tyrannical organization that doesn't even try to mask its cynical attitude toward the world around it. The fact of the matter is, for the ordinary citizen, coming to the police station just to drop off a passport application is intimidating. In addition to the building, a role must be played by the rigid, bureaucratic way the agency runs things. Out of this piss-yellow monstrosity—not to mention the rest of Länsi-Pasila, which was evidently zoned and built in an unstable state of mind, with the hand holding the pen seeking inspiration from postcards showcasing *Plattenbauten*.

Beep. 37.9. Goddamn it.

Damn you, Jessica.

The tip of the cigarette is burning his forefinger and middle finger. His ring finger is freezing in the icy wind. His pinkie and thumb are locked in an embrace.

Six months. If you begin treatment immediately.

Erne had been keeping an eye on his phone throughout the day; the private clinic had promised to call between eight a.m. and eight p.m. Generally news like this is delivered to the patient face-to-face, but due to Erne's situation at work and because the call is only a follow-up to bad news that had already been delivered, a telephone appointment was arranged.

So at eight p.m. on the dot, the oncologist Dr. Pajunen laconically recited that the CT scan of the chest cavity and the biopsies from the gastroscopy confirmed what was already considered probable: the tumor had metastasized, spreading not only to the liver and the bones but also to the esophagus.

Jessica, Jessica.

As he hung up, Erne suddenly felt curiously at peace: when he realized the thing he'd feared more than anything else in the world had finally happened, he stopped being afraid. He felt drained, and disappointed and shocked of course, but at the same time the knowledge of his own mortality set him at ease. No more questions, no more guessing. It would all be over soon.

Erne rolls the cigarette against the edge of the ashtray and lights another.

If Jessica would just have the sense to do exactly as he says.

Chapter 79

MIKAEL ENTERS, CARRYING TWO PAPER BAGS. THE SMELL of greasy pita bread, butter, garlic, and coriander wafts through the conference room.

Nina tears into the foil and styrofoam. "Lamb for Rasse—"

"I had lamb too." Mikael snatches the sandwich out from under Rasmus' nose, and Nina observes the division of the spoils out of the corner of her eye. Mikael isn't a bully in the classic sense, even though his physical presence and verbal dexterity would allow it. Rasmus, on the other hand, with his shedding scalp, bald spot, and stooped posture, is too easy a target. Sometimes it almost seems like he wants to be treated like a doormat, as if he believes it's the only reason for his existence.

But now Rasmus shoots Mikael a look tinged with resentment. Then he reaches over, grabs the other paper bag, and carefully rustles it open.

"Evidently Jessie just couldn't stay at home," Mikael says, grabs hold of his foil-wrapped pita with both hands, and takes a big bite.

"How do you know?"

"I heard Erne yelling into the phone. She headed out to the Korkeavuorenkatu scene."

"No wonder. She was on the phone with the victim when it happened." Nina continues watching the men for a second as they stuff their faces with lamb pitas.

"You think it's a coincidence?" Rasmus asks, wiping his mouth on his sleeve. Mikael turns to look at him. "Jessica has been at the center of events this whole time. Then Erne orders her to stay at home. Under strict police surveillance. But the bloodshed follows her there too."

Nina nods and looks at Mikael. Rasmus is no doubt right. Of everyone, he's been the one who's been most on top of everything from the start, not least of all because he's done the groundwork better than anyone else working from the station.

"I just hope she's safe," Nina eventually says, arms folded across her chest. She has always liked Jessica, her integrity and absolute commitment to doing what she thinks is best in a given situation. Nina has tried to get to know her better from time to time, but for some reason, Jessica has wanted to maintain a certain distance from her colleagues. Even then she's managed to do it politely, without hurting anyone's feelings.

"Jessica's a big girl." Mikael nods at the board and the new photograph Rasmus just put up. "Irma Helle."

"Victim number seven."

"The group is heterogeneous in a lot of ways," Nina says, walking over to the board.

"Like what?" Mikael asks.

"Well, in the first place, two of the victims are still unidentified. Two are men. And finally: three were wearing identical dresses. Four, if we count Laura Helminen as a victim. There's no common denominator here."

"Maria Koponen ordered five dresses. What if Sanna Porkka was dressed in one of the dresses before she was burned at the stake? Has anyone even looked into that?" Mikael asks.

"We'd better check it out." Nina writes down the question on the board. "The sizes of all of the dresses are noted in Irma Helle's order book. We can check if one of the dresses was made to Porkka's measurements."

"The fact that Sanna Porkka was the one who set out to drive Koponen to Helsinki has to be a coincidence," Mikael says doubtfully.

"Is it? Aren't you the one who spoke out against making such dangerous assumptions earlier today?" Rasmus says, drawing a murderous glance from Mikael. Rasmus has found a wholly new side to himself, a brashness that makes Nina smile in satisfaction. She loves Micke, but she gets a kick out of the occasional times someone takes him down a peg or two. Especially when the shots are fired from a completely unpredictable direction. "How could Porkka's foolproof participation have been planned, in your view? According to my recollection, the decision to bring Koponen to Helsinki was made spontaneously, by Erne."

"Who is now suffering pangs of conscience about his decision," Nina interjects.

"Exactly."

But Rasmus is on a roll: "Remember, Porkka was driving Koponen. A man who at this moment is suspected of having played a major role in the killing spree. Koponen could have somehow influenced how and by whom he was driven from Savonlinna to Helsinki in the middle of the night—"

"Motherfucker!" Mikael suddenly shouts. He stands up and spits his food out into his palm. "What the fuck . . . ? My teeth are falling out." He rubs his cheek for a moment, then pokes a finger into the half-chewed sandwich in his hand.

"What is it now?" Nina asks.

"There's a rock or something in this." Mikael shoves his forefinger into his mouth and a moment later holds up a bit of white bone for the others to see.

"That's insane."

"You lost a tooth?" Rasmus says, surprised.

"No . . . I didn't," Mikael says as his finger prods every corner of his mouth.

A moment of silence falls. Then Rasmus shoves his sandwich away, looking nauseous.

"They're in mine too." Rasmus hawks into his fist.

"What? They're what?" Nina takes her own sandwich from the table and opens the foil wrapper. She hears Rasmus' retching, and his reaction spreads to her.

Mikael stands, hands clasped behind his neck: "The man burned in the woods. Mr. X's teeth."

Chapter 80

JESSICA HAS CROUCHED DOWN NEXT TO THE WOMAN ON THE floor. The shop's large display windows have been covered with plastic sheeting, but the flash of the emergency vehicles' blue lights penetrates the space.

"Pretty straightforward," Jessica says, and rubs her fingers inside her rubber gloves. Irma Helle is sprawled on her stomach, arms at her sides; there's a large, bloody contusion at the back of her head. Only a couple of meters away lies the likely murder weapon: a brass curtain rod, one end of which is smeared with a red pulp.

"This diverges from all the other killings in the sense that nothing like it appears in Koponen's books," Yusuf says in a low voice, stepping out of the way of a technical investigator in white coveralls. The little shop is full of racks of clothes, which make moving around a challenge. The door is shut, but even so they talk in whispers, as if the walls have ears. Who knows? Maybe they do. Nothing feels impossible anymore.

"In other words, this is the first homicide that wasn't carefully planned."

"But that is still undeniably linked to the earlier killings."

"Absolutely. And, on top of everything else, the perpetrator is a woman. A woman who resembles some of the victims."

"Maybe they wanted to silence Irma Helle."

"But why wait until now? Helle could have called her tip in earlier today."

"What's the tip we're talking about here . . . the sizes of the gowns she ordered?" Yusuf asks as he makes his way to the desktop computer on the counter.

"If Maria Koponen ordered five gowns and we've only found four of them so far, we can assume one victim is still waiting to be dressed." Jessica allows her gaze to scan the shop. There's a doorway at the rear that leads down to a cellar-like workroom with two big sewing machines. "Helle mentioned a notebook on the phone. Do you see anything like that?" she then asks.

"No, but I do see a lot of pens," Yusuf says, taking pictures of the counter with his phone.

Jessica sighs and glances at her phone. Erne has called twice.

"Something else come up?"

"Erne's hot and bothered because I didn't follow orders."

"He has the stripes to shelve you like that," Yusuf says with a snap of his fingers.

"He's not going to. Not now, when things are such a mess."

"We can only hope. What do you want to do?" Yusuf asks, hands on his hips.

"Let's go to the station. And solve this before anyone else dies."

Yusuf zips up his coat. "As long as we hit the McDo drive-through on the way. You have cash?"

Jessica pulls on her hood. "Actually, I found your card. It was in my coat pocket."

Chapter 81

ERNE IS SITTING AT THE TABLE, GAZING AT HIS CLENCHED fists. It's a quarter past eleven at night, and the team is gathered in the conference room again. Rasmus is sitting at the table, looking solemn; he appears to be counting his fingers. Nina has locked her weary eyes on the fluorescent tubes on the ceiling.

Over the course of his lengthy career in law enforcement, Erne Mikson has come across many cases that, despite dogged efforts, have not been solved. But this one is too big to bury in the unsolved folder. If the worst comes to happen, the investigation will continue long after disease has claimed his life. Suddenly the terminal illness feels like a verdict of not guilty, a ticket to some better place where evil has no power.

The door opens, and Mikael enters the room.

"Well?" Erne asks. Nina and Rasmus still look pale.

"I got hold of the food-delivery guy. And I told the restaurant to close their doors. The manager assured me the food was handed off straight from the kitchen to the delivery guy, and that there's no way the teeth would have gotten into the food in their kitchen."

"At what stage—"

"At any stage. We'll be able to hear what the delivery person has to say soon." Mikael sits down. "Where are the teeth?"

"Photographed and delivered to Sarvilinna. I don't know if she's going to be able to get anything useful out of them."

The fluorescent tubes on the ceiling flicker a few times.

"This is so damn sick, Erne," Mikael says, rubbing his knuckles. "How long are we supposed to put up with this?"

Erne raises an eyebrow. "Why are you asking me? I'm not the one who sprinkled a dead man's teeth into your burger," he snaps.

"It was a pita sandwich," Rasmus mumbles.

"It could be a jerkoff sandwich for all I care," Erne thunders, then coughs a few times into his fist and continues in his earlier, hoarser voice: "Apparently you want to bring in Karlstedt and Lehtinen. I don't think it's going to change anything."

"But, Erne, you have to admit," Nina now says reflectively, without the slightest hint of disrespect, "that the clock is ticking. Having those men under surveillance might have been a good idea earlier today, but in the light of everything that has happened, I don't think we're going to win anything that way anymore."

"Especially since they know we're listening. That became clear beyond a doubt when—"

"When we listened to the recordings," Erne interrupts Rasmus, and hacks into his fist. He can taste the phlegm coughed up from his trachea, distinguish the taste of blood on his tongue.

"How many more people have to die?" Mikael asks him.

Erne looks at the trio sitting around the table and feels utterly empty. Maybe the call from the doctor really has made everything meaningless. He shuts his eyes and suddenly realizes the worst thing isn't awareness of your own death but knowing when it will come. That you can try to forget your mortality until the day you're given an excruciatingly precise timeline of the life left to you. A deadline. He might have wanted to depart the world suddenly after all, a healthy man. A heart attack on the ski track, or while he was asleep. A car crash while listening to good music.

"Let's talk about that in a minute after Jessica and Yusuf get here," Erne says, and the others grunt their approval. It's clear that the wolf pack has smelled his frailty. The sniping and ignoring of direct orders would have been unheard of just a little while ago. "Rasmus," Erne finally says, swallowing down the foul taste in his mouth.

At that moment, the door opens and Jessica steps in, followed by Yusuf.

Erne casts a pregnant glance at the principal investigator but decides to save the tirade he has prepared for a better moment. All he says is: "Sit. Rasse has the floor."

Rasmus presses his eyeglasses more firmly to his nose and picks hesitantly at the collar of his sweater. Over the day, Rasmus has scooped himself a generous serving of self-confidence from somewhere, but the way he glances around, like a dog expecting to be disciplined, hasn't gone anywhere.

"The fact of the matter is that a correlation for the seamstress' death, despite it not being a ritual murder, can also be found in the books." Rasmus reaches under a thick stack of papers and pulls out a paperback, its pages adorned with a plumage of dozens of multicolored Post-its. Then he gulps audibly and reads out loud.

But the eerie shadow drew back to where it had emerged from a moment earlier. So smoothly and swiftly that Esther was no longer sure she'd even seen it. Esther knew she was alone, because she had locked the door after her last customer left. She had never been afraid in her shop before, never allowed her imagination to gallop away with her, steer her thoughts. Something had changed. Maybe it was because of what she had seen earlier that day. Only now did she understand it was no coincidence. And then Esther feels a cold wave wash over her. Before she has time to make sense of what she has just realized, she looks out the glass doors and sees something that doesn't belong there. For a moment the contours line up with those of her reflection. But then the figure moves, transforming into a distinct entity of its own.

"In the next chapter, the police find Esther dead in her shop. She'd been killed by a blow to the head," Rasmus says, shutting the book.

"Why didn't this come up earlier? That a dressmaker—"

Rasmus laughs so sharply that Yusuf leaves the sentence unfinished.

"Esther is not a dressmaker. And there aren't any other similarities between the instances either. Only the MO. A blow to the head, which happens to be the most common way in the world of murdering someone."

"But it said in the book that she'd seen something. Something the meaning of which she understood right before someone killed her."

Hearing Jessica's voice rouses Erne from his state of deep concentration. "Yes, that's the motive for the murder in Koponen's book, but it doesn't have any similarities to what happened today. In the book, Esther sees the priest in charge of the inquisition kissing a woman suspected of being a witch."

"And the priest kills her?"

"Yes. The priest can't allow his relationship with the suspected witch to come out, so he creeps into Esther's bakery and gets rid of her."

"So Irma Helle was killed by a female priest who's having a secret affair with the cantor?"

Mikael's quip earns him a few smiles.

"It seems likely that this murder was committed for one reason: because Esther the baker was killed in the book,"

Rasmus says, rolling his tongue around his mouth as if he were searching it for something.

"One body is still missing," Erne says suddenly.

"That's true," Rasmus continues. "No one has been stabbed with a dagger yet."

Erne nods lazily, lifts his elbows to the table, and leans his head into his hands. "So we can assume that, at this moment, a man is lying somewhere in Finland—presumably the metropolitan Helsinki area—with a dagger in his chest. We just haven't found him yet."

"Who says the crime has already happened?" Rasmus counters, lowers his gaze to the table, and jots down something in his notebook.

"You heard what Rasse said, Erne," Mikael says, pulling out a brand-new pack of gum. "Bringing those two assholes into the station might help us save some poor guy's life."

Erne replies calmly: "How were you planning on extracting the information about the next victim from them? Beating it out of them?"

"If that means an innocent man doesn't die. Sure."

"Hup! Let's go with that for a minute." Erne stabs a finger at Mikael. "An innocent man. Are we sure the victims are truly innocent?"

Nina frowns. "And aren't guilty of, say, being witches?"

"Maria Koponen ordered not only her own death dress, but that of several other people as well. That doesn't sound completely innocent to me."

"I agree. It's really fucking weird," Yusuf says, tracing his lifeline with a fingertip. "But I would still start from the assumption that Maria Koponen was following someone else's instructions and didn't have the slightest idea what the black dresses she ordered from Irma Helle were for."

"Her husband's instructions, of course," Mikael interjects.

"Maybe," Erne says, and stands. "I think you guys need to talk to Laura Helminen one more time. Poke, pry, understand, comfort, pressure . . . get her to open up. Because if Helminen's hiding something, if she has a connection to the other victims, we need to find out, damn it."

"You're right, Erne." Jessica taps her fingertips together under her chin. "If whatever connects the witch hunters' victims is in some way illicit or even illegal . . . then Laura Helminen might have a reason to lie."

"Exactly."

"Yusuf and I will handle it."

"Be careful, Jessica. Nothing has changed since this afternoon. Make sure she doesn't throw a fit again," Erne says.

"What about Karlstedt and Lehtinen?" Mikael asks.

Erne turns and glowers at his subordinate. Masticating his gum, Mikael looks like a big, harmless cow. Maybe he's right. They have to start taking risks now. He might as well ditch the battle for predominance.

"Fine. Make sure they're picked up from their homes at exactly the same time."

Chapter 82

Outgoing number: +3584002512585
Time of call: 23:31:22
(dialing)

Torsten Karlstedt (TK): Hello.

(several seconds of silence)

Kai Lehtinen (KL): Does it seem to you like something is about to happen?

TK: Funny you should ask. It does. It most certainly does.

KL: Then I suppose we'd better start preparing ourselves.

TK: I still don't see anything yet . . .

KL: Just wait, *frater*.

(long pause)

TK: We might not talk for a while.

KL: That's likely.

TK: Be well, *frater*.

KL: You too.

Chapter 83

THERE'S A LOUD POP FROM THE VOLKSWAGEN'S SHOCK absorbers when Yusuf drives straight into a pothole in the frost-ravaged asphalt. Jessica's eyes are focused on the rearview mirror and the van that's following them.

"Damn it . . . There go the shocks," Yusuf curses.

"Don't worry. Our babysitters hit it too."

Yusuf turns the car into Töölö Hospital and parks right in front of the doors. A nurse smoking outside gives them a nasty look.

"Police business," Yusuf says in a discreet voice as the police van pulls up behind his car.

"An emergency?" the nurse snaps back, blowing smoke out of her nose. "If not, feel free to park where everybody else does."

Yusuf looks at the woman, laughs, and shakes his head. "What's with all the negativity these days?"

"The world's a shitty place," Jessica says.

They walk side by side through the sliding doors. The uniformed officers follow ten meters behind. Jessica and

Yusuf cross the spacious lobby, where lines of colored tape have been laid down on the floor to guide visitors.

"Listen, Yusuf," Jessica says, pressing the elevator button. "Laura Helminen seems like a young woman in a profound state of shock. So profound that it was almost impossible to question her earlier."

"And?"

Jessica lowers her gaze to the tips of her shoes and waits for the elevator doors to open. The elevator is empty, and the two of them step in. It seems odd that the patrol officers sent to ensure Yusuf's and Jessica's safety are staying in the lobby, but Erne forbade them from following the detectives up to Laura Helminen's room.

"In all likelihood, Irma Helle was killed by a woman," Jessica continues once the doors close, "who resembled the other victims, including Laura Helminen, in stature and appearance."

"Laura Helminen has been here at the hospital this whole time."

"Sure, but that doesn't mean the perp couldn't be a woman."

Yusuf grunts and then nods slowly. "Right. We assumed that the women were exclusively victims."

Jessica nods back and then shifts her gaze to the torn cuticle of her right forefinger. As she does, something about what Yusuf just said starts to nag at her. Jessica looks back up at him: "Wait. What did you just say?"

"That's what you meant, right? That we assumed that the perpetrators are men? That this is some sadistic male—"

"Yes. But the way you just put it—apparently unintentionally—is actually genius," Jessica says as the elevator rises to the sixth floor without stopping.

"What exactly did I say?"

"That women are *exclusively* victims."

"*Exclusively* victims. I don't understand—"

"We've been thinking the murderers are men who want to punish their female victims somehow. But what if it turns out they're women?"

The elevator beeps, and a mechanical female voice recites the floor number. The voice reminds Jessica of the YouTube video, the monotone repetition of the Latin words.

"But the fact that Maria Koponen ordered the clothes—"

"For some reason, we immediately assumed that Roger Koponen manipulated his wife. It's a natural explanation, of course, because no one wants to plan their own murder."

The elevator doors open; the corridor is surprisingly quiet.

"Wait," Yusuf says more softly now, and gently grabs the back of Jessica's coat. "Are you saying Laura Helminen was not only a victim; she was also a perpetrator?"

Jessica stares at Yusuf without saying a word. Then she shakes her head and laughs joylessly. "Yes, actually, that's exactly what I was saying. Am I crazy?"

"Yes. You've always been as crazy as a loon. But that doesn't mean you're not right."

The elevator doors shut behind them; Jessica sighs and eyes the corridor. The hatch to the nurses' station is closed; a bright light is blazing inside. Farther down, at the end of the corridor, a guard is posted outside Laura Helminen's room. It's still Teo.

"OK, Jessica. Let's assume Helminen knows more than she's letting on. How do you think we should approach her so everything doesn't go to shit, one way or another?"

Jessica gives Yusuf a probing look. "The idea that someone would have let someone else abduct, drug, anesthetize, and almost drown them in freezing water is far-fetched. So far-fetched, it wouldn't even occur to us as an alternative, which means we can conduct a little test of our own."

Chapter 84

NINA PULLS UP OUTSIDE A LARGE HOME IN WESTEND that, superficially at least, appears to be of an era and style similar to the Koponens' house in Kulosaari. Nina hasn't been to the Koponens; neither she nor Mikael has visited any of the several numerous scenes over the course of the case, but she has stared at hundreds, if not thousands, of photographs that the others have carried back or sent to the station. So she has grown acquainted not only with the Koponen and von Bunsdorf residences and the storefront on Korkeavuorenkatu, but ample examples of shoreline, forest, and field. Places that share nothing in common, but that are bound together by what is perhaps the grisliest series of killings in the history of Finnish crime.

"What do you think? How did Mr. X's teeth end up in our dinners?"

"I don't know. But I do know that that asshole," Mikael says with a nod toward the house, "is the one who ripped them out of the victim's mouth last night."

Nina rotates the vent to blow against the windshield, which has fogged up again.

"You coming?" Mikael asks, and makes sure the Velcro straps of his Kevlar vest are secure. They're not assuming force will be required during today's arrests, but they know not to take pointless risks with these witch hunters.

"You go ahead with the boys," Nina says, eyes glued to the house. The blue emergency lights sliding across the white plaster remind her of a work of contemporary light art. Bright lights blaze in nearly every window. "Is that him?" Nina asks, pointing at a floor-to-ceiling expanse of glass on the second floor. The man who has made his appearance there is dressed in white sweatpants and a black knit.

"Goddamn it," Mikael says, popping a piece of gum into his mouth. "That's Torsten all right."

Torsten Karlstedt raises a hand in greeting.

"Holy hell. What's he doing?"

Mikael grunts. "Hell's exactly where he belongs." He glances at his watch; it's midnight. His phone rings; he answers it with a single word and hangs up. The group that has moved into position outside Kai Lehtinen's house in Vantaa is ready to go. "When it comes to what he's doing, you'll be able to ask him yourself before long." He opens his door.

Nina feels a cold breeze on her face. Then the door shuts, and Mikael joins the group of four men in coveralls. Nina watches them advance across the front yard. Once they make it to the door, one of them starts circling around to the back. Nina notices her leg bouncing restlessly. It's hard to believe Karlstedt would try to run. But almost anything else is possible. Could this be a trap? Is he about to blow up his house and himself just to cause more chaos?

Karlstedt disappears from the window, and a moment later the front door opens. He stands there on the other side of the threshold and, as far as Nina can tell, is perfectly calm. Nina sees him vanish for a moment and then emerge wearing a red parka. She watches the escort as it makes its way to the van without incident. Once Karlstedt is finally ushered in through its rear doors, Nina shuts her eyes and lets out a long sigh of relief.

The door opens, and Mikael sits down at her side. Nina leaves her eyes closed, but she would recognize the gum-chewing in her sleep.

"What a sleazeball," Mikael says, unzipping his coat. Nina shoots him a questioning look. "You can tell he's guilty by the look his face."

"It's written on his forehead?"

"Yup. In huge letters. Besides, if you're named Torsten, there's got to be something wrong with you." Mikael holds out his hand, and Nina smiles and takes it. "Were you worried?" he asks.

"Don't think for a second that what you just did makes me think of you as an action hero. You guys might as well have been playing Barbies out in the yard. That's how dangerous it was."

"Fuck that. Weren't you watching? Our lives were at risk. Torsten tried to kill me with garlic."

Nina laughs and starts up the car. "Was the arrest in Vantaa equally dramatic?"

"Apparently. Lehtinen was led to the car without any fuss."

"And hey, dork. Garlic is for keeping vampires at bay, not witches," Nina says as the two vans in front of them pull out.

"My bad. I guess I need to brush up on my Harry Potter."

Chapter 85

WAKE UP, JESSICA.

Mom is more beautiful than she has been in ages this morning.

What, Mom?

We're going on an adventure.

Mom strokes Jessica's hair. The morning sun is flooding into the apartment through the open blinds. Jessica raises her head from the pillow. Her little brother is already up, rubbing his eyes groggily next to his own bed. Dad is standing in the doorway, looking worried. Maybe mad. Jessica has seen that look on Dad's face a lot lately.

It's Saturday.

Mom is speaking again. Jessica isn't sure what Mom means. They don't usually go on adventures on Saturday mornings. At most, they play in the pool with Dad. Lately, Mom has spent more time at work than at home.

Chop-chop, get dressed now.

Mom is still stroking her hair. Her fingers graze Jessica's earlobe, sending a warm shiver down Jessica's neck. Mom is smiling, but there's something strange about her expression.

Mom is an actor; Jessica has seen her on television lots of times. She has learned that Mom's job is to pretend to be someone else. Sometimes at a theater, sometimes on television or in movies. Mom is so good at it that there are times when Jessica doesn't even recognize her on TV.

Jessica asked Mom once how she knows how to act like she's sad. *You have to think about something sad*, Mom said.

Mom gets up from the edge of the bed and walks away. She passes Dad standing at the doorway, but they don't look at each other. It's as if they are invisible to each other. Now Jessica sees that there's a suitcase at the door. Dad comes over, hands folded across his chest, and sits down.

Jessie and Toffe. Everything's going to be fine.

Dad's smile is sad, but it's a lot more real than Mom's. It's as if, of the two of them, Dad is the better actor.

You come over here too.

Her brother clumsily pulls on a black *Ghostbusters* sweatshirt and trundles over to Jessica's bed.

Dad looks at both of them, one at a time, and pulls them in to him. Inhales their scent.

Why are you crying?

For a moment, Dad just sniffles, but then he wipes his nose on the sleeve of his black sweater.

Daddy has to go away for a little while.

Why?

Mom and I decided that would be best.

Jessica feels an enormous pressure in her chest, and she takes Dad by the wrist. She knows things aren't OK.

The enormous house has been too quiet for too long. The night before, she and Toffe stayed up late and listened to the shouting and slamming that carried through the walls, and Jessica thought: *Finally the silence is over. Finally something is happening.* But now that Dad's saying he's leaving, Jessica shuts her eyes and wishes the house were still quiet. She'd do anything, if everything could stay the way it's always been.

Come on now. Let's get a bite to eat at the airport.

The memory of a six-year-old is selective. From this vantage point, it's impossible for Jessica to guess what happened over the next few minutes. Were the conversations in the car and the words that carried to the back seat real or imagined? Were they something she has used to try to fill the gaps in her memory?

But there are some things she remembers vividly. Like her brother's fingers wrapped around her own.

And Mom's dark eyes in the rearview mirror.

Chapter 86

LOOK IN THE MIRROR. JESSICA LEANS OVER THE SINK AND gazes at her reflection in the center of the gold frame. Her dark eyes are hard to make out behind the strands of dark hair clinging to her brow. The warm water trickles down her neck to her back, and comes to a stop at the towel she has wrapped above her breasts.

Jessica walks over to the open window. The canals in Murano are quiet: there are clearly fewer tourists in October than in the summer, despite the fact that weather-wise autumn is the best time to visit the city. In Helsinki, the leaves have presumably taken on their bright colors, and wedges of migrating birds are plowing the sky.

This morning was four months to the day since Jessica first set foot in Venice. Now, summery San Michele and her plans of touring Europe feel as distant as Los Angeles, but somehow time has also passed incredibly quickly. A hazy, unreal period separates the present day from that rainy early morning when Jessica packed her bag at Colombano's apartment, arms and throat hideously bruised and crotch bleeding, was

396

stopped by him at the front door, and took his rough tongue down her throat. And hoped from the bottom of her heart that that one kiss would be enough for him. That this would be the end. That she would finally be free to leave.

Have a safe trip home, Zesika. Remember what I said. Your story is not going to move anyone, so it would be wisest to leave it untold.

A hug. Cheek against tattooed chest. Stench rising from skin. His gestures are tender, languid, as if the two of them had a sleepless but love-filled night behind them. No sign of uncertainty or regret. No rape happened. They had a brief romance and broke up. Without any disagreements, without any drama. That's the way life goes sometimes.

It's too bad things had to end this way.

A white smile. Knuckles on her cheek.

The last thing Jessica sees before the door shuts is the stringed violin resting on its stand on the console in the entryway. Then the narrow stairwell, where the wallpaper looks ugly for the first time, like a rusty well cover.

A moment later, Jessica and her bags are on a side street running along a narrow canal. She is too tired to continue, too shocked to cry. Jessica sits down on the quay stones, dangles and swings her feet above the water, and looks at the boats roped to the sides of the canal. Her primary feeling is bottomless shame. Followed by detachment, utter loneliness, and aimlessness. After all she has been through over the past few weeks, sitting on a train and flying to Helsinki feels like an impossible chore. She is too drained

397

to think about the future, about what she wants to do when she grows up. She doesn't want to see her aunt Tina, who is desperately trying to close some chasm she herself built. Jessica just wants to be. Here and now.

Like a thief, here and now has turned into three months. The autumn sea smells different: frank, fresh. Jessica returned to the hotel where she lodged when she originally arrived in Venice. She is the perfect guest: she eats at the hotel two or three times a day, is generous with tips, and pays off her tab every week. A standard room was exchanged for a junior suite at the end of July. Jessica has left the building only a few times; on those occasions, she has walked several hundred meters under cover of night before returning to the hotel. She doesn't want anyone to see her; she wants darkness to cloak her ugliness, her disgusting skin and greasy hair. A few times she has been overcome by the eerie feeling that someone is following her. Footsteps trailing her that stop when she stops. A glimpse of a shadow scurrying away when she glances over her shoulder.

She feels safe at the hotel. No one there asks stupid questions. They probably think she's a kept woman living off of some emir's fortune who has simply decided not to go home.

Jessica spends her days lying in the enormous bed, watching TV. One day, the neuralgia grows so severe that it renders Jessica totally immobile. In those moments, she clenches the sheet in her fingers and presses her eyes shut: she tries to recall that sense of overwhelming freedom she felt in the *vaporetto* the day she met Colombano for the first time. But Jessica never cries out. She will not give the world the satisfaction. The pain is often followed by a distressing thought, a flash of Mother, Father, her brother, Colombano. The episodes of pain are like stinging salt in wounds that her subconscious has ripped open. They always come together, the anguish and the pain. But not always in that order.

Jessica has put on weight, but it feels completely meaningless. When she leaves her room, she dresses in shorts and a hoodie, swipes gloss onto her lips, and pulls her hair back into a ponytail. She's like a shadow of her former self, who never went out without looking beautiful and groomed. She's a slowly dying freak in a foreign country, in a city that has turned from gloriously beautiful to abominably ugly. She is alone and, because of that, ready to give up.

What sort of idiot would Mom and Dad think she was if they were alive? Would Toffe squeeze her hand anymore? Would he even touch it?

A busker's violin sounds from somewhere. Vivaldi's *The Four Seasons. "L'inverno."* Winter truly is making its approach.

Jessica eyes the tray she ordered from room service the night before, the half-eaten entrecôte and wilted French fries. Her fingers reach for the serrated steak knife, for its wooden handle. Her wet hair drips water to the carpet. The music carrying in from outside is beautiful, its strains so timeless and ingenious.

399

Her grip slips and the knife plunks to the floor at her feet. For a moment, Jessica looks at it as if it has betrayed her trust. The strings continue to play in the background, higher and higher. Faster and faster.

Jessica closes the window and looks at her trembling hands. Maybe it's high time to do something. To go to a concert. To see the performance with fresh eyes.

Chapter 87

THE BUZZING FROM THE FLUORESCENT TUBES AT THE ceiling is so loud that it catches the attention of everyone who gets interrogated. Nina has often wondered if the lights have intentionally been left unrepaired, if the noise is a method developed by psychologists to break the human spirit.

Nevertheless, Torsten Karlstedt pays it no mind. As a matter of fact, he seems perfectly at home. He evinces no interest in his bleak surroundings; instead, he has trained his tranquil gaze directly on Nina. He's about fifty years old, visibly tanned despite the time of year, and in good shape for his age. His thick hair is a golden brown.

Nina presses the button to turn on the recorder. The interrogation has lasted only a few minutes, but for some reason, she feels like she has spent an eternity in the room.

"Where were you last night?"

"Savonlinna," Karlstedt answers, then coughs into his fist. "Why?"

"I was listening to Roger Koponen speak, of course. You know that."

"With whom?"

"Kaitsu, Kai Lehtinen. You know that too."

"You seem to know a lot about what we know."

"I don't know. But you know. I wouldn't be here otherwise, would I?"

"Why is it you think you're here?"

"Is this seriously how this goes? What sort of stupid game is this?"

Nina glances at the recorder on the table. Then at Karlstedt's black knit, which has a logo depicting equestrian sports at the breast.

"The two of you drove to Savonlinna in your Porsche Cayenne."

"Yes, we did. Is that a crime? Driving an overly provocative vehicle?"

Nina smiles wearily. "You know what? You're right, Torsten. We know all this. If you don't mind, allow me to ask you some questions we don't know the answers to."

"Be my guest."

"You never got out of the car in Savonlinna. Why not?"

"I didn't feel like it."

"So your friend Kai Lehtinen went in alone to listen to Roger Koponen speak. And you sat in the car for over an hour. Simply because you didn't feel like it after all."

"That's correct."

"Was there anyone else in the car?"

Karlstedt smiles enigmatically. "No."

"Why did you leave your cell phones at home?"

402

"Sometimes it's nice to be off the grid."

"No doubt," Nina says, arms folded across her chest. She has questioned hundreds of lawbreakers. Some have been slippery and slick, others stupid and transparent. Torsten Karlstedt doesn't belong to either group. Nina is starting to agree with Erne that the two men were brought in too soon.

Karlstedt glances at his steel watch to check the time, then unclasps it and lowers it to the table in front of him. His movements are steady and deliberate.

"Nina Ruska," he says eventually after examining the ID badge hanging around Nina's neck.

"At the service of the community," Nina says drily.

"I understand the trip Kaitsu and I made to the provinces seems strange. Especially since Roger Koponen was killed in Juva."

Nina studies the man closely. Karlstedt knows what he just said isn't true. And, most important, he has to know the police are aware of this too.

"But we have nothing to do with his death," Karlstedt continues. Absurdly enough, he's telling the truth. They have nothing to do with Koponen's death, because Koponen is alive. But they have plenty to do with the death of Sanna Porkka and the as-yet-unidentified man who died with her.

"What about the death of a female police officer Sanna Porkka?"

"I have nothing against female police officers, Nina Ruska."

403

Nina ignores the response, moistens her fingertip on the tip of her tongue, and turns the page in her notepad. *"Introduction to the Occult,"* she says.

Karlstedt smiles and crosses his legs. "An excellent work, if I do say so myself."

"You've always been interested in magic."

"In magic? No, no. The occult is about much more than magic. It's about an incredibly fascinating world of secret knowledge, in which magic plays only a small part. I'm assuming you haven't read it."

"No. But I happen to know that the work sparked criticism at the time. You didn't restrict yourself to describing a broad range of occult phenomena; you also wrote rather provocative text in which you defended their somewhat questionable history. You wrote, for instance, that the Third Reich would not have collapsed so precipitously if the Nazis had dared to put their trust in esoteric teachings. That—and this is a direct quote —'Heinrich Himmler, one of the most influential figures in Nazi Germany, should have boldly continued his explorations into the occult.'"

"Are you asking now if I'm a Nazi?"

"Potential anti-Semitism doesn't interest us at all, to be honest, unless a homicide is involved. Nevertheless, details like this support our notion that you're always hungry for attention. Just like now, here at this table, you do things to provoke. To be remembered."

"Oho. Did Nina Ruska take a few psychology classes at vocational school?" Karlstedt folds his hands on the table.

Nina smiles but doesn't look him in the eye. *Did you take a few classes on being a sleazeball asshole at business school?*

"Did you know Roger or Maria Koponen personally?"

"I'm a big fan of Roger's books."

"Answer the question."

"No, I didn't know them."

At that moment, the door to the interrogation room opens. Mikael is standing there in the doorway.

"Nina, could you step out here, please?"

Nina taps her pen against the tabletop and stares at Karlstedt. Then she stands. Slowly, because she doesn't want to give Karlstedt the impression that when someone whistles, she runs like a dog. "Could you please excuse me for a moment, Torsten?"

"Gladly, Nina Ruska," he says calmly. The fact that the prick keeps saying her full name makes Nina uneasy, which is the point, of course.

"What is it now?" Nina says, when the door to the interrogation room shuts. There's something off about Mikael. It takes Nina a second to realize that he isn't chomping on gum.

"Get anything interesting out of him?" Mikael asks, hands on his hips.

"Nothing. Maybe Erne was right."

"Shit."

"What about Lehtinen?" Nina asks, and glances over Mikael's shoulder toward the closed door behind which the other man is being interrogated.

Mikael shakes his head and waves dismissively. "Same. Cool as could be. Weird hinting between the lines. Keeps teasing but won't give it up."

"Was there anything else? Or should we get back to it?"

"There is," Mikael says quickly, and waves Nina farther away from the doors. "Wang from tech called. The anesthesia drugs used to knock the victims out . . . thiopental and pancur—well, the second one. You know what I mean. And the chloroform and even the cannulas and drip bags . . . A private clinic in Helsinki responded to our request for information. Their inventory is seriously jacked."

"Goddamn it, Micke," Nina says, feeling the tickle of enthusiasm in the pit of her stomach. "Do we know who had access to their drugs and supplies?"

"Their staff is pretty small, only twenty or so. The CEO wants to see us and clear up the matter ASAP. My assumption is to minimize any damage to their reputation if the media get their hands on the story."

"Wants to see us? At this time of night?"

"Yes. He's still at the office."

"Then we should be on our way there already."

"We're in the middle of questioning these guys."

"What's the name of the clinic?"

"*Bättre Morgondag.* On Bulevardi."

"'A Better Tomorrow'? I've never heard of it . . ."

"It's been around for about fifty years. Sounds like some sort of mindfulness hoo-ha."

"We'd better get on it right away. Can you keep an eye on these two lunatics if I grab my car and run down there?"

Mikael smiles. "Of course."

"Good. I have a hunch we're going to get on these jerks' trail tonight."

Chapter 88

TEO OPENS THE DOOR, AND YUSUF STEPS IN, TABLET UNDER his arm. Laura Helminen is awake, the television is on, and she's tapping away at her smartphone.

"Hi, Laura," Yusuf says as the door behind him shuts.

"Not again," Laura groans in a bored voice. "I already told you everything I remember—"

"I'd like to show you a few photographs."

"I'm really tired—"

"This will only take a second, Laura." Yusuf smiles empathetically, pulls a chair over to the bed, and turns the iPad screen toward the young woman. "Would you take a look at these photographs one more time? Are you sure you don't know any of these women?"

"I already looked through them once—"

"It wouldn't be unheard of for something to come to mind a little later."

Laura looks at the pictures and shakes her head. "No . . ."

"Wait a second. Whoops . . ." Yusuf says absentmindedly. "There's one picture here that doesn't belong."

Laura looks at Yusuf suspiciously. "Which picture?"

"My colleague's . . . the female detective who was here earlier. Who saved you from the freezing sea," Yusuf says, shaking his head.

Laura's face is now grave.

"You were frightened when you saw her earlier today. Do you remember?"

"Like I said, I'm exhausted."

"I'm sure you are. This has been a pretty rough day for everyone, especially you. But we police take all suspicions seriously. The fact that you reacted so strongly to Sergeant Niemi's face today led to her being shelved from the investigation." Yusuf yawns lazily.

"What?"

"Someone else is taking over for her."

"But—"

"But what?"

"As you can tell, I was clearly exhausted. I didn't recognize her just a second ago—"

"Don't worry about that. The decision has already been made."

Yusuf stands and turns to leave.

"Wait," Laura says, now looking shocked. "She has to stay on the case—"

"What do you mean?"

"I take it all back. I never saw a painting of her."

"What do you mean, you didn't see a painting of her?"

"I wasn't even in a basement," Laura says, and tears start streaming down her cheeks.

Yusuf pulls his phone out of his coat pocket. "Did you hear that, Jessica?"

The door opens, and Jessica steps in. "Try not to scream this time," she says, shutting the door.

Laura looks at each of the detectives in turn.

"Start talking, Laura. What do you mean, you weren't in a basement? You described everything you saw there in pretty exact detail. Including a painting of me," Jessica says, walking up to the bed.

Laura looks around in a panic, tries to press the call button hanging next to the bed, but Jessica pulls it out of her reach.

"Talk. Or you're going to find yourself in even deeper trouble."

"They'll kill my family."

"They who?"

"I don't know. They gave me simple instructions . . . I was supposed to make up a story."

"Why didn't you just tell the truth, Laura? They can't find out what you tell us. No one can hear us."

"That's not true!" Laura says tearfully.

"What do you mean?"

"Because they said there's someone close to you who will find out everything."

"What the hell?" Jessica murmurs, and glances at Yusuf, who looks equally confused. "Close to me? Who? A member of the police force?"

"I don't know . . . I swear I don't know."

410

"Why was it so important to you that I not be removed from the case?"

"They said it had to be you."

"It?"

"The one who solves the case."

Jessica knocks a tray from the nightstand to the floor. Then she raises a forefinger at Laura. "You're going to tell us the whole story now! What else did you lie about?"

"The only thing I lied about was the basement. Because they told me to! All I remember was that I was leaving the house . . . And then I came to in a strange place and got instructions from a masked man. He told me they would let me live as long as I stayed calm and did exactly what they told me to."

Jessica sits in the free chair next to the bed and buries her face in her hands. "All right, Laura. You're safe; they can't hurt you." She touches Laura's shoulder, then nods at Yusuf. "Let's go."

"There's one more thing," Laura says.

"What?"

"Something I heard—"

"What did you hear, Laura?"

"That all you saw was the message stamped into the snow, but you didn't see the most important thing."

"Something from the window?"

"Yes."

"Nothing else?"

411

"They said my family is dead if I tell the truth . . . You have to protect my parents, my brother . . ."

"We'll take care of it." Jessica walks past Yusuf to the door and opens it.

"You girls don't seem to get along very well," Teo says with a dry smile as Jessica and Yusuf step into the corridor.

Jessica glares at him sourly. "We have a little job for you."

"I almost feel like telling you to review the chain of command, Ms. Niemi. I take my orders—"

"I'll have these orders faxed to you, with all the necessary stamps. While you're waiting, do me a favor." Jessica steps up to the brawny man, arms folded across her chest. She catches the scent of a citrusy cologne. She used to like the smell, but now it makes her nauseous.

"What do you need, Jessie?"

"First of all, be careful with that patient. We don't trust her. Secondly, confiscate her phone. Tell her it's for security purposes. Make sure it gets to Rasmus Susikoski at HQ. Have someone pick it up."

"Why don't you just take it yourselves?"

"Because we're in a hurry. And because I want to know if Helminen makes a call over the next fifteen minutes."

Teo smiles, revealing a row of straight teeth. "Fine. You can forget the fax. But you could return the favor and go for an ice cream with me someday." He stares intently at Jessica.

"I'd love to. Be sure to bring the wife and kids."

Jessica turns toward the elevators. Yusuf follows along behind like a tentative shadow.

Chapter 89

THE BUZZER SOUNDS, AND NINA GRABS HOLD OF THE wooden door handle. The ornamental stairwell is granite or some other expensive stone; the white veins in its gleaming surface crisscross a light brown background. A few handsome pillars stand between the door and the elevators, emphasizing the lobby's height. Nina glances at the engraved-brass list of tenants. The clinic takes up the first three floors; the administrative offices are on the third.

Nina's soft-soled sneakers don't make the tiniest sound on the sturdy red runners. She strides up the stairs to the third floor and knocks on the oak door, which has clearly been updated to a burglary-resistant model recently. It stands out in distinct contrast to the rest of the hundred-year-old Jugendstil building. Nina notices that, in addition to the offices of the Bättre Morgondag clinic, a foundation of the same name is housed on the floor too.

A moment later, the door is opened by a clean-shaven but incredibly stressed-looking man of about forty wearing a pink dress shirt, a navy tie, and dress trousers. A sizable, more or less heart-shaped birthmark covers his forehead.

413

"Nina Ruska. Police," Nina says, and glances at her watch. The time is nearly two a.m., but CEO Daniel Luoma is still at the office. "Thank you for agreeing to meet at this hour—"

"I took a nap while I was waiting," the man says, extending a hand. "Daniel Luoma."

Nina shakes his hand and steps in. The offices smell of freshly sawn wood and varnish.

"You've remodeled recently?" Nina asks as she follows Luoma down the hallway. Bright lights sparkle at the ceiling.

"Completed just a couple of months ago. We gradually redid the floors, doors, and window frames. Both up here in the offices and in the clinic on the lower floors."

"So the clinic has been around for a while?"

"Yes. We've been in the same location since nineteen sixty-nine. Fifty years, next autumn. The entire building belongs to the Bättre Morgondag Foundation, which also owns the medical clinic."

They have paused at the door to an office, and now Luoma gestures for Nina to go on in. She eyes the neat room: windows giving onto Bulevardi, snow falling in the glow of the streetlamps. Then she enters and seats herself in a leather chair across from Luoma's desk.

"I'll get right to the point. You indicated that both drugs and the equipment needed to administer them are missing from your stocks." Nina rubs her eyes. She's dead tired, but now she just has to keep going. They're close to a breakthrough.

Luoma scratches his bare chin with the nail of his forefinger and then, after a pause that lasts a hair too long, nods.

"And you noticed while you were conducting an inventory?"

"Today, when the police . . . when you contacted us. I performed the inventory myself."

"You didn't trust anyone else to do it?"

"To be honest, if you assign a task like that to someone else, regardless of who they are, you can never be a hundred percent confident in the accuracy of the results."

"So you're saying that any one of your clinic's sixteen employees could have taken them?"

"Theoretically. Fifteen, if you discount me. And I'm the one who noticed and reported the missing items, so I hope I'm not on the list of suspects."

"Are you a doctor?"

"I am. I specialize in psychiatry."

"Could I have a list of all of your employees?" Nina says, and a moment later, she has a fresh printout in her hand. Not a single name on the list rings any bells. Each employee's job title is listed after the name and birth date: five doctors, six nurses, and five people in administration.

Nina looks back up at Luoma, who is now gazing out the window pensively. His left earlobe looks a little funny; it was torn at some point and scarred over.

"Psychiatry . . . Does the Bättre Morgondag clinic specialize exclusively in mental illness?"

"Oh . . . I thought you knew that." Luoma leans forward slowly. "Yes. We specialize in treating psychotic patients."

"A private clinic for psychotic patients? And you have enough business?" Nina says skeptically, still staring at the list of names.

"I suppose you could say unfortunately we do." Luoma crooks his fingers slowly, to almost hypnotic effect. "Let's take one illness that causes psychosis: schizophrenia. In Finland, the prevalence is around one percent. In Helsinki alone, there are several thousand people who suffer from schizophrenia. And some of them, or their loved ones, are prepared to invest in the quality of their care."

"One percent? That sounds pretty high."

"I understand. You're thinking about movies now: Norman Bates, John Nash, delusions, imaginary friends . . . Not all patients suffer equally strong delusions. Sometimes the sole symptoms of the disease are depression and mood swings."

"So medication and medical equipment required for anesthesia have been stolen from the clinic. What do you use them for?" Nina asks, gripping her chair's armrests. Despite the recently completed remodel, the air in the room is in some way sticky.

Luoma looks at his computer screen for a moment and then gives Nina a tired smile. "Now and again, psychotic patients require anesthetization."

"I see." Nina glances mechanically at her watch. "Do you have any idea, any idea at all, which one of your employees might have taken the drugs?"

"No." Luoma looks back at Nina grimly. Or not exactly directly at Nina, but more like through her.

"All right." Nina stands, list in hand.

"Please, sit for just a moment longer," Luoma says calmly, gesturing at the chair.

Nina hasn't let go of the armrest yet. She sits back down without taking her eyes off Luoma. "So you have a suspicion after all?"

"Not exactly. I don't believe the person who took the drugs was an employee."

"Who, then?"

"There's something you ought to know." Luoma shuts his eyes. He has suddenly gone white. "You're investigating the death of Roger Koponen—"

"Yes?"

"He's one of our oldest patients, and what I'm about to say may sound completely insane . . . but I'm almost certain I saw him standing across the street from our clinic today," Luoma says, looking more surprised by his words than Nina is.

Chapter 90

YUSUF TURNS OFF THE EXPRESSWAY AT THE KULOSAARI exit. The clustered gray-and-black clouds have parted for the moon, and a strong wind tosses the crowns of the tall trees. Finnish rap is playing on the radio.

Jessica glances at the text message she just received. She doesn't recognize the number, but the drunken, suggestive contents and the signature kingdick88 leave no doubt as to the sender's identity.

"We *'missed the most important thing'*? What the fuck does that mean?" Yusuf says after a lengthy silence, making the gears shriek by shifting into second mid-ramp when he's still going well over sixty.

"Tech went up to that bedroom to take pictures too," Jessica says, browsing her iPad screen. "I don't see anything out of the ordinary here."

"What if the old lady hadn't noticed the writing?"

"Someone would have noticed it when the skating track was combed by helicopter."

"But were Helminen's abductors specifically referring to Adlerkreutz's window? What we saw from there? The

418

Koponens' house, the house next door, the street, the yards, the hedges . . ."

"The sea, the island opposite . . ."

"Which was scoured with a fine-tooth comb."

"Maybe there was something on the ice? A figure or text we didn't notice?"

"They would have seen that from the chopper."

"Damn it. Is there still a patrol outside the Koponens' house?"

"Yes. I can call in reinforcements if you're nervous."

"I'm not nervous," Jessica says as Yusuf drives past the former Iraqi embassy and toward the shore. "What about what Helminen said about someone close to me?" Jessica says flatly.

"Could just be a scare tactic."

"But what if it's true? Think about it. The writing that appeared in my notebook. The teeth in the sandwiches delivered to the police station. What if these witch hunters have a mole at the station?"

"Eww, creepy." Yusuf pulls over between the Koponen and Adlerkreutz residences. A police van is still there. He opens his door. "OK, let's go give this old lady a heart attack."

Chapter 91

NINA GAPES AT DANIEL LUOMA. HER NOSTRILS ARE PICKING up a pungent smell. Whatever it is, it's getting stronger. Either that or her senses are on high alert.

"Roger Koponen?" she asks, tilting her head.

"When I received the request for information from the police earlier today, I knew right away it had something to do with the murders of Koponen and his wife. I just had this inkling. And then, when I saw Koponen out on the street . . . Could it be possible?"

"Tell me: why was Koponen being treated here?" Nina says, dodging the question that is, considering all that has happened, infinitely relevant.

"Roger Koponen fell into a difficult, long-term psychosis in the late nineteen nineties. At the time, he was diagnosed with paranoid schizophrenia. In other words, he experienced paranoid fantasies that were incredibly strong on some days, on others mild or nonexistent."

"Wait a minute." Nina pulls out her phone. "Can I record this? Purely for investigative reasons."

Luoma shrugs. "I don't see why not."

Nina clicks on the recorder.

"I was Roger's doctor from the start. Generally, these sorts of cases are treated with antipsychotics, with the aim of suppressing activity in the central nervous system. But antipsychotics have numerous harmful side effects that can have a limiting effect on living a normal life. Ever since Bättre Morgondag was established, our treatment path here has been slightly different: in addition to a light-handed approach to medication, we focus on a model of open dialogue based on constant interaction with the patient."

"Dialogue? Does that really help if someone is suffering from severe delusions—"

"It has proven extremely effective."

"OK." Nina pricks up her ears; she thinks she catches sounds coming from the hallway. Almost as if someone were wiping their feet in the entryway.

"Roger Koponen has been a very unusual case in many regards. In terms of open dialogue, the treatment results have been excellent. According to my own reports, the illness has been more or less managed, with the exception of the occasional brief psychotic episode after months, or even years, of absolutely no symptoms at all."

"But why—"

"Koponen has succeeded in living a relatively normal life and keeping his illness a secret, at first from those close to him and later from the public. But his psychotic episodes have always been incredibly strong. As if the illness would claim its due when it remanifested. With interest."

421

"And how is this evident?"

"In addition to schizophrenia, Roger suffered from dissociative identity disorder. The lay term for that is *split personality*, and it's an accurate term to describe Roger's state. When he slides into psychosis, Roger turns into a different person. A totally different personality."

Nina looks at the man sitting across from her, who seems somehow relieved. As if a huge burden had suddenly been lifted from his shoulders.

Goddamn it. Suddenly it all makes sense. "Do you think Roger took the drugs?"

"I hope you believe me. I mean, I know it sounds totally crazy, if he's been murdered."

Nina stands. "I need to make a couple of phone calls. Is there somewhere private I could talk?"

"The entire floor is empty. There's a conference room at the end of the hall."

Nina taps in Erne's number and walks toward the door at the end of the hall. There's no one to be seen, but the lights are blazing in almost every room.

Erne answers in a dry voice. "Nina?"

"I have something big, Erne. I'm talking big big," Nina says, shutting the door behind her.

"Well?"

"I'm with the CEO of Bättre Morgondag. It's the clinic where the drugs used to subdue and anesthetize the victims were stolen from—"

Nina turns and loses her train of thought when she sees the painting hung at the head of the long conference table. What she sees there makes her momentarily forget that Erne is on the line. She curses so softly that he can barely hear her: "What the hell . . . ?"

"Hello? Nina?"

Nina lowers the phone from her ear and tentatively walks along the table toward the painting. Erne's demanding voice carries from the phone, and Nina whispers back something reassuring.

The large painting is about a meter wide and a meter and a half tall and hung in a gilded ornamental frame. It depicts a beautiful woman in a black dress sitting at a coffee table, her thick hair jet-black.

"I'll be damned . . ."

The work could just as easily be of Maria Koponen, Lea Blomqvist, Laura Helminen—or Jessica Niemi. But the face doesn't belong to any of them. It's the face of a beautiful thirty-year-old woman. Strong, pronounced features.

"Erne . . . there's something really damn weird going on." Nina registers that her voice is trembling. She looks at the brass plate screwed to the lower edge of the heavy frame.

CAMILLA ADLERKREUTZ, 1969, CHAIRMAN, BÄTTRE MORGONDAG FOUNDATION.

Chapter 92

THE STRINGS FADE. A MOMENT OF SILENCE FOLLOWS, during which both the performers and the audience seem to hold their breath. Then hands strike together, first one pair, then another, and eventually the clapping spreads through the auditorium like wildfire. The musicians bow. Colombano receives the applause; he raises the hand holding the bow high, then looks back at the orchestra standing behind him like a band of loyal soldiers, ordering them to bow with a wave of his hand. Colombano is like a god whose touch cannot be discerned by the eye, but who controls the musicians like marionettes. People whistle, enraptured, cry *bravo bravissimo*, even though the event was only a competent tourist concert. Colombano seems to relish the attention. The pride and self-satisfaction that spread across his face during the applause are so tangible that they cannot be contrived.

Jessica doesn't take her eyes off of Colombano.

Look at me, my love.

Jessica is sitting in the middle of the auditorium, presumably the only member of the audience who hasn't joined in the effusive applause.

I know you see me.

Colombano leads his troops in a second theatrical bow, then shifts his bow into the hand holding the violin and presses his free fingers to his chest.

Look at me, my love.

And, in the end, it happens: Colombano's gaze rides across the sea of faces, then stops as if speared.

Now you see me.

Colombano looks terror-stricken, as if he has seen a ghost. Even so, the smirk falls away slowly, as if something were preventing him from fully grasping what's going on, from recognizing the face he's seeing. Then he forces his eyes to move on from Jessica and smiles again, this time the corners of his mouth forcibly drawn up to his ears, like those of a sad clown. Colombano descends from the dais with a few brisk steps, strides toward the door at the rear of the hall, and glances once more at Jessica as he passes the middle row.

I'll be waiting for you.

People stream out the doors of the concert hall, burbling in delight at what they just heard. A middle-aged blond man in a beige blazer and jeans glances over his shoulder at Jessica before he vanishes through the doorway. He looks somehow familiar, but Jessica pushes the thought from her mind.

A moment later, the room is quiet. The woman with the sharp cheekbones gathers up the programs, water bottles, and other debris strewn across the chairs. The moment is a repeat of the evening a few months ago when Jessica sat in the auditorium for the first time, listening to the irresistibly gorgeous man play. Just like then, the auditorium first filled and then emptied. Then Colombano disappeared into the back room, and silence fell. Just like then, all Jessica can hear is her own pulse, that and the footfalls of the brusque woman echoing in the deserted concert hall.

"You've been here before," the woman says suddenly in Italian. She has stopped behind Jessica.

Jessica answers without turning around: "I have." She has not spoken with anyone in a long time, and her throat feels dry.

"You were . . . you were with Colombano," the woman continues, gradually entering Jessica's field of vision.

"I was," Jessica says. She doesn't know what to make of this woman, her questions, the empty auditorium, anything. But this time she has no intention of beating a retreat like a wounded animal, of stumbling across the cobblestone road and being rescued by Colombano. Jessica feels like she has the upper hand; she knows she is in the right place tonight. For the first time in months, she feels alive.

The woman brushes a strand of hair from her strong brow, glances uneasily at the closed doors at the rear of the

426

hall, and lowers the large trash bag to her feet. She looks at Jessica apprehensively. "You should go," she finally says. Her voice is not rude; the words sound more like friendly advice.

"I know," Jessica says, not taking her eyes off the other woman.

"I don't think you—"

"I *am* going. Away. Finally. I came to say goodbye to him."

The woman hides her nose between her clasped palms for a moment.

Time out. If you have something to say, say it.

"Listen," the other woman says at long last, and then steps closer. Her voice has dropped to a whisper. "I understand you."

"What do you mean?"

The eyes are now mournful, even pitying. Jessica knows she looks atrocious; not even the beautiful black evening dress can hide the fact that she hasn't had the energy to care for her appearance lately. The woman has seen enough of life to understand that all this is because of Colombano. Jessica is not the first. She is not the only one.

"It's none of my business," the woman says, still glancing toward the door as she seats herself a few chairs away, "but you clearly aren't doing well—"

"You're right. It's not your business."

Everything feels unreal, as if she were observing this conversation from a distance.

The woman sighs but doesn't make any sign of backing down. "Colombano . . . this is what he does. I mean . . . he destroys everything."

"Really?" Jessica asks indifferently. She feels a pain in her knee, but she doesn't let it disturb her concentration. *Of course he does. Do you think I'm an idiot?*

Now the woman looks sad. She knows she's saying too much, revealing something she shouldn't, but she simply can't stop herself: "And you're here because you . . . you want to understand. Forget about this. There's no understanding Colombano. There's something wrong with him. Very, very wrong."

For a moment they sit there in silence. Jessica's eyes relentlessly bore into the woman, who searches for the right words as she looks at the floor.

"What? Did you learn the hard way?" Jessica says without a trace of emotion. She spent the whole morning looking at herself in the mirror. Trying to feel compassion, fear, pity, hope. She wasn't able to capture any of them.

The woman bites her lip as if to keep it from trembling. "No. But I've known him for a long time."

"So his charms didn't work on you?"

The woman shakes her head in short, jerky movements. "You misunderstand. Colombano is my little brother."

At that moment, the door opens, and the echo of heavy footfalls reverberates through the space. The woman stands and scurries off, like a dog caught doing something naughty.

428

Chapter 93

NINA RUSKA ENDS THE CALL. SHE SNAPS A FEW SHOTS of the painting and then hurries back into the corridor. The name Camilla Adlerkreutz sounds vaguely familiar, as if someone had mentioned it during the investigation, but no matter how she racks her brain, she can't remember the context.

She strides toward Luoma's office, but slows down when she hears voices inside. *Luoma is talking to a woman.*

She knocks on the open door, pushes it wide, and discovers a woman in a heavy coat and a beanie sitting across from Luoma. She looks like she's been crying. A shock of sorts is also blazing from Luoma's face.

Luoma hurries to explain: "I'm sorry. This is . . . from the police—"

"Ruska. Nina Ruska."

"That's right. This is my wife, Emma Luoma."

"Hello," Nina says anxiously, and shifts her gaze to the list of names; it's still on the desk in front of the woman, where Nina left it a moment ago. Then she looks at the woman blowing her nose. Her red cheeks are covered in freckles.

"Emma works here as a doctor too," Luoma says awkwardly.

"What about Camilla Adlerkreutz? Is she also a doctor?"

"Yes, but she retired ages ago. Maybe fifteen years ago."

"Was she ever Roger Koponen's doctor?"

"Yes. Camilla founded this clinic."

Nina watches Luoma rub his forehead. She doesn't know what to make of all this. "I have to get going." She's already taking a step toward the door when she realizes she neglected the crying woman. "I'm sorry. Did you have something you wanted to tell me?"

"This might be my fault—" the woman says softly.

"What?"

"Koponen getting his hands on those medications."

"What do you mean?"

"He's extremely persuasive."

"What happened?" Nina asks, returning to the desk. So much is happening right now that it's hard to keep her thoughts straight.

Emma Luoma turns her bloodshot eyes to Nina. "Some time ago, Roger showed up and said he needed something. That I should open the door to the dispensary and look the other way for a second."

"Something?"

"I thought he was talking about sedatives. Roger took them in addition to alcohol. He knew what he was looking for. And I trusted he would just take a few pills for his own use. But never in a million years did I suspect—"

"I don't understand. Why didn't you just write him a prescription?"

"Because they were having an affair," Luoma interjects abruptly. He buries his face in his hands, then sighs deeply and continues more steadily. "There. It's out now. My wife and Roger Koponen were seeing each other. Contrary to every damn professional code of conduct, moral stricture, and marriage vow."

"Daniel . . ." Emma wails softly.

"Telling half-truths isn't going to fly, Emma. We have to be honest with the police."

Nina draws the stuffy air into her lungs. She should head back to the station and take Emma Luoma with her. The doctor needs to be interrogated thoroughly.

"I know where he's hiding," Emma blurts out.

"What? Where?"

"Roger has a hideout in Laajasalo. Another house—it's not in his name. He writes there. And meets women."

"Do you know the address?"

"No . . . but I've been there a few times."

"Would you be able to show us where it is?"

"Of course." Emma reaches across the desk and tries to take her husband's hand, but he doesn't respond. "You said it yourself, darling. No half-truths."

For a moment, the couple hold back their tears.

"Is Roger mixed up in those murders? Did his kill his wife?" Emma finally asks.

Nina doesn't respond; she is furiously considering her next move. "OK. I want you to show me the other house. Right now." She starts wrapping her scarf around her neck

"Now?"

"Now."

"All right," Emma says, wiping her eyes on her sleeve.

Luoma rises from his chair. "I'm coming with you."

"Fine. Put on your coats," Nina says as she brings up Erne's number.

Chapter 94

ERNE TAKES LONG STRIDES DOWN THE CORRIDOR, ARMS squeezed against his sides. It makes him look like a flightless bird more than anything, but right now any movement in his chest or shoulder muscles sends pain shooting through his lungs.

He stops between two interrogation rooms, thinks about which man is being questioned in which, then knocks on one of the doors. A moment later, the door is opened by Mikael, who seems peppy, considering the time of day and the ongoing situation. Mikael draws the door shut behind him, but before he does, Erne catches a glimpse of Kai Lehtinen: a bald man with a gaunt face who looks as creepy as Erne imagined.

"Get anything?" Erne asks.

"Not yet. I told Nina you might have been right. Maybe we should have kept them under surveillance for a while longer." Mikael speaks softly even though the door is soundproofed.

"What's done is done. Let's do our best to make the most of the situation. Besides, it looks like Nina might have found something over on Bulevardi." Erne glances back to make sure no one is listening. "Press the jerkoff a little longer. I'll see you in the conference room in fifteen minutes." He gives Mikael a pat on the shoulder.

Mikael grunts. "Sounds mysterious."

"And hey, Micke." Erne turns back around. "Does the name Camilla Adlerkreutz say anything to you?"

"Huh? Adlerkreutz? Bunsdorf? All we're missing are the Romanoffs."

"Does it?"

"Can't say that it does. Who is she?"

"I'll tell you soon," Erne says, and continues on his way. He accelerates to full speed but slows down again before he steps into the open-plan office, where half a dozen data miners sit at their desks.

Erne walks over to a youngish woman staring intently at her screen, iPhone to her ear. He lowers a printout to her desk; it's of the photograph Nina took of the painting.

"Find out if this woman is still alive and where she lives."

"She looks like a witch."

"That's exactly why."

Chapter 95

RASMUS SUSIKOSKI LETS HIS CHIN REST ON HIS CROSSED
fingers and studies the collage of photographs and text
snippets arranged on the wall. The conference room is still.
There's not the tiniest hint of Mikael's gum chomping,
Nina's sighing, Yusuf's whistling, Erne's raspy breathing,
or Jessica's fingernail drumming. He is finally alone. He's
always been happiest by himself. Even at law school, he
preferred to delve into his books and leave the strutting
and socializing to those for whom it came more naturally.
He's a lone wolf. He has never felt like he belonged, even
at work.

Rasmus knows he's different from the others in a lot of
ways: an introverted bookworm who can never manage to
open his mouth when he ought to. He has always been
struck dumb at those very moments when verbalizing his
thoughts would take life in the desired direction. It's the
greatest tragedy of his life. He has often wondered if his
lack of success with women is the reason for or a conse-
quence of this. Probably both.

There's a knock at the door.

"Hey, Susikoski."

Riikka Woodward steps in to the room, and Rasmus' heart skips a beat. Not because the investigative assistant has new information regarding the case, but because Rasmus, emboldened by a few shots of candy-pink liquor, approached her with romantic intentions during a team-building cruise the unit took last October. And got a bitter smackdown in return.

"Yes?" The simple response almost catches in Rasmus' throat.

"The report from the water utility came in."

"Anything interesting?" Rasmus takes off his glasses; the temples feel sweaty in his fingertips. He rubs his eyes, and for a moment, the room looks blurry. It's what he was hoping for. Maybe Riikka won't be able to see him now either.

"I looked for consumption spikes of about twenty-five hundred liters. One challenge is that most of the old apartment buildings and homes in the area have old-fashioned meters, the kind that is read once or twice a year. The meters with remote capability that upload information directly to the cloud—"

"Well? Did you find any?"

"Yes. A cottage in Kaitalahti. Water consumption about zero otherwise, but five days ago, it was a serious deluge. About three, four thousand liters."

"What—"

"And guess whose name is on the mortgage? Maria Koponen."

Rasmus puts his glasses back on. "You're kidding. How the heck could we have missed that?" Suddenly it feels hard to sit still; Rasmus stands. "Unless a pipe burst . . ."

"And was repaired the same day—"

". . . that's the tub we're looking for. There's not a doubt about it. We have to get a SWAT team out there."

Rasmus opens the door and lets out an incredulous laugh.

"What's so funny?"

"Now we're going to get those assholes. And it's thanks to Micke's idea, goddamn it."

Chapter 96

NINA TURNS UP THE HEATER AS THE CAR CROSSES THE bridge between Herttoniemi and Laajasalo. The tension between the couple in the back seat is palpable; it's like an enormous iceberg that refuses to melt despite global warming. Nina looks at the teary woman through the rearview mirror. It's incomprehensible to her that a psychiatrist would not only enter into a sexual relationship with a schizophrenic patient, but would also help that patient steal lethal drugs from her place of employment. Regardless of what happens, Emma Luoma's career in medicine is, in all likelihood, over. The marriage is tougher to predict. But things don't look so good in that department either.

Nina glances at the navigator on her phone. She's supposed to meet two vans of SWAT officers armed to the teeth at the Neste service station in Laajasalo. The convoy will continue from there to Koponen's presumed hideout, with Emma Luoma showing them the way. They're taking no more risks. From now on, they're going in hard.

Erne's name appears on the phone. Nina removes the phone from its stand; she doesn't want to use the hands-free function with the Luomas listening in the back seat. "Hey, Erne, I'm almost at the rendezvous."

Aside from one oncoming Defense Forces van, the road is deserted.

"Can your passengers hear me?"

"No."

"Good. We have some new information. The water utility found a spike in consumption in Kaitalahti. A few days ago they turned on the taps and went to town. It's some sort of summer cabin, and it's in Maria Koponen's name. Based on the Maps' street view, the structure's profile is a match: stone foundation, narrow windows at ground level. We got a blueprint from the city. The cabin has a big basement, and it's on the water."

"Fuck."

"It has to be the same one our good doctor is taking you to."

"It does. But should we still confirm?"

"What I want you to do is leave the Luomas with a police escort at the service station. We'll go in with the SWAT team and raid the cabin at Kaitalahti, and if we don't find anything there, we'll reassess the situation. It's better not to bring civilians if it turns out to be a crime scene."

"Roger."

Nina glances in the rearview mirror again. The doctors are now holding each other's hands. Forgiveness is a formidable power. Especially in moments like these, when chaos is on a rampage, drowning sorrows and troubles that would otherwise feel overwhelming.

Chapter 97

ERNE ENDS THE CALL AND CLICKS OPEN A TEXT MESSAGE that arrived just a moment earlier. It's from Jessica.

```
Helminen has been feeding us lies.
We're going to check on something.
I'll call you after.
```

Rasmus is sitting at the conference room with his laptop open in front of him.

"Fuck me," Erne says, plopping down next to Rasmus. "Does Micke know Nina is headed to Kaitalahti?"

"Not yet. He's still taking turns interrogating those two assholes. Did something new come up?"

Erne shakes his head and digs his lozenges out of his pocket. He watches Rasmus tap in www.battre-morgondag.fi and bring up the medical clinic's website.

"Something about this place is seriously wrong if outpatients can get their hands on deadly drugs."

"That woman is going to be facing charges for pulling that stunt." Erne shuts his eyes. He hopes from the bottom

440

of his heart that Roger Koponen is at the cottage, and this hellish snarl will begin to unravel. He considers the scale of the case, how small they all are in this universe. How ultimately minor the earthly destruction those sick assholes have managed to cause. And how they will die in the end too, fade into oblivion. When this case is closed, Erne is going to throw in the towel and take sick leave from which he will never return.

Erne feels a jab in the ribs; Rasmus' voice is little more than a whisper. "Erne . . . look."

"What?" Erne opens his eyes. He can tell he was only seconds from falling asleep. The disease has sapped his strength, his capacity to tolerate exhaustion. "What is it now?" he repeats grumpily.

Rasmus has opened the website's Staff tab, which features photographs of the Bättre Morgondag staff. He's holding his forefinger next to the face of a dark-haired woman with a warm smile.

"Doesn't Emma Luoma look familiar . . . ?"

Erne focuses his eyes on the screen, which Rasmus turns toward him.

"Now that you mention it . . . maybe a little. We've seen quite a few women who look like that over the last twenty-four hours." Erne falls silent and looks at Rasmus. "Wait . . . What are you getting at?"

For a second, Rasmus stares at the photograph as if he were waiting for the Emma Luoma staring out of the screen to blink first. Then he jams his thumbnail between his teeth. "I'm pretty sure that ... Wait," he says, and stands. Rasmus walks over to the large board, where a mind map of photographs, call data, meetings, and contacts has been patched together.

"Who are you looking for?"

"Goddamn it, Erne. If I'm right ... goddamn it ..."

Erne watches alertly as Rasmus takes down a photograph from the board. Then he walks back to the table on unsteady feet and holds it against the screen, next to the photograph of Emma Luoma. Rasmus is comparing a close-up of the woman crushed to death by stones to the neutrally smiling face on the website.

Erne looks at the two images side by side. At first, the idea seems too impossible to be true. It's so pivotal that he has to start rebuilding the entire chain of events from the end.

"Emma Luoma is Mrs. X, the victim from Haltiala," Rasmus says.

A pungent smell assaults Erne's nostrils. Rasmus has started to sweat again.

"She was never reported missing," Erne mutters. Silence. They both know what this means. Even so, seconds pass in utter paralysis.

Erne reaches for his phone with both hands. Nina has to be at the service station by now, where the SWAT team is waiting for her. She has to be safe.

"Because ... her husband is dead too," Rasmus says in shock, and looks at the take-away bag lying on the table. *Mr. X's teeth. Daniel Luoma's teeth.*

442

"The couple Nina met were not doctors."

The seconds that pass in the silent room feel like an eternity. A pop-up window advertising Nicorette gum appears on the screen, and Erne has the sudden urge to smoke.

"Dear Christ Almighty," he says, phone at his ear. He jumps up. "Nina's not answering her phone."

Chapter 98

JESSICA RAPS INSISTENTLY ON THE DOOR. YUSUF IS standing behind her. It feels bad, dragging an old woman out of bed at three in the morning, but right now they don't have any choice.

Jessica looks at the dark green door and its bright white frame. The paint job looks surprisingly fresh, almost brand-new. The big ornamental wooden house on the crest of the hill is like something out of a different time and place. It has to be one of the oldest houses still standing on Kulosaari, an evocation of the past. Through the small window, Jessica sees a light come on in the entryway. Then she hears a fearful voice through the door.

"Who is it?"

"Police. Detectives Niemi and Pepple. We were here last night."

For a moment, it seems as if nothing is happening. Then the door slowly opens, and the old woman is standing in the entryway, looking scared and sleepy, in a light blue robe with a nightgown in the same shade visible underneath.

"I remember you," she says but doesn't step aside. The cold wind tousles her curled bangs.

"Mrs. Adlerkreutz, may we come in? It's important."

"What's wrong?"

"May we?" Jessica repeats as calmly as possible, and nods toward the hall inside.

"For goodness' sake, you certainly chose quite a time," the old woman huffs, then gestures for Jessica to come in.

"I'm sorry to have to wake you up like this, but it's urgent."

"I daresay," Mrs. Adlerkreutz says as Yusuf pulls the door shut behind him.

Jessica is about to step off the doormat when Mrs. Adlerkreutz points at her shoes and wags a finger. "Could you please remove your shoes?"

"I . . . Of course," Jessica replies with a frown. The night before, Mrs. Adlerkreutz's views on the matter had been completely the opposite.

"I need to take another look in your bedroom."

"You can't see the text from there anymore—"

"If you don't mind, I'd like to take another look anyway." Jessica pulls off her other shoe and sets the pair side by side on the doormat. She is enveloped in the smell of old wood and damp.

"I'll wait here," Yusuf says, hands on his hips. He glances at his shoes; he's too lazy to unlace them just to lace them back up again.

"Fine," Jessica says, and turns toward Mrs. Adlerkreutz, who seems a little put off as she belts the robe more tightly around her waist.

"For goodness' sake. I suppose we'd better go upstairs, then."

"Have you made any progress?" she asks as they shuffle up the stairs at a leisurely pace. So leisurely that Jessica has time to study the photographs hanging in the stairwell. Just like upstairs, the majority are black-and-white group portraits.

"You can put your mind at ease, ma'am. This is one case we're going to solve," Jessica says, herself unsure why she wants to make empty promises to the old woman. The stairs creak beneath her feet, and she hears the woman yawn as she climbs one slow tread at time.

Finally, Jessica sees light beaming through the open door at the end of the hall.

"So you wanted to have another look at the Koponens' house . . ." Mrs. Adlerkreutz mutters.

"I just need a moment at the bedroom window. Then we'll let you get back to sleep," Jessica says, following the doddering woman toward her bedroom.

"All right, be my guest. I haven't made the bed, for understandable reasons."

Jessica smiles at Mrs. Adlerkreutz and enters the bedroom. She walks slowly to the window and lowers her fingers to the frame.

They missed the most important thing . . .

Chapter 99

THE WHITE WALLS OF ERNE'S OFFICE FEEL LIKE THEY'RE closing in on the desk where he's sitting, a red radiophone to his ear. It has a direct link to a special telephone network reserved for authorities; with its long antenna, it resembles the first heavy-duty cell phones of the nineties. The sweat dripping down his cheeks signals that the combination of stress and the inflammation festering in his body is sending his temperature up again. It must be over 38 at the moment. It has to be. Not that it makes a difference anymore. Now that he has received his death sentence, he can stop taking his temperature.

"How do you want to proceed?" The low male voice at the other end of the line belongs to the SWAT team leader. Nina, who Erne a few minutes ago designated the officer in charge of the operation in the field, didn't arrive at the rendezvous and isn't answering her phone.

For a few seconds, Erne stares out at the sleeping construction site surrounded by a siege of construction cranes, which will come back to life in a few hours. He grips the phone and glances at Rasmus, who looks back at

447

him apprehensively from the other side of the desk, arms folded across his chest and fingers buried in the folds of his sweater. Erne should be sending the SWAT team out to look for Nina. She can't have gotten far in her red Škoda.

"You have the address?" Erne says. He registers that his voice is trembling; the decision is the most difficult one of his career.

"Yes."

"Proceed according to the plan. Report to me in real time."

"Roger. Over and out."

Erne lowers the radio to the table and grabs his mobile phone.

"Rasse, I need you to file a report on a missing police officer immediately. I want any and all patrols available to be looking for Nina's Škoda, which is probably in Laajasalo. Nina did manage to communicate that she was in the immediate vicinity of the rendezvous."

"Roger." Rasmus pops up from his chair more quickly than one might think possible, based on his appearance.

"And, Rasse, have Micke come in here. He gets to go out into the field."

Rasmus nods and vanishes through the doorway.

Erne presses the phone to his ear again and listens to the dial tone for a second. *Goddamn it, Jessica! What the fuck is going on?* He rubs his chest to slow his galloping pulse. He brings up Yusuf's number. No response.

Something is seriously awry.

448

Take it easy. One of them will call you back any minute now. Jessica and Yusuf are together. They aren't in any danger . . .

Why the hell didn't he stick more firmly to his decision to keep Jessica home and under guard until this unprecedented murder spree was solved?

Jessica is going to call any minute. Or Yusuf.

"Erne? I reported the missing officer, and the patrols have been alerted," Rasmus says from the doorway. "A roadblock is being set up on the bridge leading from Laajasalo to Herttoniemi."

"Good. What about Micke?"

"I didn't see him—"

"Find him, goddamn it!" Erne's growl ends in a cough. Rasmus vanishes into the corridor again.

Erne wiggles his fingers over his keyboard, then enters bättre morgondag helsinki into the search engine and clicks the first result. He opens the Staff tab and scrolls to first Daniel and then Emma Luoma. Waves of nausea roll through him.

The Luomas are dead. Daniel Luoma was driven to Savonlinna the day before last in Torsten Karlstedt's trunk. Alive, as the medical examiner has confirmed. They stopped Sanna Porkka's car, set her and Daniel on fire. Meanwhile, someone sowed his DNA around Koponen's waterfront house. Emma Luoma was abducted, probably at the same time as her husband, and taken to Haltiala. In the end, whoever these people are entered the Bättre

449

Morgondag offices on Bulevardi with the couple's keys, called the police, and met Nina. And now—

Everything has gone to hell.

Erne opens the About Us tab and reads the brief history presented there.

```
Specializing in the treatment and
therapy of psychotic patients, Bättre
Morgondag . . . operated by a founda-
tion of the same name established in
1969 . . . founder and chair, psychi-
atrist Camilla Adlerkreutz, MD, PhD
. . . Alternative, drug-free forms
of treatment . . . a model of open
dialogue.
```

The comprehensive history is studded with a dozen black-and-white photographs. The topmost one is of the first clinic, Villa Morgon. Then a portrait of the foundation's founder dating from the nineteen sixties. Her face looks exactly the same as it does in the painting; only the background is different.

"Six minutes to target," a voice blares from the radio-phone.

Erne acknowledges receipt of the message and buries his face in his fingers

Chapter 100

THEY MISSED THE MOST IMPORTANT THING . . .

What the hell am I supposed to see from here?

Jessica bites her lip and tries to concentrate. She is exhausted, but she'll stand here staring out this damn window until dawn if it's going to help them solve the case. The *Malleus Maleficarum* stomped into the roof of the Koponens' house is nothing more than a wan memory in the wake of above-zero temperatures, a fresh layer of snow, and the technical investigators, like graffiti someone tried to scrub off and paint over. She sees the street, the surrounding houses, the Koponens' large lot. The frozen sea, the islands hundreds of meters out. *What the hell am I not getting?*

Jessica looks at the street outside the Koponens' house, where she gave chase to the murderer in white coveralls the night before. The hedge. She imagines the horned figure on the ice raising his hand to greet her from the darkness.

Gradually, Jessica grasps that the light in the room is preventing her from seeing clearly. Everything outside mingles distractingly with the reflection of Mrs. Adlerkreutz's bedroom: the bed, mirror, the writing desk, the chair. The

Persian rug, the small chandelier, Mrs. Adlerkreutz standing in the doorway. Jessica herself.

"Excuse me, ma'am. Could you please turn off the lights?" Jessica says in passing, and tries to focus her vision out the window.

A few seconds pass, but nothing happens.

"Could you please turn off the lights, just for a moment?"

Jessica takes another look at the old woman's reflection in the window. Then at herself. The mirror image is blurry, a bad copy who only remotely resembles a woman named Jessica von Hellens. A woman who doesn't exist. Her eye sockets are like two enormous black saucers, deep wells that lead to some strange dark place. She sees horns sprouting from her head. And then she sees a girl lying motionless on the bed in the hotel room in Murano, every single cell of her body on fire, from her fingertips to her toes. It's as if she were lying in the middle of an inferno. She stares at the ceiling, the stucco detailing, and hates herself and her life. The fact that she has a vast fortune doesn't make it the least bit more tolerable, maybe just the opposite. Everything she touches turns to shit. Jessica feels the steak knife from room service at her wrist—the knowledge that she could put an end to all of this at any moment is a relief. All that's needed is a tiny movement, and she could rest forever in this suite of a mediocre hotel in this city that stinks like a fish market.

Tears well up in Jessica's eyes. Not from sorrow or poignancy but fear.

She now understands that she has come to this room to see her own reflection. Just as her mother had urged her to do in the dream. She is looking in the mirror.

Jessica slowly turns around and lowers her hand to her holster. Mrs. Adlerkreutz is still standing in the doorway, hands crossed over her breast. She is not looking at Jessica. She is looking around the bedroom in apparent satisfaction. Then Mrs. Adlerkreutz lowers her eyelids, inhales the old-house smells of wood and tar.

Jessica hears her phone ring, but she doesn't answer. She knows she needs two free hands now. She has to get out of here. Yusuf is still downstairs.

Jessica gulps and takes a step closer to the old woman. "We're going now."

"You're just like your mother." Now Mrs. Adlerkreutz smiles almost tenderly.

Jessica senses the goosebumps form on her skin, feels her heart skip a beat and then compensate by pounding like crazy. "What?" she mumbles, unlocking her holster.

The old woman is no longer frail and sleepy. "You have it too."

"What are you talking about?"

"Your brain. It's unique. It's why you are the way you are."

"I'm leaving now. Yusuf!" Jessica shouts hoarsely, but there's no response from downstairs. "Yusuf!" she shouts again, more loudly this time, and steps toward Mrs. Adlerkreutz.

453

Then footfalls carry from somewhere. But they aren't coming from the stairwell; they're coming from somewhere closer. A door creaks.

"Theresa was ill," Mrs. Adlerkreutz says as Jessica wraps her hand around the pistol.

"Yusuf!"

"And even so, she was still my favorite pupil." The old woman lets out a little laugh.

"What the hell are you talking about?" Jessica's voice is trembling. She aims the gun at Mrs. Adlerkreutz and the doorway behind her. *My favorite pupil.* The photographs from the corridor and the stairwell crash into Jessica's consciousness. Her grip on the pistol tightens. "Move!"

At the same instant, two figures appear in the doorway. Jessica can make out curved horns in the darkened hallway, and a wail escapes her lips. The gun becomes an unsteady extension of her hand as she backs up to the window.

"Yusuf!"

"Yusuf isn't coming," Mrs. Adlerkreutz says as one of the men steps past her and into the room. "And that pistol of yours . . . you might as well lower it. It has been rendered harmless."

Jessica feels panic wash over her; her ears roar, and her vision blurs. Then she feels the pain. She aims her pistol at the leg of the slowly approaching horned monster, but the trigger won't move: the firing pin is jammed. *What the hell? Micke checked the gun.* The pistol falls to her feet. She feels a large man's arms around her and a wet towel on her face. As she struggles with every ounce of strength she can muster, she senses herself gradually sinking somewhere deep: into an ever-murkier pond impenetrable to the sun's rays.

Everything's fine, sweetheart.

Chapter 101

ERNE LOOKS AT HIS MUTE PHONE AND LOCKS HIS FINGERS behind his neck. Nina's life is in danger, and even if half the Helsinki police force is going to be looking for her in a second, something inside Erne tells him this isn't going to end well. Soon he's going to have the privilege of sitting in the conference room, explaining to Mikael why he sent Nina out for a drive with two murderers. This is the second time in forty-eight hours when Erne has encouraged someone to give a murderer a ride. *And where the fuck is Jessica?* He hasn't heard a peep out of her since her text message.

"Two minutes to target," a voice says through the radiophone on the desk.

"Roger." Erne swallows a few times.

Rasmus appears in the doorway. The look of concern on his face has turned into something resembling bewilderment.

"What's wrong?"

"I can't find Micke—"

"What do you mean, you can't find him?"

"He . . . he left."

Erne pulls his glasses from his furrowed brow. "What are you talking about?"

Rasmus takes a few steps until he's standing in the middle of the room, hands on his hips. His voice wavers uncertainly. "That's what I was told. That Micke left with Karlstedt and Lehtinen in cuffs. Apparently they were on their way to the elevators. Downstairs, I was told they exited the building. With their coats on—"

"Where the fuck would Micke be taking our prime suspects in the middle of the night?"

"Maybe he heard Nina's in trouble? Maybe he went to find her."

"And took the suspects with him? That doesn't make any sense. Besides, where would he have heard about Nina? Did you tell him?"

"I didn't even find him . . . Maybe Nina called him directly?"

"This is bizarre. I'm going to call him."

Rasmus shakes his head. "I already did."

There's a knock at the door, and Riikka Woodward peers in, a pen between her teeth. "Here's the information you asked for, Erne," she says, and hands the paper to Rasmus, who has extended his hand. Rasmus takes a few steps toward Erne but then stops, frowning, as he reads the document.

"Camilla Adlerkreutz? The director of the foundation?"

"I asked Woodward to find out . . . What does it say?" Erne is now on his feet, leaning against the desk with his full weight.

Woodward disappears into the corridor, and Rasmus hands the piece of paper to Erne.

"That her address is in Kulosaari. This is right across from the Koponens' house."

"Just a second . . ." Erne dives back into his chair and grabs his mouse. He pulls up one of the photographs from the foundation's history. It shows an old ornamental wooden house. *Villa Morgon.*

Erne turns the screen to Rasmus. "Could this be the same house Jessica and Yusuf entered to see the Koponens' roof—"

"The address is a match."

"But . . ." Erne has risen to his feet again. He reaches for his gray sweater, pulls it on, and then slides his arms into the sleeves of his dark green coat. "I asked Micke a little while ago if the name Adlerkreutz meant anything to him. He said he'd never heard it before."

A signal echoes from the radiophone. Erne picks it up and raises it to his chest. *Point to HQ.*

"But Micke got a list of all the neighbors from Yusuf," Rasmus mutters.

"Maybe it slipped his mind."

"Or else . . ."

Point to HQ.

"I hope that's what happened, Rasse," Erne says, and raises the radiophone to his mouth. "This is HQ."

Chapter 102

JESSICA OPENS HER EYES TO FLAMES FLICKERING IN THE gloom. She can sense damp in her nostrils, mingled with the pungent odor of burning fuel. Aside from the whisper of the flames blazing at the tips of the wooden posts, the room is utterly still.

Her eyelids feel heavy. But she doesn't hurt anywhere. She feels as light as a butterfly resting on a lily pad. A few meters away, a large red blanket is spread across the floor, covering something underneath.

"Jessica von Hellens," a woman's voice says behind her.

Jessica replies almost against her will. "What?"

"Welcome."

Jessica can't see anyone. She tries to look and discovers that her head is locked in a wooden neck support that prevents her from turning her head.

De primo, fratribus et sororibus.

Jessica hooks her fingers; her wrists press against restraints.

Meanwhile, a group of half-naked people appears. They walk past her to either side of the chair she's trapped in.

There are four, five, six, eight of them. They're wearing black capes; hoods cover their faces. A quiet rustle echoes as the bare feet shuffle across the stone floor.

Now Jessica realizes she's wearing a black evening dress. A pair of high heels has been placed next to her feet on the floor. Her thoughts begin to clear. Her breathing feels shallow; the air catches in her throat. "What's going on?"

"Be still, Jessica," a woman's voice says.

Jessica stares at the thin, naked body; the drooping breasts are streaked with fat blue veins.

Then the woman raises her frail hand and slides back her hood. The smile revealed under the disguise is tender and a touch absentminded. Just like a moment ago in the bedroom.

"I'm not sure if we've ever been properly introduced. My name is Camilla Adlerkreutz." The woman takes a step closer to the chair Jessica is sitting in. The others remain standing in place. Jessica allows her eyes to wander across the naked bodies. The group consists of both men and women. "You must have many questions."

Jessica's tongue feels heavy, and there's a strange industrial taste in her mouth. Jessica closes her eyes. Everything is confusing. It's hard to pin down her thoughts.

"I want to leave," she says softly. "I want to see Erne."

"I know we don't have much time. My own time in particular is running out," Camilla Adlerkreutz says, then steps aside so Jessica can see across the room. A painting of a beautiful raven-haired woman hangs on the far wall. "Do you see it? It could just as easily be of you."

She's right; the resemblance is astonishing.

"But it's not you, Jessica. It's me." Some of the warmth in her voice has dissipated.

"I want to leave," Jessica whispers.

"You want to leave. The problem is, Jessica, that you don't know what you want. You're just like your mother." Camilla Adlerkreutz takes a few steps toward Jessica and stiffly kneels before her. "She was a beautiful, unspoiled soul, but she was also a stubborn bitch who turned her back on us."

"I don't know what you're talking about," Jessica says. She realizes her breathing has grown rapid and shallow.

"Of course not, sweetheart. How could you . . . ? Like your mother, you have been blessed with a mind of extraordinary qualities. With a brain that simply refuses to be ruled by banalities. With understanding that repels society's force-fed truths." Camilla Adlerkreutz raises her hand theatrically to her forehead. Her movements are fluid; the frail, wrinkled hand rises into the air and then returns to stroke the gray hair.

"My mother?"

"You still see her, don't you? Late at night when you can't sleep? We—me and my sisters and brothers here . . . The actions we have taken over the past two days may strike you as heartless, but, in reality, all we want is a better tomorrow. That is what we represent. *A better tomorrow.* Every single

461

one of the brothers and sisters you see standing before you has sworn to protect this ideology to the bitter end."

"What the hell—" Jessica stammers.

"Would you care to take over from here, *frater*?"

Camilla Adlerkreutz shuts her eyes, and the man standing at the far right edge reaches for his hood and slips it back, revealing his face. Although she has never seen him in the flesh, Jessica recognizes him.

Roger Koponen's pupils are as big as plates, and his face is bright red. He looks as if he might explode at any second.

Chapter 103

ERNE HEARS THE MAN'S WORDS BUT DOESN'T WANT TO understand them. "Please repeat."

"The target is empty."

The words echo in Erne's ears. The radiophone mouthpiece smells of dried spit, and Erne realizes his heart is pounding. "What about the tub?"

"There is no tub. The basement is full of junk."

"What the hell—"

"At first glance, I'd say this isn't the house we're looking for."

"But it has to be," Erne says softly.

"We'll take a look around the immediate vicinity," the voice says over the radio.

"Roger."

Erne lowers the radiophone to the table; his heart is beating as fast as a baby chick's. The phone on the table rings again. *Internal line.* Another number appears on the screen of his mobile phone: Lönnqvist from the Police

Board. "What the fuck is going on here?" Erne mutters, too distracted to answer either call.

"I think I know," Rasmus says with a frown. He's engrossed in his own phone.

"What now?"

"There's a new video online . . . on Instagram this time." Phone in hand, Rasmus walks over to Erne.

"What the hell is this?"

They see a dimly lit hospital bed with a beautiful dark-haired woman lying in it.

"Is that—"

"It's Laura Helminen."

A constant stream of new comments is appearing at the bottom of the screen.

"Is this live?" Erne asks in a hushed voice. The blare of the phones ringing in his office seems to be coming from somewhere in the distance.

"Yes . . . *at malleusmaleficarum* . . ."

"Someone's transmitting a live stream from Helminen's room. What happened to the security at the door, god-damn it?" Then Erne remembers the message Jessica sent him. *Helminen has been feeding us lies.*

He points at the figure at the bottom of the screen. "Are those . . . What's that number?"

"The number of people watching right now."

"What the hell . . . ?"

Tens of thousands of people are watching. #malleus-maleficarum. There are hundreds of comments, most of them in English.

"The comments are responses to something she said at the beginning of the video."

"Can you rewind—"

But at that instant a muscular man in a dark suit appears at the bottom of the screen. He stops next to the bed.

"That's the guard—"

"Shh. Listen."

Unfortunately, I'm going to have to confiscate your phone.

Why?

Orders. Where is it?

Over there, on the shelf.

The woman points directly at the camera, and the security guard turns around.

"Teo . . ." Erne whispers. He knows Teo from ministry gigs. Competent guy, even though Jessica thinks he's a cocky asshole. Teo calmly takes a few steps toward the phone.

"What the hell?" Rasmus whispers.

It takes Erne a second to understand what he's referring to. Laura is not lying in her bed anymore; she has crept up behind Teo. Her snarled black hair hangs in her eyes. "What is she—"

Erne raises his hand to his mouth.

It happens fast. Teo's hand is reaching for the phone when the movement abruptly stops. The look on his face turns from self-confident to confused, and an instant later dark red liquid starts spurting from his neck.

And then the only one standing in the shot is Laura Helminen, a cold smirk on her face.

Malleus Maleficarum.

Chapter 104

FOR A MOMENT, THE ROOM IS SO STILL THAT JESSICA can once again hear the flicker of the flames dancing at the tips of the wooden torches. The smell of fuel reminds her of childhood, of asphalt shimmering in the heat.

"Mater pythonissam," Roger Koponen says with a bow to the old woman. Then he turns his shocked eyes to Jessica. "Everything has a purpose, Jessica. A second ago, we uploaded a succinct but profound manifesto that expresses our concerns about contemporary society and the ways in which it has been degraded." He speaks without intonation, like someone reading a speech from paper.

Jessica feels her body go limp again, as if a toxin were pumping through her body. "You . . . killed your wife?" Jessica says, and gulps. Her throat feels numb.

"Maria sealed her own fate. Her work represented resistance against freedom of the mind and a better tomorrow. I had no say in it. I didn't even know it had to happen. I would have done everything in my power to prevent it;

after all, Maria was my wife . . . But, in retrospect, it all seems perfectly obvious."

Jessica tries to wrench free of her bonds. She tenses her muscles as hard as she can, but her hands and ankles are firmly shackled to the wooden chair.

"Look, Jessica. Everything has already been written. Just like Roger's books. It has all been plain from the start," Camilla Adlerkreutz says.

"But . . . why?" Jessica asks. Fear has broken through the sensation-numbing medication; she feels a tear roll down her cheek.

"This may all feel a little perplexing, Jessica dear . . ." Camilla gestures to the row of people standing behind Roger Koponen. "You don't actually have to understand what it is we hope to achieve; delving into our teachings requires years of intense study. Roger's disgust with contemporary society and its restrictions inspired him to write the most engrossing of stories, stories infused with our ideology and practices. Tens of millions of people around the world have read them and are now unwittingly open to our way of thinking. It would be downright foolish to not take advantage of this set of circumstances. Thanks to Roger's books, we have scores of possible new believers, and we must intensify the learning process. Do you have any idea how many people are discussing the Better Tomorrow movement as we speak? *Malleus Maleficarum.* The hammer of the witches is a matter of burning interest in millions of Western households now. Missionary work is incredibly effortless these days; all it requires is knowing how to wield all the instruments at one's disposal."

"But—"

"The secular world we live in today tries to silence those to whom God has granted the gift of an open mind. And as we know, a genuine ability to think critically and creatively, to see the forest for the trees, is a threat to organized society. Society wants to label these individuals as crazy: diagnoses are developed for them, and they are given drugs that slow their thinking. My life's work has been to ensure that their potential is harnessed, instead of them being left to rot in hospitals and neglected in the homes of loved ones. I've never treated sick people, Jessica. I have, of course, played my role and employed terms society embraces. But only to be able to conduct my work in peace. No, I have not treated the sick, because these people, all of you standing here around me, are anything but sick. You are a ray of light in the midst of a chaotic hell overrun by narrow-minded elitists."

Jessica tastes salt: a tear in the corner of her mouth. The old woman's bony hand wipes it away. Jessica feels her breath catch. She feels a tingle in her back and tiny bursting lightning bolts in the nerve endings of her leg muscles. Now she sees a gleam in the glow of the burning torches. It's a dagger.

"Am I the seventh victim? The last witch?" Jessica whispers.

"You?" Camilla Adlerkreutz says, amused. "Do you still not understand why we have done all this?"

It's getting harder and harder to breathe. Jessica's nostrils are full of mucus, and an enormous lump weighs in her throat.

"I've saved dozens of souls, Jessica. Prevented their minds from being poisoned. I've ensured that not a single one of my patient's lives has been stunted by a diagnosis concocted by a so-called expert in the field. No one deserves the label of mentally ill. Not even those who turn their backs on me. Imagine! Thanks to me, all these poor souls who would have been pumped full of drugs and shackled with restraints can freely choose their subject of study and career path. They can obtain positions of power, of influence. My children do not settle for grunt work. They are everywhere. On the land, at sea, in the air."

"My mother—" Jessica says softly, but her voice catches on the lump in her throat.

"The Luomas were our best doctors at Bättre Morgondag for years. But they lost their grip; they sold their souls to the pharmaceutical industry. As did Albert von Bunsdorf. Albert gradually came to join that group of people who believe that extraordinary brain function always demands a diagnosis, treatment, and medication. Terms like 'split personality,' 'illness,' 'disease,' 'delusions,' 'psychosis' . . . they are assaults on difference."

Camilla Adlerkreutz appears to think for a moment. Then she lets out a bark of mischievous laughter as if she had just remembered something amusing.

"Not to mention that Blomqvist minx," she continues, still smiling. "One of the most outrageous academic studies of recent years was this young woman's dissertation asserting that non-mainstream brain function is not only an illness—it is supposedly caused by some ridiculous parasite."

"But—"

"Haven't you grasped how the system works, Jessica? Apparently not, because there was no need for you to. Do you think you would have made it this far without my having exerted my influence? Do you think you would have ever passed the background check necessary to join the police force? Now, as you rise through the ranks, you can help us advance our goals and right the wrongs that society has created out of ignorance. I watched you grow up, dear. I know that you can do what your mother could not, or would not, do."

"What?" Jessica whispers, and begins to cry.

Camilla Adlerkreutz lowers her chin to her chest, and for a moment, she appears to be praying. Then she stands up and raises her hand into the air.

"Detego."

One at a time, the naked figures standing in a semi-circle pull back their hoods. The clean-shaven man with a birthmark blazing on his brow. Torsten Karlstedt. Kai Lehtinen. A beautiful dark-haired woman Jessica doesn't recognize. Presumably the same one who knocked on the window of Irma Helle's shop last night and killed her. And last of all . . .

"I'm sorry, Jessica," Mikael says, and crosses his hands at his chest.

Jessica can't breathe. *Because they said there's someone close to you who will find out everything. Who's watching and controlling things.* She feels like an idiot. Suddenly everything is so damn obvious. The water meter, the pistol, the notebook. Mikael pressuring Erne to bring in Karlstedt and Lehtinen. And the way Mikael, after one two-hour session in a hotel room the night before last, wanted to go for a drive with Jessica. To make sure she was the first detective at the scene of the crime in Kulosaari when the patrols on duty got the call.

"Help me, Micke," Jessica says softly as the shock gradually turns into anger. But the words feel pointless as they escape her lips. "Get me out of here, you fucking asshole!" she screams.

Mikael looks back at her without batting an eye. "Jessica, my friend. Our journey ends here, but yours will continue."

"What the hell, Micke? Have you lost your mind? Did you kill—"

"Calm yourself, Jessica." Camilla flashes a circumspect smile. "You're falling into the trap of thinking like the majority of the population. You're adopting their narrow way of viewing the world. To them, we are evildoers. But to so many others, we are heroes. Our movement is much

472

vaster than you can imagine. We have brothers and sisters around the world who welcome us with open arms. And, before long, there will be many more. Roger's books are flying off the shelves, and our online manifesto has been seen hundreds of thousands of times."

"You are fucking insane—"

"You see? You're doing it again, Jessica. Please, try to understand that the sole purpose of all this, this treasure map drafted with such exquisite care, is to spread our message. To disseminate knowledge."

Camilla Adlerkreutz turns around and walks over to the red blanket. Her skin looks surreal in the torchlight, like papier-mâché that has been formed around a frame of bent wire. Her uncloaked body crouches over the blanket, her black fingernails take hold of it, and a moment later, two naked figures are revealed beneath.

Jessica bellows in horror.

"The dagger is not for you, Jessica dear," Camilla Adlerkreutz says, and then laboriously works her way back up to her feet. "Your destiny is not to die but to continue living even after we are all dead."

"Yusuf! Nina!" Jessica shouts, but neither one answers. Both of them are lying, unconscious and eyes shut, on the same cold stone floor Jessica can feel against the soles of her feet.

"Maria had five beautiful dresses made, Jessica. Perfectly identical to the one your mother wore to her first awards gala.

473

Of course, Maria didn't know what I, the old lady next door, would do with the dresses, but she agreed to help me out."

"Nina, wake up! Yusuf—" Jessica stammers, but deep down she knows it's useless.

Suddenly there's indeterminate thumping overhead. Mikael eyes the ceiling beams. "They're here."

The thumps on the ceiling grow louder.

"We must make haste, *mater pythonissam*," someone in the room says, but Camilla Adlerkreutz looks composed, not the least bit hurried.

Jessica wants to cry out, to make sure the police find this space, which must be in the basement of the big wooden house. But her voice has caught in her throat. Not one of the naked people standing in the semicircle makes the tiniest sign of trying to escape.

Jessica sees the dagger's gleam again, this time in the old woman's hand.

"Some of us will remain. Some of us will depart. But you will go on. Because, just like your mother, you, Jessica von Hellens, are *mater pythonissam*."

Jessica hears the people behind her begin to sing. A melody she recognizes vaguely. Then there's the sound of metal sinking into flesh somewhere nearby. Tears stream down her cheeks. Heat spreads through her body, and she shuts her eyes.

It is the song Mom was singing that morning.

Respice in speculo resplendent, Jessica.

Chapter 105

JESSICA OPENS HER EYES BUT DOESN'T TURN TOWARD THE man who just entered the auditorium. She waits until her nostrils catch the scent of his sweet aftershave.

"Zesika," Colombano says. His voice bears a hint of sarcasm, presumably in an attempt to mask his surprise and confusion.

Jessica opens her eyes and turns. Colombano is looking at her with his hands deep in the pockets of his khaki trousers, his white dress shirt unbuttoned nearly to his navel.

"You've come back to Venice," he says as the woman Jessica now knows is his sister slips through the door and shuts it behind her. The two of them are alone now.

Jessica notices her voice is shaking. "I never left."

Colombano chuckles. "What?"

"I've been in Murano this whole time."

For a moment, Colombano shakes his head as if Jessica were utterly mad. Maybe she is. And not because she's been lying, paralyzed, in a hotel room for months on end, but because she has come back.

"Listen. I'm sorry we ended the way we did."

"I don't believe you."

"Oh, Zesika. Look at yourself . . . You look terrible, frankly. How did such a beautiful, well-dressed girl turn into such a . . . fat, dowdy troll?"

"So I'm not your princess anymore? Something you want to share with your friends?"

Colombano bursts out in a rollicking laugh. "I never shared you with anyone."

"No, you didn't. Your friend just watched while you raped me."

"You're talking crazy. Come on, now, let's go out from here."

"I know Chiara's death wasn't an accident."

"What the hell are you talking about?"

"I know she committed suicide because she couldn't take it anymore. Because you're a narcissist who sucks up all the oxygen in the room. You have a way of making a person feel important, desirable. But you're even better at dragging them back down to earth, stripping them of all self-respect and self-esteem—"

"Shut your mouth."

"But I wanted you to know," Jessica says, and now her eyes grow moist from tears for the first time in weeks, as if the numbness that took over her mind and body for months releases its grip during one sentence, "that I see through you. And I despise you. And so does your sister."

Colombano guffaws. "You have some nerve."

"Go ahead, laugh. We both know it's an act."

"You don't know anything, you fucking whore." Colombano stalks over and grabs her wrist, yanks her to her feet. "You know what I think? I bet you're still so in love with me that you couldn't leave. And in the end you came back to me like a junkie craving their fix. Am I right? You came back for more of what you think you hate . . . but that you really love."

Colombano says these last words right at the base of Jessica's ear, spraying warm spittle onto her throat. She looks him in the eye and feels a swelling panic inside. Colombano's powerful fingers are wrapped around her slender wrist. She came here of her own free will, put herself at the mercy of this sadistic man. The two of them are alone in the auditorium. No one is going to come to her aid.

"Come." Colombano wrenches Jessica down the row of seats toward the door. Her knee bumps painfully against a chair, knocking it over. She is clutching her little purse in her free hand.

"No!" Jessica cries, her voice echoing in the deserted space.

Colombano's grip on her wrist tightens, and Jessica feels a tingling in her fingers where the blood isn't properly circulating. He yanks her past the tall pillars into a smaller room and across it to a door at the far side.

"Let go of me!"

"Don't pretend you came here just to talk . . ."

Colombano opens the door and shoves Jessica in so hard that she falls face-first to the floor. She catches a glimpse of the room: it's an office of some sort, its walls covered with old concert posters; there is a desk with computers in the middle of it, a threadbare sofa, and an outside door on the opposite wall.

Jessica hears a rustling and clinking in Colombano's hands, then feels a leather belt around her throat.

"You show up here just to fuck with me! To spoil my concert . . . to ruin my concentration."

Jessica tries to breathe; her fingers fumble for her throat and the belt tightened around it. She feels Colombano raise her black dress and sink his fingers deep into the flesh of her buttocks. Jessica screams and reaches for her purse, which has fallen to the floor. Her fingers grab at the strap, at the wooden handle jutting out from inside.

"You don't deserve any answers . . . You were just a girl at the cemetery. Do you think you're the only one? You're all so fucking predictable and weak. And stupid! Coming here alone to pester me, ask dumb questions. Am I sorry? No, you dumb cow. Look at yourself. You're fat! A twenty-year-old slut . . . If I didn't have to discipline you, I wouldn't touch you with a ten-foot pole anymore—"

Colombano's sentence ends in an abrupt thud. For a moment, all is utterly still; then he roars and rises. Jessica feels the belt around her neck give, and she rolls over onto her back.

Colombano takes a few dazed steps backward, tries to see where his gaze can't fully turn, spies the handle of the steak knife sticking out under his collarbone. Farther up, on either side of his Adam's apple, blood pumps from two stab wounds. For a second, it looks as if he has horns, but when he steps forward, it turns out to be a poster for the opera *Faust*.

"What the fuck . . . ?" he rasps, and grabs the knife handle. Blood drips between his fingers. He and Jessica look at each other in astonishment, as if they were seeing each other for the first time in some wholly unexpected place and time. He manages only to pull the blade out an inch and grimaces in pain. "You fucking whore!"

All calculation and resolve have evaporated from Colombano's eyes. All that's left is pure rage. He takes a few strides and lunges at Jessica with all his strength. Jessica feels his blood drip to her face, his powerful, rough fingers around her throat. His animal roar in her ear. And only now does Jessica understand why she returned to this accursed building, why she wanted to confront this monster again: she believed Colombano would do what she hasn't been capable of during these months alone in her hotel room. Soon everything will be over.

But then Colombano's grip slips.

Jessica opens her eyes. The man who was on top of her, bearing down on her with all his weight, is gone.

Oletko kunnossa?

Jessica doesn't recognize the voice, but the words are Finnish. *Are you all right?*

479

She hears a faint cry from Colombano. A stranger steps across her. Jessica lies there, letting her breathing steady. Eventually she wipes her blood-smeared face and sits up. The leather belt is lying on the floor, but she can still feel it choking her.

Colombano is lying a few meters away, knife in his chest. Next to his wheezing carcass stands a man, about forty years old. The same man Jessica saw earlier that evening in the audience. His fingers are wrapped around a small statuette, which he presumably used to wallop Colombano in the back of the head.

"Who . . . who are you?" Jessica asks, and notices how foreign the Finnish words sound when she utters them. She hasn't spoken Finnish in ages.

"Jessica. Listen," the man says, wiping the blood from his forehead. "It was self-defense."

He speaks calmly, and Jessica thinks she can make out a dialect of some sort.

"Is he—"

"I don't know. I don't know, damn it . . ."

At that instant, Colombano's body goes limp, and his hands fall lifelessly to his sides. Jessica bursts into silent tears.

"We have to get out of here," the man continues, glancing around nervously. He stalks over to the door he entered through a moment earlier and makes sure the auditorium is still empty. Then he locks the door and walks over to the outside door. He carefully cracks it, thrusts his head out, and returns to Jessica.

"You don't want to hang around to figure this out with the Venice police. And I don't either. We have to leave this mess behind. Go back to Helsinki."

"We? Who . . . who the hell are you?"

"I came to bring you home. People are worried about you."

"What people?"

"Your aunt."

"But—"

"Jessica," the man says, and squeezes Jessica's shoulders. He smells of stale tobacco and faintly of whisky. His face is hard and deeply grooved but gentle. "There's a sink over there," he says in a firm voice. "Wash your face and walk out that door. It leads to a little canal. The street looked empty when I looked out. But check to be sure before you step out. No one must see you, under any circumstances."

"But what . . . ?" Jessica stammers, as the man shifts his worried face to the prone Colombano. The violinist's eyes are open, staring into eternity.

"I'll clean up this mess. Go to your hotel in Murano and wait for me there. I'll come as fast as I can. And then we'll leave. I promise you, everything is going to be OK."

Jessica starts sobbing as she looks at the man. Only now does she realize that what she hears in the man's voice is not a dialect, but a foreign accent. "Who are you?"

"Erne," he says, pulling his police badge out of his breast pocket. "You can trust me."

Chapter 106

ERNE MIKSON SQUATS NEXT TO THE BODY LYING ON THE concrete floor and wipes the sweat from his brow. The flames from the wall torches are making the low-ceilinged room warm. Despite the chills shuddering through his body, the heat has glued Erne's shirt to his back. He doesn't even want to guess the reading the thermometer would give if he stuck it under his armpit now.

One of the men from the SWAT team walks up to Erne: "It's going to take a while to clear the mouth of the tunnel."

"They're not in the tunnel anymore."

"No, they're not," the man replies, rogers a short radio message, and makes for the far wall. A three-foot-tall chasm yawns at the center of it. Leaning against the wall next to the hole is the enormous oil painting of the young Camilla Adlerkreutz.

Erne shuts his eyes and opens his nostrils to inhale the cloying scent of gunpowder. He hears the chatter of the dozens of police officers, medics, and CSIs, as well as a pair of uncertain footsteps dragging themselves down the stairs.

"Erne."

Erne hears Rasmus' voice but doesn't immediately respond.

"Erne," Rasmus says again.

"What?"

Rasmus steps into the room, hands thrust deep into the pockets of his brown parka. "The ambulance took off."

Erne sighs and opens his eyes. "And Jessica has security with her this time?"

"Yes."

"Good."

Rasmus shifts his gaze to the tips of his shoes. "I don't think . . . I mean . . . if they wanted to kill Jessica, they would have done it while they had the chance."

Erne slowly rises to his feet and looks at Rasmus. He feels like telling his subordinate to knock it off with the hypothesizing, but deep down he knows Rasmus is right. Adlerkreutz had her reasons for going through so much trouble to first lure Jessica into her trap and then decide to release her unharmed. Jessica must have some understanding of what's going on; Erne has been too shocked to reflect on the matter himself. They'll have time to get to that later—alone. Just he and Jessica.

"I managed to get drawings from the city—"

"Of the tunnel?"

"Yes. There are no official documents, just a blueprint and a building permit from the nineteen fifties. The city has no record of the tunnel actually being built, no year, no builder—"

"Which is why we didn't know to look for it in the first place."

"According to the blueprint, it runs under the bay bridge to the bomb shelter at Kulosaari. The SWAT team just checked it out, but they're gone. There must have been a car waiting for them."

"Cameras?"

"Negative," Rasmus says, scratching the back of his head.

"Under the bay bridge . . ." Erne says softly. "That explains how Laura Helminen popped to the surface right off the Koponens' property."

"And how Maria Koponen's killer vanished without a trace." Rasmus pulls a tiny jar out of his pocket. Erne looks on in disbelief as his subordinate, otherwise impressively negligent in matters of personal hygiene, dabs his fingertips in the ointment and spreads it reverently across his dry lips. "The cold dries them out—"

Erne cuts him off and takes a few steps toward the other body. Just like the first corpse: a bloody stab wound in the chest. There's no sign of a knife.

"Any other news from the outside world?"

"Bättre Morgondag—the Better Tomorrow movement—has set off a social media frenzy. Instagram has taken down the video Helminen streamed from her hospital room, but it's already living a life of its own on the internet. The manifesto uploaded to Roger Koponen's YouTube account is one of the most-viewed videos today—in the world."

"What does it say?"

"It's pretty long—"

"In a nutshell, Rasmus."

"I'd like to say it's anarchy, if not in the most traditional sense. But it's actually just hypocrisy disguised as anarchy."

"What do you mean?"

Erne looks at Rasmus and sees something rare on his face: an expression of anger and disgust.

"It's pretty obvious," Rasmus starts after a brief pause and continues: "that Camilla Adlerkreutz has been taking advantage of these people. She has been controlling neuroatypical individuals by making them believe that she has their best interests at heart. Many of them from a very early age on."

"And not just any individuals," Erne sighs.

"Exactly. People in positions of power. She is taking advantage of them with her so-called philosophy. Rather than them being helped by medication, standard treatment, they are enslaved by her to change the 'world order.' And think about all the money these people would otherwise spend on treatment and medication."

"It all went to her pockets," Erne says. He speaks in a low voice as he squats next to the second body: "If Roger

Koponen was in on this the whole time, is it possible he wrote the book with this plan in mind?"

Rasmus responds quietly: "I don't think so. If that were the case, he would have had to have been able to predict their enormous success."

Erne nods and pulls a pack of cigarettes from his pocket. "Or else he just hoped for it."

Erne plucks a cigarette from the pack, places it between his lips, leaves it unlit. He looks at the two dead men lying side by side on the ground. And now Erne can't help thinking there's always been something damn peculiar about the faces of Roger Koponen and Mikael Kaariniemi, some inscrutable message written on them. As if they'd always been concealing some big secret within.

Chapter 107

JESSICA OPENS HER EYES; HER LIDS FEEL HEAVY. SHE SEES a painting of a sailboat, a wood-grain closet, a wide door to a wheelchair-accessible toilet, and a little television hanging from the ceiling. She knows she's still in the hospital and that Yusuf and Nina are alive, recuperating in the neighboring rooms. Erne told her so this morning as soon as she woke up.

"Jessica?"

Jessica turns and sees a familiar face, a tightly pulled bun, and lone strands of hair against the bright sunlight.

"Tina?"

A wrinkled hand squeezes hers. A tear trickles down the lean cheek.

"It's so wonderful seeing you after so many years . . ."

Jessica studies the other woman. She has dyed her hair a reddish tint and, despite numerous face-lifts, looks much older than Jessica remembered. Pride and an imposing presence have been replaced by frailty and an air of melancholy.

"You have no idea how much I've thought about you, Jessica."

487

"What do you want?" Jessica turns to the window, and silence falls over the room. Tina clearly doesn't have an answer prepared. Maybe she tried to come up with one and couldn't.

"What I want is for you not to think of me as the enemy," she finally says, wiping her teary eyes on a lace handkerchief she pulls from her purse.

Jessica shakes her head. She has a hard time understanding why her aunt has come to see her now, after all these years. It's been so long since they last saw each other that Jessica wouldn't have recognized Tina's voice if she hadn't seen her face.

"I don't. But I don't think of you as a friend either, Tina." Jessica's throat feels tight; it's surprisingly hard to say what's on her mind.

"But—" Tina whispers, and Jessica swats the air dismissively.

"Mom didn't trust you." Jessica hears her voice dropping to a whisper too.

They both fall silent.

"Your mother was sick," Tina eventually says, her voice trembling. "Your mother was the most beautiful and gifted person in the world, but she was also very, very sick."

Jessica turns away and shuts her eyes. She has heard this before, but can't remember where. "What do you mean?"

For a moment, Tina looks as if she were going to back down and refrain from saying what's on her mind. Lock her chest of confessions for the next thirty years. But a deep sigh leads to stammered words.

"Your mother was mentally ill. She was diagnosed with paranoid schizophrenia at a very young age," Tina says, and her delicate smile speaks of relief. Starting is always the hardest part. "But thanks to medication, she was able to live a rather normal life, and her work as an actor . . . well, you could say she was extraordinary at it, not in spite of her illness but perhaps because of it. On the other hand, in an upper-class, aristocratic Sweden–Finn family like the von Hellens, there was no way their daughter's mental illness would be spoken of publicly in the nineteen seventies. In order to keep it a secret, Theresa was taken to a private psychotherapy center for children and adolescents directed by Camilla Adlerkreutz."

"But . . ." Jessica mumbles, feeling a heaviness spread from her gut toward her chest.

"If you don't count the mild paranoia and sudden fits of rage, Theresa managed daily life quite well. To our parents' horror, at the age of twenty, she applied to, and was accepted at, the Theatre Academy, and before long she launched an acting career that, as you're well aware, remains unparalleled by Finnish standards. Theresa met your father, who was working as a set designer for the Helsinki City Theatre. You were born soon after and, two years later, Toffe. Then you moved to the States." Tina takes a sip of water from her plastic mug. The wrinkles at her scrawny throat remind Jessica of a turkey wattle.

"Why are you telling me this now?"

"Your father didn't want to go to the States. He felt staying in Helsinki would have been the wisest course of action, hands down. If for no other reason than for your and Toffe's sake. By then your parents had inherited so much money that financial success on the other side of the pond wouldn't have made a difference one way or the other."

"Mom went to chase her dreams—"

"That wasn't the primary reason. Your mother left because she was afraid to stay."

"What was she afraid of?"

"Camilla Adlerkreutz." Tina holds a brief pause. The clink of a dining cart carries in from the corridor. "Adlerkreutz dismissed Theresa's claims by saying she was delusional. You can guess who everyone believed: a schizophrenic or a well-respected psychiatrist."

"But . . . what did Mom say?"

Tina looks at Jessica for a long time, then grunts as if it were all too incredible to be true.

"That Adlerkreutz practiced occult arts aimed at brain-washing children and adolescents. Theresa said Adlerkreutz forced her patients to participate in rituals where they were submerged in water . . . They were abused physically but even more so mentally. And that what Adlerkreutz did to her patients truly worked. Everyone seemed to be in her power."

"Except Mom?"

"At least based on how stubbornly she resisted and tried to tell our parents what was really happening during her therapy."

Tina bursts into silent tears. She turns her gaze toward the sunlit window, wipes her nose, and gathers her thoughts.

"When she came of age, your mother refused to attend any more sessions. But Adlerkreutz's circle wouldn't leave her alone. Theresa said people were following her at night, that she was getting strange phone calls. That they threatened to do something terrible if she didn't return."

"Things a paranoid person would say."

"Exactly. I don't know if you can blame my parents for never taking Theresa's accusations seriously. And that's why she wanted to get away. As far as possible."

"Did Mom ever say why she was so important to the cult?"

"According to Theresa, Adlerkreutz had handpicked her to be the future leader of the cult and carry on her work. Adlerkreutz saw something unique in Theresa, perhaps something to do with Theresa's sensitivity, the charismatic energy she radiated, her ability to sway people's emotions. The same traits that later made her an influential movie star. Perhaps your mother possessed too much potential to waste. She could have been a valuable asset, a tool of her propaganda."

For a moment, Jessica stares ahead blankly. She experiences shock, anger, and sadness, but none of these emotions manages to take root inside her. Finally she whispers: "Did . . . did Dad know?"

"Theresa didn't want your father to know the truth. Your father no doubt came to know your mother's unstable side over time, but I don't believe he had the slightest idea what caused the sudden mood swings and the intermittent loss of perspective. So he hung in there."

"For my and Toffe's sakes?"

"Of course! I'm certain he loved Theresa too," Tina says, then drains her water mug. "All that success . . . life in the spotlights and on the red carpet . . . I'm not sure if it made your parents' life harder or easier in the end, but within a few years, things had gotten so impossible that your father decided to move away."

Jessica's heart skips a beat and suddenly her throat feels incredibly dry. "That morning . . ."

"The night before the accident, I got a phone call from your father in Los Angeles. I hadn't heard a word from either of them for years, so it took me completely by surprise. Your mother had done her best to paint me and the whole von Hellens family as villains, but as home life grew more difficult, your father gradually came to realize that the problem lay elsewhere. He briefly told me that the marriage had run its course some time ago, that he had fallen in love with someone else, and that he was moving to Palo Alto to be with this other woman. Your mother was just preparing to shoot a new film, and your father had hoped he could take you children with him, but Theresa was adamantly opposed. In any case, your father called and begged me to fly out and support Theresa and lend a hand with the children."

"You flew to Los Angeles?"

"Of course. Theresa was my sister. But unfortunately I arrived too late . . ."

"The accident had already happened," Jessica says, and looks out the window. The freeze has folded a beautiful symmetrical star on the windowpane.

"When it happened, I was still in the air . . . flying over Nevada, to be precise." Tina wipes away a tear with the ball of her thumb. "I didn't find any of this out until I'd been waiting two hours in the back seat of a taxi at the entrance gates to Bel Air. Eventually the police came, explained the situation, and brought me to the hospital. You weren't expected to pull through, Jessica . . . I'll never forget how little you looked, surrounded by all those machines . . ."

"So you were there—"

"Every day for four weeks while they patched you back together. Your grandparents also came over. It was incredibly hard for them . . . especially since they had to say goodbye to their elder daughter and her family after such a long period of estrangement. Without a chance to make up, to repair the damaged relationship. But they still didn't know to blame themselves for not having believed what Theresa told them about Camilla Adlerkreutz's therapies."

"So you believed her?" Jessica says, and turns her gaze out the window again. The sun is shining more brightly than it has in weeks.

"Listen, Jessica," Tina says. "I wanted to take you in, but it simply wasn't possible."

"Because you didn't like children?"

"I was too young to adopt, and due to breast cancer, your grandmother wasn't in a stable condition. Your father's sister was the only logical choice. And although she wasn't exactly fond of us von Hellenses, I knew she was the best alternative for your sake. The Niemis were good people."

"They were. Do you think I haven't spent every other day of my life thinking I'm cursed? That I've lost both sets of parents? Who the hell under the age of twenty has lost a brother and both their biological and adoptive parents? I'm the one here who must really be a witch." Jessica can no longer hold back the tears. "Do you think money makes it any easier?"

"If anyone knows that it doesn't, it's me, Jessie." Tina strokes Jessica's hair, and to her surprise, Jessica doesn't recoil from the gesture. "I'm sure you don't remember anymore, but we tried to maintain contact with you even after the Niemis adopted you. We truly thought that one day you'd forget all your bitterness toward us, and we could go for an ice cream, to the amusement park . . . do something fun."

"And when your husband died, you didn't have anything better to do than track me down in Venice—"

"Everyone was worried, Jessica. I had to send someone after you."

"Why are you here now?"

"Because you've lived over thirty years of your life without knowing the truth. Brooding over all sorts of theories about your parents' accident. You knew your mother hated us. I'm sure you heard dozens of reasons for it, the majority of which were no doubt the product of her imagination. And now you know the truth, that she hated us because we didn't believe her. We thought she was a paranoid schizophrenic—which she was, absolutely—and we didn't believe her when she told us what Camilla Adlerkreutz had done to her."

Tina picks up her gray purse from the floor and pulls out a folded piece of paper. Jessica looks at it for a second, then takes it suspiciously and unfolds it.

State of California motor vehicle collision report
Place: Los Angeles, 4280 Lincoln Blvd 33°58' 41.1"N 118°26'08.9"W
Time: 7:45 a.m. 05/04/1993

For a moment all is silent: there's a pause in the machine's hum, no footfalls echo from the corridor. Jessica realizes that she has always known but hasn't wanted to believe it. That if you push something deep enough, it's out of sight but never truly goes away. Jessica feels her brother squeezing her hand harder and harder. She sees Mom look at her in the rearview mirror. And Mom's eyes aren't sad anymore; they're hopeful. Mom's dark eyebrows rise; her mouth draws up in a smile. The sorrow is gone, and it even seems as if her eyes are laughing. *Soon everything will be fine, sweetheart.* Her father, who is staring out the window, comes out of his reverie when the car crosses the median. Her father turns, roars, and tries to grab the steering wheel.

Soon we'll be happy again.

A silence that goes on and on. An endless silence, white in color and smelling of hot asphalt and exhaust, an emptiness that follows her into this hospital room, where it all takes on meaning again.

Chapter 108

ERNE ASKED ME TO SAY A FEW WORDS TODAY. IT'S A GREAT honor, and I told him I'd planned on doing it whether he wanted me to or not.

We all loved Erne. Expressing that doesn't require a long speech or thousands of beautiful words. Because Erne is sitting somewhere out there, glancing at his watch. And, as we all know, that sight always lit a fire under the butt of whoever was speaking. So I'll keep my comments brief.

The last investigation I worked on with Erne ended up being a case where one of the criminals was a famous writer, which is why—as horrible as it might seem—I want to talk to you about writing.

You see, I believe that each of us is the author of our own life. We write our own story each and every day by simply living it. By seeing, hearing, experiencing, by making mistakes and hopefully learning from them. The stories of some inspire admiration and envy; those of others, pity or even disapproval. The number of literary tastes is infinite, and so are the critics who feel it's their job to criticize the way in which others write their lives.

I myself have always thought that my book doesn't need to be a bestseller. The critics can make what they want of it. My story doesn't need to reach tens, hundreds, or thousands of people. A limited audience is better: you see, I don't want my book to be thought of as dull or trivial just because the reader doesn't know me well enough. That's why, in this matter, as in many others, quality is more important that quantity. I want whoever opens my book to appreciate and respect the author, regardless of what is written there. I want someone who asks to keep reading even when there's nothing more to say. I want a reader who is dedicated to my text. A faithful reader.

Erne was the reader, editor, and critic of my life all wrapped up in one package. We didn't always see eye to eye about everything, but I knew he respected my text. Despite my meandering and erratic style, he always seemed to somehow know where the text was going. And the fact that he usually read it with a restful look on his face told me that, in spite of everything, I'm going to be just fine. Even with my punctuation errors.

Now that you're gone, continuing to write feels hard. But that's exactly why it's important to keep doing it. The rest of our stories keep going, and your story lives on inside them.

Thank you, Erne. And bon voyage.

"I'm speechless," Erne says as Jessica lowers the piece of paper to the table. Both of them wipe their eyes. Erne's speech is labored, and it's apparent that every utterance demands incredible effort.

Jessica blows her nose and then smiles at the gaunt man whose stick-thin hands are resting peacefully on the armrests of his wheelchair.

"You really know how to write, Jessica."

Jessica lets out an involuntary laugh and blows the hair out of her eyes. "That doesn't make me happy. Not now."

"Thank you for reading it to me."

"If felt somehow"—moved, Jessica takes Erne's hand—"somehow important for you to have a chance to hear it. Because everyone else gets to. So you don't miss out on anything. Especially because it's about you."

Erne smiles between wheezing coughs and waves dismissively. "Well, we'll see if anyone shows up."

"Of course they will. Don't be an idiot." Jessica pats Erne's hand. The water is bubbling in the kettle. Frank Sinatra's "Fly Me to the Moon" carries from the living-room speakers. It's Erne's absolute favorite.

"You want tea?"

"No, thanks. I think I'll go rest now."

"Are you sure? Maybe a sandwich?" Jessica says, and catches the panicky tone in her voice. She doesn't want the moment to end. Erne seems so frightfully calm and sure. Ready. He appears to be at peace with the world around

ne has accepted his own smallness and microscopic
e in its continuum of millions of years.

"I need to go lie down."

"Sure . . . let me help you."

"Jessica . . ." Erne says, then takes Jessica gently by the
wrist and steers her back into her chair. For a moment
they just sit there, Erne looking Jessica deep in the eye.
"Thank you, Jessica."

Jessica's voice quavers: "You ought to get some rest now.
Your boys will be here tomorrow."

Erne smiles wearily. "So now they're coming, to say
goodbye . . . I haven't seen them in ages."

Erne lowers his gaze to his hands. The sparrows chirp
cheerily in the park across the street, where green has just
appeared at the treetops. Spring is at its most beautiful
right now.

"Thank you for letting me stay with you these few
weeks," he finally says, and smiles. He lets his placid gaze
roam around the large kitchen, then shuts his eyes. The
lids look so heavy when they're closed; opening them again
must take a lot of effort.

Jessica gulps and looks at the memorial speech resting
on the table. Next time, Erne won't be around to hear it.

"Do you like that guy?" Erne suddenly asks.

"Who? Fubu? I guess. He's fun. And uncomplicated."

"Fun is good."

"But it's not enough?"

Erne smiles and shakes his head. "Promise me one thing, Jessie."

"What?"

"Never look back. Only forward . . ."

"Because life only lies ahead."

"Exactly."

There's a short beep, and Erne laboriously digs the thermometer out from his arm.

"You have a fever?"

A euphoric smile spreads across Erne's face. "Thirty-six point five."

"Fantastic. Come on, Ser Davos. I'll help you get into bed," Jessica says, pinching Erne's cheek. "Tomorrow is a new day."

Chapter 109

JESSICA.

Jessica opens her eyes. The living room is dark; the timer turned off the television. The time on the cable box reads three thirty a.m. The wind is howling outside, setting the windows creaking.

Someone has called out to Jessica again. The voice was Erne's. Healthy Erne's, not that frail man laid low by an agonizing, rapidly advancing illness. Erne, on whose grave she laid a dandelion bouquet.

Jessica.

Now Jessica is no longer sure if the voice is a man's or a woman's. Suddenly she finds herself on her feet. The towel she wrapped around herself after her evening shower has slipped to the floor. Jessica takes a step. And then another. Her limbs feel light; nothing hurts. It's as if she were gliding above the hardwood floor. Levitating, without any friction between the soles of her feet and the floor, no contact with material.

Come here, sweetheart.

e person speaking is both man and woman. It could be ne, Nina, Yusuf, Tina, Dad, and Mom together.

Je ca walks toward the long dining table, the straight-backe eople sitting around it. The beautiful black evening dr is spread out in the center of the table, pressed and cle The fifth dress. Next to it, a pair of high heels, lustrous exquisite. They have to be the most beautiful shoes in tl vorld.

Jessica st in the midst of her weightless movement and turns he ice to the mirror. Something isn't right. It feels as if the flection staring back at her were repeating her movem ts at a slight lag, as if, instead of being a precise copy, it re reacting spontaneously to the reality Jessica represents

Respice in specul splendent.

It's me.

Of course it is, swee art.

Out of the corner her eye, Jessica sees the woman in the black evening d s sitting at the head of the table, reading from a thick b . Next to her sits Camilla. Not frail old Mrs. Adlerkre , but the young Camilla, the force of her physical prese e extending all the way to the mirror.

Remember what I did, Jess . Remember that I saved you and your friends. It's a gift I ca take back whenever I want.

Jessica nods. Camilla giv an almost imperceptible smile and turns her gaze away.

Suddenly a powerful wave of childish love and affection for her parents surges over Jessica; she wants to please them. She wants her mother to be proud of her.

The woman slowly stands. It looks like her mother, but her movements are stiff and mechanical. She's like a marionette in the hands of an unskilled puppeteer who has tangled the strings.

Jessica closes her eyes, and when she opens them a moment later, her mother has appeared behind her. Mom's face is anything but beautiful. It is mangled, almost unrecognizable; blood trickles down from the crushed scalp, over one eye, and toward the chin.

Jessica feels tears welling up in her eyes.

Why are you crying, sweetheart?

I know what you did, Mom. That morning in the car.

I didn't mean to make you cry, darling.

Her mother's cold hand is on the skin of her shoulder.

No. I'm not crying because you did it.

Why, then?

Because I understand.

Chapter 110

I'M LOOKING IN THE MIRROR.

THANK YOU

Sergeant Marko Lehtoranta, instructor, Police University College

My editor, Petra Maisonen

The folks at Tammi

Family & friends

Elina, Nicole, Toomas, and Julia at Elina Ahlback Literary Agency

Michelle Vega at Berkley

Jon Elek at Welbeck

Rhea Lyons at HG Literary

The man in the mirror

ABOUT THE AUTHOR

MAX SEECK IS AN AUTHOR AND SCREENWRITER WHOSE interests include well-conducted research, reading Nordic Noir and listening to movie soundtracks as he writes. He made his debut in 2016 with the award-winning *The Angels of Hammurabi*, which met with great critical acclaim and commercial success. *The Witch Hunter*, the first in a new series, has now sold in 38 territories, with a TV adaption in production and more Jessica Niemi thrillers to come.

🅵 🅾 🆅 @maxseeck

WELBECK

PUBLISHING GROUP

Love books? Join the club.

Sign-up and choose your preferred genres to receive tailored news, deals, extracts, author interviews and more about your next favourite read.

From heart-racing thrillers to award-winning historical fiction, through to must-read music tomes, beautiful picture books and delightful gift ideas, Welbeck is proud to publish titles that suit every taste.

bit.ly/welbeckpublishing